Praise for Donna Andrews's
Meg Langslow Mysteries

Owls Well That Ends Well

"It's a hoot . . . A supporting cast of endearingly eccentric characters, perfectly pitched dialogue and a fine sense of humor make this a treat." *—Publishers Weekly*

"Death by yard sale epitomizes the 'everyday people' humor that Andrews does so well . . . For readers who prefer their mysteries light . . . Andrews may be the next best thing to Janet Evanovich." *—Rocky Mountain News*

"Andrews delivers another wonderfully comic story . . . This is a fun read, as are all the books in the series. Andrews playfully creates laughable, wacky scenes that are the backdrop for her criminally devious plot. Settle back, dear reader and enjoy another visit to Meg's anything-but-ordinary world." *—Romantic Times* (starred review)

We'll Always Have Parrots

"Laughter, more laughter, we need laughter, so Donna Andrews is giving us *We'll Always Have Parrots* . . . to help us survive February." *—Washington Times*

"Perfectly showcases Donna Andrews's gift for deadpan comedy." *—Denver Post*

"Always heavy on the humor, Andrews's most recent Meg Langslow outing is her most over-the-top adventure to date." *—Booklist*

"I can't say enough good things about this series, and this entry in it." —*Deadly Pleasures*

"Hilarious . . . Another winner . . . keeps you turning pages." —*Mystery Lovers News*

Crouching Buzzard, Leaping Loon

"There's a smile on every page and at least one chuckle per chapter." —*Publishers Weekly*

"This may be the funniest installment of Andrews's wonderfully wacky series yet. It takes a deft hand to make slapstick or physical comedy appealing, yet Andrews masterfully manages manages it (the climax will have you in stitches.)" —*Romantic Times*

Revenge of the Wrought-Iron Flamingos

"At the top of the list . . . a fearless protagonist, remarkable supporting characters, lively action, and a keen wit." —*Library Journal*

"What a lighthearted gem of a juggling act . . . With her trademark witty dialogue and fine sense of the ridiculous, Andrews keeps all her balls in the air with skill and verve." —*Publishers Weekly*

"Genuinely fascinating. A better-than-average entry in a consistently entertaining . . . series." —*Booklist*

Murder with Puffins

"Muddy trails, old secrets, and plenty of homespun humor."
—*St. Petersburg Times*

"The well-realized island atmosphere, the puffin lore, and the ubiquitous birders only add to the fun." —*Denver Post*

"Another hit for Andrews . . . entertaining and filled with fun characters." —*Daily Press* [Newport, Virginia]

"Andrews's tale of two puffins has much to recommend it, and will leave readers cawing for another adventure featuring the appealing Meg and Michael." —*Publishers Weekly*

"The puffin angle proves very amusing . . . an enjoyable flight of fancy." —*Booklist*

Murder with Peacocks

"The first novel is so clever, funny, and original that lots of wannabe authors will throw up their hands in envy and get jobs in a coffee shop." —*Contra Costa Times*

"Loquacious dialogue, persistent humor . . . a fun, breezy read." —*Library Journal*

"Half Jane Austen, half battery acid . . . will leave you helpless with heartless laughter . . . Andrews combines murder and madcap hilarity with a cast of eccentric oddballs in a small Southern town." —*Kirkus Reviews*

"Andrews's debut provides plenty of laughs for readers who like their mysteries on the cozy side." —*Publishers Weekly*

Owls Well That Ends Well

Donna Andrews

St. Martin's Paperbacks

OWLS WELL THAT ENDS WELL

Copyright © 2005 by Donna Andrews.

Excerpt from *No Nest for the Wicket* © 2006 by Donna Andrews.

Library of Congress Catalog Card Number: 2004051437

ISBN: 0-312-99790-6
EAN: 9780312-99790-8

Printed in the United States of America

St. Martin's Press hardcover edition / April 2005
St. Martin's Paperbacks edition / March 2006

St. Martin's Paperbacks are published by St. Martin's Press, 175 Fifth Avenue, New York, NY 10010.

10 9 8 7 6 5 4 3 2

For Dad,
who inspired Meg's dad, and still inspires me

Acknowledgments

Thank you!

To the folks at St. Martin's/Minotaur who make this all possible—to Ruth Cavin for all her guidance and support, and for never letting me get away with less than the best book I can write; to her assistant, Toni Plummer, for her efficiency in keeping the book on track; and (long overdue) to the art department for doing such wonderful covers with whatever bird I foist upon them.

To Ellen Geiger and Anna Abreu at Curtis Brown for taking such good care of the business side of my writing career, so I can do the fun part.

To the friends who critiqued the manuscript—as usual, on short notice, during busy times in their own lives: Ellen Crosby, Kathy Deligianis, Suzanne Frisbee, Dave Niemi, and Rosemary Stevens.

And to the readers who take the time to tell me how much they like reading about Meg and her family. Sometimes, when real life seems determined to interfere with your writing, it really does help knowing that someone out there is waiting impatiently to see what happens next.

Chapter 1

When the doorbell rang, I stumbled to the still-dark window and poured a bucket of water where the front porch roof would have been if it hadn't blown away in a thunderstorm two weeks ago.

"Aarrgghh!" screamed our visitor. A male voice, for a change.

Ignoring the curses from below, I poured another gallon jug of water into the bucket, added a scoop of ice cubes from the cooler, and stationed it by the window before crawling back into the sleeping bag.

"I have an idea," Michael said, poking his head out from under his pillow. "Next time let's just hire someone to do this."

"There won't be a next time," I said. "We are never, ever having another yard sale."

"Works for me," Michael said, disappearing under the pillow again.

Within thirty seconds I heard the gentle not-quite-snores that told me he was fast asleep.

A point in Michael's favor, the non-snoring. The list

was long on points in Michael's favor and very short on flaws. Not that I normally keep ledgers on people, but I suspected that after several years together, Michael was tiring of my commitment phobia and working up to a serious talk about the "M" word. And no matter how much I liked the idea of spending the rest of my life with Michael, the "M" word still made me nervous. I'd begun making my mental list of his good points to defuse my admittedly irrational anxiety.

Not something I needed to worry about right now. Now, I needed to sleep. I settled back and tried to follow Michael's example. But I didn't hear a car driving away, which probably meant our caller was still lurking nearby. Perhaps even trying to sneak into the yard sale area. I wished him luck getting past our security. But odds were he'd eventually ring the doorbell again. Or another early arrival would. If only someone had warned me that no matter what start time you announce for a yard sale, the dedicated bargain hunters show up before dawn.

My family, of course, had been showing up for days. Every room that had a floor was strewn with sleeping bags, and my more adventurous cousins had strung up hammocks in some of the floorless rooms.

From downstairs in the living room, I heard the thumping of Cousin Dolores's morning aerobics and the resonant chants Cousin Rosemary emitted while performing her sun salutations. Perhaps this morning they would both keep to their own separate ends of the living room. If not, someone else would have to restore peace between East and West today.

Michael was definitely fast asleep again. What a wonderful gift, being able to fall asleep like that. I felt envious.

Just envious, the cynical side of my mind asked. Not even a teeny bit resentful? I mean, it's no wonder he can sleep so soundly. He hasn't spent every waking moment of the last two months getting ready for this weekend.

In late August, we'd bought The House—a huge Victorian pile, three stories high plus attic and basement, with three acres of land and assorted outbuildings, including a full-sized barn equipped with a resident pair of nesting owls. The only way we'd been able to afford it was to take the place "as is," which referred not only to the property's run-down condition, but also to the fact that it still contained all of the late Edwina Sprocket's possessions. And Edwina had been a hoarder. The house had been merely cluttered, the attic and basement downright scary, and the barn . . . apparently when the house became overcrowded, she'd started shoving things into the barn. When she'd run out of space on the first floor of the barn, she'd placed a ramp up to the hayloft and begun pouring junk in from above. She'd filled the barn and moved on to the sheds by the time she'd finally died, leaving her various grandnieces and grandnephews with a hideous clearing-out job that they'd avoided by selling the place to us. "As is." With a clause in the contract entitling them to ten percent of whatever we made by selling the contents.

Eventually, I assumed, I would come to share Michael's conviction that this was a marvelous deal. Perhaps tomorrow evening, when the yard sale was history. Right now, I just felt tired.

I heard a car engine outside. Probably another caller heading for our doorbell.

I crawled out of the sleeping bag and stumbled over to the window. I rubbed my eyes, opened them, and found myself staring into the pale, heart-shaped face of one of our resident barn owls, sitting on its favorite perch, a dead branch in the oak tree just outside our window. Apparently I'd interrupted its bedtime snack—the tail of an unfortunate field mouse dangled from its mouth.

"Ick," I said. "Are you trying to put me off spaghetti for good?"

The owl stared at me for a few seconds, and then twitched its head. The tail disappeared.

"That branch has got to go," I said, to no one in particular. Certainly not to the owl, who wasn't likely to give up his customary feeding station simply because I objected to having our front porch whitewashed with owl droppings and sprinkled with leftover rodent parts every night. Perhaps I could delegate the branch removal to one of the many uncles and cousins who kept asking what they could do to help, assuming I found one who could be trusted with sharp implements.

Just then our latest caller rang the bell, and I emptied the bucket out the window, still staring at the owl.

No screams or curses this time. Only a very familiar voice.

"Meg? It's me, Dad."

I closed my eyes and sighed.

"I brought doughnuts."

I stuck my head out of the window, startling the owl into flight. A very wet Dad stood on our doorstep. Water beaded on his shiny bald head, and he was trying, with his chin, to brush several ice cubes off the stack of boxes in his arms.

"I'll be right down." I said.

I pulled on jeans and a sweatshirt and headed down the hall for a quick visit to the bathroom. But when I was still ten feet away, a bathrobe-clad man carrying a bulging shaving bag emerged from the last bedroom on the right, waggled his fingers at me cheerfully, and disappeared into the bathroom.

The only bathroom on this floor. Chalk it up to lack of caffeine, but I was so irritated it took me a few seconds to realize that I had no idea who the heck the man in the bathrobe was.

Yet another visiting relative, obviously. But no one I recognized. I thought I knew all the relatives who'd invited themselves to stay at the house. I racked my brain to figure out which aunt or cousin might have brought a new husband or boyfriend along.

Meanwhile, I headed for the third floor bathroom. I reminded myself that this was a temporary inconvenience. First on our long list of remodeling projects was creating a real master bedroom suite with a private connecting bath. And we weren't inviting any more houseguests until we'd solved the bathroom shortage.

Just then I heard the strains of Puccini's "Un Bel Di Verdremo" wafting down from the third floor, which meant that Mrs. Fenniman, another visiting relative, had taken possession of the bathroom for her usual long and tuneful ablutions. I went downstairs instead.

I followed voices to the kitchen. Apparently someone else had let Dad in. He'd put on water for coffee and was sitting cross-legged on the kitchen floor, sharing his doughnuts with my brother, Rob, and a petite middle-aged woman who looked vaguely familiar—although it was hard to tell, because she was wearing a set of Groucho Marx glasses, complete with the fake nose and mustache.

"Morning," I said.

The bathroom off the kitchen was, of course, occupied. But since it was only a half bath, turnover should be faster than upstairs. I stationed myself by the door.

"Morning, Meg," Dad said, raising a cloud of powdered sugar as he waved at me. "You remember your mother's cousin, Emma. From Wichita."

"Kansas?" I asked.

Emma nodded, and raised her Groucho mask briefly so I could see her face. She wasn't wet, so I deduced she'd come in with one of the family instead of ringing the bell.

"Mother said her relatives were coming from all over for the yard sale," I said. "But Kansas?"

Whatever Emma started to say was drowned out by the loud thud and subsequent howl of agony from the bathroom.

Chapter 2

"Claude!" Cousin Emma shrieked, and leaped toward the closed door.

"I brought my medical bag," Dad said. Though semiretired, Dad kept his state medical license current so he could treat family, friends, and victims of interesting accidents—like the one happening behind the bathroom door. Though once angry curses and loud thuds replaced the howls, I deduced it wasn't a serious one.

"See if you can open the door," I called to the bathroom's unlucky occupant.

The downstairs half bath was tucked under the stairs, in a space that should have remained a closet. We called it the quarter bath. Most people avoided bumping their heads on the four-foot ceiling over the toilet, but unless they were very short, they usually hit the five and a half foot ceiling over the sink when they straightened up after washing their hands. The fact that you couldn't sit down without bumping your knees against the sink was another strike against it. No wonder Michael, at six-four, refused to use this bathroom. I had trouble enough myself at five-ten.

Rob ambled over and gave the bathroom doorknob a sharp tug, which not only opened the door but tore it completely off its hinges, revealing a small, plump, middle-aged man crouched inside.

"Oops," Rob said.

"This is my husband, Claude," Emma said.

"Are you all right?" I asked. Claude nodded. He was also wearing a Groucho mask. Was this some peculiar Kansas custom?

I noticed that Claude was clutching his trousers closed with one hand. He probably didn't have elbow room to zip them up, since the bathroom was slightly under three feet wide. I turned away to make polite conversation with Emma while Dad and Rob pried Claude out and exclaimed over his bruises.

"All the way from Kansas," I said.

"Well, we didn't come just for the yard sale," Emma said. "But since we were here . . ."

"Emma does love a good yard sale," Claude said, limping over to collapse beside the doughnut box.

"Wonderful," I said.

"What should I do with this," Rob said, holding the door toward me.

"For now, shut it behind me," I said, as I ran in.

"It's going to be splendid!" I heard Dad say outside.

I looked at the bags under my eyes and my Bride of Frankenstein mane and thought maybe I should borrow Emma's Groucho disguise.

"But why in October?" I heard her saying outside. "I mean, luckily you have the weather for it this weekend, after all those weeks of rain, but isn't it rather late in the season?"

The loud flush of the ancient toilet drowned out much of Dad's reply, but I gathered that he was telling Emma and Claude about Edwina Sprocket's clutter. I washed my hands without bonking my head for a change and then, after dragging my fingers uselessly through my hair, I gave up.

"But, of course, everyone knows that a multifamily yard sale's a much bigger draw," Dad was saying as I heaved the detached door out of my way and set it carefully beside the doorway. "So a few of the family decided to join in and make it a bigger event."

"I think seventeen is more than a few, Dad," I said, plunking myself on the floor beside the doughnut boxes.

"You have seventeen other people participating?" Emma exclaimed.

"Seventeen other households," I corrected. "Heaven knows how many people that means. And that's just the family. We also have thirteen of Michael's friends and colleagues from Caerphilly College selling their stuff."

"Goodness," Emma exclaimed. "It must be enormous!"

"Two acres' worth," I said, gesturing toward the back yard.

"My," Emma said. "How exciting!"

She went over to the kitchen window and peered out.

"Now, Emma," Claude said, with a nervous laugh. "You know we can only take so much on the plane."

"There's always UPS," Emma said.

"Go out and take a closer look if you like," Dad said. "But don't go inside the fence. The security's still active."

"If it's all right," Emma said.

She hurried outside, followed by an anxious Claude.

I sighed, and rubbed my aching forehead.

"What's wrong, Meg?" Dad asked.

"I know I should be happy that she's so excited," I said. "The more people who show up with a cheerful, ac-quisitive attitude, the more stuff we'll unload."

"And the more money you'll make," Rob said.

"I don't care about the money," I said. "I just want all

the stuff gone. And I can't believe anyone would want to buy any of that junk."

"Junk!" Dad exclaimed. "You have a wonderful collection out there. I can't understand why you're selling most of it."

"No one can," Rob said. "Just ignore her; she's been like this for weeks."

"Like what?" I asked.

"Grouchy," Rob said.

"I prefer to think that I've achieved a more enlightened and detached attitude toward material possessions," I said.

"Grouchy," Rob repeated, nodding. "You don't want her coming over to your house right now. First she starts cleaning the place up—"

"And you're complaining?" I exclaimed.

"But then she starts trying to throw your stuff away or take it for the yard sale. It's seriously annoying."

"Look, I'm sorry," I said. "I admit I've been grouchy. It's probably just that I've been spending too much time dealing with stuff. I'm down on stuff. I'll get over it after the yard sale."

"Probably," Rob said. "I remember one time I had the flu after I'd been eating too much pizza and—"

"Rob," I said. "No one wants to hear this."

"Okay," he said. "It's just that for a couple of weeks, I didn't even want to look at a pizza, much less eat one. And you know how I love pizza. You'll get over it."

Just then we heard a loud crashing noise from above.

"Someone forgot he was in a hammock?" Rob suggested.

"Sounds more like someone taking the back stairs," I said.

Sure enough, Cousin Bernie stumbled into the kitchen a few seconds later, looking indignant and slightly worse for wear.

"Did you know there are three steps missing right in the middle of those stairs?" he asked.

"Yes," I said. "That's why there's that board nailed across the doorway with the KEEP OUT sign on it."

"Someone could kill themselves on that thing," he muttered. He walked over to the quarter bath and absently reached out to yank on the nearby doorknob, bringing the loose door down on top of himself.

"I've got my bag," Dad exclaimed, as he and Rob leaped to Bernie's assistance. Dad liked nothing quite as much as the chance to patch up an accident victim, so he was looking quite cheerful.

He also looked different. Obviously I needed caffeine if it took me this long to notice that he was wearing a peculiar brown garment made of damp feathers. Though I was probably responsible for the damp part.

"What is that you're wearing?" I asked, as he and Rob struggled with the door.

"My costume," Dad said. He picked up a wad of feathers lying on the floor beside him and jammed it over his head. "I'm a great horned owl," he said, his voice slightly muffled by the plumage that hid his mouth.

Apparently Rob and Dad had been working at cross purposes. Without Dad's involvement, Rob finally heaved the door off Cousin Bernie. Bernie popped up, saw Dad, closed his eyes, and lay down again.

"Concussion," he muttered. "I must have a concussion."

"Oh, dear," Dad said. "I hope not. Open your eyes and let me see your pupils."

"Are you going straight from the sale to an early Halloween party?" I asked, as Dad fished a small light out of his bag.

"Meg!" Dad exclaimed. "The yard sale. Remember how we decided, with Halloween coming up so soon, to make it more fun by offering a discount to anyone in costume?"

"She forgot," Rob said, as Dad shone the light in Bernie's eyes.

"It's on all the posters," Dad said. "The pupils look fine. How many feathers am I holding up?"

Bernie shut his eyes again and moaned.

"Here," Rob said. He reached into a grocery bag at his side and handed me a Groucho mask.

I remembered Dad suggesting the costume discount, but I didn't recall agreeing to it. But what would be the point of complaining? It was on all the posters. Dad would know—he'd made and distributed the posters; one of the few yard sale chores I'd successfully delegated. I put on the mask. The day was bound to bring moments when I failed to keep a polite, friendly expression on my face. Maybe the mask wasn't such a bad idea after all.

"Where's the nearest working bathroom?" Cousin Bernie said, popping his eyes open and scrambling to his feet.

"Second floor," I said. "That way!" I said, throwing myself in front of the door to the unsafe back stairs. Cousin Bernie whirled and ran out toward the front hall.

"Good luck," I muttered. I glanced over to see that Rob had plopped a slouch hat and a blond fright wig on his head and was beaming happily.

"You do realize that Harpo never speaks," I said.

He beeped his bicycle horn at me and batted his eyes. Okay, not a bad resemblance, which was pretty odd, since my tall, blond Adonis brother was always considered the best looking in the family and Harpo was—well, Harpo.

"All the SPOOR members will be in costume, each as a different kind of owl," Dad said. SPOOR—Stop Poisoning Our Owls and Raptors, a local conservation group—was Dad's new ruling passion.

"So we'll have a whole gaggle of owls," Rob said.

"A parliament of owls," Dad corrected. "You only use gaggle for geese."

"It's too dark to see much yet," Groucho Emma exclaimed, returning to the kitchen. "But it's going to be simply marvelous."

Groucho Claude, who followed her in, looked less enchanted. Groucho Meg knew just how he felt.

"A parliament of owls . . . a murmuration of starlings," Dad went on. Collective nouns were one of his many hobbies. "A muster of storks . . ."

"Morning," said a voice behind me. I turned to see the man who had beaten me to the upstairs bathroom earlier, now clad in jeans and a dark sweater. He strolled over to the coffeepot and poured himself a cup. Then he looked at Rob and Dad, sitting on the floor beside the doughnuts. Rob beeped his horn.

"An exaltation of larks," Dad recited. "An unkindness of ravens . . ."

The man frowned slightly, and strolled back out.

"And, of course, a murder of crows," Dad said. "I've always liked that one."

"You would," I said. "Who was that man, anyway?"

"I have no idea," Dad said. The feathers rustled slightly as he shook his head. "Not one of your friends from up here?"

"I've never seen him before," I said. "I thought he was a relative I'd never met."

"He's not family," Emma put in. "His eyes are too close together."

"He's a Sprocket," Rob said, through a mouthful of doughnut.

"Oh, God; not another one," I said.

Chapter 3

"Another what?" Emma asked.

"Another Sprocket," I said, sitting down and helping myself to a doughnut. "The family who used to own the house."

"But they sold it, right?" Emma said.

"They get a piece of the action," Dad said.

"Ten percent of whatever we make from selling the contents," I elaborated. "I've spent the past two months hauling stuff out of the house and barn, calling in appraisers, and negotiating to sell things at the best price possible, and all the time, I've had Sprockets underfoot."

"A plague of Sprockets," Rob said.

"Lacks alliteration," I said. "How about a surfeit of Sprockets?"

"Actually, that's used for skunks," Dad said. "A surfeit of skunks."

"It fits, then," I said, nodding.

"I'm sure they just wanted to help," Dad said, glancing at the door through which the latest Sprocket had disappeared.

"Yeah, right," I said. "It's no wonder the sales contract took so long. The only thing they ever agree on is their paranoid suspicion that Michael and I are stealing some priceless Sprocket family treasure. The best thing about this yard sale won't be getting rid of so much junk but seeing the last of the whole annoying family."

"Hear, hear," Rob said, beeping his horn vigorously.

"There now," Dad said, patting me on the arm. "It helps to get it out of your system, doesn't it?"

"Have another doughnut," Emma suggested.

"Why is he staying here, anyway?" I said. "Plenty of motels in town; I usually make the Sprockets stay in one."

"He got in late last night, and all the motels were full," Rob said. "He was pretty stressed out, so I told him he could stay here."

"Where he can cause even more trouble," I said, with a sigh. "That's the reason there's no furniture here," I added, to Emma and Claude. "If we bring anything into the house they assume it belonged to their Great-Aunt Edwina and start accusing us of trying to cheat them by leaving it out of the inventory. So we don't move anything in until all her stuff is gone."

"You're not keeping anything from the house," Emma said, rather plaintively.

"What we're keeping is locked up in an off-site storage bin," I said. "After we inventoried it, photographed it, and paid the Sprockets ten percent of whatever inflated price they thought it was worth."

"Goodness," Emma said. "They sound very trying."

"You have no idea how glad I'll be to see the last of the Sprockets," I said.

Just then, frenzied barking and snarling erupted from the backyard.

"What's that?" Emma exclaimed.

"Not again," I muttered.

"Our security system," Dad said, rubbing the tips of his wings together. "Works just as I planned."

"Looks as if the last of the Sprockets was trying to get inside the fence," Rob said, peering out the kitchen window.

"Oh, I see," Claude said, joining Rob at the window. "The pit bull and the Doberman are the security system."

"No, they're just for show," I said. "Spike, the little fur ball, is the security system."

"That would be the black-and-white dust mop thing dangling from Mr. Sprocket's ankle?" Claude asked.

"Don't worry," Rob said, ambling toward the door. "I'll rescue him."

"Poor little puppy," Emma said, shaking her head.

"I think he meant Sprocket," I said.

I peered out. Dad had shown up several days ago with enough eight-foot black plastic deer-proof fencing to enclose the entire two-acre yard sale area, as well as a collection of tents and multicolored fluttering banners—all of it borrowed, or so he claimed. I suspected the tents and banners had come from two of Mother's cousins who ran car dealerships, but the fencing worried me. Dad's definition of "borrowing" was questionable at times, and I kept expecting some neighboring farmer to show up irate, waving a bill for his deer-razed crops.

But the crowning touch was the short chicken wire fence that ran outside the main fence, leaving a small area where we'd turned loose as many dogs as we could round up on short notice. The pit bull had turned out to be a devout coward, the geriatric Doberman slept most of the time, but Spike, Michael's mother's dog, more than made up for their shortcomings.

I nodded with approval as Rob used a piece of doughnut to bribe Spike into detaching himself from Mr. Sprocket's left ankle.

"Meg, I have the signs for the barn," Dad said.

"Signs?" I echoed. "Why, what are you doing with the barn?"

"Making it off-limits," Dad said. "So no one will disturb the owls."

"Fine, Dad," I said. I'd have plenty of time later to explain that the barn would be my blacksmithing workshop, not a sanctuary for his beloved endangered barn owls. If the owls couldn't tolerate a reasonable amount of hammering, they could relocate to any of the other run-down outbuildings on the property.

"Oops; there's the doorbell again," I said.

I strolled toward the front door, followed by Dad, still chattering about the owls. By now, it was light enough that I could see our caller. He was peering through the glass sidelight to the left of the front door. I deduced from a half-dozen greasy triangular nose marks that he'd already exhausted the possibilities for snooping through the right side.

"Oh, great," I said. "It's Gordon-you-thief."

"Who's that?" Dad asked.

"Gordon McCoy. He runs the Antique and Junque Emporium on Main Street."

"Why do you call him Gordon-you-thief?"

"Everyone does," I said, opening the door. "No, Gordon, you can't go in early; you'll have to wait until nine like everyone else."

Gordon straightened up and smirked at me. You couldn't call it a smile when his beady eyes weren't involved at all, and he had an awkward way of trying to open his mouth as little as possible to hide his front teeth, which were oversized and underbrushed. His appearance would improve enormously if you could swap his nearly nonexistent chin with his exaggerated Adam's apple, and he'd be much more pleasant to have around if he'd stop using aftershave by the quart. I deduced from the red bandanna knotted over his head, the red sash around his waist, the painted-on handlebar mustache, and the single gold clip-on hoop earring that he'd typecast himself as a pirate.

"Shiver me timbers and call off the dogs," he said, throwing up his hands. "I'll come clean."

"Very funny, Gordon," I said, and started to close the door.

Gordon's foot got in the way.

"I'm here for the yard sale," he said, in an injured tone. "And you've got all these dogs running around loose."

"They're not loose," I said. "They're inside a fence, with a BEWARE OF THE DOGS sign."

"Well, how am I supposed to get in with all those dogs running around?"

"We'll be removing the dogs when the yard sale starts," I said. "At nine."

"But that's two hours from now," Gordon complained. "What am I supposed to do for two hours?"

"Go have breakfast somewhere," I suggested.

"Aw, come on," he said. "After all I did for you when you were getting ready for this? What's the harm?"

"See you at nine, Gordon," I said. I raised my foot and took deliberate aim, as if about to stomp on the foot he still had stuck in the door. He jerked his leg back and I shut the door.

Good riddance.

Chapter 4

"After all he did for you?" Dad repeated. I turned around to find that he had his back to me and was attempting to peer over his left shoulder at me.

"What are you doing?" I asked.

"Owls can rotate their heads a full 270 degrees," he said.

"I expect their necks are built rather differently from yours," I said. "You'll pull something if you keep trying that."

"Yes, they have several extra vertebrae," Dad said, rotating his head and trying to peer over the right shoulder. "Exactly what did Gordon do for you?"

"Beats me," I said. "He gave us estimates on some of the books and antiques, but since everyone else's estimates were at least twice what he offered, we didn't sell him anything."

"That doesn't sound helpful," Dad said.

"What's more, he missed every appointment he made with us," I added over my shoulder as I headed back to the kitchen. "And then he'd show up at some maximally inconvenient time and get huffy when we refused to leave him alone in the house. I'm surprised he waited until seven to show up."

"If you mean the weasel in the pirate costume, he was skulking around the yard earlier," Rob said.

"How can you say something like that about a perfectly nice animal like the weasel?" I asked.

"The sewer rat in the pirate costume, then," Rob said. "He was the one who set off the dogs in the first place, but somehow he managed not to get bitten."

"That's Gordon," I said. "How is Mr. Sprocket?"

"Please; Barrymore," the man in question said, offering me his hand to shake.

"Sorry," I said. "Mr. Barrymore, of course."

"No," he said. "Just Barrymore. Barrymore Sprocket."

"Nice to meet you," I said, with more enthusiasm than I felt. "Have some doughnuts; I hear the doorbell again."

As soon as I was out of sight, I dried my now-damp hand on my jeans leg and made a mental note to introduce Barrymore to my cousin Leo, the mad inventor, who might still be looking for guinea pigs to test his revolutionary new antiperspirant hand cream.

"Has this been going on all morning?" Dad said, as I appeared in the hall again. He had perched on the newel post at the bottom of the banister, the better to practice his head-swiveling.

"Only since five-thirty," Rob called from the kitchen.

"Five-thirty isn't this morning, it's last night," I muttered, on my way to the door. "If it's Gordon-you-thief again, I'll kill him."

A pleasant-looking woman in her fifties, wearing a flowered dress and a flower-decked hat, stood on the doorstep. Overdressed for a yard sale—she even held a pair of white kid gloves in her left hand. If this was a costume, it was too subtle for me. But there was no mistaking her purpose. She had that now-familiar acquisitive gleam in her eye and she clutched a copy of the *Caerphilly Clarion,* open at the classifieds.

"Excuse me," she said, with an ingratiating smile. "Is this where the yard sale is being held today?"

I pointedly looked past her to the road. Yes, the half-dozen yard sale signs Dad had tacked up several days earlier were still there, and even though it wasn't quite fully daylight, they were clearly readable even from here. For that matter, while driving up to the house, she could probably have spotted the fenced-in sale area. The multicolored tents and awnings were hard to miss.

I focused on her face.

"Yes, we're having a yard sale, but it doesn't open till nine a.m.," I said.

"I'm so sorry," she said. "I did so want to come, but you see, we're having a luncheon at church today, and I have to be there at nine."

"For a luncheon?"

"I'm in charge of preparations," she said. "Anyway, I just wanted to see if you had any little bits of china."

"Little bits of china," I repeated.

"Yes," she said. "I just love little china figurines. But I can't afford to buy many of them in stores—fixed income, you know. And between church events, and Scout meetings, I just never seem to have a Saturday free for yard sales. So I was wondering—if you had anything like that, maybe I could just slip in and take a peek. I won't take much of your time, really. And I'd be so grateful."

By this time, I realized I'd encountered another well-known fixture of local yard sales—the Hummel lady, who'd built her enormous collection for peanuts by using her sharp eye and sharper bargaining skills at flea markets and yard sales. And, of course, by conning her way into yard sales before anyone else.

"Oh, no, I don't really think we have anything like that," I said. "Not anymore, anyway. Well, we did find a box of figurines my great-aunt picked up when her husband was stationed in Germany in the fifties, but they weren't anything fancy. Just these cutesy little kids with lambs and puppies and things."

Her expression had grown strangely fierce and the fingers holding the newspaper twitched slightly.

"But I sold the whole box for a dollar to a guy who showed up a few minutes ago," I said. "Sorry."

"But– but–," she sputtered.

I had a hard time not laughing at the look of astonishment on her face. Okay, I suppose it was mean of me, but I was running on too little sleep, thanks to the likes of her.

Suddenly I saw her expression change to one of cold rage. She pursed her lips and her eyes narrowed. I stepped back involuntarily, but then I realized she wasn't looking at me.

She'd spotted Gordon-you-thief, lurking about the yard, craning his neck to see something inside the fence that surrounded the yard sale.

"I see," she said, in clipped tones, already turning away. "Thanks anyway."

I stayed to watch for a few moments. Seeing how quick she'd been to jump to conclusions about him, I suspected that she'd encountered Gordon before and that it might be fun to watch her accost him. But, instead, she marched over to the outer edge of the yard and stood there, close to the bushes that separated the yard from the road, staring at him.

I shrugged. Perhaps there would be interesting fireworks later.

"How does this sound?" Dad asked, and then demonstrated an owl's hoot.

"Fabulous," I said. "If I were a vole, I'd be terrified."

"I don't think it's resonant enough," Dad fretted.

When I returned to the kitchen, I found that several more relatives had joined the crowd—out-of-town ones who'd never met Michael before, and were inspecting him as frankly as if he were going on sale along with the eight-track tapes and Ronco gadgets outside. I considered asking Dad for the best group noun for an excessively large collection of family members—a chattering of cousins, or an unkindness of relations? But I stifled the impulse. After all, Mother would probably hear about it if I said anything insulting about her family.

Michael was pretending not to notice. Instead, he was looking with a puzzled expression at the impromptu kitchen table some of the family had constructed by propping the detached bathroom door up on some of the bricks left over from the chimney that had collapsed in September.

"Someone was trapped in the bathroom," I said.

"Ah," he said, nodding. "Well, we were planning to demolish the quarter bath anyway."

He sounded calm about the damage, though I couldn't tell what his face looked like. He'd donned a mask—Groucho never looked half as good—and began giving Claude and Emma the grand tour of the house. The tour was a lot safer than it used to be, now that I'd cleared all the stuff out. Also a whole lot less interesting, at least with me as tour guide. All the decluttering had temporarily dulled my enthusiasm for the house, so my tour consisted of a series of apologies for the house's present decrepitude; warnings about what not to touch, walk on, or stand under; and a dispiriting inventory of the repairs needed to make the house habitable.

Perhaps I should tag along more often on Michael's tour, I thought, as I sipped my coffee. If I listened with my eyes closed, I could almost see our future kitchen, with its deft blend of period charm and modern functionality, instead of the battered, dated 1940s room I was actually sitting in. The formal dining room next door certainly looked a lot better in the candlelight of Michael's imagination, with all its plasterwork and parquet painstakingly restored. He was particularly effective at evoking a vision of our library-to-be. You could almost overlook the fact that the actual room was boarded off until we could replace the floor that had collapsed into the basement a couple of decades ago.

Dad chimed in with his vision of what we planned to do with the yard, though I seriously doubted if we had room on three acres for free-range cows, sheep, and poultry along with the organic vegetable garden and the orchard of endangered heritage fruit trees.

At least Mother wasn't around to share her decorating suggestions. Presumably she was still working on her beauty sleep back at the Cave, as Michael and I called the tiny, dank basement apartment we were about to leave behind for the new house.

I tried to tune all this out. Not that I wasn't, at least in theory, equally excited about all these projects—the ones that didn't involve livestock, anyway—but the sheer number of them overwhelmed me, and the only thing that kept me from panicking was that they were all neatly jotted down in the notebook-that-tells-me-when-to-breathe, as I called my giant to-do list. Once they were in the notebook, I could manage not to think of them all the time. And this morning, just thinking about them made me tired.

And maybe just a little worried.

People had warned me that buying a house together

was one of the most stressful things you could do to a relationship, and renovating it was another, so doing both together probably constituted a death knell for couples less firmly grounded than Michael and me.

At least I hoped we were firmly grounded. We'd only had a few minor arguments so far. Minor because, after one of us had stormed off—me to my rented forge or Michael to his office at the college—the other had quickly gone running after to apologize, and we'd always mended the quarrel quite satisfactorily by bedtime. Then again, so far we hadn't gotten very far with the renovations. We'd only gotten as far as working through the clutter.

And what's this "we" stuff? the cynical part of my brain put in. You're the one doing all the work.

While Michael works two jobs so we can afford it, the kinder, gentler part of my brain replied. Instead of whining, I should be proud of how well he juggled the conflicting roles of drama professor vying for tenure and regular cast member on a syndicated TV show.

The cynic tried to suggest that money wouldn't be such a problem if Michael hadn't committed us to buying such a money pit of a house. Kinder-gentler would then protest that if Michael hadn't taken the house, we'd still be trying to make do with his tiny basement apartment.

I was tired of the whole argument. I smacked both voices back into their cages and told them to shut up, at least for today and tomorrow. I had a yard sale to run.

And the doorbell was ringing again.

Chapter 5

Over the next hour, the sixty or seventy people who'd be staffing booths at the yard sale arrived. Michael's faculty colleagues fit in so perfectly with my family that I kept mistaking them for distant cousins, which boded well for the harmony of the yard sale, but made me want to re-think living in Caerphilly.

At least the faculty members already knew Michael, or thought they did, and had no interest in asking him probing questions that relatives thought suitable for evaluating potential in-laws. So far he'd dodged questioning from several of my uncles about his political and religious af-filiations, but a particularly nosy aunt had surprised him into giving her an inventory of which optional body parts he still possessed: tonsils and wisdom teeth absent, ap-pendix and gall bladder still present and accounted for, and so forth. She didn't believe that he only wore glasses to read, though, and had taken to following him about and peering at him from various angles, trying to spot the contact lenses she suspected he was wearing. Although

Michael usually enjoyed my family rather more than I did, today he was starting to look slightly frayed.

And every time I opened the door to let in a yard sale participant, I could see that the crowd of waiting customers had grown larger. Spike's bark was beginning to sound hoarse.

"Amazing," I muttered, peering out of the window.

"What's amazing?" Rob asked.

"Look at all the customers," I said, shaking my head.

"Is there an official term for a whole lot of customers, like there is for owls and such?" Rob asked. "I know I'll get in trouble with Dad if I call them the wrong thing."

"I'd suggest a gaggle, like for geese, but I don't want to insult them," I said. "Though I can't imagine why this many people would want to spend a perfectly good Saturday at a yard sale."

"Maybe Dad took my suggestion," he said.

"What suggestion?"

"To spread a rumor that Captain Ezra Sprocket hid his pirate loot somewhere in the house," Rob said.

"Oh, good grief," I said. "Even if he had and we'd found it, do they really think we'd absent-mindedly put it out for the yard sale along with the empty plastic flowerpots and worn-out linens?"

Rob shrugged.

"And didn't you and Dad make up Pirate Ezra anyway?"

"Yeah," he said. "But I can see the Sprockets having a pirate or two in their family tree, can't you?"

"They're all pirates," I grumbled. "I still don't get it."

"Well, you wouldn't," Rob said.

"No," I said. "I've lost the ability to look at Edwina's clutter in a detached fashion, as a mere collection of inanimate objects—annoying, perhaps a little sad, but essentially benign. I've started to see it as a hostile force occupying the house—a force against which I've been doing battle for weeks."

"Battle?" Rob echoed.

"And while I've evicted the Army of Clutter from the house, and even banished some of it entirely to the dump or the local antique stores, most of its forces are now encamped on our lawn," I went on, waving my hand at the yard sale area. "In fact, they've gotten reinforcements from other households and are even now plotting revenge. Planning sieges and ambushes, and beaming hostility at us so strongly that I'm surprised you can't see a visible, tangible haze floating up and drifting malignantly toward the house."

"Wow," Rob said. "I want some of what you're on."

So much for explaining how I felt to my family.

At eight-thirty my mother showed up, dressed as a flapper, with a candy cigarette in a foot-long antique holder. She looked impossibly elegant, and I fought off one of my occasional moments of resentment that I'd inherited her height, but not her blonde hair or slender model's build.

She also looked calm and rested, and I wondered if it had been a good idea, camping out here in the house so she and Dad could stay at the Cave. Then I reminded myself that it had been my suggestion. The cramped, cluttered Cave had been giving me claustrophobia for weeks.

"Hello, dear," she said, pecking me on the cheek. "Sorry I'm so late. Is there anything I can do to help?"

"Actually, there is," I said.

Mother looked startled. No doubt she'd been making one of those obligatory social offers that one is supposed to decline with polite assurances that everything is under control. After more than thirty-five years, she should know I have no social graces.

"We're not opening the sale until nine," I said. "People have been ringing the doorbell since before six, badgering us to let them in early. Can you do something about them?"

"Of course, dear," Mother purred. She drew herself up, adding a full inch to her height, and headed toward the front door with her sternest face on. I wasn't sure if it was the chance to play Miss Manners and boss people around or the fact that the would-be early birds were trying to get into the sale ahead of her, but she threw herself into her assigned task with enthusiasm. Ten minutes later, when I had a moment to glance out one of the side windows, I saw that she'd chivvied the arriving crowds into a neat line leading up to the gate of the yard sale area, and was lecturing Gordon-you-thief on the rudeness of cutting in line.

Hundreds of people, and at least half of them in costume. Although many of the costumes consisted solely of masks bought from Rob, who'd set up a table by the driveway, right beneath one of the posters announcing the costume discount. He didn't have a lot of variety—in fact, apart from Groucho, he only had Richard Nixon and Dracula. I suspected he'd bought the masks in bulk and was selling them at a steep markup. At least he wasn't charging immediate family, but still, I wasn't sure I liked the new entrepreneur Rob who'd emerged since his computer-game company had become successful. I'd actually begun to miss the old feckless Rob who couldn't be bothered with boring practical details like money.

Someone should talk to Rob, I thought, with a sigh. Preferably someone other than me. I'd recently overheard two aunts praising my willingness to tackle the unpleasant, thankless jobs that no one else would, and realized that no matter how happy it made my aunts, this wasn't

entirely a positive character trait. Neither was being considered the most efficient and organized person in the
family. And when you combined the two, you got things
like this giant yard sale. Maybe when the yard sale was
over, I would work on expanding my vocabulary to include the word "no."

I'd worry about that later. After the yard sale. For the
moment, I made a mental note to keep an especially
sharp eye on the several women in hoop skirts that
seemed like a shoplifter's dream.

At nine sharp, Rob, Dad, and Michael ceremonially
led the dogs away and we opened the gates.

Gordon-you-thief was among the first half dozen to
enter—even Mother couldn't work miracles.

I stood inside the gate, trying to make sure no one got
knocked down and trampled, and nodding greetings to
anyone I recognized—which included most of the local
antique and junk dealers. But unfamiliar faces outnumbered the familiar ones. I wondered how many were ordinary customers, lured from all over the adjacent dozen
counties by our 30-FAMILY YARD SALE ads, and how
many were antiques dealers and pickers.

No matter. Amateurs or professionals, they could
come from Timbuktu if they liked, as long as they all
left with their arms full of stuff. And they all seemed intent on doing so. By the end of the first hour I could see
major traffic congestion up and down the aisles, as the
people in bulky costumes encountered the even larger
numbers of people dragging boxes or baskets of stuff
along with them.

At the far end of the fenced-in area we'd placed a dozen
ramshackle card tables and several of Mother's relatives
had set up a concession stand. Cousin Bernie and Cousin
Horace—the latter in the well-worn gorilla suit that his
new girlfriend didn't often let him wear to parties these

days—were already lighting fires in half a dozen grills and checking their supplies of hamburger patties and hot dogs, while Aunt Millicent and Cousin Emily set out plates of sandwiches and cookies and bowls of fruit and salad. We didn't want anything as mundane as hunger to make people check out early. Cadres of Grouchos and Draculas were already lining up for chow. We'd even arranged to rent two portable toilets, which were tucked discreetly behind the shrubbery in another corner of the yard sale area.

So far, not a lot of people were checking out at all. That's where things would get sticky. Most of the sellers had organized an elaborate, color-coded system of price stickers so customers could go through a single checkout at the exit. We'd be weeks coming up with an accurate tally of everyone's sales, and even then half the sellers would still think they'd been shorted. The sellers who collected money themselves were supposed to issue receipts that their customers could show at checkout, but I already knew they'd forget, and I'd spend way too much time straightening out the resulting problems. And the ballerina and the white rabbit who were currently serving as cashiers were proving unfortunate choices. Harvey seemed terrified of the cash register, and Pavlova of the customers. It was going to be a long day.

"What's wrong?" Michael asked, when he returned from his dog delivery mission.

"Oh, dear," I said. "Do I look as if something is wrong? I thought I had on my welcoming hostess face."

"I'm harder to fool than most of these people," he said. "I know you too well."

"I'm just wondering who in the world will buy all this stuff?"

"Are you worrying about the quality of the stuff, or just the sheer quantity?"

"Both," I said. "Take that, for example."

I pointed at a lamp shade on a nearby table.

"Ick," he said.

"Ick" summed it up pretty well. The lamp shade was huge—three feet tall, and equally wide at the base, though the sides curved in as they went upward and then flared out again, making it look like an inverted Art Nouveau birdbath. Its dominant colors were orange and purple, though at least a dozen other hues appeared here and there in the trimmings. And as for the trimmings, I had nothing against lace, fringe, braid, bows, beads, tassels, appliqués, rosettes, silk flowers, rhinestones, prisms, or embroidery, but I thought inflicting all of them on one defenseless shade was unforgivable.

"I can see why someone would want to get rid of it," I said.

"I'd have dumped it ages ago," Michael said, after glancing behind him to make sure the seller was truly out of earshot.

"Who in the world was so devoid of taste that they'd make such a thing?" I exclaimed. "And more to the point, who will ever buy it?"

Michael shrugged.

"Beats me," he said. "But odds are someone will buy it, and if not, we've got the truck from the charity coming Monday morning, and then the Dumpster from the trash company in the afternoon. One way or another, it'll all be gone by Monday night."

"And good riddance," I said. "Meanwhile, why is Mrs. Fenniman shaking her fist at Cousin Dolores?"

"Damn," he said. "I thought I'd calmed them down. Apparently Dolores is selling a spectacularly ugly vase Mrs. Fenniman gave her as a wedding present. Mrs. Fenniman is peeved."

"Dolores dumped the groom a good five years ago," I said. "If you ask me, she's allowed to unload the baggage that came with him. Should I go and explain that to Mrs. Fenniman?"

"Strangely enough, that's almost exactly what your mother said just now when I asked her to mediate," Michael said. "Ah, there she is."

As usual in our family, Mother's arrival shut down hostilities instantly, as both combatants scrambled to avoid her wrath.

"Thank God for Mother sometimes," I said. "Though whenever I find myself saying that, I always wonder if I should take my own temperature. And what is Everett doing with his boom lift, anyway?"

I pointed up, where one of the portable toilets had been lifted forty feet in the air on the platform of the boom lift. Everett, one of Mother's more enterprising cousins, had brought the boom lift over two weeks ago to help with our roof repairs. It was a multiperson model, with a six-foot wide metal platform on the end of a forty-foot extension arm. The arm so dwarfed the tractor base below that I kept expecting the whole contraption to topple over. So far even Mother's family hadn't achieved that in any of the boom lift's previous outings, though several had broken limbs by slipping through the railings and falling off the platform. At least whoever had put the portable toilet on the platform seemed to have loaded it securely.

"I heard him threatening to play a joke on your Uncle Floyd," Michael said.

Just then, the portable toilet's door slammed open and a portly man, still fumbling with his fly, stepped out, looked down, and abandoned his pants to clutch the rail of the boom lift.

"I think Everett picked up the wrong toilet," I said. "That's not Uncle Floyd."

"No, it's Dr. Gruber," Michael said. "Chairman of the Music Department. I'd better go rescue him."

Michael took off running. Uncle Floyd emerged from the other toilet and joined the crowd gawking up at the airborne professor.

"Good heavens," exclaimed a voice behind me, in an English accent.

"Morning, Giles," I said, turning to greet him. Giles Rathbone was one of Michael's closest friends on the Caerphilly College faculty, not to mention a member of his tenure committee.

And he wasn't wearing a costume. I liked Giles.

"I had no idea yard sales were so . . . lively," he said, staring up at the boom lift with visible alarm.

"This isn't your typical yard sale," I said.

"Or that so many people would be out this early," he added, looking around as if the crowd unnerved him as much as Dr. Gruber's plight.

I had to smile. Giles's tall form, loosely draped, as always, in tweed and corduroy, was hunched protectively and his eyes behind the thick glasses blinked and watered as if unused to this much brightness. Seeing Giles out-of-doors always reminded me of the scene at the beginning of *The Wind in the Willows* where Mole emerges into the sunlight.

"A bit overwhelming," I said, and Giles nodded in agreement. He looked half ready to bolt back to his car. I suppressed a sigh of exasperation. How had Michael ever befriended such a recluse? I'd spent the first six months I'd known Giles convincing him that it was okay to call me Meg rather than Miss Langslow. Though come to think of it, perhaps I'd only gotten him to drop the Miss. I couldn't remember if he'd ever actually called me Meg.

Friends had warned me that it could be hard work, getting your significant other's male friends to accept you, but I hadn't expected the process to be quite so much like coaxing a small nocturnal animal out of its hole.

Though that reminded me: I had bait today. I fished around in my pocket until I found a small slip of paper I'd stuck there.

"Here," I said, handing it to Giles. "I jotted down a map of which tables are selling books."

"Ah, thanks," he said. "I'm sure I'll find that helpful." I hoped so. Sooner or later, I was sure, I could break through Giles's reserve and turn polite acceptance into real friendship.

"It's only fair," I said. "You were an enormous help dealing with Edwina's library. Without you, we'd have put a lot of valuable books out for the yard sale."

Giles nodded absently and turned his attention to the map. Well, so much for bonding with Giles today.

I heard a small commotion to my right, and turned to see Gordon-you-thief, attempting to drag two oversized boxes through the crowd.

"Hey, Guiles," Gordon called. It took me a second to realize that he was talking to Giles, and mispronouncing his name, with a hard "G" rather than a soft one.

"I think he's calling you," I said to Giles, in an undertone.

"Maybe if I ignore him he'll go away," Giles said, through clenched teeth.

"No such luck," I said. "He's headed this way."

"Hey, Guiles," Gordon repeated, coming up to stand in front of Giles with his back toward me. "Glad I ran into you."

"Hello, Gordon," Giles said, edging back slightly.

"You're still collecting R. Austin Freeman, right?" Gordon said, taking a half step to close up the distance between them.

"What's that?" I asked.

"R. Austin Freeman's an early-twentieth-century mystery author," Giles said turning to me and, not accidentally, edging farther away from Gordon. "His protagonist was both a lawyer and a doctor—sort of a late-Victorian Quincy. I've been collecting his books for years. My collection's nearly complete, though," he said, turning back to Gordon and stepping away slightly when he realized that Gordon had again closed the gap to what was, for Giles, uncomfortably close quarters.

I couldn't decide whether to laugh or feel sorry for Giles. I'd done this dance with Gordon myself, backing away half a step at a time as he kept inching closer than I found comfortable. At first, I'd assumed that we just had very different senses of personal space, but eventually I'd realized that Gordon did it deliberately, to keep people off balance in a negotiation.

Or perhaps just to annoy them. At any rate, once I knew what he was doing, I'd figured out how to stop him. Whenever he tried to crowd me, I'd step even closer and peer down my nose at him. At 5'10", I was a good five or six inches taller than Gordon, and he didn't like having to crane his neck to see me.

I was tempted to try it on him now, and rescue Giles, but Gordon was already turning away.

"Still, you might want to take a look at what I found on the dollar table over there," he said, jerking his thumb over his shoulder. "I bet you'll want it when you see it in the shop."

He sauntered off, still smirking.

Giles sighed.

"The maddening thing is, I probably will want whatever he's found," he said. "The bastard has a damned good idea what's in my collection."

"He sold you most of it?" I guessed.

"No, only a few, and those some years ago. As soon as he finds out you're collecting something, the prices start creeping up. More than creeping, really. Skyrocketing. I usually do better elsewhere. But he stops by my office from time to time. That's where I keep my detective fiction collection, you see. And the science fiction and fantasy stuff. To annoy the old fuddy-duddies who look down their noses at genre fiction."

I fought to hide my smile. To look at him, you'd take Giles for a fuddy-duddy himself. I had a hard time imagining that beneath his stodgy tweed beat the heart of a rebel. A pedantic rebel, perhaps, and one who preferred to keep his rebellion subtle enough to avoid offending the administration.

"So while Gordon's in your office, he sneaks a peek at your shelves."

Giles snorted.

"Sneaks a peek! I came back from a class one day and found him taking a detailed inventory. Not only which books, but in what condition. So he could be on the lookout for better copies that might tempt me to trade up."

"At sky-high prices," I said. This was a longer and more natural conversation than I could ever remember having with Giles. Perhaps I should bone up on this Freeman person. Or was our shared dislike for Gordon the stronger bond?

Giles nodded.

"The only Freemans I'm missing are a few relatively rare ones. I suspect he's found one of those or perhaps what he thinks is a better copy of one I already have."

"So he'll probably be extracting more money from you soon," I said.

"Not necessarily," Giles said. "Last fall, I made a resolution not to deal with Gordon anymore. I decided it spoils my enjoyment of the books, just knowing they've passed through his hands. Haven't been in his shop for over a year now."

"Maybe he hasn't found anything after all, then," I

said. "Maybe he's just trying to lure you back into his den of literary temptation."

"Let's hope I have the strength of will to resist, then," Giles said.

"Get thee behind me, Gordon!" I said.

Giles chuckled at my joke, though as usual I couldn't tell if he found it funny or just wanted to be polite. I wondered, suddenly, if I wasn't the only one making an effort to become friends. Perhaps, in spite of thinking me entirely too boisterous and independent, Giles was, in his own stuffy way, making heroic efforts to get to know me. Or perhaps I was just overreacting to his normal British reticence. No way to tell.

"Well, I suppose there's a chance Gordon has overlooked a few books worth owning," he said. "Be seeing you."

I was surprised to see him stop briefly at the table where Dad, still in his great horned owl disguise, was selling off Edwina Sprocket's collection of owl tchotchkes to benefit SPOOR. I hadn't pegged Giles for a birdwatcher or a collector of ceramic owls. But I had to smile when I saw him pick up a pair of owl-shaped bronze bookends and tuck them in the crook of one arm before heading off toward the books.

Just then, a squabble broke out between Scarlett O'Hara and a middle-aged Gypsy, who'd each grabbed one of a pair of brass andirons, and my day really began going downhill.

Chapter 6

Where were my volunteer helpers, I wondered. Scarlett backed off when I threatened to expel her from the yard sale, but I had to sit on the Gypsy for ten minutes to calm her down. And no one lifted a finger to help me. I had recruited a dozen relatives to help, but apart from my two increasingly demoralized cashiers, none of them were nearby. I hoped they were off taking care of other problems. We had plenty of problems to go around. In addition to squabbles between customers, I was starting to notice squabbles among the sellers, as various people suddenly noticed which priceless treasures their spouses, parents, children, or siblings had decided to unload.

"She's selling my high chair," my forty-something cousin Dermot announced, pointing to his sweet, gray-haired mother as if he'd just spotted one of the FBI's top ten wanted criminals lurking in our backyard.

"If you want it, why don't you just buy it?" I asked.

"I'm not selling it to him," Dermot's mother said. "He'd only stick it back in my garage again."

"I don't have room for it in my apartment."

"And I don't have room for it in my garage."

I left them to sort it out. Up and down the aisles, similar battles were being waged over rusting tricycles, battered reclining chairs, and moth-eaten scraps of clothing. If I'd known how traumatic yard sales were for the sellers, I'd have arranged to have a family therapist on hand.

Mother was being unusually helpful, but she couldn't be everywhere at once, and she had her hands full dealing with the shoplifters. She knew who all the family kleptomaniacs were and exactly what mix of threat and cajolery to use with each of them. And long experience with the light-fingered members of our clan had given her a second sense for spotting strangers intent on pilfering, whether for professional or psychiatric reasons.

For once in my life I wished I had more family members like Mother. I could use a dozen more of her, at least.

I'd assign one just to keep people out of the barn. I didn't quite share Dad's passionate concern for the welfare of the nesting owls, but I had other, more practical reasons for declaring the barn off-limits. Including the fact that we weren't entirely sure parts of it were structurally sound. The last thing we needed to inaugurate our life in the house was a lawsuit from some disgruntled customer who'd wandered in where he had no business being and gotten injured by falling beams or rubble. So I'd posted a variety of threatening signs on the barn doors, everything from "Keep out!" and "No Trespassing!" to "Warning! Falling debris!" and Dad had added his "Keep out! Owls nesting!" signs, which were probably less effective but a lot more picturesque.

And yet less than an hour into the sale, I saw Gordon ducking into the barn, dragging a large cardboard box. And then he came out empty-handed. Several times. Okay, he probably wasn't attempting larceny. For one thing, both of the ground floor doors to the barn were inside the fence, and if he tried to lower stuff out of the hayloft door, which did overlook the outside world, someone would surely notice. So he was probably only doing what people had warned me the greedy and inconsiderate customers would do—dragging large quantities of stuff off to one side to sort through at their leisure before returning the unwanted items to the sale area. Not a big problem if they did their sorting and returning relatively soon, but if they waited till near the end of the sale, when you started reducing prices across the board . . .

Well, Gordon might be in for a nasty shock. For one thing, we weren't reducing prices today—this was a two-day event. And for another thing, as soon as I had a moment I planned to slip into the barn, drag out everything Gordon had hidden away there, and put it back out for anyone who wanted it.

Unfortunately, every time I set out toward the barn, some new crisis intervened. A lost child. A lost purse. More scuffles between overeager Grouchos and Nixons.

I caught Eric and one of his little cousins charging admission to the portable toilets and ordered the young entrepreneurs to exercise their capitalistic instincts by helping Cousin Horace at the hamburger stand.

"You'd be amazed what you can find at yard sales," I overheard one woman telling another. "On *Antiques Road Show,* people are always bringing bits of junk they bought at yard sales and finding out they're worth thousands of dollars."

"That's true," the second woman said. Just then they spotted my shadow. They hunched protectively over the table in front of them and glared at me until I moved on. I fought back a smile. Would it reassure them to know that I was not a competitor? That I had no intention of buying

anything at the yard sale, and particularly not from that
table, which was filled with some of the worst junk I'd
cleared out of Mrs. Sprocket's attic? Probably not. And I
certainly didn't want to discourage them by mentioning
that seventeen keen-eyed antique appraisers had already
turned up their noses at the contents of that particular
table. For all I know, if I'd called an eighteenth dealer he
might have spotted a hidden treasure among the clutter.
Perhaps the cracked chamber pot had once stood in the
servants' quarters in Monticello, or perhaps Eleanor Roo-
sevelt had crocheted the toilet paper roll covers as part of
the war effort. I wished them luck.

Cousin Deirdre, the animal rights activist, had begun
splashing paint on every moth-eaten fur coat and taxider-
mied mongoose in sight. I confiscated her paint and explained to the unhappy fur owners that she only used
nontoxic washable paint, but most of them didn't calm
down until Mother promised to see that Deirdre reim-
bursed their cleaning costs.

"Meg, we're out of Spike's dog food!" Rob exclaimed,
appearing at my elbow while I was trying to calm an elderly lady whose sense of decency had been violated by
her discovery that one of the booths was selling back is-
sues of *Playboy*.

"Get him a hamburger from Horace," I said.

"Okay," Rob said. "How does he like them?"

"Ask him," I said.

"Roger," Rob said, turning to go.

"While you're going that way," I called after him, "Could
you tell that man with the grandfather clock that he doesn't
have to carry it around the whole time he's shopping; we'd
be happy to keep it behind the checkout counter for him."

"I've already told him that, twice," Rob said. "He says
he doesn't mind carrying it."

"Let me rephrase that. Tell him if he whacks one more

person in the head with the clock, I'll take it away from him and kick him out of the yard sale."

"Roger."

I returned to my irate customer.

"I'm sorry, ma'am," I said. "I'm not sure we have the right to keep someone from selling his *Playboy* magazines, but if you can point out the booth, I'll ask him to keep them out of sight."

"Hmph," the woman snorted, as she turned and marched away. After a few feet, she stopped and turned back, hands on her hips.

"And don't let me catch you selling any of that trash to that worthless husband of mine!" she shouted.

I turned to the checkout counter. The white rabbit and the ballerina looked stricken. Michael, standing nearby, wore the intensely solemn look that always meant he was trying not to crack up.

"And does anyone have any idea who she is, and what her worthless husband looks like?"

"No," Michael said. "But I know who's selling the *Playboys*. Your cousin Everett."

"Can you talk to him?"

"Sure," Michael said. "I'll tell him to keep his *Playboys* under the counter with the *Penthouses* and *Hustlers*."

"Good grief," I said. "I thought all he had was forty years of *National Geographic*."

Just then I heard a loud altercation nearby. Not the first of the day, by any means, but the voices sounded familiar, so I waded through the crowd to see what was going on.

"It's mine!"

"No, it's not!"

"Yes, it is!"

"I saw it first!"

"But I touched it first!"

"Liar!"

"Thief!"

"Let go!"

"Take that!"

Typical. I'd heard so many quarrels already today that I'd given up intervening unless the participants came to blows, which these two seemed about to do.

And to my dismay, I realized that the latest combatants were two of my aunts—elderly, respectable women who didn't hesitate to rap my knuckles at Thanksgiving dinner to correct minor flaws in my table manners.

They were playing tug-of-war over an antique purple cut-velvet piano shawl with foot-long fringe. Not tugging very hard, of course, since the material was fragile; but both of them were obviously determined not to let go. Aunt Gladys, her stout form encased in a vintage beaded opera gown, had both ring-encrusted fists clamped firmly around her end of the shawl and looked as if even the boom lift would have trouble dislodging her. In a fair fight, I'd have bet on her. But Aunt Josephine didn't fight fair. Looking uncannily authentic in her wicked witch costume, complete with a pointed hat and a toy cat wired to her shoulder, she was only holding the shawl with one hand while with the other she whacked Aunt Gladys in the derriere with her broomstick, throwing in an occasional kick to the shins for good measure.

I took a deep breath and was about to wade in on my one-woman peacekeeping mission when a streak of black-and-white fur appeared and launched itself at the shawl. Spike. He couldn't quite leap high enough to reach the shawl, but he managed a good mouthful of the swaying fringe. My aunts watched in horror as he hung suspended from the shawl for a few seconds and then dropped when his weight ripped the fragile fabric in half.

"Sorry," Rob said, running up and clipping the leash back onto Spike's collar—an easier task than usual, with

Spike's fangs muffled in fringe. "I was taking him over for his hamburger, but he got loose."

"A Solomon among dogs," I said. "Does either of you want this?"

I held out the remaining half of the shawl. Both aunts shook their heads. They gathered up their dignity along with the objects they'd apparently dropped in the fray and strode off without looking back.

"Bring the other half back when Spike finishes with it," I told Rob. "Maybe Aunt Minnie can use it for her quilting."

"And who's paying for that?" said a woman at a nearby table. Presumably the wounded shawl's owner.

While I was settling up, my irritation surged again when I spotted someone else going into the barn. The latest in a long series of someone elses who'd been shuffling in and out of the barn.

This one I even recognized—the Hummel lady. Apparently she'd decided to skip out on her church luncheon after all. I'd also seen a man I suspected I'd recognize when he no longer wore a cartoon-sized sombrero. And a tall man in a brown jacket and a Dracula mask. One of the Gypsies—we had about a dozen, since it was one of the easiest costumes for a woman to throw together at the last minute; this one was tall and slender and less gaudy than most. Even poor Giles. Perhaps he'd decided to talk to Gordon-you-thief about the Freeman book after all.

"We have a problem you need to deal with," Barrymore Sprocket announced, stepping into my path so I either had to notice him or kick him.

I counted to ten before answering. And then I continued on to twenty. Sprocket had been reporting problems for me to deal with all morning, and creating more problems than he solved. He'd fingered two people as professional shoplifters casing the joint. By the time I'd

drummed it into his head that his two suspicious characters were not only cousins of mine, but off-duty police officers I'd drafted to help with security, everyone at the
sale had also gotten the message, thus seriously under-
mining their effectiveness as undercover operatives. He'd
pitched a major fit when a small Groucho broke a cheap
vase, and mortally offended the child's mother, who
changed her mind about buying several hundred dollars'
worth of stuff. When he'd reported that one of the portable toilets was out of toilet paper, I'd told him where we
kept the extra supply and assigned him to janitorial duty.
He'd been making himself scarce since. I should have
known it was too good to last.

"What now?" I asked, through gritted teeth.

Chapter 7

"That Gordon person is hiding stuff in the barn," he said. "He's got boxes and boxes of stuff in there and—"

"Did you tell him the barn is off-limits?" I asked.

"Yeah, but he wouldn't listen to me," he said, shrugging. "He said you told him he could use it."

"He's lying," I said.

"Well, then maybe you should go and tell him to get out," Sprocket said, with a shrug. "He won't listen to me."

Who would, I thought, but I decided it wouldn't help to say it.

"I'll deal with it as soon as I can," I said aloud. "Of course, I could deal with it now if you could take over doing something for me for a few minutes."

As I expected, he disappeared as I finished my sentence.

But he was right; I needed to deal with it. Or find someone who could. I finally escaped from the checkout and made it as far as the SPOOR table, where Dad had just finished signing up one of the Nixons as a new member.

"Thank you!" Dad said. "And as promised—everyone who signs up today gets a dozen genuine owl pellets."

He handed the new SPOORite a baggie full of something, and they shook hands, laughing.

Dad had a whole bowl of the somethings on the table. I picked up one and examined it. It was lumpy and gray and vaguely resembled the remarkably unappetizing organic trail mix he was fond of making during his health food kicks.

"What is this, Dad?" I asked when his customer had gone. "Some kind of special, nutritionally balanced owl kibble? I have to tell you, Michael and I aren't up for cosseting our owls with an expensive special diet. Free-range owls, that's what we want."

"Very funny," Dad said. "You don't mean to tell me that I never taught you and Rob about dissecting owl pellets when you were kids?"

"Not that I recall," I said. I glanced at the pellet uneasily and dropped it back in the bowl. "Why is that so interesting?"

"Because you can tell exactly what an owl's been eating from the pellets!" Dad exclaimed.

"Oh," I said, wiping my hand on my jeans. "Pellets are droppings."

"Not precisely," Dad said. "Owls regurgitate rather than excrete them. But the principle's the same. See, here's an example of a pellet that contained the entire skeleton of a vole!"

Dad was flourishing a sheet of poster board to which he'd glued dozens—perhaps hundreds—of tiny rodent bones, along with a lot of little tufts of ratty-looking fur. Glancing behind him, I could see that he had at least a dozen more owl pellet posters.

"Fascinating Dad—but right now, we have an owl crisis. Gordon-you-thief keeps sneaking into the barn. I'm sure he doesn't mean to upset your fledgling owls, but—"

"I'll go and talk to him immediately," Dad said.

He put a sign on his chair that read Owl Be Right Back and hurried over to the barn.

"Excuse me," someone said, tugging at my elbow. "I think a quarter apiece is too expensive for these."

I turned to find a middle-aged version of Goldilocks standing at my side, pointing her porridge spoon at a collection of tiny china owls on one corner of the SPOOR table.

I stifled the impulse to say that I agreed and would give her a quarter to take the whole lot of them off our hands. Then an evil thought hit me.

"I could let them go at three for a dollar," I said, feigning reluctance.

"Okay," Goldilocks said. She snatched up the whole collection, all twelve of them, handed me four dollar bills, and hurried off, as if afraid I'd retract the offer. A second too late, I realized that I'd just broken my own rule about giving everyone receipts.

"Aunt Meg?"

I looked down to see my nephew Eric dressed as Superman. He was staring at Goldilocks's retreating back with a puzzled look.

"Aunt Meg, three for a dollar—"

"Yes, I know," I said. "I'll explain it to you later. Or your grandfather will when he gets back—do you want to watch his table for him?"

"Okay," Eric said, with a grin. Then he stood behind the counter, puffed out his chest so the "S" showed to better advantage, and assumed a serious, responsible expression.

On my way back to the checkout counter, I ran into my cousin Basil. Or possibly Basil's identical twin, Cyril. No one in the family could tell them apart and I'd given up trying after I figured out that no matter what you called one of them, he'd claim to be the other twin anyway. At any rate, he was trying to shove an enormous box of stuff along in front of him by kicking it, while carrying a moose head in each arm.

"Let me help you with that," I said.

"Thanks," he said, as I divested him of the moose heads. "That's my pile over there."

He indicated a huge pile of stuff over by the fence. Enough stuff to fill a two-bedroom apartment, which was what Basil and Cyril had. But their lair was already crammed to the ceiling with books, computer equipment, war-gaming paraphernalia, and assorted junk. Where could they possibly put all this stuff? Not to mention that every item he'd collected was either broken, perfectly hideous, or both.

"What in the world are you doing with all this stuff?" I asked.

I tried to keep my dismay from showing, but apparently I failed.

"Oh, don't worry," he said. "We're getting rid of it all really soon."

"Getting rid of it?" I echoed. "Then why buy it in the first place?"

"You know that TV show that comes to your house and organizes it?"

"Yes," I said. Actually, I knew of several such shows, and watched them all religiously, a guilty secret I hid from everyone but Michael. I hoped it was a phase I'd grow out of once we unloaded Mrs. Sprocket's clutter.

"We want to get on that show," he said. "But the first thing they do is make you get rid of half of your stuff. And we don't want to get rid of anything; we just want them to organize us."

"I see," I said. "So you're trying to put enough extra stuff in your house that they won't touch yours."

"Exactly," he said, beaming.

While I wanted to ask, what if they didn't get on the show, I hated to spoil his fun.

"Good luck with it," I said instead, and left him with his loot.

Back at the checkout area I found to my relief that Mrs. Fenniman and Michael had taken over as cashiers. Michael would remain calm and genial no matter what the customers said or did, Mrs. Fenniman took no guff from anyone, and both of them could do a halfway decent Groucho voice to go with their masks. Things were looking up.

In fact, I suddenly realized that I was feeling cheerful again. Dad would take care of Gordon-you-thief, and in the meantime, I was surrounded by people made very, very happy by the yard sale.

"Meg, this is wonderful!"

I turned and saw my twenty-something cousin Rosemary, from the Keenan branch of the family. I had a quick moment of panic, because I couldn't immediately remember what I was supposed to call her these days. Morgana? Ecstasy? Cassandra? She'd been through all of those, but I didn't think any of them were current. Rob had taken to calling her simply "Not-Rosemary." She had changed her name five or six times in the last decade, usually to symbolize some new breakthrough she felt she'd achieved in her path to wisdom or enlightenment or however she currently defined her goal. Not-Rosemary had never met an Eastern religion or a new age fad she didn't like, and she always dressed to enhance her already uncanny resemblance to the Woodstock-era Joni Mitchell.

I reminded myself that I didn't actually have to call her anything at the moment. And even if someone she didn't know joined us, a free spirit like Not-Rosemary wouldn't expect a formal introduction.

"Wonderful?" I repeated. "I'm not sure how wonderful it will be, but I hope it's productive."

"Oh, it will be," she said. "Look at the blessing you're giving all these people."

"Blessing?" I echoed, distracted by a passing shopper. I wasn't quite sure how much of a blessing it was to tempt anyone into buying a surplus milking machine and a dozen vintage 1960s troll dolls.

"Are you familiar with feng shui?" she said. "It's the ancient Chinese art of placement. The literal translation is 'the way of wind and water,' and—"

"Yes, you gave Mother a book about it for Christmas, remember," I said. Although considering the effect the book had had on Mother, I would have guessed the literal translation of feng shui was "Come, let us drop everything and rearrange the furniture another seventeen or eighteen times before dinner."

"Clutter is very significant in feng shui," she said. "At least in dealing with Western homes. If you want to feng shui your house, the first thing you should do is get rid of clutter."

"Really?" I said, with genuine interest. Had Not-Rosemary finally taken up a fad that I could relate to?

"Yes," she said. "Clutter is bad. Blocks the house's chi—the energy flow—and can also hold negative energy from past residents, or past owners of the clutter. If you ask me, clutter is probably the root cause of half the problems in our culture."

"I see," I said. I was glad to see that she'd finally stopped blaming television and refined sugar, since I rather liked both of those.

"So look at what your yard sale will accomplish," she said. "What a wonderful energy clearing! Imagine all the bad karma and negative energy everyone's getting rid of!"

She drifted off, beaming cheerfully at everyone she

passed. I wonder if it would eventually occur to her that the sellers couldn't get rid of their cosmically blighted stuff unless some other poor soul bought it. Did the buyers get the seller's negative energy along with the stuff, or did being sold reset an item's karma count to zero?

But she had helped me realize why the sellers were so happy: they were removing unwanted burdens from their lives. Okay, some of them thought it was more about making money than dry cleaning their chi, but surely even they were starting to feel not just richer but lighter and freer.

I had a harder time understanding why the buyers were so happy, but as Mother frequently remarked, I hadn't inherited her shopping gene. I decided to assume that everything the customers were carrying around would meet some long-felt want. Better yet, some dire need that their perilous finances would never have allowed them to meet if not for our yard sale. That would solve the karma count problem, too.

Of course, I kept spotting the occasional person who threatened to overturn my newly created illusion—what long-felt want or dire need could my elderly aunt Catriona have for a fully functional crossbow and a video on firming her buns? I pushed the thought out of my mind.

And I also saw a few people who seemed genuinely upset by something. I tried to suppress the urge to go and ask them what was wrong. No matter how much I wanted everyone to have a lovely time at the yard sale it wasn't my responsibility to make it happen. I couldn't fix everyone's problems. I shouldn't even try.

"What's wrong?" I asked Cousin Morris a few minutes later.

"I think it's over," he said, his words slightly muffled because his head was buried in his hands. "The passion has gone out of our marriage."

Too much information, I thought, and scrambled for

the right thing to say. Cousin Morris was a pleasant, mild-mannered man with gently receding hair and a gently growing tummy. Cousin Ginnie, his wife, was responsible for the tummy. She was a plump, cheerful woman whose life revolved around cooking, thanks to her career as the dessert chef for an upscale Williamsburg restaurant. They were older than I was—in their fifties—but I was fond of Morris and Ginnie, and never passed up their dinner invitations. Still, I didn't think of them as close friends. Why was Morris confiding in me? Or was he going around saying the same thing to everyone he met? That didn't sound like Morris.

And I had to admit that if I had to pick a word to describe their marriage, "passion" wouldn't be the first thing that came to mind. It wouldn't come to mind at all. "Comfortable, though slightly boring" would have been my diagnosis—the sort of relationship so many married people fall into after a while. Did this have anything to do with my inexplicable reluctance to take the plunge with Michael? The fear that we'd eventually settle into comfortable-but-boring?

Cousin Morris didn't seem either comfortable or bored at the moment. He looked miserable. He had raised his head to stare at something.

I followed his glance, and my jaw dropped. I knew Cousin Ginnie had taken a table for the yard sale but, until now, I hadn't inspected her wares—the most incredible collection of racy lingerie I'd ever seen outside of a Frederick's of Hollywood catalogue. As I watched, she took a pouf of black and fuchsia lace from a shopper half her age, demonstrated that the young woman had been holding it upside down, and gestured, with the same sweet smile she used when urging you to have another scoop of freshly whipped cream on your chocolate soufflé, toward the small tent that served as a dressing room.

"Oh, my," I said.

"You see," Morris said, shaking his head. "It's as if she's auctioning off our marriage, one romantic moment at a time. I thought she loved my little presents."

"Oh, they're all presents from you?" I said.

"So many wonderful Christmases, birthdays, anniversaries," he intoned.

"That's very sweet," I said.

"Mother's Days, Valentines Days, Easters, Halloweens, Thankgivings, Fourth of Julys, May Days, April Fool's Days, summer and winter solstices . . ."

I had to admire Cousin Morris's romanticism, though if I were Ginnie, I'd have tried to channel him into a more diverse range of gift ideas. Still, his heart was in the right place, I thought, as he progressed from holidays to special occasions.

". . . and graduations, and back-to-school weeks. Promotions, and awards, and of course as a welcome home whenever I return from a trip . . ."

Every trip? Morris spent about half his work life on the road.

"I think it's wonderful," I said. "But don't you think that perhaps she might have decided she has too much . . . um . . ."

"How can you have too much love?" Cousin Morris asked, sounding slightly shocked. He pulled out a handkerchief and blew his nose vigorously.

I wanted to suggest that even if you couldn't have too much love, you could definitely have too many black lace negligees trimmed with marabou feathers. But before I could figure out how to say it tactfully, he wandered off, still shaking his head and muttering softly.

I should do something, I thought, but nothing came to mind, so I made a mental note to worry about it later. Considering what a hard time I had remembering mental notes just now, this amounted to the same thing as deciding not to worry about it, only with less guilt.

As I turned to leave, I noticed a nun shopping at Cousin Ginnie's booth. Of course, given the costume discount, she probably wasn't a real nun, but it was still disconcerting to see her perched on the counter, her habit hiked up well over her knees as she tried on a pair of fishnet stockings.

"Everything going okay?" I asked Michael, when I arrived back at the checkout counter.

"Just dandy," Michael said. "Your out-of-town relations will never grow bored while I'm around. In the past hour alone they've asked if I've ever been married before, was I breast-fed, and what were my College Board scores."

"Good grief," I said. "Just tell them to mind their own business."

"I just say 'not recently' or 'I don't remember,' whichever fits my mood," he said. "That keeps them happy."

"Apart from that, how's everything going?"

Mrs. Fenniman shook the cash box at me. I took this to mean it was filling up. Michael, who had a much better sense of my priorities, pointed to a man staggering away from the checkout counter with three large boxes of stuff. I smiled. Yes, stuff was leaving. Lots of stuff.

I took a deep breath. Maybe everything would turn out fine after all.

"Meg?"

I turned to find Dad and a man I didn't recognize, carrying a large trunk toward the cashier's table. I noticed several customers already in line glaring at them, and heard a few mutinous comments about people waiting their turns. In fact, the whole crowd was beginning to mutter.

I decided to avert trouble by meeting the trunk procession before it reached the checkout table.

"There's a line, you know," I said to the man.

"This lady wants to buy the trunk," Dad said.

"But only if you can find the key," said a short, blonde woman, appearing from behind the trunk. "It's no use to me if I can't even get it open."

The mutinous comments from the line were growing louder.

"It had a key when we put it out," I said, frowning. "Did you look around where you found the trunk?"

"Someone had dragged it into the barn," Dad said.

"Gordon-you-thief," I said, nodding. "Put it down while we look for the key. No, don't block the cashier's line—it could take us some time to find the key."

Following my gestures, Dad and the other man maneuvered the trunk down behind the cashiers' tables, into the small roped-off area we'd set aside so we'd have a place to put our own stuff and hide from the customers.

Pacified, the customers in line grew quiet again. For now.

The man dropped his end before Dad did, and I heard something thump inside the trunk.

"We definitely need the key before I can sell you the trunk," I said. "It was empty when we put it out; the price doesn't include the contents, whatever they are."

"I don't want the contents," the woman said, with a sniff. "I didn't put them there. I just want the trunk. In working order. With a key."

She's a customer, I told myself. I tried to smile, and then decided not to bother; the Groucho mustache hid my mouth anyway, and the smile wasn't likely to reach my eyes.

"Dad, could you go and see if you can find Gordon McCoy," I said. "The jerk probably locked some stuff he wanted into the trunk and took away the key."

The woman remained, tapping her foot and looking pointedly at her watch while Dad and Rob went up and down the aisles, looking for Gordon. I began to worry. What was Gordon trying to pull? I didn't think there was any way he could get out of the yard sale area without our seeing him—certainly not with anything valuable. Anyway, despite the nickname, literal larceny wasn't really Gordon's style, only sharp business practices.

"Maybe he went to lunch," Dad suggested, returning after his third or fourth sweep through the grounds. "But I got these from your cousin Fred's table. I suspect those trunk keys don't have too many variations—see if any of these fit."

He handed me a shoebox full of keys—probably several hundred of them, in a variety of sizes—and dashed off again.

Cursing Gordon-you-thief under my breath, I sat down beside the trunk with the shoebox in my lap and began trying keys. The metal plate around the keyhole was slightly scratched. It hadn't been when I'd put it out, which meant that she'd probably tried to pick or force the lock before bringing the trunk to me. A fact I'd bring up if, as I anticipated, she tried using the scratches to dicker over the price when I finally got the damned thing open.

To my complete astonishment, the seventeenth key I tried actually fit.

"Victory!" I exclaimed.

"It's about time," the woman who wanted to buy the trunk exclaimed.

I heaved the lid up and looked inside.

"It's Gordon," I said.

"Yes, he's probably the one who locked the trunk," Michael said, over his shoulder. "What did he put inside?"

"No, I don't think he locked the trunk," I said. "I mean, it's Gordon inside the trunk."

Chapter 8

"Gordon?" Michael exclaimed, leaping up from his chair. "In the trunk? Is he—?"

"Definitely," I said. "I think his head's bashed in."

I hoped I sounded calm. I'd seen dead bodies before, and as a doctor's daughter, I like to think I have a pretty strong stomach. But there's a difference between hearing your father prattle on at the dinner table about dead bodies, real or on the pages of the mystery books he loves, and finding one in your own backyard. I inhaled deeply, as my yoga teacher always recommended in moments of stress, and then decided to postpone further deep breathing until later. Even through the reek of Gordon's aftershave, I could smell the unmistakable odor of blood.

Gordon's red pirate bandanna was askew, revealing his thinning, straw-colored hair, and both bandanna and hair were clotted with clumps of darker red.

"Someone probably hit him with that bookend," Michael said, pointing to an object lying at the other end of the trunk, by Gordon's feet.

"Oh, damn," I muttered. The last time I'd seen that owl-shaped bookend, Giles had been carrying it.

The woman who wanted to buy the trunk looked in, shrieked, and fainted. I looked around. The people in line hadn't been paying much attention to what I was doing before, but now, thanks to the unconscious woman, they were starting to gawk.

"Shut the trunk," I said, and then followed my own orders. "Mrs. Fenniman, can you take care of her? We need to keep people behind the ropes—maybe if they don't see what's happened we won't have a panic. And can someone go tell Dad not to let anyone in the barn?"

"We should call the police," Michael said.

"No need to call," Mrs. Fenniman said. "I saw Chief Burke a few minutes ago, looking over some fishing gear at Professor Hutson's table. Shall I get him?"

"I'll do it, and then enlist Meg's dad," Michael said, shoving back his Groucho mask as he turned. "You make sure no one leaves the scene of the crime."

"Will do," I said.

Not hard, since the only people planning to leave were the dozen standing in the checkout line, and at least for the moment, most of them seemed enthralled at having a front row view of what would doubtless be the most exciting thing to happen in Caerphilly in months.

Though they didn't know about the murder just yet. At the moment, they were watching Mrs. Fenniman minister to the fallen customer. Some of them looked puzzled—probably the ones who knew that the Heimlich maneuver wasn't necessary or even useful in cases of fainting. Of course, Mrs. Fenniman knew that, too, but she'd been dying to practice the technique ever since Dad had taught her how a few weeks ago. Thank goodness he hadn't yet taught her how to perform a tracheotomy.

I scanned the crowd, looking for Giles. I couldn't

imagine him killing anyone, and I suspected he'd absent-mindedly set the owl bookend down someplace. If he could remember where, that might help us—correction, help Chief Burke—identify the killer.

"I'm off duty, you know," said a mellow baritone voice at my elbow.

"Chief Burke, thank—" I began, and then my mouth fell open. Apparently the chief had decided to take advantage of the costume discount—if not for the familiar voice, I'd never have recognized him. He wore a black leather coat, wraparound shades, and at least a foot of glossy Afro. Was he supposed to be Shaft, I wondered. I thought Shaft was bald, though, so I wasn't sure who Chief Burke was impersonating, but he dwarfed the miniature Darth Vader who stood beside him, tugging on his hand.

"If you have a shoplifting problem, I can have one of the duty officers cruise by," he said.

"It's not a shoplifting problem," I said. "It's a murder problem. I thought you'd want to be the first to know."

I'd spoken too loudly. I could hear gasps and whispers from the people in line, and several of them ran off, presumably to tell their friends.

"Lordy," the chief said, shaking his head. "I wish I thought you were kidding. Frankie, you go find your Grandma and tell her she'll have to find you some lunch. Grandpa has to work."

Darth Vader nodded and scampered off.

"So where is this alleged murder?" the chief said.

I pointed to the trunk. He walked over, used his handkerchief to lift the lid, and peered in.

"That poor rascal!" he exclaimed.

"I see you know Gordon," I said.

"Well, of course," he said. "He's had that eyesore of a shop on Main Street nearly fifteen years. I'm not surprised, really. Lord knows, no one deserves to be murdered, but if anyone could provoke Saint Peter himself into forgetting that fact, it would be Gordon."

With that, he pulled out his cell phone. Calling the station for reinforcements, I hoped.

Michael returned.

"Your Dad's got the barn under control," he said.

"Great," I said. "Now all we have to worry about is them," I said, pointing to the crowd. The line snaking away from the checkout table was becoming obscured by the increasing numbers of people showing up to gawk, and they'd begun shoving the ropes inward, a few inches at a time. "If Chief Burke doesn't get some officers here pretty soon for crowd control . . ."

"Don't worry," Michael said. "Also under control." Just then the crowd parted, and Mother appeared, took up a position just inside the rope, and began issuing orders. Within two minutes, she had the ropes back to their original position and the crowd arranging itself in several rows, by height, so everyone would have the best possible view. Which might not be optimal in the chief's eyes, but I thought it was an improvement over being trampled by curious onlookers while guarding the trunk.

But while the gawkers were happier, the shoppers had grown surly.

"Maybe I should start writing up people's sales tickets while they're waiting," I said. I rummaged through the stuff on the checkout table for one of the little pads of sales receipts. "That's what really takes time, and if they see things are moving—"

"I'll do it," Michael said, plucking the receipt pad from my hand. "I'll round up some of our elusive volunteers to help. You stay here and help Chief Burke."

He flagged Mrs. Fenniman and the cousin dressed as a white rabbit, and the three of them began working their way down the line. As soon as they started, I could see a decrease in the number of frowns and annoyed glances at wristwatches.

And not only was morale improving, but I figured that once people had their sales slips all neatly written up, they'd be less likely to change their minds and leave us stuck with the junk they'd picked up. The man carrying Mrs. Sprocket's near life-sized reproduction of the Venus de Milo, for example. I really wanted to see that leave.

First things first. Murder trumped our yard sale, no question. I turned back to the chief. He had pulled off his wig and sunglasses and was struggling out of his leather jacket with one hand while holding his cell phone in the other. I went over to help him out. That doing so allowed me to eavesdrop was, of course, purely incidental.

From the frown that crossed his face when he saw me, I deduced that he'd neither forgiven nor forgotten my so-called meddling in the last murder case we had in Caerphilly.

"Yes, I know I gave Clyde the day off for his cousin's wedding," he was saying into the phone. "But we've got a situation here. You tell him to head on over here as soon as they're safely hitched. And—hold on," he said, with a look of alarm. "I'll have to call you back."

I followed the chief's gaze and saw a short, plump African-American woman swathed in white robes and wearing a Cleopatra-style headdress. She held Darth Vader's hand and frowned at the chief.

"I declare," she said. "If you're too triflin' to buy your grandson a measly hamburger . . ."

"Minerva," the chief said, in a stage whisper. "We have a serious crime going on here."

"Dad, it's probably time for Eric's lunch," I said. "Why don't you take the chief's grandson along and feed them both?"

Dad looked crestfallen. He wanted to stay at the crime scene.

"We'll make points with the chief," I whispered to him. "And with Mother; she won't want Eric to see this. Come back when you've found someone reliable to watch them both."

Dad's expression lightened.

"Come along, Frankie," he said, offering Darth Vader his left wing. "Do you like hamburgers or hot dogs?"

"Yes," Darth Vader said.

Minerva Burke nodded approvingly and returned to whatever table interested her. Chief Burke looked relieved.

"Thank you kindly," he said. "Of course, she'll want to take Frankie home when she learns we have to shut the shopping down for the time being."

"I was afraid you'd say that," I said, with a sigh.

"Ladies and gentlemen!" the chief shouted. "Ladies and gentlemen!"

I hadn't realized before how loud the yard sale was. And it wasn't a single, identifiable noise, but the general hum of several hundred people bargaining, conversing, and trading rumors about the murder with their friends and neighbors, mixed in with the louder, more sporadic noises of children playing, parents calling or scolding, radios pumping out tunes or talk shows, grills sizzling, and the occasional honking of my brother's Harpo horn. About a third of the people in the yard seemed intent on ignoring the murder and continuing to shop. Another third clustered around the edge of the roped-off area, arranged in height order, frankly staring at the crime scene. The rest dashed back and forth, trying to do both at once and annoying everyone.

The chief tried several times to make himself heard, with no success. Shoppers and rubberneckers alike ignored him.

"Allow me," Michael said. He stepped up onto the cashier's table and drew himself up to his full height.

"Attention, shoppers!" he proclaimed, and his resonant stage actor's voice cut through the general noise and silenced it as a hawk's cry would cut off the normal cheerful chatter around a bird feeder.

"Attention shoppers!" he repeated. "Due to an unfortunate occurrence, we regret that we have to suspend the yard sale temporarily, by order of the Caerphilly Police Department. If you'll all please take the items you now have and form an orderly line leading to the checkout area and stand by for instructions from our chief of police . . ."

Murmurs of mingled outrage and curiosity ran through the part of the crowd still shopping, while the ones gathered around the murder scene pretended to think the announcement didn't apply to them.

People began to comply. At least the ones still shopping. They didn't go happily, and they weren't quick about it, and I suspect no power on Earth could have kept them from picking up a few more items as they passed various tables, like horses snatching a mouthful of grass every time their riders dropped the reins. But they began gradually ambling toward the checkout line. I overheard the chief making another phone call and ordering someone to stop by the station on his way here to pick up the departmental bullhorn.

Mother, still keeping the onlookers in order, took a moment to draft Rob to take her place in the checkout line. I noticed, with alarm, that she handed him the orange and purple lamp shade I'd found so hideous. I hoped she was only holding it for someone else. Or maybe she liked the shape and was planning to strip off all the ghastly trappings and recover the frame with a nice unobtrusive beige. Surely the lamp shade couldn't possibly be part of her decorating plans for Michael and me.

I'd worry about that later. The first two of the chief's officers had arrived. Given the speed of their arrival and the fact that they wore civvies with what appeared to be folded Nixon masks shoved in their pockets, I suspected they'd been here all along as customers. Burke assigned them to search the barn. I hoped the chief would assign the next arrivals to crowd control. Even Mother could only do so much.

"Meg, your cousin Horace has found something," Dad said, appearing at my elbow.

"And just what has he found?" Chief Burke said, stepping between me and Horace.

Cousin Horace stepped forward, holding a charred object at the end of a set of barbecue tongs.

"We found this in one of our grills," he said. "And there are some stains on the cover that might be blood spatter."

"And just why are you so familiar with blood spatter?" Chief Burke asked, frowning at Horace. "Been watching *CSI* too often?"

"Cousin Horace's a crime scene technician with the sheriff's department at home," I said.

"Ah," the chief said, nodding with approval. I blinked in surprise at his ready acceptance of Horace's credentials, and then realized that among so many costumed revelers, Horace's habitual gorilla suit looked perfectly normal. The chief had already focused on the object Horace was holding.

A book. The side toward me was so badly charred that I could only just make out the faint suggestion of pages, but Chief Burke found his side more interesting. I edged closer to look over his shoulder and found that the book's front cover was only slightly scorched and perfectly recognizable, its faded red cloth binding stamped in gold and black with a chessboard motif and the book's author and title.

The Uttermost Farthing, by R. Austin Freeman.

Chapter 9

"Damn," I muttered. A little too loudly.

"What is it?" the chief said, looking back at me.

"This is turning into a zoo," I said, waving at the crowd of rubberneckers and interrupted shoppers, pretending that they rather than the book had inspired my exclamation. "I don't suppose you'd let us collect their money so they could all haul their stuff away."

The chief lowered his head and peered disapprovingly over his glasses.

"And you're positive none of their stuff is evidence?" he said.

"It was just a thought," I said. "How about if I get my volunteers to go down the line and box up everyone's stuff—we'll have the carbons of the sales slips for an inventory. And then we can store everything until your officers are finished with it, and you could question people and get them out from underfoot."

He looked at me suspiciously, then nodded.

"That should work," he said, sounding faintly surprised that I'd come up with a good idea. "Get Sammy to help you," he added, as a tall, gangling young redheaded officer strode up, still trying to button one of his uniform cuffs.

Help me or make sure I didn't pull anything?

I added Sammy and the cousin dressed as a ballerina to the checkout line detail. Michael and Sammy did the heavy work of boxing up the items while Mrs. Fenniman, the ballerina, and the white rabbit continued writing up sales slips.

I tried to recruit Horace, but the chief had already deputized him to help with the crime scene examination, since Caerphilly only had one part-time evidence technician. Dad, who devoured mysteries and loved the idea of being involved in a real-life crime, kept dashing around, trying to be everywhere at once. I hoped he'd found someone reliable to watch Eric and Frankie. I couldn't tell if he was seething with jealousy that Horace was participating in the investigation or vibrating with eagerness at the thought of interrogating Horace later. He'd badger me with questions, too, I thought, with a sigh. Dad had convinced himself and almost everyone we knew that I was a brilliant amateur sleuth. Unfortunately, Chief Burke was one of the few holdouts. The more I could keep Dad out from underfoot, the happier the chief would be.

For that matter, I planned to be as helpful as possible to the chief when I couldn't stay out of his way entirely. I raced to clear one of our two checkout tables when he asked for some place to serve as a collection point for the evidence they found—so far, only the half-burnt book.

"You go on down to the barn and get started," the chief told Horace—who had shed his beloved gorilla suit, apparently in the interest of looking more professional.

"And be careful," I said.

The chief raised an eyebrow at me.

"Tell all your officers to be careful in there," I said. "The barn's old, and run down, and we're not sure it's structurally sound. No one was supposed to go in there."

"Ah," the chief said. "That's the reason for the KEEP OUT signs. Makes sense. Knowing those Sprockets, it's a mercy the whole thing didn't fall down years ago."

"If Gordon had paid any attention to the signs, maybe he'd be alive today," I said. "Of course, a whole lot of other people ignored them as well."

"Such as?" the chief said, taking out a small notebook.

"I don't know all their names," I said. "Barrymore Sprocket probably knows more than I do—he went in and tried to chase Gordon out, with no success."

"We'll talk to him," the chief said, scribbling notes. "Right now, just tell me who you saw."

"The Hummel lady, for one," I said, pointing to her. "I don't know her name, but that's her, over there in the flowered dress."

The chief nodded, and scribbled in his notebook. Why couldn't he satisfy my curiosity by exclaiming, "Oh, you mean Mrs. So-and-so?"

"Then there was a man in a gigantic Mexican sombrero," I said. "He's probably still around somewhere. And a tall man in a brown jacket. And one of the Gypsies—we have quite a lot of Gypsies, so I'm not quite sure which one. Oh, and Giles might have gone in to talk to him about a book."

He couldn't claim I'd left out Giles. But had my casual manner made Giles seem less suspicious or more? The chief just kept scribbling.

"Of course, I didn't necessarily see everyone who went into the barn," I said. "I was trying to keep the yard sale running. There could have been dozens of others."

"Hmm," the chief said, looking up from his notebook. "Somehow I suspect you didn't miss much."

Just then Horace returned, escorting a uniformed officer who held something in his latex-gloved hands.

The other owl-shaped bookend.

"We found it in the barn, sir," the officer said, placing it on the evidence table. "Appears to be a match for the murder weapon."

Of course, Giles picked that moment to stroll up.

"I didn't know you were closing so early," he said, blinking with confusion at the general exodus toward the checkout line. "I don't suppose—oh, there it is. Have you found the other one as well?"

He was pointing, of course, at the owl-shaped bookend.

"Is this yours, sir?" Chief Burke asked, with narrowed eyes.

"Er . . . no, not exactly," Giles said, blinking with confusion. "Not yet anyway. I suppose it belongs to Dr. Langslow. I got it from his table, anyway. I was planning to buy it."

I winced. To someone who didn't know him well, Giles's stammer and his unwillingness to meet the chief's eyes probably smacked of guilt. I realized that this was simply his normal behavior when forced to talk to anyone he didn't know very well about any subject other than nineteenth-century English poetry, but just how well did Chief Burke know Giles?

"And just what did you do with it in the meantime?" the chief asked.

"Carried it around with me," Giles said. "Them, actually—there's another one someplace. I don't suppose you've found it, eh? Anyway, I'm afraid I threw them down after I lost my temper with that beastly Gordon McCoy."

"And one of them struck Mr. McCoy," the chief said, nodding.

"Good heavens no!" Giles exclaimed. "Just threw them down—over there in the barn. Although a few minutes ago, when I returned to look—"

He took a step or two in the direction of the barn and the

chief headed him off by stepping in his path, the way a Border collie would guide a large and rather flustered sheep.

"The barn's off-limits," the chief said. "Just what were you and Mr. McCoy quarreling about?"

"It wasn't a quarrel," Giles said. "He offered to sell me a book at an exorbitant price, and I told him I wouldn't pay that much even if I wanted it, and I already had a copy. And then he said something rude, and I replied in kind and threw the bookends down in a temper. And when I returned later to apologize and reclaim my bookends, I couldn't find him or them."

I sighed. Giles sounded less nervous now, and more like his usual dry, precise self. Unfortunately, under the circumstances, dry and precise sounded more like stuffy and condescending.

"Is this the book?" the chief said, indicating the Freeman book on the evidence table.

"Good heavens," Giles said. "The swine. I didn't think he'd actually do it."

"Do what?"

"Burn it," Giles said. "He said if I didn't buy it, he might as well burn it—I thought he was just joking. I never imagined . . ."

He reached out to touch the book—I had the impression he wanted to comfort it—but the chief grabbed his arm.

"Hands off," the chief said. "That's evidence."

"Evidence?" Giles echoed. "What—?"

"I hear you have a body for me," said a voice behind us.

"Coroner's here, chief," Sammy announced, unnecessarily.

"Body?" Giles looked pale.

"We're investigating the murder of Gordon McCoy," the chief said. "I'm afraid I have a few more questions for you, Professor Rathbone."

Giles didn't faint, but I suspect it was a close call.

Chief Burke looked up and noticed that the small crowd of kibitzers had grown larger. He frowned.

"Meg," he said. "I need a place where I can talk to these people. Someplace more private."

"You can use the house," I said. "The dining room would work. There's no furniture, though."

"Can we have a room with furniture, then?" the chief asked.

"None of them have furniture yet," I said. "At least the dining room has a floor. I can haul in one of the card tables and a few folding chairs; we have plenty of those."

"That would be fine," the chief said, and waved his hand as if dismissing me to go set up his interrogation room.

I'd have been more irritated if I hadn't seen Mrs. Burke, standing behind him, hands on her hips, and a frown on her face.

"Henry," Mrs. Burke began, in a warning tone. "What kind of high-handed stunt are you pulling, shutting down the yard sale like this? Don't tell me there's some county ordinance about yard sales that you've suddenly decided to enforce."

"Don't start with me, Minerva," the chief said. "It's not my fault that no-account Gordon McCoy managed to get himself murdered right in the middle of these good people's yard sale."

"Gordon McCoy!" Mrs. Burke exclaimed. "Well, God rest his soul, but if we had to have someone murdered . . . I suppose there's no help for it, then; you can't argue with a murder, can you?"

With that, she trotted off to take her place in the checkout line.

I went over to snag a few folding chairs from some of the now-idle sellers.

As I was picking up the chairs, I overheard someone talking in the checkout line.

"If I were the chief, I'd take a good look at that wife of his," a voice said.

Chapter 10

I froze so I could hear better, all the while envying dogs their ability to swivel their ears in any direction.

"His own wife?" a second voice exclaimed. "You can't really think Minerva—"

"No, silly, Gordon's wife."

"Carol? I thought she and Gordon split up two years ago."

I pretended to find something wrong with the chair I was about to fold, and risked a look over my shoulder. One of the Marie Antoinettes we'd been watching so closely as a possible shoplifter was leaning toward a stout, gaudily dressed Gypsy.

"It was five," Marie Antoinette said. "And they reconciled; but now they've split up again, and this time it looks permanent."

"Very permanent, with him dead and all."

"Well, naturally," Marie Antoinette said. "I mean it was looking permanent, before Gordon was killed. They were fighting over property, and Carol swore he was hiding assets from her."

"And was he?"

"For heaven's sake, it's Gordon we're talking about," Marie Antoinette said, tossing her fluffy white wig. "Of course he was hiding assets."

"Troll," the Gypsy muttered.

"But she's been going about it the wrong way. She should have just hired a private investigator to follow the jerk. But she's been trying to do it all herself."

"Maybe she can't afford to hire anyone?"

"Well, that's possible. But at least she shouldn't have run around doing things that probably made the judge think she was a nutcase."

"What kind of things?" the Gypsy asked.

"She broke into his house," Maria Antoinette said. "And got caught."

They both shook their heads.

"So if you ask me, Chief Burke is barking up the wrong tree, hassling that poor Professor Rathbone," Marie Antoinette continued, jerking her head toward where the chief was still talking to a stricken-looking Giles. "They should look at Carol."

"How does killing Gordon help Carol find his hidden assets?" the Gypsy asked.

"If he's dead, and they're still married, she doesn't need to worry about finding them, silly. They're all hers now."

"Unless he's hidden them so well that no one ever finds them," the Gypsy suggested.

Or unless she was the one who murdered him.

"Wouldn't that be something?" Marie Antoinette exclaimed, and they both giggled. I suspected that however much they disliked Gordon they weren't overly fond of Carol either.

I folded the chair and turned toward the house. I realized that I might have a very good chance of prying information out of Carol, since I probably had a good idea where Gordon had hidden his assets. Several times, while delivering things to the bin we'd rented at the Spare Attic, an off-site storage place, I'd run into Gordon coming from or going to a nearby bin. He'd looked anxious when he noticed I'd seen him. If I could find Carol, maybe I could trade her this information in return for the inside scoop on what she'd seen in the barn.

Of course, the ethical thing to do was to tell the chief what the two women had been saying and share my knowledge of Gordon's storage bin with him.

Later. Assuming I could pry the chief away from his intense conversation with Giles.

"Damn!" I muttered.

"What's wrong, Meg?"

I looked up to see that Dad had returned. Alone.

"Eric and Frankie—" I began

"Taken care of," he said, waving genially.

"Fine," I said. Giles was still talking to the chief. I shook my head and stuck a folding chair under each arm.

Giles was pointing toward the barn.

"Damn the man," I muttered.

"What's wrong?" Dad asked.

"Someone should tell Giles not to talk to the police without a lawyer," I said.

"You think he had something to do with the murder?"

"No," I said. "I can't imagine him having anything to do with the murder, but I don't think Chief Burke agrees. If Giles doesn't watch out, he'll get arrested."

"Oh, dear," Dad said. "He seems like such a nice man."

"Very nice," I said. "And he thinks Michael deserves tenure."

"So do I, naturally," Dad said.

"Yes, but you're not on his tenure committee," I said. "Giles is."

Dad frowned.

"But I thought Giles was an English professor," he said.

"He is," I said. "So is Michael, technically. The drama department, being small, is technically a subgroup of the English department."

"How odd," Dad said. "Is that a good thing or a bad thing?"

I sighed, and rubbed my forehead. The slight headache I'd been trying to ignore suddenly felt worse. I could have sworn I'd explained this to most of my family several times already. Maybe I'd just fretted about it so much that it seemed as if I'd told them.

"Depends on your point of view," I said. "If you ask me, most of the English professors—the tenured ones, anyway—are stuffy, pompous bores. Of course, I could be prejudiced by the fact that they all look down their noses at their colleagues in the drama section of the department."

"That must be annoying."

"Worse than annoying," I said. "Every year or two, they try to eliminate all but the driest and most academic of drama courses. Which would also let them eliminate all those déclassé theater people like Michael."

"Oh, dear," Dad said. "So Michael's job isn't safe?"

"Well, it is and it isn't," I said. "The college administration always reinstates the canceled classes—they're too popular to kill. But while the administration wants the prestige of having an award-winning theater arts program and the fees the drama classes bring, they could care less if any of the faculty responsible ever get tenure. So far, in the past thirty years, not a single one has."

"That doesn't sound promising," Dad said, staring at the house as if the connection between Michael's tenure and our ability to continue paying the mortgage had begun to dawn on him.

"Doesn't mean Michael would be unemployed if he didn't get tenure," I said. "He'd almost certainly be welcome to stay around indefinitely, as a lecturer or something. On a suitably tiny salary, with no benefits to speak of. That helps the bottom line almost as much as those popular courses he teaches."

"The college's bottom line, you mean."

"Yes," I said. "It wouldn't help our bottom line at all—not that that's the most important thing. I could make up the difference with my blacksmithing if I had to, though that would certainly slow down the house project. But if Michael doesn't get tenure, he might not want to stay on, and it can be hard for someone refused tenure to get a good teaching job anywhere else. And much as he likes acting, it's teaching he really loves."

"So this is where Giles comes in," Dad said. "He's pro-Michael."

"Exactly," I said. "When Michael arrived, they took a look at his background—the soap opera stuff, mainly—and made the mistake of assuming he was a lightweight. So they didn't figure they had to pack his tenure committee with curmudgeons—they gave him a bunch of honest, if slightly pedantic, professors. And so far, Michael has won them over. He has the credentials; he publishes regularly; he's jumping through all the hoops. His committee loves him—he and Giles have even become friends—but the department is running scared. If Chief Burke arrests Giles and gives the department fuddy-duddies an excuse to force him off the committee, they'll replace him with one of the hardliners, and Michael will have no chance at tenure."

Just then, Chief Burke looked up from his conversation with Giles and frowned at me. I picked up the chairs, waved them, smiled, and then turned toward the house.

"Don't worry," Dad said. "I'm sure there are other suspects."

"A whole flock of them," I said.

"No, not a flock," Dad said, frowning. "Ah! I've got it! A skulk. Like a skulk of foxes."

"A skulk of suspects," I said. "Works for me. But just in case Chief Burke disagrees, get Michael to call that defense attorney he knows."

"The one who represented Rob when he got arrested?"

"That's the one," I said.

Dad scurried off and I focused on the chairs.

As I lugged them along, I realized that it had been several weeks since Michael had complained about anything going on in his department. Not a good sign. When he was feeling generally optimistic about how his career was going, he'd vent about small day-to-day irritations. When he thought something was going badly, he clammed up about work. Which was what he'd been doing recently. If I hadn't been so crazed over the upcoming yard sale, I'd have noticed. I should have noticed.

I vowed to make up for this as soon as possible, thus fending off a full-scale attack of the guilts that I didn't have time for right now.

While I was crossing the soaring front hall, I heard the patter of sneaker-clad feet from the landing above.

"Bang!" piped a small voice.

"Argh! You got me!"

Chapter 11

I glanced up to the second floor landing and saw Frankie, Chief Burke's grandson, minus his Darth Vader mask but still swathed in the long black robes, standing at the head of the main stairs, clutching his side. Then he fell over and bumped slowly and noisily down the whole twelve-foot length of the main staircase before landing with a thump in the front hall.

"Frankie!" I exclaimed, racing to his side. "Are you all right?"

"I'm fine," he said, frowning with impatience at this typically annoying grown-up interruption.

"It's your turn to be the detective," Eric called from the top of the stairs.

"Is there an adult around here . . . taking care of anything you need?" I asked.

"Rob," Eric said, racing up the stairs toward the third floor.

"Where is he?" I asked.

Frankie leaped up from the floor, pointed toward the living room, and ran off after Eric.

Evidently Dad's definition of someone reliable to watch the boys differed greatly from mine. Rob lay on the floor of the living room with his Harpo hat pulled down against the glare from the enormous front windows. He had a tiny portable TV on his stomach and was watching a football game.

"You'll need cable," Rob said. "Assuming you can even get cable here in the back of beyond. You may have to get a satellite dish. You might want to think about that before you decide whether you're actually moving way out here."

Did he really think we were likely to change our minds at this point?

"Aren't you supposed to be babysitting the boys?" I asked aloud.

"They're fine," he said, as he fiddled with the miniature TV's rabbit ear antenna. "Having a great time."

"Ya got me!" Eric yelled, and then I heard something bumping down the stairs from the third floor. I stuck my head back out into the hall. Not content with a single flight of stairs, when he finally hit the second floor landing Eric improvised a series of picturesque twitches and convulsions that propelled him to the head of the main stairs and then over the edge of the top step for another histrionic descent.

"A great time." I echoed, when the noise of Eric's descent had subsided.

"Kids are pretty resilient at that age," Rob remarked, eyes still glued to the tiny snow-filled screen.

"And you call this watching them."

"I told them not to leave the house."

"And you think that will stop them?" I said. "Would it have stopped you at their age?"

"I told them we'd have Popsicles at one," Rob said. "They won't go far. They show up every ten minutes or so to ask how much longer till one."

"Clever," I said. Of course, no one had ever accused

Rob of being stupid. An underachiever with no common sense, perhaps, but definitely not stupid. "What happens after one?"

"I'll figure something out," Rob said. "Maybe I'll shove a watermelon in the refrigerator and tell them it'll be ready to cut at two."

"You don't have to keep them in the house, you know," I said. "Just out of trouble."

"In the house is better," Rob said. "Did you know those two were running a protection racket?"

"Eric and Frankie?"

"Demanding a quarter to keep an eye out and prevent Everett from picking up the portable toilets while people were inside."

"Those rascals!" I said. "They were there when I told Everett he was banned from the yard sale if he even tried to pick up another toilet."

"Little thieves," Rob muttered. "No Popsicles for them until I get my quarter back."

"Just keep them out of the dining room," I said, heading back out into the hall. "Chief Burke's using it for his interrogations."

"Roger," Rob said.

I deposited the chairs and went outside to liberate a reasonably empty table. One of the card tables from the picnic area would do, I decided.

"You do realize that costume is a slur on devout Paganism," I heard a voice say at my elbow. I turned to see a small, plump woman dressed in flowing pastel tie-dyed robes and wearing several pounds of ankhs, peace symbols, pentagrams, yin-yang signs, and other assorted amulets around her neck.

I was about to ask her what devout Pagans had against Groucho, until I realized she wasn't talking to me but to Aunt Josephine, in her traditional witch costume. A bit stereotypical but effective, since even in ordinary dress Aunt Josephine bore a strong resemblance to the movie version of the Wicked Witch of the West.

"I beg your pardon," Aunt Josephine said, looking down her long, pointed nose at the woman. "Were you casting aspersions on my personal appearance?"

I left them to it. Aunt Josephine was quite capable of defending herself verbally, and for all I knew, equally capable of turning her attacker into a toad.

I made my way to the far end of the fenced-in area, past the line of people waiting to check out. I nodded with satisfaction to see that many of them were still avidly perusing the tables at a distance—some of them were even taking notes. Or were they watching the police? Probably both. I collided with one woman dressed as a pregnant angel, who had inched forward a good six feet from her assigned place in line to stare avidly at one of the tables of books.

"Sorry," she said, straightening her halo, which had been knocked askew. "My fault. Any idea when they'll let us get on with it?"

"I wish I knew," I said.

"Damned shame if they arrest that professor," she said. "Doesn't look like the type who would hurt a fly. Of course, it's a damned shame they have to arrest anyone. Ought to give whoever did it a medal for performing a public service."

"I take it you weren't fond of Gordon-you-thief," I said.

"Gordon-you-thief!" she exclaimed. "That's perfect."

"You've bought books from him, too?"

"Competed with him, actually," she said. "I'm a bookseller. Used to go on the occasional booking expedition with him, until I found out what he was like. Do you know what he did to me?"

She stopped peering at the books and turned to me.

"We were visiting a couple of used bookstores—the

kind where they don't really know what's valuable, and you can pick up something for a few bucks that's worth much more. In the first one, he told me the parking meter was about to run out, but he could use some more time—so how about if he fed the meter another hour's worth of quarters, and then after that hour we could go on to the next store, a mile or two away. But the minute we walked into the second store, the owner said, 'Gordon, what's wrong—did you forget something? You just left a couple of minutes ago.' "

"Sneaky," I said, shaking my head.

"That was the last time I went booking with him."

"So it wasn't just his customers who might want to kill him," I said. "Any other dealer who knew him would, too."

"Definitely," she said, with a laugh. "Maybe I should work on my alibi."

She turned away and resumed her long-distance book scanning.

"You want to know who I think killed him?" she said, over her shoulder. "Ralph."

"Ralph?"

"His ex-partner," she said. "Ralph Endicott."

"They didn't part on good terms?"

She laughed.

"Have you seen him here today?" I asked.

She straightened up, shaded her eyes with one hand, and scanned the crowd.

"Over there by the lemonade stand," she said. "The tall man in the brown corduroy jacket and jeans."

"Thanks," I said. I smiled to myself. I recognized Ralph, the ex-partner, as one of the people who'd gone into the barn, presumably to see Gordon.

I stopped off long enough to point out the bookseller and the ex-partner to Sammy as possible suspects, then wrestled the card table into the house and lugged it into the dining room. Of course the dining room was the only logical choice for the chief's interrogations. With a house full of relatives, we weren't giving up access to the refrigerator, so the kitchen was out. The living room didn't have a door to close it off from the hallway, only a wide, open archway, so even if we convinced Eric and Frankie to rehearse their Tarzan yells and hyena laughs outdoors so the chief would have peace and quiet, he wouldn't have much privacy. No, the dining room was the place.

Especially since the chief probably didn't know that we had a dumbwaiter running from the basement up to the dining room and then on to the master bedroom above. A dumbwaiter that carried sounds reasonably well. I set the table right in front of the dumbwaiter door, then went to the kitchen, filled a pitcher with ice water, and set it on the table, with a couple of glasses. A nice hospitable touch to make it less likely that the chief would move the table.

I was about to check to see if the dumbwaiter door was latched—it had an unnerving habit of drifting slowly open if we left it unlatched—when I heard the chief coming down the hall, so I hurriedly leaped away and was standing across the room, gazing out the window, when the chief entered.

"Will this do?" I asked.

"Just fine," the chief said. "Where's your phone, anyway? My cell phone's not getting great reception out here."

"We don't have one yet," I said.

"I'd have thought you'd find a phone pretty useful, all the time you've been spending out here," he said, frowning.

"We did," I said. "And so did the Sprockets. After paying several hundred dollars in long distance charges that we knew but could not prove were made by various visiting Sprockets, we had the line disconnected."

The chief frowned and nodded.

"Sounds about par for the course with those Sprockets," he said. "Can't tell you how relieved I was that none of them were moving in here."

Considering how much I annoyed the chief, that certainly said a lot about the Sprockets.

"Anything else you need?" I asked. "Shall I fetch anyone?"

"Sammy can do that," the chief said. "Don't worry; if we need anything, we'll let you know."

He smiled, and stood in the center of the room, motionless, in what I deduced was a subtle hint that my presence was no longer needed.

I walked out of the room slowly, looking behind me as I went, in a deliberate show of reluctance. Of course, I hadn't really expected the chief to let me stay, but he'd be suspicious if I didn't at least try to lurk nearby.

I decided to check outside to make sure no one needed me before taking up my eavesdropping vantage point. And if the chief saw me outside, all the better.

Outside, I saw that the fenced-in area was nearly empty—of people, that is; the Army of Clutter was still there in all its glory. Two acres, covered almost entirely with stuff. Tables piled high with stuff. Boxes filled with stuff. Aisles and rows and huge messy clusters of larger stuff. Enough racks of clothes to stock a department store, if any of the garments were still in style and in reasonable condition. Several thousand books, though that number would probably shrink to several hundred if we didn't count duplicate copies of *The Da Vinci Code* and a handful of other recent bestsellers. Three or four houses' worth of furniture, some of it actually sound enough for use. All lying peacefully in the autumn sunshine, undisturbed except for the small area where the local evidence technician was industriously photographing the contents of a table while Cousin Horace meticulously dusted the contents of the adjacent table for fingerprints.

I hoped that there was something special about those particular tables. If they followed the same process with the whole two acres, Michael and I would have to bequeath the chore of finishing the yard sale to our grandchildren.

The job of clearing out the customers was going much faster. Michael and his checkout crew were nearing the end of the line, and most of the open space inside the fence, along with the corner we'd planned to use as a picnic area, now contained neat, orderly rows of boxes, each carefully labeled with the name of the person who'd either bought the contents or would be buying them, if they bothered returning when the police allowed us to open again. The uniformed officers were progressing more slowly with questioning the departing customers, but still making visible progress. As I watched, they let two uncostumed people go free, while an officer escorted a Nixon up to the house—presumably for further questioning by the chief.

Of course, that didn't mean that our lawn was in any danger of becoming deserted. Most of the people who'd been allowed to leave the yard sale area were still hanging around outside the fence, watching the police, and window-shopping. I wondered if the police inside found the circle of impassive Nixons, Draculas, and Grouchos as unnerving as I did.

From the size of the crowd I suspected some of the people milling around our yard had only arrived after news of the murder spread through the county. Especially the ones wielding cameras and binoculars. The cousins who'd been running the concession stand inside the fence had scrounged up more grills and food, and were doing a brisk business. The occasional squeal of feedback emanated from the side yard, where the as-yet-unnamed band formed by one of Eric's older brothers was tuning up and preparing to satisfy their largely unfulfilled passion for playing to a live audience. Apparently the medical examiner had departed without allowing Dad to accompany him, and Dad had consoled himself by organizing an owl pellet dissection project. Several dozen children and teenagers and even a few bemused adults were diligently hacking and sawing on owl pellets with disposable plastic knives borrowed from the concession stand. Mother, by contrast, was circulating like the hostess at a floundering party, apologizing for the disruption and urging people to have some lemonade while they waited for the yard sale to reopen.

The press had arrived in force. I recognized the reporter from the *Caerphilly Clarion,* and the crews from the local TV and college radio stations stood out in the crowd because of all the equipment they were lugging. I had to chase several of the television trucks out of the side yard, though not before they had destroyed what little resemblance it had to a grassy lawn.

"Ah, well," Michael said, when he saw me staring at the impressive new ruts. "We probably needed to rototill that part of the lawn anyway. By the way, is that one of the uncles who shouldn't be wandering around by himself?"

"Uncle Ned? Not that I know of," I said, looking over at the uncle in question. "Why, what's he been doing?"

"Coming up and spouting gibberish at me," Michael said.

"Oh, that's not gibberish," I said. "Farsi, Arabic, and I think I heard he'd taken up Mandarin. He's testing to see if you react. Always on the lookout for foreign spies, Uncle Ned."

"Probably not a good time to practice my French or Vietnamese, then," he said.

"No, and probably just as well to keep him away from

Giles," I said. "Uncle Ned still hasn't forgiven the British for burning the White House in the War of 1812."

"Right," he said, nodding. "Should those people be climbing on the fence?"

Dozens of people were spread-eagled against the deer fencing, like bugs on a windshield, as if pressing every square inch of their bodies as close as possible to the barrier would get them inside faster. We'd had a cat once who did that with screen doors when she wanted to come inside. She'd even leap up to plaster herself as high on the door as possible, the better to be seen, which hadn't done a whole lot for the condition of our screen door. Sure enough, one of the onlookers started to do much the same thing, but the deer fencing began to collapse under his weight, and Michael went over to help the uniformed officers remove him from the fence.

Cousin Everett was doing a brisk business with the boom lift, sending small groups of people up on the platform and then waving them gently over the yard sale area. Hard to tell, at this distance, whether they were reporters, avid bargain hunters scoping out the merchandise, or just thrill-seekers, but he had dozens of people waiting in line for their turns.

Everett had apparently found time, before he began giving rides, to deposit a party of volunteer roofers on top of the house. As I watched, several of my uncles rolled back one of the tarps, ready for another attempt to patch the last of the roof leaks. I suspected we'd eventually have to break down and replace the entire roof. But the longer we postponed that, the better we would be able to afford it. In the meantime, the uncles were having fun; they'd found a productive use for all the leftover shingles everyone had in their garages and sheds, and I had decided that the random mixture of shingle colors gave the house a festive patchwork look.

But none of this chaos was bringing us any closer to getting rid of our mountains of stuff, I thought, with a sigh.

"Meg?"

I turned to see Cousin Horace and a uniformed officer standing behind me.

Chapter 12

"Horace," I said. "How's the forensic examination going?"

"Now, Meg," he said. "You know I can't reveal confidential information."

"I wasn't asking for confidential information," I said. Not yet, anyway. "I just asked how it was going. If you want to cheer me up, tell me you're almost finished and we can restart the yard sale soon."

"You don't want me to lie to you, do you?"

I sighed.

"We're supposed to get some reinforcements from Richmond," he said. "More technicians to help us process the crime scene. But even when they get here, it'll go a lot faster if we aren't interrupted by all those people hanging on the fence and knocking it down. Not to mention trying to sneak under it."

"Fat chance doing that," I said. "Did you see the length of the pegs Dad used to tack the bottom down? We'll be lucky if we ever get some of them up; we'll probably have to cut the damned fence away."

"Yeah, we expect when they figure out they can't pull

it up, they'll start trying to cut it," Horace said. "We were wondering if you could help us keep them away."

"Me?"

"Well, you did it before the yard sale started," Horace said.

"Wasn't me," I said. "But I'll go get Spike. Find a bull-horn or something and tell the crowd to step behind the outer fence, or I won't be responsible for the conse-quences."

Spike was exiled to his pen beside the barn, though they'd shut the doggie door we'd installed in the barn wall, which would have let him go inside to spy on the crime scene. He seemed bored, and almost glad to see me. At least he only bit me once while I was snapping the leash onto his collar, and even that was rather perfunc-tory. The Doberman and the pit bull, who'd been cower-ing at the far side of the pen, looked quite relieved to see him go.

"Attention, ladies and gentlemen," came Horace's am-plified voice. "We'd like you to step back behind the short outer fence. Please step behind the outer fence, or Meg won't be responsible for the consequences."

Titters ran through the crowd, and rose to a crescendo when I appeared, half-pulled by the eager Spike. When we'd opened up the sale, we'd simply moved part of the outer fence aside. I made sure the ends were closed off so Spike couldn't escape, leaving a long crescent-shaped area for him to run in. I lifted him inside and let him have the full length of the leash. He lunged toward the nearest people who'd ignored Horace's command, barking and snarling in his best *Exorcist* fashion. Only my weight at the other end of the leash slowed him enough to keep the first few malingerers from being bitten, and after that, people got the message. As Spike hurtled along, the path cleared magically before us. Well, before him. A few people stepped back in after we passed, but when we got to the far end of the run, I undid the leash and declared open season on anyone who ignored Horace's very reasonable request. Spike quickly cleared the open space and then trotted up and down inside, defending his territory against invaders.

"That should work," Horace said. "See, I told you Meg would know what to do," he added to the other officer, as they headed back to the gate.

"Just give us our yard sale back as soon as possible," I huffed after them.

Michael spotted me, and came over to talk through the fence.

"Great idea," he said. "And I promise, I won't tell Mom what you're doing with her dog."

"She said he needed more exercise," I said, still panting. "Best exercise in the world, running. Look how lean and fit greyhounds are. You seem to have everything under control."

"We should be finished with the customers in half an hour," he said. "Then I thought I'd take your mother into town to keep her entertained—want to come?"

"Keep her entertained how?" I asked. Call me suspicious, but I had a hard time imagining what entertainment Mother could find in Caerphilly. The town didn't have that many elegant shops and restaurants to begin with, and she'd already exhausted the charms of those in the past week while staying with us.

"She has some new ideas for decorating the house," he began.

I winced.

"I'm not in the mood to talk about decorating with Mother," I said, trying to keep my tone light. "If you want to take her, that's fine; just please don't bring back any stuff right now. I'm not sure I could take adding any more clutter before we get rid of all the junk that's already here for the yard sale."

"She was talking about paint colors," he said. "I don't think that's apt to involve much clutter."

"Paint's fine," I said. "I like paint. We could decorate entirely with paint. If we painted the various rooms with really beautiful colors, we wouldn't even need all that much furniture. Just elegant, uninterrupted expanses of color."

"Uh . . . right," Michael said. "I'll tell her to suggest some nice self-sufficient colors. If you're not interested in going, maybe I can just drop her off and pick her up later."

"She should be used to that," I said. "It's what Dad always does. And I really think someone should stay here to keep an eye on things."

"And snoop," Michael said, nodding.

"I'm not snooping," I said, in as dignified a manner as I could manage.

"Well, maybe you should start," he said. "I like Chief Burke, but I have this sinking feeling he'll take the path of least resistance and arrest Giles, and even if the attorney gets him off, it won't help his career any."

"Or yours," I said.

"True," Michael said. "Though my career's not as important as clearing Giles."

"Maybe not," I said. "But it all amounts to the same thing, so I plan to provide the police with whatever unofficial assistance I can."

"Good," he said. "Happy snooping. I'll be back as soon as I can."

With that, he returned to inventorying the departing

customers' junk collections and I headed back to the house.

I found Barrymore Sprocket and several of my relatives sitting around the makeshift kitchen table, eating hamburgers and mountains of potato salad while Rob doled out Popsicles to Superman and Darth Vader.

"This interruption won't help the yard sale," Barrymore said, through a mouthful of burger. "Weeks of preparation and advertising, all at great expense, and now this!"

"Yes, I'm so sorry," I said. "If I'd been thinking, I would have scheduled the murder for some other weekend."

"Rescheduling the yard sale will double the expenses," Sprocket grumbled. And diminish the Sprocket pirates' haul, since they took their ten percent of the net profits.

"Actually, this will probably help the yard sale," Rob said, as he unwrapped a grape Popsicle for himself. "No amount of advertising could possibly match the publicity value of a really juicy murder."

He'd been saying that a lot recently—repeating something I'd said to him, some months before, when a murder had occurred on the premises of his computer game company. He'd become convinced that the notoriety of the murder had contributed significantly to the success of *Lawyers from Hell II,* the game they'd released shortly thereafter. I made a mental note to drop by his office and see if his muttering about the publicity value of homicide was making any of his employees nervous.

For now, I let Barrymore Sprocket ponder Rob's words while I headed for the stairs. With all those people sitting around the kitchen, I'd probably need to snag the dumbwaiter at the top of its route, in the master bedroom. Even my family might start asking questions if I disappeared into the basement for several hours.

As I passed the dining room, I could hear the chief talking to someone, but the old plaster walls were thick and reasonably sound-resistant. In the living room I saw a random collection of witnesses and suspects, some in costume and others in civilian clothes. About half of them were sprawled on the floor, while the other half stood, leaned, or paced up and down the room, all under the watchful eye of a police officer.

Upstairs, I slipped into the master bedroom, closed the door, and tiptoed over to open the dumbwaiter door. I'd hoped that the sound would travel up the shaft. It did, but not well enough for me to hear more than one word in ten. The intermittent hammering from the roof didn't help, either. Ah, well—I hadn't expected it to be that easy.

When we'd found the dumbwaiter, during one of our tours of the house before buying, I'd considered it a useless though harmless toy. But Michael had been enchanted, and now I was glad he'd spent an entire afternoon replacing its frayed ropes—one of the few actual repairs the house had received so far.

When I tried tugging the rope, I did find myself wishing Michael had oiled the pulley at the top while he was at it. But the pulley was way up in the attic, and I hoped if Chief Burke heard its squeak, he'd just mistake it for part of the hubbub outside. Or, more likely, assume we had bats in our belfry literally as well as figuratively.

I pulled the dumbwaiter up, slowly, so it wouldn't bang around in the shaft. On the third try, I found a way to fit myself in the dumbwaiter and still leave my arms free to reach outside and tug on the ropes. Luckily for me it was an oversized dumbwaiter. I wondered if in some bygone era the Sprockets had been legendary for the size and splendor of their dinner parties—I had a hard time imagining even a restaurant needing a dumbwaiter quite so large.

I lowered the dumbwaiter, hand over hand, until its top was only a foot above the bottom of the door, which gave me as little distance as possible to cover if I had to get out of sight quickly. I could still hear fine. And while the doors that opened from the shaft into the dining room were closed, they didn't fit all that well, and the right panel had a number of cracks and splits, so I could even see out, though at the moment the only thing in my field of vision was the chief's leather coat, slung over the back of one of the folding chairs.

Apparently I arrived in the middle of an interesting interrogation.

"And you expect us to believe that!" the chief exclaimed.

Chapter 13

Believe what? I wanted to shout. But whoever Chief Burke was questioning didn't answer, and the chief's favorite interrogation technique was to sit and stare reproachfully at his subjects until they threw up their hands and talked. Which worked a lot of the time, but wasn't very amusing for anyone trying to eavesdrop.

Or perhaps he was interrogating someone with a hearing problem. Perhaps, even now, penetrating questions, harsh accusations, and frantic denials were flying back and forth at breakneck speed in sign language. Just as I began to imagine the killer blurting out a halting confession with trembling, exhausted fingers, a voice broke the silence.

"I don't know what else you want," an unknown man said. "When I realized I was wasting my time, I told him to call me when he was serious about doing business, and I left. That's it."

"And Mr. McCoy was still alive when you left."

"Alive and well."

The other man's voice sounded vaguely familiar, but I couldn't put a name or a face to it. I peered out, and saw the crisp black shoulder of the chief's shirt. Then the shoulder shifted, and I caught a glimpse of the giant sombrero I'd seen one of Gordon's barn visitors wearing.

"These papers he wanted to sell you—were they valuable enough that someone else would kill him for them?"

"Since I never got to see them, I have no idea," Sombrero said. "I can't imagine that they would be. Where would Gordon have gotten something that valuable?"

The voice was precise, dry, and slightly pedantic; it teased my memory.

"And there's no one who had a reason to kill him?" the chief asked.

"From what little contact I had with him, I can imagine there might be all sorts of people with ample reason to kill him," Sombrero said, sounding slightly testy. "But I'm afraid I have no idea who could have done it."

"And there's nothing else you can think of that might help us?"

Silence. I assume Sombrero must have shaken his head, or perhaps shrugged.

Chief Burke sighed.

"Thank you, Professor Schmidt," he said.

Professor Schmidt. I remembered him now. One of Michael's colleagues at the English department. One of the stuffier ones he avoided. Okay, I could probably find a way to run into Professor Schmidt again if I wanted to find out more.

"Is that all?" Schmidt asked.

"I'll call you if we think of anything else. Show him out, Sammy."

I heard the folding chair scrape across the floor and a depressing number of boards that squeaked as Sammy and Professor Schmidt walked over them. I wished I had room to take out my notebook-that-tells-me-when-to-breathe. I needed to make a note to find out how to fix squeaking floorboards.

"He could have done it," a slightly hoarse tenor voice said. "He clearly hated the victim."

"Sammy, Sammy," the chief chided, softly, in his musical baritone. "Everyone hated him. We wouldn't have standing room in the jail if we arrested everyone who hated him. But this isn't an Agatha Christie novel. They didn't all gang up and stuff him in that blasted trunk. Bring in that ex-partner of his."

More squeaking. Squeaking door hinges, too, as Sammy ushered the ex-partner in.

"Ralph Endicott," the partner said, introducing himself to the chief. Again I wished I could scribble in my notebook, as Endicott rattled off his address and phone number. Never mind. Caerphilly was a small town. If he wasn't in the book, someone I know would know where to find him.

"Tell us what you were doing here today," the chief said. "And how you happened to be in the barn with the deceased."

I heard the folding chair creak slightly, and I suspected Chief Burke had leaned back, lacing his hands over his slightly rounded belly and staring at Endicott with half-closed eyelids. I'd been on the receiving end of the chief's interrogation technique myself some months ago.

"The yard sale," Endicott said. "I was here on business."

"You were selling things?"

"No, buying things," Endicott said, with just a hint of impatience in his voice. "For my shop. Yard sales are good hunting grounds for anyone who sells antiques, as I'm sure you know. After all, why do you think Gordon was here?"

"For your shop, yes," the chief said. "This would be a new shop? I understand that when you and Mr. McCoy parted company this past November, he kept the shop the two of you had been running."

"That's true," Endicott said. "His name was the only one on the lease. Careless of me, but what could I do?"

"And you didn't resent that?"

"Enough to kill him, you mean? Certainly not," Endicott said. "I resented it at the time, of course, but from what I've heard recently, the owner's planning to jack the rents up sky-high when the leases are up. Ironically, Gordon did me a favor, hanging onto the shop."

"So where have you opened up your new shop?" the chief said. "The one you were buying things for. I don't recall seeing it yet."

"That's because I haven't opened it yet."

"Having trouble finding suitable premises?"

"I can find plenty of suitable premises, thank you," Endicott said. "Frankly, I don't want to open my new business until I'm sure I'm well and truly rid of Gordon. Purely in a business sense, of course."

"Oh?"

"The man was a total sleazeball," Endicott said, his voice growing slightly heated. "If I'd known what he was like, I'd never have gone into business with him in the first place. I haven't been actively involved in the shop for two years, and I sold him my interest outright a year ago, and yet every time I turn around someone's filing another suit against him and naming me as a codefendant. Not to mention the bill collectors."

"Seems like a motive for wanting to get rid of him," Chief Burke said. "Dead, he can't do anything else that'll get people fired up to sue him."

"Dead, he's not earning any more money to pay judgments," Endicott said. "I suspect some of the plaintiffs will try to come after me instead."

"So you're telling me you're actually worse off with him dead?"

"I could be," Endicott said.

"So why did you go into business with him, if he's such a disreputable character?" the chief asked.

Endicott sighed.

"I didn't realize then how disreputable he was," he said. "I only saw his good qualities."

"And those were?" the chief asked.

I was curious, myself.

"He was brilliant, in his own way," Endicott said, his voice sounding oddly melancholy. "He had an encyclopedic knowledge of antiques, collectibles, and especially rare books. That's how he started out—in books—and then he added other things as he figured out how to make money out of them. And he didn't just have academic knowledge. He could walk into a room and sort the treasures from the junk at a glance. A phenomenal eye—and the ability to con the owner of a piece into letting it go for a fraction of its value. If he'd just had an ounce of integrity . . ."

A pause. I heard the chief's chair creak.

"So what were you doing in the barn with him?" he asked.

Endicott laughed.

"Curiosity killed the cat," he said, his voice returning to its normal tone. "Or in this case, made him a suspect. I wanted to see what he'd found at the sale. I waited till he left and then ducked in."

"Just to see what he'd found?" the chief said. "You weren't appropriating anything for yourself?"

"Just to see what he'd found," Endicott said. "One of the few things I miss about having Gordon around was that he had an uncanny knack for spotting trends before

anyone else. If he was stockpiling something, that probably meant he expected the value to soar. Or, if he was
passing up something that looked hot, it might mean the
bottom was about to fall out of that particular section of
the market. So I was snooping in Gordon's stash. He
came in and caught me at it."

"Thought you were stealing, did he?" the chief said.

"Oh, he knew what I was doing," Endicott said. "Had
himself a good laugh at my expense. I said a few unpleasant things in return, and left."

"And you have no idea who might have killed him?"

Silence, but I assumed Endicott must have shaken his
head, because I heard the chief sigh.

"That's all for now, then," he said. "I'll be in touch if I
think of more questions."

"Oh, come now," Endicott said, over the scraping
sound the folding chair made as he stood up. "Don't you
mean *when* you think of more questions?"

It didn't sound as if he waited for Sammy to show him
out. The floor squeaked, the door opened and closed, and
Chief Burke sighed again.

"Sad, isn't it?" he said.

"Sir?" Sammy said.

"For a man to quit this earth in the prime of his life and
leave behind nothing but enemies," the chief mused.
"That's a sad, sad thing."

"Well, sir," Sammy said. "Maybe if he hadn't made so
all-fired many enemies while he was here on this earth, no
one would have been in such a hurry to help him quit it."

"An excellent point, Sammy," the chief said. "And let
that be a lesson to us all. So who else have we got out
there?"

Sammy answered, but I didn't catch what he said. Just
as he was speaking, the dumbwaiter lurched, banged
against the side of the shaft, and jerked up a foot.

Chapter 14

I reached out and grabbed the ropes to stop the dumb-waiter from moving any farther.

"What the dickens was that?" the chief exclaimed.

A good question.

I felt a series of jerks, and the dumbwaiter strained against my hold. Someone was trying to raise it. No, now they were trying to lower it.

"Probably those guys on the roof," Sammy said.

"That came from the walls," the chief said.

"You don't suppose it's rats?" Sammy asked.

"Give me a hand, Frankie," piped a voice beneath me. "Pull on this."

I took a tight grip as the dumbwaiter strained down-ward, presumably because Frankie had joined Eric's at-tempt to retrieve it.

"Sounds too mechanical for rats," the chief said. "Check that little door over there."

Damn. With their first tug, Eric and Frankie had jerked the dumbwaiter up so it was squarely in front of the door. The second Sammy opened the door he and the chief would see me. I loosened my hold on the rope so the boys' tugging would pull me down again, out of sight.

Unfortunately, they chose that moment to give up.

I heard Sammy walking toward the dumbwaiter door.

I was reaching out to grab the ropes and haul myself away when the dumbwaiter lurched and then sailed upward, as the boys reversed their tactics and pulled on the other rope. I banged my hand hard on the side of the shaft, and then my head against the ceiling when the dumbwaiter reached the top of its course.

"Okay, I know what we can do now," the small voice from below piped.

Something that didn't involve the dumbwaiter, I hoped. If only they'd start up their protection racket again. But at least I was out of sight when Sammy opened the panel and peered in.

"It's a toy elevator," he said, his voice echoing up the shaft.

"That's a dumbwaiter, you ninny," the chief said.

"What's it for?" Sammy said.

"When the rich people who used to live here gave dinners, they'd haul the food up from the kitchen in that."

"But the kitchen's on this floor," Sammy objected.

"Well, maybe it used to be in the basement in the old days. Or maybe they used it to haul wine up from the wine cellar. Shoot, maybe it was just for show. I can just see old Mrs. Sprocket—Edwina's mother-in-law—making her poor cook run all the way down into the basement to put the food in the dumbwaiter. Mean as a snake, she was. Shut the damned thing and bring in Mrs. McCoy."

Presumably he meant the disgruntled soon-to-be-ex-wife, Carol. I waited a few seconds for Sammy to shut the dumbwaiter door, and then began carefully lowering myself again.

Carol had taken her seat by the time I had returned to

my listening post. I peered through the cracks in the dumbwaiter door and then nodded. Carol was the slim, elegant Gypsy I'd seen going into the barn. While I'd largely gotten over being jealous of slender women, in no small part thanks to finding Michael, who appreciated my more normal female shape, I had no trouble understanding why the plump Marie Antoinette and the stout older Gypsy disliked her. She looked rail-thin; remarkably self-possessed for someone who had just lost a husband (even an unwanted one); and altogether too chic to have anything to do with Gordon in the first place. I wondered how such an odd couple had ever gotten together.

"No, I don't remember exactly what I said," she was saying. "It was just like a thousand other conversations we'd had since we began the divorce proceedings."

"Give me the general gist, then," the chief said.

"I think I started by asking him why he hadn't returned some papers he was supposed to sign. Of course, the bastard never has done anything on time or right the whole time I've been married to him, so I don't know why I expected him to change after we filed for divorce. But usually, if I nag him enough, he eventually signs things. So we exchanged a few insults, for old time's sake, but I could see his heart wasn't in it. He was up to something— some deal, some bargain—so I left him to it."

Just then, I felt the dumbwaiter jerk up slightly. Damn, the boys were trying to haul it up from above. I reached out and grabbed the ropes to keep myself in place.

"I take it you parted on unfriendly terms?" the chief asked.

"We're getting a divorce, aren't we?" she said. "Oh, you mean today? No more than usual."

The boys were pulling more strongly—it was all I could do to stay in place.

"Did you see anyone else there in the barn?"

"Not that I remember," Carol said.

The pulling stopped, but the dumbwaiter began jerking oddly. What was going on?

The chief wasn't saying anything. I peered through the cracks. I could see his glasses, lying on the card table, and one elbow, moving up and down as if he were rubbing his face.

Just as he picked up the glasses, I heard—and felt—something land on the top of the dumbwaiter.

"What was that?" Sammy said.

"This is cool," came a small voice from above me, as another small thud hit the top of the dumbwaiter.

"What in tarnation?" the chief said.

I heard footsteps. I reached over, grabbed the ropes, and pulled the dumbwaiter down. I'd just gotten myself below the level of the door when I heard it open.

"What the Sam Hill are you boys doing in there?" the chief demanded.

I remained motionless while the chief chewed out the two boys and sent them packing with orders to stop fooling around with the dumbwaiter and stay out of trouble.

Luckily for me, he didn't inspect the dumbwaiter to see if anyone else was fooling around with it.

I inched the dumbwaiter back up after he'd dismissed the boys, but the rest of his interview with Carol was pretty tame, and I was wondering if I should try to sneak the dumbwaiter back up to the bedroom and leave when, after escorting Carol out, Sammy ushered in Cousin Horace.

"So, have you found anything interesting?" the chief asked.

"Nothing we didn't expect," Horace said. "Professor Rathbone's fingerprints are all over both bookends, but then he admitted that he'd been carrying them around half the morning. He tells us we'll probably find his fingerprints on that half-burned book, too."

"How very forthcoming of him," the chief muttered. "Anything else?"

"Well," Horace said, sounding sheepish. "Turns out the spatter marks on the book weren't blood spatter after all."

"What were they?"

"Barbecue sauce," Horace said. "Sorry. It was definitely spatter, and I was right about it being organic, but it wasn't blood."

So did this help Giles? I couldn't decide.

"Hmph," the chief said. "Any sign of the missing items?"

"Not yet," Horace said. "We're still looking. It's a big yard sale."

Dammit, why couldn't they name the missing items? And missing from whom?

"What about the trunk?" the chief asked.

"Only prints we found were from Dr. Langslow and that couple who wanted to buy it," Horace said. "Apart from that it was remarkably clean."

"Maybe someone polished it up nice for the sale."

"Yeah, but at least we would have found Gordon's prints, from when he dragged it into the barn. And there are those marks on the key plate. Someone was definitely trying to pick the lock."

"That woman who wanted to buy it, like as not."

"She says not," Horace said. "Not that I necessarily believe her. But I'm thinking the killer wiped it clean after stuffing the body inside. If Professor Rathbone was the killer, isn't it odd that he'd be so careful about wiping the trunk clean and not do anything about the bookends?"

"Not really," the chief said. "Typical of these professors, from what I've seen. All brains and not one lick of common sense."

"Or maybe he's more devious than you think," Sammy put in. "Maybe he realized that people had seen him carrying the bookends and thought it would look suspicious if his prints weren't on them."

"Hmm," the chief said. "Sammy, what's that racket going on outside?"

"They're looking for Meg Langslow," Sammy said. "Some problem only she can handle, apparently."

Chapter 15

Damn! Just my luck that someone would start looking for me now. And not just looking for me, but kicking up enough fuss that the chief heard about it.

I needed to see what the problem was. Perhaps if I moved the dumbwaiter very slowly . . .

"Could be the fingerprint technician," Horace said. "We need to take her fingerprints, for elimination purposes, and no one's seen her for over an hour."

The chief made a noise that sounded surprisingly like a growl.

"I'll go help them find her," Horace said, hastily. Under cover of the squeaks he made getting to the door, I began pulling up the dumbwaiter.

"Make sure she's not in the barn," the chief called after him. I paused to find out why the barn was so interesting.

"The barn?" Sammy repeated.

"We've had to chase her father out of the barn twice already," the chief grumbled. "He won't say what he's looking for—just gives some cock and bull story about an owl's nest in the barn, and wanting to check on the fledgling owls."

"Cock and bull story?" Sammy said. "Why wouldn't he just be telling the truth about wanting to check on the owlets?"

"And here I thought you were a birdwatcher, Sammy. It's October, remember? Everyone knows that birds nest in the spring. So even if they did have an owl's nest in the barn, the baby owls would have flown away by now, right?"

"Not necessarily, chief," Sammy said. "Barn owls can breed any time of year. In fact, if conditions are favorable, they may produce two broods a year."

"You don't say," the chief said.

Perhaps Sammy didn't notice the note of impatience in the chief's voice.

"It's primarily a question of food supply," Sammy said, warming to his topic. "You see, a grown barn owl eats five or six voles a night, and the fledglings can eat twice that much, so you need a fair number of voles to keep a family of barn owls going. Course it doesn't necessarily have to be voles. Mice, rats, shrews, moles, frogs, lizards, bats, baby rabbits, other birds, insects—they're pretty omnivorous. I dissected an owl pellet once that contained—"

"Sammy, do you belong to that SPOOR group of Dr. Langslow's?"

"Yes, sir," Sammy said. "Except Mrs. Sprocket founded it, you know; we only just elected Dr. Langslow as our new president last month. He—"

"Whatever," the chief said. "Seeing as how you're a SPOOR member and all—"

"I assure you sir, that I will in no way allow my membership in SPOOR to interfere with the proper performance of my duties as a police officer," Sammy said, in his most earnest voice.

"I'm sure you won't," the chief said. "Do you suppose you could convince Dr. Langslow to let you inspect the fledgling owls in his place? Seeing as how you're a SPOOR member in good standing as well as a police officer? Then maybe we could get him out of our hair and let him go bother the coroner the way he usually does."

"Yes, sir," Sammy said. "Want me to go do it now?"

"The sooner the better."

"Right, sir."

"I'll take a break while you're out doing it," the chief said. "On your way out, tell Fred to give me five minutes and then send up the next witness."

Perhaps I was in luck. If I could sneak out while Sammy was inspecting the owls and the chief was on his break, I wouldn't have to haul myself back up to the bedroom.

I waited impatiently for the door squeak that would tell me they were safely out of the room, and then reached out to open the latch.

With no luck. Sammy must have done a better job of wedging it shut than I usually did. I could see the wooden latch crossing the crack between the dumbwaiter door and the surrounding frame, and if I'd had something long and flat, like a nail file, I could easily have knocked it free. Unfortunately, lock picking hadn't been in my plans when I crawled into the dumbwaiter.

Ah well. At least I could take advantage of the chief's absence to haul the dumbwaiter up to the bedroom. With luck, his break wouldn't take him someplace where he'd hear the pulley squeaking.

I arrived safely at the bedroom level, and was reaching out to open the dumbwaiter door when I heard voices.

"Hold the other end right next to the wall, dear,"

Mother was saying. "That's eight feet, three and a half inches. I was thinking about chintz."

Mother often did. And she was wielding her perennial tape measure. Always a danger sign, that tape measure. She'd offered to help us decorate, a dozen times or more, but so far we'd put her off with one excuse or another. I hoped she wasn't planning to surprise us by redecorating the bedroom. I'd long ago figured out that while Mother had wonderful taste, it wasn't my taste or Michael's. So just why was Mother taking measurements in our bedroom?

"What next?" Michael asked.

And why was Michael helping her?

"I want the distance between the ceiling and the top of the window frame," Mother said.

"Right," Michael said. "I could ask Meg about that, if you like."

Did he think I'd memorized every detail about the house?

"About the chintz? No, I don't think it's a very good idea to bother her just now."

I thought it was a great idea, actually. At least if they were talking about something they planned for the house in which they expected me to live.

"Twelve and a quarter inches," Michael said.

"I think it would be better if we just surprised her," Mother said. "Now give me the distance between the window frame and the corner."

"It's just that I don't know what chintz is," Michael said.

I did. I didn't like it.

"It's a sort of flowered fabric, with a shiny finish," Mother said.

"Doesn't really sound like something Meg would like," Michael said.

Good call.

"Wait until you see it," Mother said. "It's the overall effect that matters. How do you feel about Louis Quatorze?"

"Is that another kind of fabric?" Michael asked.

I wanted to shriek "No!" but I held my tongue. Apparently Mother had some plan to decorate parts of the house without my permission or even knowledge. Right now, I had an edge, because she didn't know that I'd overheard her plans. If I confronted her, she'd apologize and promise never to do it again, and then come up with an even sneakier plan.

And why was Michael aiding and abetting her?

Of course, perhaps I was overreacting. Perhaps he was only humoring her. After all, some days, humoring Mother felt like a full-time job, and we both knew that Michael was better at it than I was.

I'd wait to see if he mentioned anything about her plans.

Meanwhile, I needed to go before they realized I'd overheard them.

"That's odd," Michael said. "They're yelling for Meg outside—I wonder where she's gone."

"She and her father are probably somewhere, playing detective," Mother said.

"No, Dr. Langslow is outside," Michael said. "One of the television people is interviewing him."

I winced. Chief Burke would be furious if Dad said anything outrageous on television about the murder. Definitely time to get moving. I began slowly lowering the dumbwaiter.

Chapter 16

I paused at the dining room level long enough to confirm that Chief Burke was back and see who he was interrogating.

"So, Ms. Mason," he was saying.

"Just Maggie, please."

I recognized the voice of the bookseller who'd told me about her negative experiences with Gordon. Was she a suspect, too? Good! Not that I had anything against her, but the more other suspects the chief had, the better for Giles. I decided to eavesdrop for just a few more minutes.

"You say this book wasn't all that valuable?"

"It's hard to tell from what's left," she said. "But as far as I can see, no. Even with the scorching, you can see that it wasn't in very good condition to begin with. See that discoloration on the pages? Dampstaining; that was there before the fire. The binding—what's left of it—is in lousy shape. And a bookplate on the inside cover; that lowers the value. No dust jacket. Not signed."

"So it's not worth anything?" the chief asked.

"Now? No," she said. "Not much of a market for half-burned books."

"Before it was burned," the chief said, sounding testy. "Was it worth something then?"

"Probably—it's a pretty rare title. Maybe forty or fifty dollars, even in that condition. The pre-burned condition, anyway."

"I see," the chief said.

He sounded disappointed. I could see why. The less valuable *The Uttermost Farthing* was, the less convincing a jury would find it as a motive for Giles to murder Gordon.

"Don't just take my word for it," Maggie said. "I can give you the names of some experts. Ask them."

I left her reciting rare book experts' names, addresses, and e-mails to the chief. I squeaked my way as gently as possible down to the basement. Just as I was about to fling open the door, I heard voices, and froze.

"Are you okay?" My brother Rob.

"I'm fine." Cousin Horace. Sounding very far from fine.

"Yeah, right," Rob said. Evidently he agreed with my diagnosis. "Come on, what's wrong?"

"It's Darlene," Horace said.

"Your girlfriend?"

"Not anymore," he said.

"Bummer," Rob said. "When did she dump you?"

"She didn't dump me," Horace said, somewhat indignantly. "I dumped her. She sold my suit!"

"Your gorilla suit?"

No answer, but I assumed Horace had nodded because Rob let out a long breath and then said, "Man, that stinks."

Although they couldn't see me, I nodded. No one in the family quite understood why Horace insisted on wearing his battered gorilla suit on every possible occasion, but we all knew how important it was to him. Recently, he'd discovered that he wasn't the only person in the world with this hobby, and had begun attending occasional conventions of people dressed in animal costumes. I had no idea what else they did at these conventions, but they made Horace happy, which was more than I could say for Darlene. Unfortunately, he had met Darlene at a Fraternal Order of Police social, not one of his furry conventions.

"I took it off because I was working," Horace went on, "and gave it to Darlene for safekeeping, and she sold it."

"Well, ask her who she sold it to."

"I did," he said. "She won't tell me."

I closed my eyes and sighed. Much as I disliked Darlene, I understood how she felt. And the idea of never having to look at Horace's threadbare old gorilla suit again was appealing. But dammit, that wasn't her decision or mine to make.

And how had she sold it so fast, with the yard sale still closed?

"Damn," Rob said. Then, after a pause, he added. "I bet Meg could get her to tell."

"You think so?" Horace asked.

I was torn between wanting to kick Rob for putting something else on my plate and agreeing that yes, Darlene would tell me. And I might even enjoy making her do it.

Of course, if I was going to interrogate Darlene, I had to get out of the basement one of these years.

I left Rob to commiserate with Horace and began slowly hauling myself up again. Back to the bedroom. I'd lose the advantage of surprise in my battle against Mother's unilateral decoration schemes, but at least I wouldn't embarrass Horace or get in trouble with Chief Burke.

All this hauling up and down was getting exhausting. Maybe we should put in an electric motor for the dumbwaiter.

But then, perhaps mechanization was overkill. After all, I wouldn't normally be using the thing for transportation, and a couple of well-placed locks would prevent any visiting urchins from doing the same. If only Michael weren't so charmed by it, I could see removing the dumbwaiter and turning the shaft into a laundry chute.

Luckily, by the time I hauled myself up two stories, Mother and Michael had vanished. Though Mother had probably gone off to buy chintz, I thought gloomily.

"Hey, Meg!"

I looked out the window and saw Cousin Everett peering in. Standing on the platform of his boom lift, presumably.

"Come on," he said. "They've all been looking for you outside."

As busy as Everett had been, I figured this might be my only chance for a ride in the boom lift, so I crawled out the window onto the platform.

"Hang on," Everett said. I grabbed the railings and looked down. And then I started when I saw Eric down on the ground, standing beside the boom lift controls.

"You're not letting Eric drive this thing," I gasped.

"Of course not," Everett said. "I'm running it—see?"

I looked over and saw that the platform did contain a complete duplicate control panel.

"Oh," I said, as we began moving. "I didn't know you could drive it from up here."

"Yeah," he said. "Pretty cool, huh?"

"Uh . . . yeah," I said. Instead of merely lowering me to the ground in the front yard, Everett lifted the platform up to its full forty-foot height, then rotated it ninety degrees so we were facing the backyard before lowering it again. The crowds on the ground looked like ants, and even relatives mending the roof looked doll-sized. Very cool, unless you happened to be slightly afraid of heights, which I hadn't realized I was until we hit the thirty-foot level.

"Thanks a million," I said, when Everett finally deposited me just outside the yard sale entrance.

"Any time," Everett said.

I stepped off into chaos.

"Meg!" Sammy exclaimed. "There you are! We need your fingerprints!"

"Meg!" Mrs. Fenniman called. "Where's the key to the cash box. We need to lock up."

"Meg!" Dad shouted. "What channel is CBS on up here? And when do they have the local news? We have to watch it tonight; they just interviewed me about SPOOR!"

"Hey, Meg," Rob said, appearing at my side. "I've got the lawyer on the phone. He's having trouble finding his way here—can you come and talk to him?"

"Meg, dear," Mother said, on my other side. "Are you sure you don't want to come shopping with me? It's for the house."

"Aunt Meg! Come look what I found in my owl pellet!" Eric called.

For a moment, I seriously considered running back inside, crawling down the dumbwaiter shaft, and dumping myself out at Chief Burke's feet. Maybe he'd arrest me for interfering with his investigation and I could spend the rest of the day in a nice, quiet jail cell.

Chapter 17

By the time I'd turned over the cash box key, sent Dad to guide the lawyer, given Mother my regrets, admired a small rodent skull that Eric had found, and allowed Sammy to ink and print my fingers, another dozen small crises had piled up, and I thought I'd never have a chance to continue what Michael called my snooping. Then I noticed a particular face appear in the circle surrounding me. Professor Schmidt. Just the person I wanted to talk to, although it looked as if I might have to solve a dozen other people's problems before I got the chance.

"Dad," I said, when he reappeared from his conversation with the lawyer. See if you can help some of these people. I'll see what I can do for Professor Schmidt; he's been waiting a long time."

Schmidt didn't even thank me for letting him jump ahead of the others who had, technically, been waiting longer than he had.

"Someone has blocked my car in!" he exclaimed.

"Okay," I said. "Do you have the make and model and license plate number?"

He frowned.

"It's an SUV," he said. "Black. Or maybe dark blue."

"Show me."

He turned and headed toward the road, and I followed. I resisted the urge to say how idiotic it was, coming to complain about the SUV blocking him in without bringing full information. After all, it gave me a chance to get him away from the crowd and extract some information.

"So, the police finally let you go?" I said, with deliberate casualness.

"Finally let me go?" he said, starting. "What do you mean by that?"

"I didn't mean anything by it," I said. I tried to look innocent, though I knew that wasn't my forte. "I just assumed they'd question you pretty closely."

"Me?" he said, looking even more alarmed. "Why?"

"I thought you were Giles's competitor for the rare book Gordon found. Isn't that why you were in the barn, talking to him?"

"Good heavens no," he said, with an exaggerated wince. "From what I heard, it was a *mystery* book. I'm a professor of *literature*!"

His tone reminded me of my great-aunt Hester, whose complete lack of firsthand knowledge about pornography hadn't diminished her passion for condemning it. As far as the family could tell, a *Wonder Woman* comic and a few mildly titillating historical romances were the closest things she'd ever seen to an obscene book. I wondered if Professor Schmidt's knowledge of mysteries was equally sparse.

"That's odd," I said. "I overheard that you were trying to buy a book from Gordon."

"Papers, not books," he said.

"Papers, then," I said. "And they had nothing to do with Giles's mysteries?"

"It was about Mrs. Pruitt," he said, with injured dignity.

"Mrs. Pruitt," I repeated, trying to sound both encouraging and noncommittal while racking my brain to think who Mrs. Pruitt might be.

"Mrs. Ginevra Brakenridge Pruitt," he said, in a withering tone.

"Oh, that Mrs. Pruitt," I said. "I thought you meant someone living."

"I am the world's leading scholar of Mrs. Pruitt's oeuvre," he said, sounding slightly offended.

Ginevra Brakenridge Pruitt was a late-nineteenth-century poet whose name had been largely (and justifiably) forgotten outside her hometown of Caerphilly. She'd probably have been forgotten here as well if she hadn't inherited a whacking great fortune from her robber baron father and doled out large portions of it to the college over the years in return for naming buildings after her and various members of her family.

"I heard a rumor that Gordon had acquired a cache of Mrs. Pruitt's papers," Schmidt went on. "I wanted to find out if it was true."

"And was it?"

"I still don't know for sure," he said. "I went into the barn to talk to him privately, but it was a waste of time. He was noncommittal. I suspect if he had the papers, he was probably putting out feelers to find out where he could get top dollar for them."

"Didn't that make you mad?" I asked.

"Irritated, perhaps," he said. "But, of course, I knew he'd have to come back to me eventually."

"When he figured out there was nowhere else he could sell them," I said, nodding. "Not if he wanted to get top dollar for them," I added, hastily, seeing the offended look on his face. "I mean, he should have known that no one could possibly match your dedication and commitment to Mrs. Pruitt's legacy."

"Yes," Schmidt said. "We did some verbal sparring—he refused to admit he had any papers, and at the same time, kept asking me to estimate what they'd be worth if he did have them. As if I could put a value on something I'd never seen. I lost patience and left. Not a very good atmosphere for a negotiation anyway. He was clearly itching to get back to the yard sale. I thought I'd talk to him later."

"Too bad," I said. "Guess you'll have quite a wait now."

"Why?" he asked, frowning.

"The police won't release anything of Gordon's until they've solved his murder, will they?" I said. "It could be weeks, even months. To say nothing of the delay until the estate goes through probate and you can start dealing with whoever inherits."

Schmidt smiled.

"Mrs. Pruitt has been dead nearly a century," he said, in a lofty tone. "I think I can wait a few more months to find out about these papers. If there are any papers to begin with. That's just the sort of rumor Gordon would have loved starting."

"And the murderer's done you a favor, too, hasn't he?" I said.

Schmidt looked startled again.

"Favor?" he said.

"Hard to think of anyone who wouldn't be easier to deal with than Gordon, isn't it?" I asked.

"Quite," he said, with a dry chuckle. "Now, about my car . . ."

I took down the SUV's license plate—as it happened it was neither black nor blue, but a dark green Ford Expedition—and returned to make a few announcements to the crowd. I offered Schmidt a glass of lemonade, on the house, while he waited, but he declined. He seemed relieved to see me walk away.

He was anxious about something. Or hiding something. I'd made him visibly nervous a couple of times, but he'd recovered, which probably meant I wasn't asking the right questions. I made a mental note to see what Michael knew about him. Could there be some juicy departmental scandal involving Arnold Schmidt that would crack the whole case wide open?

Chapter 18

I borrowed the police bullhorn and strolled around announcing the SUV's license plate number and politely asking the owner to move it. At first, I didn't mind the excuse to wander around and see what everyone was up to. But about halfway through my second circumnavigation of the fence, my stomach growled, and I realized I was starving. My mellow attitude abruptly changed to annoyance at the inconsiderate SUV owner. So I reworded my announcement. Instead of "Will you please return to your vehicle and move it so others can leave," I began saying, "This is your last chance to move your vehicle before the tow truck arrives." Almost immediately, a stout, red-faced man sprinted toward the road. I deduced that I had accomplished my mission, so I headed for the grills to pick up a burger for lunch—although it was getting closer to dinner time, so I made it two burgers.

"Meg?"

I turned, still chewing my first mouthful of burger, to find Cousin Sidney standing before me with a reproachful look on his face.

"You called another towing service? When you knew I was here?"

Fortunately, with my mouth full, I couldn't easily utter my first response—that even if I had the slightest idea which of Mother's hundreds of relatives were here, I wouldn't necessarily have remembered that one of them currently ran a towing service. By the time I finished chewing and swallowing, tact had returned.

"There you are!" I exclaimed. "No, I didn't call another towing service, because I knew you were around here someplace, and I figured I'd run into you before too long. There's such a crowd here that people who want to leave are starting to get blocked in by the new arrivals."

"I can take care of that," Sidney said, beaming.

Of course, I was wary of just towing cars without any posted signs warning of the possibility—just my luck that we'd tow a newly fledged lawyer who wanted practical experience in litigation—but Cousin Sidney happily agreed to tow a few of the family cars back and forth at random intervals, and after his first few passes, I saw people heading for the road, so I figured our tactic was working. I also noticed fewer Grouchos, Nixons, and Draculas in the crowd—apparently people were realizing that the yard sale wasn't starting up again soon and shedding their unneeded costumes.

"Meg, can I have some money for a funnel cake?"

I looked down to see Eric gazing up at me plaintively, as if the prospect of a funnel cake was the only thing that gave him the strength to continue.

"I'd give you the money, but where on earth are you going to buy a funnel cake?" I asked. "This isn't the county fair, you know."

"The funnel cake truck is out front," he said. "And the Sno-Cone stand, too. Come and see!"

I followed him around to the other side of the house

where, indeed, a brightly painted funnel cake truck and a mobile Sno-Cone stand had set up and were dispensing their wares to a long line of customers.

"Can I have one? Please?"

I handed over the money for a funnel cake. Eric looked at it dubiously.

"What about Frankie?" he asked. "Can't he have one, too?"

"He can't share yours?"

"He's our guest!" Eric said. "Wouldn't it be more polite to let him have his own funnel cake?"

"Okay," I said. "But you'll have to hit up someone else for Sno-Cones."

"Oh, Frankie's grandma is getting us those," Eric said. "Thanks, Meg!"

Nice to know I wasn't the only soft touch in town.

"That was a good idea," said Dad, who happened to be standing nearby.

"Giving the boys another sugar high?" I said. "Since it's Rob watching them, not me, I suppose so."

"No, I meant having the food vendors come out," Dad said.

"And compete with the family run concession?"

"I don't think it will hurt," Dad said. "Your cousins already have more customers than they can keep up with."

"Maybe I'll have a funnel cake, then, if it won't look disloyal," I said. "I wish I could take credit, but the funnel cake and Sno-Cone people appeared on their own."

"Probably similar to the way flies and carrion beetles appear on a dead body," Dad said, nodding. "It only takes minutes for the faint odor of beginning decay to attract scavenger insects."

"I would have said the way ants find a picnic," I said. "Maybe I'll wait on the funnel cake."

"I think I'll indulge," Dad said, and joined the funnel cake line.

You'd think I'd have gotten used to Dad's metaphors by now, I thought, with a sigh.

I spotted Cousin Rosemary. She'd been one of the people I'd had to turn down when they asked to join the yard sale at the last minute. Apparently she'd brought her stuff anyway, and now that the real yard sale was unavailable, had set up a booth in our front yard, near the Sno-Cones and the funnel-cake, between an aunt selling quilts and Horace's ex-girlfriend Darlene, who crocheted afghans in remarkably loud colors. I glanced around, and saw that several other card tables had appeared, like mushrooms after a rain. A black market yard sale and craft fair was growing up outside the gates of the one still held captive by the police.

Well, like the food, it would be something else to keep people entertained until we could let them back into the yard sale. And maybe Not-Rosemary was still selling the bath oils and bath salts she'd started making when she discovered aromatherapy. I actually liked some of her bath concoctions. And I realized that she'd hung a sign at the front of her booth with her new name conveniently blazoned across it: ROSE NOIR.

Unless that was the name of her business. I stopped in front of her table.

"Rose Noir," I said. I figured if that was her new name, she'd think I was greeting her, and if it wasn't, she'd just assume I was reading her sign.

"Yes—do you like it?" she asked.

"Very nice," I said, while reaching into my pocket for the notebook-that-tells-me-when-to-breathe.

"I think I've finally found a name that really captures the true essence of my nature," she said.

"Yes, it certainly does," I said, while scribbling a

memorandum to myself: "Note: Rosemary = Rose Noir" and today's date. "You're still selling the bath oils, I see."

I picked up a jar of her lavender-scented bath oil.

"How much for these?"

She frowned.

"Here," she said. "Try this instead."

She tried to hand me something called "Scheherazade." I could tell from the name, without even reading the label, that it would be dripping with musk.

"No thanks," I said. "I'd rather have the lavender. Lavender's good for dealing with stress, remember? And that's certainly something I have plenty of today. Stress, I mean, not lavender. I'm all out of lavender."

"I'm sorry," she said. "But I can't sell you that. I just don't see you as a person who should be using lavender."

"Why not?"

"Scents have personalities, too, you know," she said. "And if you're wearing the wrong scent for your personality, it's as bad as wearing the wrong color for your skin. It creates all kinds of psychic conflict."

"So what scent should I wear?"

"Here, let me try something," she said, rummaging among some small brown bottles on her table with one hand while she tried to grab my wrist with the other.

"No, tell me what scents you recommend first," I said, pulling my hands back out of reach.

"Strong, forceful scents," she said. "Cinnamon. Clove. And musk."

"Cinnamon and clove are all right," I said. "But not musk. I hate musk."

"See!" she said, as if this proved something. "I knew it! You're fighting your true sensual nature."

"Musk makes me sneeze, and I'd sooner just roll in a compost heap," I said. "I don't see why you won't sell me some of that lavender bath oil you sold me the last half dozen times I've seen you. I promise not to wear it out in public and embarrass you. I just want to take a nice, hot, relaxing bath in it tonight. It's good for relaxing, isn't it? And—"

I stopped myself when I realized, from the look on poor Rosemary's face, that I was raising my voice. I took a deep breath.

"Never mind," I said. "If you won't sell me any lavender, how about rose?"

She shook her head.

I gave up.

Time I got back to more important things. Like trying to get the yard sale back on track. And trying to keep Chief Burke from arresting poor Giles.

I realized that I hadn't seen Giles recently. Not since before my travels in the dumbwaiter. Dad was just stepping away from the funnel cake booth with his prize in hand, so I fell into step beside him.

"Seen Giles lately?" I asked.

"Not since the lawyer got here," he said. "They went upstairs somewhere to talk."

"Well, that's a relief. That he's talking to his lawyer, for a change, instead of the cops. No thanks," I said, as Dad held out his funnel cake. "I don't want to deprive you."

"Don't worry," he said. "I've had a couple already."

"Ah, so that's why there's already powdered sugar all over your costume," I said, nodding. "If you keep this up, you'll look more like a snowy owl than a great horned owl."

Dad's hearty laugh raised a cloud of powdered sugar, and he went off to share my joke with the rest of the family.

I was momentarily distracted by a table at which one of our neighbors was selling what looked like a lifetime supply of organizational tools—every kind of box, bag, tote, basket, shelf, and bin I'd ever seen and some I hadn't. Had she won a free, all-you-can-carry shopping binge at The Container Store and decided to sell off the surplus? I could still feel the seductive promise—that everything would be okay if I just organized my stuff, and here were the tools that could do it. But I broke the spell and walked away. Probably because Edwina Sprocket had built up her own impressive collection of organizational gizmos, and they hadn't kept clutter from taking over the house while she'd lived there. We'd put most of the bins and totes out with the other yard sale loot, and they'd been one of the first things people snapped up and fought over.

Back to business, I told myself. I decided to go inside and see if I could talk to Giles.

I found him and the lawyer in the dining room—apparently the chief was finished with his interrogation. The lawyer was talking to someone on his cell phone, or at least trying to—he stood over by the window, shouting into it. Giles sat slumped on one of the folding chairs.

He didn't look up when I came in, so I went over and tapped him gently on the shoulder.

"Good God, what now?" he snapped, but the anger faded as soon as he saw it was me.

"Sorry," he said. "I thought you were one of the coppers again. My nerves are shot. I'm not used to being treated like a common criminal."

I nodded. I wanted to say that I hoped he'd kept his temper better in check with the cops, but I could understand if he hadn't, under the circumstances. And Giles's brief, uncharacteristic flare of temper only made him seem more vulnerable when it passed.

"I've been trying to find out what really happened," I said.

He nodded. I felt momentarily annoyed—didn't he realize that I'd spent most of the afternoon trying to help him? But then, perhaps he didn't. Even if he did, I could hardly expect him to share Dad's inflated confidence in my sleuthing abilities.

"How has it been going here?" I asked.

"Apart from the fact that they're about to arrest me, you mean?" he asked.

"They're not!" I exclaimed. I was hoping Chief Burke would have found some evidence to suspect someone other than Giles. After all, I'd been trying to steer him to every other possible suspect I could think of.

"I was in the barn, and they have my fingerprints on the murder weapon, and probably the blood-stained book, too."

I opened my mouth to mention that the book hadn't been bloodstained after all, but then remembered, in time, that I had heard that while eavesdropping. And I didn't think it would be a bad thing if Giles made the same wrong assumption in front of the chief.

"And I admitted quarreling with the man," Giles went on. "Not to mention throwing the bookend at him."

"Everyone quarreled with Gordon," I said. "Including two people with a much better motive for killing the jerk—his ex-partner and his estranged wife."

Giles nodded.

"Just what happened in the barn?" I asked.

Giles frowned, and for a moment, I thought he was angry at me for questioning him. Then his face fell and he sighed. Probably just sick to death of answering that question.

"You went into the barn to talk to Gordon?" I prompted him.

"Yes. Twice," he said. "Once when Gordon was still alive, and once, I suppose, after he was already dead, since I didn't see him. If only I'd known it would make me a suspect."

"You're not the only one," I said. "Tons of people were traipsing in and out of the barn all morning. So who did you see there?"

"Gordon, of course," Giles said. "The first time, anyway. The second time, there was no one there at all."

"Did you notice anyone going in or out?"

Giles thought briefly.

"The second time, someone was leaving as I came in," he said.

"Who?"

"No one I know," Giles said.

"Describe him, then," I said.

"Her," Giles corrected.

"What did she look like?"

He shook his head.

"Giles—" I began. And then I stopped myself. No sense taking out my frustration on poor Giles. It wasn't really his fault that the stress of being a suspect sent him retreating behind the rather stiff, chilly exterior of his English reserve.

Though I shuddered to imagine how an American jury would react to his demeanor. I hoped things wouldn't get that far. And come to think of it, maybe it would reduce the chance that they would if someone had a word with Giles about softening his prickly manner when dealing with the police.

Probably a better job for Michael.

"Look, I'm sorry," I said. "I'm just trying to help. Isn't there anything you can tell me about the woman?"

"All I remember was the hat."

"What kind of hat?"

"It had all these bobbling flowers all over it," he said. "Frightful object, really; I remember wondering why anyone would put such a thing on her head. I'm sorry; that's not much help, is it?"

"No, it's a great help," I said. "I think I know who it is. The Hummel lady."

"Hummel lady?"

But just then, Chief Burke strode in. He frowned at me before turning to Giles.

"Giles Rathbone," he said. "You are under arrest. You have the right to remain silent. . . ."

While the chief read Giles his Miranda rights, I slipped back out into the hall. I went up to a short section of wall we were planning to demolish anyway and gave it several swift kicks.

"Idiot!" I snarled, and then added a few choice words. Only a few, and fortunately I didn't specify who I was talking about. I heard smothered titters from overhead and glanced up to see Eric and Frankie peering down at me.

"Don't either of you dare tell your grandparents what I just said," I warned them.

The dining room door opened, and Giles walked out. The police weren't precisely leading him away in handcuffs, but two burly officers escorted him out the front door, down the steps, and along the path to the waiting police cruiser. Though perhaps the burly officers were there not to prevent his escape, but to keep him from accidentally killing himself. He stumbled several times over the cracked concrete of the walk, and I mentally moved "new front walk" much higher on the list of repair and remodeling projects that already occupied seventeen pages in my notebook-that-tells-me-when-to-breathe.

Giles looked miserable as he ran the gauntlet of curious onlookers and eager reporters. Not that being arrested is a picnic for most people, but I suspected it was pure hell for someone as self-effacing as Giles. If only he'd stand up straight and look calm and professorial. Unfortunately, cameras on either side were taking pictures so rapidly that their flashes blurred into the almost constant glare you see at celebrity press conferences, and the barrage of light made him squint and hunch his shoulders in a way that looked furtive and guilty. He may not have been tried in a court of law, or even in the court of public opinion, but in the camera's eye he'd already been found guilty, guilty, guilty.

"Wow! Would you look at that?" Rob said, at my elbow. "It's like watching the movie stars arrive at the Oscars."

"More like watching celebrities arrested on *Court TV*," I said.

"They didn't have this many reporters at my arrest," Rob said, sounding envious.

"I'm sure they would if you were arrested today," I said. I meant it sarcastically, but Rob took my words at face value.

"I suppose so," he said. "*Lawyers from Hell II* did significantly raise our public profile."

"Hey, if you want to put it to the test, why don't you confess?" I said. "You could always say you did it out of compassion for Giles, and in the meantime maybe it would be good publicity for your next game."

"Hmmm," he said, and walked away wearing what I'd come to think of as his serious, corporate look—the one that usually inspired Mother to take his temperature and Dad to lecture him on the importance of dietary fiber. Fortunately, he didn't remember to wear it often. For that matter, he often let whole weeks pass without remembering to show up at the offices of the company he ostensibly ran, to the great relief of his staff, who could get a lot more work done when he wasn't underfoot, and knew that they could always rely on me to hunt him down if they needed him to sign something or impress a client.

I turned back and watched as the officers guided the stunned-looking Giles into the backseat of their patrol car and drove off.

Chapter 19

Most of the police vehicles drove off in the wake of the car carrying Giles. I hoped the media would follow suit, but unfortunately, only a few of them did. Which probably meant that the local reporters had all too good an idea of how little newsworthy material they'd get from Chief Burke and preferred to stay here and work the crowd. Since the crowd contained a fair number of my family, the odds were good that they'd eventually do something entertaining, though not necessarily related to the murder. My more exhibitionistic relatives were already jockeying for their chances.

Including Dad. He and half a dozen of his fellow SPOOR members, all dressed as various species of owls, had appropriated the front stoop and were giving a presentation on the importance of owls and other predators to the ecosystem. Dad was the only one enjoying his costume. The rest huddled together and hunched their shoulders with embarrassment, which gave them an unfortunate resemblance to a flock of cartoon buzzards waiting for a new supply of carrion.

Should I tell Dad? No, I didn't want to spoil his fun; and besides, his exuberance more than made up for the lugubrious effect of his troops. Even in my current tired state, the sight of him pacing up and down his impromptu stage, waving his wings with excitement, made me smile.

That was about the only thing that did, though. What do you do when you throw a party and the guests refuse to leave? It was getting close to dark; surely they'd leave then. Or would they?

I went into the kitchen and rummaged through my supplies until I found the markers and large sheets of paper I'd brought for making any last minute signs. I printed two notices that read YARD SALE CLOSED UNTIL FURTHER NOTICE. As an afterthought, I added a smaller note at the bottom of each, advising readers that the reopening would be announced on the campus radio station.

"Won't work, you know," Rob said, looking over my shoulder.

"Worth trying," I said, handing him the signs and a roll of masking tape. "Would you do me a favor and stick one of these on the gate to the fenced-in area and the other on the mailbox?"

He nodded and sauntered out. I poured myself a glass of iced tea, sat down in a corner of the kitchen, closed my eyes, and did my yoga breathing exercises. Breathe in on four counts. Breathe out on eight. In on four counts and out on eight. As usual, the breathing helped me tune out the surrounding chaos, and as usual, I nearly jumped out of my skin when a person whose arrival I'd tuned out suddenly spoke to me.

"Meg, dear," Mother said. "I'm sorry; I didn't mean to startle you."

"I was resting," I said.

"That's nice," she said. "You just stay there and rest. I only wanted to ask you a couple of questions."

"Ask away," I said. "Though my brain's pretty fried right now."

"Michael has been *so* nice about taking me places and helping me with my designs for your house."

I winced, suspecting from her tone that she was finding me annoyingly uncooperative.

"But it's hard to work in a vacuum, dear," Mother went on, with a slight edge to her voice. "If you'd just give me some idea what kind of décor you want, I could work a lot more effectively. Without any guidance, I'm left to guess what you'd like, so it's no wonder you're not happy with my suggestions."

"At the moment, I don't know what we want," I said. "I'm waiting for the house to tell us."

"The house?" Mother said, after a pause. "You're waiting for it to talk to you?"

"Not literally," I said. "I mean, I don't expect a voice to emerge from the mantel chanting 'Art Deco' or 'lime green' or anything. But I think you have to live with a place for a while before you can figure out what kind of décor would suit it."

"Living with it's going to be uncomfortable without furniture," she said. "Are you sure you're not beginning to get some idea what's on the house's mind?"

"At the moment, it's very focused on all the repairs and renovations it needs," I said. "And it's been so full of so much clutter for so long that I think it finds emptiness very restful." Also silence, but I decided I'd better not go that far.

"I see." Mother said. Her expression bore a strong resemblance to the look she used to get when one of her children—usually Rob, of course—claimed to have a stomachache on a school day.

"I suspect if we force it to give us design ideas right now, it would want something very spare and minimalist," I said. "Like those elegant Japanese rooms with nothing in them but a tatami mat and a single flower in a simple vase. Or Shaker décor. Did you know that after every meal they'd pick up the kitchen chairs and hang them from hooks on the wall, so they'd have as few things as possible to interfere with sweeping the floor? Doesn't that sound nice?"

"If you say so, dear," Mother said. "You'll let me know when the house comes up with any less extreme decorating ideas?"

"Of course," I said, but she was already sailing off. Was she admitting defeat, or just regrouping for another attack?

Regrouping, definitely. I squeezed my eyes shut again.

The next interruption to my breathing was more welcome. A pair of strong hands began massaging precisely the area between my shoulders where the muscles had knotted up from tension.

"You can relax," Michael said. "Rob's putting up your signs."

"Thanks," I said, leaning into the back rub. "Of course, that doesn't mean anyone's paying the slightest attention to them."

"No, but people do seem to be leaving, now that it's getting dark and there's not a lot to see."

"Good," I said.

"I broke up another fistfight. None of your family were involved this time."

"You sound surprised."

"I was," he said. "Not about your family. I just didn't expect two very dignified faculty members to come to blows over ownership of a Weed Whacker. And a nonworking Weed Whacker at that."

Rose Noir could probably have said something eloquent on the insidious effects of clutter and materialism on the human character, but all I could muster was a tired head shake.

"I was thinking maybe we could go pick up Giles when they release him," Michael said after a moment. "They have to release him before long, right? We could be there to bring him back to his car."

"Okay," I said. "Ready when you are."

"Hang on while I pack a few things we'll need," Michael said.

The hands disappeared, alas, but I had to admit that my shoulders already felt better.

I wondered if the police really would release Giles soon or if he'd have trouble getting bail on a weekend. But I didn't want to depress Michael. Especially since he was packing a picnic supper to take with us. Even if he was thinking of Giles's missed meal more than ours, he was definitely packing enough for all three of us, and then some.

"Signs up," Rob said, wandering back in. "Maybe we should threaten to turn Spike loose on anyone who isn't gone by six."

"Where is Spike, anyway?" I asked.

"Um . . . the cops had me put him in his pen when the crowds started dying down," Rob said. "I guess he's still out there."

"Rob! You know he's supposed to come in before dark!"

I hurried outside.

We'd had to placate Michael's mother, Spike's absentee owner, when she'd first heard about the pen, and explain that no, Spike wasn't living in the barn. But since I'd spent so much time there getting ready for the yard sale and would spend just as much after we moved in, working in my forge, Dad and Michael thought it would be a good idea to have Spike there with me.

"You can keep each other company," Dad had said.

"Some company," I'd said, frowning at Spike, and

from the expression on his face, I suspected Spike felt the same. A pity he couldn't talk, or he'd set them straight by explaining that he could care less about human company as long as his food bowl was full.

"Besides, he can warn you of trespassers," Michael had said. "It's pretty isolated out here."

So far, the one time we'd had a trespasser—a rather shabby character who tried to enter the house through an unlocked window—Spike slept through the whole thing, including my chasing the would-be thief away with a large (though unsharpened) broadsword. But even if Spike had barked when the guy began trying doors and windows, I'd probably have ignored the noise, since I'd long since gotten used to him barking at every legitimate visitor who turned into our driveway, every car or truck that passed by on the road, every mouse or squirrel that showed its nose in the barn, the owls every time they came or went, and the occasional shadow of a cloud or hawk passing overhead.

Still, I had to admit that Spike enjoyed his pen. A Spike-sized doggie door let him go at will from the large, outside area, which we'd nicknamed the barking lot, to a small inside enclosure along one wall of the barn, where we kept his spare bed and a set of bowls. The main problem was that we couldn't leave him out at night, to howl at the moon or mourn its absence, for fear of owls getting him.

"The barn owls probably wouldn't try it," Dad had said, eyeing Spike judiciously. "Unless they were really starving, and clearly they aren't, if they've had a second brood. But a great horned owl wouldn't hesitate to attack Spike."

"It would if it knew him the way we do," I'd said, out of loyalty. But I had to admit, Dad had a point. Spike's craving for outdoor nightlife would have to remain unfulfilled.

I only hoped the police on duty would let me in to whisk him away before the owls did.

Chapter 20

Outside, I spotted Dad and Eric talking to Sammy, the young uniformed officer, at the gate of the yard sale area.

"Meg!" Dad called. "Do you want to come with us?"

"That depends on where you're going," I said. "I need to get to the barn to fetch Spike."

"Then come along," Dad said. "We're checking on Sophie."

"Sophie?" I spent a few minutes racking my brain to remember who Sophie was and how she fit into the murder investigation or the family tree. Or had someone once again made the mistake of thinking that Spike needed feminine companionship? If so, this time I'd send the vet bills to the idiot responsible.

"I give up," I said, finally. "Who's Sophie?"

"One of your owls," Dad said, in a reproachful tone. "The female of the nesting pair in the barn."

"Oh," I said. "I don't think we were ever formally introduced. But isn't the barn still off-limits?"

"Not as long as Sammy's escorting us. I thought you might like to see the barn. Since Sophie's there," he added, with a look of such perfect innocence that I knew he was up to something.

"Ah," I said. "Yes, just for a minute."

"Come with me," Sammy said. "But remember, don't touch anything."

I started guiltily when he said that. He'd probably noticed me scrutinizing the various boxes and piles lined along the fence. I decided it wouldn't be a good idea to explain that I was only wishing for someone to steal the hideous orange and purple lamp shade from Mother's stash, not actually planning to do it myself.

"Have you heard anything more about that great horned owl sighting?" Dad asked Sammy.

"No, but I've asked the night shift to keep their eyes open," Sammy said.

"For an owl?" I asked.

"Night time is when you find them out, owls," Sammy said.

"Not just an owl," Dad added. "A great horned owl!"

"Cool!" Eric said.

"Is this a good thing or a bad thing?" I asked.

"Depends on your point of view," Dad said. "It's a fascinating species, of course, and like the barn owl, endangered, so in theory it's a good thing, spotting one. But not so close to the barn."

"It could eat Sophie's fledglings," Sammy said.

"It could eat Sophie!" Dad exclaimed. "They're two to four times the size of full-grown barn owls."

"Can someone take Spike inside now?" I asked.

"Poor Sophie!" Eric exclaimed, looking very worried. "We have to do something!"

I deduced from Dad's silence and the solemn look on his face that there wasn't much we could do to save Sophie from becoming some larger owl's dinner if she were unlucky enough to encounter one.

Inside the barn, I was relieved to see that Spike was fine. Dad, Eric, and Sammy hurried over to the far corner, where the owls had their nest high up in the rafters, while I followed more slowly, studying my surroundings. The barn was going to be my forge—my workspace. I felt possessive about it. I felt a stab of guilt when I realized that I harbored some resentment toward Gordon. Okay, I could blame him for trespassing, but it wasn't his fault he'd gotten murdered in the barn. And was it selfish to hope that his murder wouldn't affect my ability to work here?

But looking around, I felt reassured. I probably couldn't get past what had happened here until the chief had arrested someone for Gordon's murder—arrested the real killer, that is, not poor hapless Giles. But the barn already felt like home again. More so than the house, I realized, with a pang of guilt. In fact, while my decluttering labors had dimmed my appreciation for the house, they hadn't touched my love of the barn.

Perhaps because the barn didn't need much more work. No one expects a blacksmith's forge to look like a *House Beautiful* photo shoot. All I had to do was move my tools and equipment into the least ramshackle end of the barn and I was set. The odd falling board or shingle wouldn't hurt my iron and tools. They'd survive if the whole barn fell down on them, which two expensive structural engineers had separately warranted wouldn't happen.

I'd planned to set up my forge Monday, as soon as I packed off the unsold yard sale debris to charity or the dump. Maybe I should still do that, even though we might not be finished with the yard sale. I'd be a lot easier to live with after a few hours of pounding on things with my hammer.

I stood with my eyes half closed, appreciating the barn, while the owl fanciers, having reassured themselves that Sophie hadn't fallen victim to a hulking feathered bully, began searching the barn floor beneath the nest. For pellets, I assumed.

I suspected Dad was prolonging our stay in the barn so I could examine the place for clues, but I wasn't sure there were any to find. I saw all the stuff Gordon had accumulated, neatly arranged along one wall, much of it still dusted with fingerprint powder. We'd have to clean the powder off before we put the stuff back on sale. If they even let us sell it.

And if the police dusted the entire two-acre collection for prints, maybe I should just call Goodwill now.

"Sammy, they're not dusting everything for fingerprints, are they?"

"No, mostly just the stuff in here," he said.

"That's good," I said. "So why aren't Horace and the rest still working on the stuff outside?"

"They will be tomorrow," Sammy said. "Right now, they're searching the suspect's house."

"For what?" I asked. "They have the murder weapon."

"Yes, but they haven't found the victim's keys and wallet."

Aha! So they were the mysterious missing items I'd overheard Horace mention.

"And they won't find them at Giles's house, I can tell you that," I said.

Sammy shrugged.

"They have to search, anyway," he said. "You've got to be thorough in a murder investigation."

I decided to suppress my honest opinion of the investigation so far. Instead, I drifted to the corner where they were searching and looked up toward the owls' nest.

Sophie sat on a rafter, gazing down at us. Her face, with its heart-shaped ruff of white feathers and long, flat beak, looked deceptively mild. I was relieved to see that she wasn't bobbing her head. I'd seen her do it once, when I was up in the hay loft clearing things out some weeks before, and thought it rather cute how closely she resembled one of those bobble head dolls. Only later did Dad break the news to me that I'd probably gotten closer to her nest than she liked, and that the head bobbing was a sign that she was getting ready to attack.

She wasn't bobbing tonight. She only stared down at me and blinked, in slow motion, as if asking me what I was doing here. Good question.

"Dad, can you keep an eye on things here while Michael and I go into town to see Giles?" I said, still watching Sophie.

"Don't tell me the jail has visiting hours this late," Dad said.

"Not until morning," Sammy said.

"Actually, we hope the lawyer will get him bailed out soon, and we can take him home," I said.

"Can't the lawyer do that?" Dad asked.

"The lawyer could," I said. "But Michael thinks Giles would appreciate seeing a few familiar faces, and I want to hear Giles's side of the story."

"Ah," Dad said, nodding. "Get him off his guard and interrogate him. Good plan."

"Not exactly," I said. "We're on his side, remember?"

"That's right," Dad said. "But I have to admit, in a way, it's a pity. Giles would make such a perfect defendant."

"That's not fair," I said. "Just because he's a bit stiff and pompous—"

"I didn't mean that at all," Dad said. "Do you really think he's pompous? I thought he was a friend of yours."

"Sorry," I said. "I shouldn't have jumped to conclusions about what you meant. It's just that I've noticed that people who don't know him get that impression."

Including me, when I first met him.

"I just meant that he would be a very distinguished defendant," Dad said. "Cultured, well-spoken, and . . . well, handsome doesn't apply, I suppose, but he's . . ."

"Appealing, in an untidy, bookish, professorial fashion," I suggested.

"Yes, that's the ticket," Dad said. "And very suitable, too. I mean, it's a much classier murder than most, isn't it? Killing someone over a book, instead of drugs or money or infidelity or any of those typical motives. And a vintage mystery book, to boot—I really like that part."

"I'm sure it will be a comfort to Gordon at that great yard sale in the sky, knowing he made an atypically classy exit. And to Giles when he's put on Death Row."

"Laugh if you like," Dad said, in a tone of mild reproach. "I'm just saying that when you finally identify the real culprit, I hope it's someone . . . um . . ."

"Equally classy, but not so nice?" I suggested. "I'll remember that tomorrow when I start auditioning candidates for the role of the real killer. Meanwhile, I want to interrogate—I mean talk to Giles. Just to see if he knows anything we can use to shake Chief Burke's belief in his guilt. You know, if I were an evil person, I'd point out to the chief that there was probably an eyewitness to the murder."

"An eyewitness!" Dad exclaimed.

"Meg," Sammy said, very solemnly. "You should have mentioned this to the chief earlier."

"It wouldn't do any good," I said. "You'll never get him to talk."

"Who?" Dad asked, while Sammy shook his head with a worried air.

"Him." I pointed to Spike.

"Hmm," Dad said, looking at Spike. "You're right. He could very well have been in the barn when it happened."

"And look how cheerful he is," I said. "He's not usually this happy unless he's bitten someone quite recently. He probably enjoyed the vicarious bloodshed."

"You could be right," Sammy said. "Do you suppose we should test him for blood spatter?"

"What good would that do?" I asked. "For one thing, he probably does have blood spatter on him; he must have bitten three people today alone. But even if you found Gordon's blood on him, all that would prove was that he might have been in the barn at the time of Gordon's murder, which isn't exactly relevant. That bookend weighs more than Spike, and I'm pretty sure the murderer had opposable thumbs."

"I should tell the chief, though," Sammy said. "Don't give him a bath until I find out if we need to test him."

"A bath? Do I look like a masochist?" I said. "But if you like, you can take him into protective custody."

"No, thanks," Sammy said.

"Released on his own recognizance," Dad said.

I was about to leave them to their fun when I saw Sophie close her eyes and shudder slightly.

"Dad," I said. "I think something's wrong with Sophie."

Chapter 21

Dad, Eric, and Sammy hurried back to the corner and stood at my side. I pointed. Sophie's face took on a pained expression. Her eyes closed, her features scrunched up, and she shifted uneasily from foot to foot.

"Grandpa?" Eric said, looking slightly uneasy himself.

"Should we leave her alone?" I asked, jerking my thumb at Eric, trying to communicate to Dad that if Sophie were about to keel over at our feet, maybe we should lure Eric out before her demise.

"No, let's stay a little longer," Dad said.

"She hasn't been poisoned, has she?" I asked. "That is what SPOOR is worried about, right? Farmers using poison on their rodents and killing the owls?"

"No, I don't think she's been poisoned," Dad said. "Watch."

We watched for a few more minutes. I was already working on how to explain Sophie's death to Eric if Dad stuck me with the job, and wondering whether we had a box the right size to serve as a coffin for the owl funeral that I could see in our future.

Suddenly Sophie stretched out her neck, opened her beak, and spat out a pellet.

"There," Dad said, beaming proudly, as if Sophie had done something particularly clever. "You see, she's fine."

"Co-o-ol!" Eric said, running to retrieve the pellet. For the SPOOR collection, no doubt.

"Ick," I said.

"Can she do it again?" Eric asked.

As if this were her cue, Sophie launched herself into the air and swooped gracefully out the open door.

"Isn't that fascinating?" Dad said.

"At least she makes a lot less fuss than a cat with a hairball," I said. "Take Spike inside, will you? I'll see you when I get home from jail."

"Is there anything else I can do to help?" Dad asked, as he headed over to Spike's pen.

"No," I said. "Then again—if you wouldn't mind. It's not something you can do tonight, but if you wouldn't mind tomorrow . . ."

"Just say the word," Dad exclaimed.

Dad was disappointed at his secret assignment—obtaining lavender and rose bath products from Cousin Rosemary—but the warning that she must on no account know that he was buying them for me satisfied his taste for cloak-and-dagger operations.

Michael and I had plenty of time to cool our heels and eat our share of the picnic supper when we got down to the police station, but shortly after ten, Chief Burke let Giles go. Probably a good thing we'd come to collect him. The defense attorney was having a splendid time, arguing with the chief and threatening to file various motions. He wasn't eager to leave. We hustled the tired and disheveled Giles out of the station.

"Enthusiastic sort of chap," Giles said, when we were safely in the car.

"Well, this is what they live for, defense attorneys," I said. "A nice, challenging case."

"And he's very good," Michael put in. "Whenever any of the law school professors need a defense attorney, he's the one they call."

"That's encouraging, I suppose," Giles said. "Just as a point of information, do the Caerphilly law faculty get arrested often?"

"Not really," Michael said. "But I'm told that when and if they were, he's the very man they'd call."

Giles nodded.

"Think positively," I said. "As a mystery buff, don't you find it exciting to experience the criminal justice system firsthand, instead of just reading about it?"

"No, I think reading about it is infinitely preferable," Giles said, looking at me with alarm. "For that matter, I suspect it will be a good long while before I really enjoy reading mysteries again. Especially police procedurals."

"You'll feel better in the morning," Michael said.

"Better, perhaps; but not differently," Giles murmured.

Giles lived in a quiet neighborhood, only minutes from the police station—and, for that matter, only minutes from campus. You had to move out of town, as we had, to find anyplace that wasn't only minutes from anyplace else in Caerphilly.

Our original plan was to ferry Giles back to his car, but he looked so beat that Michael suggested that we just take him home and worry about the car tomorrow. Giles didn't protest.

Though when we arrived at his small, mock-Tudor house, he insisted on inviting us in for sherry and, despite the late hour, I didn't protest. I wanted to hear Giles's side of the story. And I didn't mind finally getting to see Giles's study, where Michael had spent so many happy hours. I understood Michael's point that Brits were more reserved than Americans, and didn't invite people to their homes as readily, but I thought it was about time.

Giles went to fetch the sherry and Michael collapsed into a shabby but comfortable-looking green plush armchair while I prowled around exploring. Giles had four of the chairs clustered together in the center of his study—the walls being completely occupied by more square feet of bookshelves than most town libraries could boast. Giles's book collection still overflowed the shelves. Stacks of books marched along the base of the bookcases, and more mountains of books occupied every open space. Small mounds surrounded each armchair, and here and there large Indian brass trays balanced on book stacks of suitable height to form side tables, while battered corduroy cushions thrown atop low heaps of books took the place of footstools.

Comfortable clutter, I found myself thinking. Earlier in the day, I'd have called that an oxymoron, but Giles's study reminded me that not all clutter was irretrievably bad, and suggested that maybe some collections of things, however large and apparently disorganized, didn't qualify as clutter. Should I feel guilty for having a double standard about clutter?

Since nearly every square inch of wall space was occupied by books, Giles had improvised a way to display the decorations most people hung from picture hooks. He'd used those hooks designed to hold Christmas stockings on a mantel without driving a nail into the wood to suspend various objects from the front of the bookshelves. Two silver stars supported a small oil painting, a team of brass reindeer towed a pair of antique dueling pistols affixed to a polished wooden board, and a series of framed certificates of appreciation from various arcane societies floated beneath a series of brass letters spelling out the cryptic message ACNE ELOPE. I puzzled over the sequence for several minutes before realizing that he'd combined the letters in two sets of holiday hooks, one reading PEACE and the other NOEL.

Now, I settled into another faded green chair and waited for the sneezes. Giles's study reminded me of his office, which I had seen before. I always sneezed half a dozen times shortly after entering his office until my nose adjusted to the prevailing atmosphere of book dust and left me alone. I expected his study would have the same effect.

"I want our library to look like this," I said, when I'd gotten past the sneezes.

Our future library, that is. Right now most of our books were packed in boxes and stored in Michael's office at the college, in the Cave, or at my parents' house. But we'd already designated one huge room on the ground floor as the library, with an adjacent room for Michael's office. It had the potential to look just as cool as this, I thought, looking around. In fact, even cooler.

To my surprise, Michael only looked around wistfully and nodded. Odd. Normally I was the one who would have trouble visualizing what the library could look like once we replaced the missing floor, mended the water-damaged ceiling, and put new glass in all the boarded-up windows. Was he just tired, or was something else wrong?

"I don't know how to thank you," Giles said, for the hundredth time, as he came in carrying three reasonably clean sherry glasses. "Bail bonds, criminal defense attorneys—I'm afraid it's all rather foreign to me."

"No problem," Michael said, accepting a glass of sherry.

"Always happy to share our vast personal experience

with the criminal justice system," I added, as I held out my hand for a glass.

"Er . . . right," Giles said, handing me the sherry.

We sipped in silence for a few minutes, while Giles wandered about the study, making minor corrections to how various books and knickknacks were arranged, muttering something about jackbooted thugs as he did so. Not really fair—the room looked in very good shape for a place the police had just finished searching from top to bottom. And he was lucky that they hadn't felt it necessary to use fingerprint powder.

I wondered briefly how long one should wait before asking one's host how his arrest had gone, and then decided to dive in. If Giles hadn't gotten used to my impatient nature by now, it was time he learned.

"I'm amazed that they actually arrested you," I said, which I thought was a pretty tactful opening.

"I don't blame them," Giles said. "You have to admit, the evidence looks bad for me."

"But what about motive?" I asked. "I mean, can you really imagine someone killing someone else over a book?"

"Well, yes," Giles said. "I can imagine it."

Chapter 22

"Giles!" I exclaimed.

"Your lawyer will probably be happier if you don't go around saying things like that," Michael suggested.

"I don't condone it," Giles said, sounding uncharacteristically melancholy. "It's abhorrent to consider taking a human life for any reason, but for a mere material object? Unspeakable. But unimaginable? No. I can imagine it. A great deal more easily with a book than with some other object. Isn't that strange?"

"Not really," Michael said. "You value books. I'm not sure you care about any other material objects."

"But not that book," Giles said, in something closer to his normal precise manner. "For one thing, I already have a copy of *The Uttermost Farthing,* thank you very much. The copy Gordon found isn't even in particularly good condition. You can see that just by looking at it."

"Not anymore," I said.

"True," Giles said, looking pained. "I wonder if there's enough left to judge the condition. For all I know, they only have my word on its poor condition before he tried

to burn it. Stupid thing to do. It was badly worn and dis-
colored, but it would have done for a reading copy.
Though not at the price he was asking for it."

"What was he asking?" Michael said.

"Eight hundred dollars," Giles said, with some heat.
"Outrageous, even if it were in mint condition. He'd have
been overcharging to ask fifty for it, the blackguard."

He blinked suddenly, as if he'd surprised himself with
the strength of his emotion. He'd certainly surprised me.
Normally Giles didn't go much beyond mild indignation.

He shook his head and sipped his sherry.

"I don't know why the poor blighter annoys—annoyed
me so much," he said, in something closer to his normal
dry tone of voice.

"I do," I said. "I heard him say he'd found a book you
wanted on someone's dollar table."

"Nothing wrong with that," Giles said. "That's his
business. Buying books cheaply and selling them for as
much as he can get. He has a right to make a living. Why
should I resent the fact that he has the time and energy to
go book hunting and the expertise to recognize a valuable
book when he finds one?"

"Annoying that you didn't get to the dollar table first,"
Michael said.

"But that's not his fault," Giles said.

"Says you," I put in. "You didn't see him shoving his
way to the head of the line."

"He happened to get to that table first," Giles said.
"And however annoying it would be to pay full price
when he'd paid a dollar, I could afford it. If I'd wanted the
book in the first place, and I didn't. So I feel bad about re-
senting him so much."

"Don't," I said. "He didn't have to gloat."

"Gloat?" Michael said.

"If Gordon had been a decent salesman, he would have

glossed over the fact that he only paid a dollar for the book. But he didn't. He was gloating. Hell, if Gordon had been a really good salesman, he'd have hidden the fact that he got it at a yard sale at all."

"How could he, when we were at the yard sale?" Giles asked.

"He could have just bought it and taken it to his shop. What if he'd told you that he found it in another bookstore, and paid more than he should have, but he knew it was one you wanted for your collection? You'd feel differently then, wouldn't you?"

"If you ever open a used book store, I shall be very skeptical of every word you utter," Giles said, with a pained look.

"There's a reason she does so well at craft shows," Michael said.

Giles nodded. I noticed that his face wore the forced smile that generally meant he was trying to ignore some ghastly and peculiar bit of American barbarism. I felt a fleeting twinge of irritation and realized, in one of those painful moments of self-knowledge, that I was intent on rescuing him less for his sake, or even for Michael's, but for my own satisfaction. Once I cleared him, he'd damn well have to be grateful to me. Not that I planned to gloat or anything.

"Getting back to the murder," I said. "Have you remembered seeing anyone in the barn apart from the Hummel lady?"

Giles shook his head.

"Well, I'll start with her tomorrow," I said.

"She seems an unlikely suspect," Michael said. "Would someone really kill another human being for a Hummel figurine? Or even a whole box of them?"

"Beats me," I said. "Of course, I don't even know why people would pay any money for them."

"You dislike Hummel?" Giles asked.

"I don't have anything in particular against Hummel," I said. "Or Fiesta Ware. Or Depression glass. Or old books or seventy-eight RPM records or mint nineteen-fifties-era Barbie dolls or any of the other material possessions people collect. I just don't get it. Sorting through Edwina's Sprocket's stuff for the last two and a half months makes me want to get rid of the things I have, not go out and buy more."

"The sense of profound estrangement from the material world," Giles said, nodding. "In the Middle Ages, people who experienced it would give away all they had to join a convent."

"Or, in the nineteen-sixties, a commune," Michael added. "Having a yard sale's the twenty-first-century equivalent. Much less extreme."

"But much less satisfactory," I said. "At least when the police interrupt it less than halfway through, before even a fraction of what we need to get rid of has been sold."

"If only I'd stayed home," Giles muttered.

"And miss all those bargains?" Michael exclaimed.

Giles laughed ruefully, and I looked at Michael with a frown. I wasn't sure he was kidding. I'd heard of sane people who developed gambling fever after a trip to Vegas. What if Michael developed an unhealthy obsession with yard sales as a result of ours? I had a sudden vision of him coming home weekend after weekend, covered with dust and smelling of book mold, bearing random objects that had caught his wandering eye. Faded plaster garden ornaments. Ramshackle bits of furniture that he would announce needed only a bit of work to make them good as new. Quaint vintage grocery tins and bottles, still reeking pungently of their original contents.

No. I was thinking of Dad. Not Michael.

Though I'd long since deduced that one thing I loved

about Michael was that he shared some of Dad's more charming enthusiasms and eccentricities, without going overboard on them.

Yet. Was he going to age into Dad-hood? I suddenly felt a rare surge of sympathy for Mother.

I shook myself and returned to the conversation. Or the lack of conversation. Giles and Michael were both staring into their sherry.

"Poor blighter," Giles muttered.

He sounded rather melancholy. Perhaps even sad. How ironic that the only person who seemed the least bit sad over Gordon's murder was the one Chief Burke had arrested for it.

But then, underneath Giles's irritation with Gordon, I sensed that they shared a deep love of books. That was one of the reasons I'd kept trying to work with Gordon when I was selling the valuable books to dealers. Every so often something—maybe just the way he'd touch an old, rare volume—would remind me that the man really did love books.

Of course, the next second he'd do something that proved his love of books took second place to his lust for money, so I'd eventually given up trying.

For that matter, the love of books was one of the reasons I kept trying to get to know Giles better—that and the fact that Michael liked him. So, despite my impatience, I followed their example, and sipped my sherry in silence for a few moments.

Giles was looking around his study, as if memorizing it. "I shall miss all this," he said, finally.

"What do you mean, miss all this?" Michael asked.

"They won't want me around," Giles said, taking a rather large sip of sherry—more like a gulp. "You know how they are about any kind of notoriety."

"Tell me about it," Michael said, gulping his sherry as

well. Michael's brand of notoriety was to appear on national television every week, wearing tight black leather pants and a black velvet robe in his role as Mephisto, the lecherous sorcerer on a cheesy television show. It wasn't Shakespeare, but it paid a lot better than being an assistant professor. I suspected the administration might almost prefer a nice respectable murderer.

At least now I could feel reasonably sure that worry over tenure, not anything I'd done, was causing Michael's down mood.

"But Giles, you're tenured," I said aloud.

"They'll find a way," Giles said, staring into his sherry. "Put me on administrative leave. Assign me all the eight A.M. freshman survey classes. Force me into retirement."

"No, they won't," Michael said, reaching over and clapping Giles on the shoulder. "We'll find some way to prevent it."

"Chief Burke's the one who could prevent it," I said. "If he'd just hurry up and find the real killer, instead of wasting time on Giles."

"So we'll find the killer instead," Michael said.

"How?" Giles asked.

"I'm sure Meg will think of something," he said.

From we to me, I thought. I was tempted to say something sarcastic, but Giles reached over and grasped my hand.

"Thank you," he said. "If you knew how much . . . I mean, I can't possibly explain . . . I mean."

"Please, you don't have to thank me," I said. And I wished he'd stop trying. Much as I'd wanted to break through his dry exterior, I found I didn't enjoy seeing normally taciturn Giles struggling with the unfamiliar task of expressing an emotion. What should have been moving only felt horribly embarrassing for both of us.

Besides, I hadn't actually done anything yet.

Giles fell back into his chair and stared into his sherry again.

"We should be going," I said. "After all, we have a long day of sleuthing ahead of us."

"Right," Giles said.

"She's right," Michael said. "To say nothing of the yard sale."

He and Giles stood up and headed for the front door.

Before following them into the foyer, I hung back long enough to do a bit of quick redecorating, changing ACNE ELOPE to ENLACE POE, something I'd been itching to do the whole time I'd been here. I wondered how long it would take Giles to notice.

"Sorry you have to do all this," Michael said, as we pulled out of Giles's driveway.

"All this yard sale stuff or all this proving Giles innocent stuff?" I asked.

"Both."

I nodded. I was sorry, too, but anything I said would only sound like complaining. I leaned back against the headrest and closed my eyes.

"I wonder how many divorces this yard sale will cause," I said, and then wondered if it was wise to drop something quite that ominous into the conversation. So, I told him about Morris and Ginnie.

"Good grief," Michael said. "When I saw the booth, I assumed she had one of those home selling franchises. Like Tupperware, only with lingerie."

"No, it's all from her own wardrobe," I said. "I can't imagine selling that stuff."

"So you side with Morris, then?"

"No," I said. "I understand why she wants to declutter, but I wouldn't set up a booth at a yard sale to do it. And I can't imagine anyone buying the stuff."

"Why not?" Michael asked.

"Secondhand lingerie?"

"It all looked brand-new to me," Michael said. "After all, they're not the sort of garments you'd keep on for long, and given how large a collection she has, I doubt if she wears any one piece very often."

"Still, it's the idea. Who could possibly be buying it all?"

"Just look for the lavender bags with silver trim," Michael said. "You can't miss them."

"And you know this because . . . ?"

"I'm highly observant," Michael said. "I would never think of insulting you with secondhand lingerie."

"That's good," I said. "But I'm worried about Morris."

"If you like, I could talk to him," Michael offered. "Try to get him to see it as a positive thing. That what matters is the whole experience—buying the presents, opening them, putting them on, and taking them off. Not the actual garments."

"Precisely," I said. "That would be great."

He nodded.

"Wonder if Ginnie takes returns," he said, after a few moments.

I smiled faintly at the joke. At least I hoped it was a joke. We rode for a couple of minutes in silence, and I was close to falling asleep when he spoke up again.

"I was really hoping you could come with your mother and me tomorrow," he said. "But I suppose it will have to wait for a while."

A long while.

"Your mother really does have some interesting ideas for the house."

Had I ever mentioned to Michael that "interesting" was what Mother had taught us to say instead of nasty words like "ugly" or "hideous?"

"I think if you took a look at what she has in mind—"

"Could we talk about it later," I said. "I'm pretty tired."

"Sure," he said. But I sensed something off in his tone. I felt a sudden flash of anger—not at him, though. And not really at Mother. At life, which keeps throwing stuff at us at the wrong moment. I took a couple of breaths and swallowed the impulse to snap at him.

"Sorry," I said aloud. "I know it's important. Too important to talk about when I'm so tired I'm not really coherent. Not to mention so cranky I wouldn't blame you if you let me walk home."

"I understand," he said. "I just thought, while she's up here, that this might be a good chance for you and your mother to do some bonding."

"Bonding?" I echoed. "Mother and I don't need bonding. Mediation, occasionally, or possibly therapy. Have you been spending too much time in the psych department?"

"Just a thought," he said.

But he meant well, I knew. He just hadn't figured out yet that Mother and I could squabble noisily over everything under the sun without being really mad at each other. He and his mother hardly ever raised their voices, but when they did—look out. Mother and I rarely saw eye to eye, but we understood each other.

"Maybe we could do something nice for Mother when the yard sale is over," I said aloud. "Like that antiquing trip she's been talking about."

"Good idea," he said. And this time I could hear the hint of a smile in his voice. More like the normal Michael. A few seconds later he reached out and took my hand. A nice gesture, however transient, since his car had a standard transmission, and he'd probably have to downshift in a minute or two. Still—another quarrel averted. Or was it only postponed?

Part of the problem was our difference of opinion on how to handle my parents when they came up with the sort of peculiar ideas my family specialized in, particularly when it came to how other people should run their lives. Michael favored humoring them as long as possible, while I thought it worked better if you set them straight immediately. Humoring them only hurt their feelings more in the end, not to mention creating a very real danger that they'd go out and do whatever strange thing you were trying to talk them out of.

And the house caused more of these conflicts every week.

Damn the whole house project anyway. I wondered how we could possibly get safely through the next few months, or even, God help us, years of repairs and renovations.

Of course, looking on the bright side, next to surviving the house with our relationship intact, proving Giles innocent of murder looked remarkably easy.

Despite the late hour, as we approached the house we could see lights blazing on every floor. And when we got closer, I heard shrieking from somewhere in the house. Barrymore Sprocket stood on the front step, smoking a cigarette.

"There you are," he said, as I ran toward him. "They've all been looking for you."

"What's wrong?" I asked.

He shrugged, and just then another chorus of shrieks rose up, so I raced past him into the house, and then up to the third floor, where the shrieking came from.

Chapter 23

I arrived in time to see a dozen of my relatives, clad in bathrobes and bedroom slippers, stampede past the head of the stairs, all shouting variations on "Watch out! Here it comes!" as they passed. They all vanished into the last two rooms along the corridor, slamming the doors behind them.

Here what comes? The hall looked empty from where I stood—I'd stopped two steps below the third floor landing. I stuck my head into the hall and peered up and down. Nothing.

"What is it?" Michael asked from the second floor landing.

"No idea," I said. "But something has them scared."

"So I gathered from Barrymore," he said, arriving at my side. "But he hasn't a clue what."

We couldn't see anything ominous from our post, so we stepped out into the hall. No fearsome monster appeared to threaten us. The corridor was an empty line of closed doors, except for the last door on the right, which hung open.

"Shall we check there?" Michael said.

Just then I heard a soft hissing noise. I looked up and saw a small barn owl sitting on the ceiling light fixture at the end of the hall. I pointed it out to Michael.

"Sophie?" he asked.

"Too small. One of the fledglings, I suspect."

And quite possibly the fledgling who'd gotten in the habit of having its bedtime snack outside our window. The fledgling was bobbing its head as if warning that it was about to attack, but when I stepped closer it fled through the open door. Screaming erupted from the darkened room beyond.

When Michael and I stuck our heads in, we found that the screaming was coming from under a sleeping bag, while the owl fluttered around the edges of the ceiling, its ghostly white face luminous in the faint light from the door.

"Come out from there!" I ordered the unseen screamer on the floor.

No response. I fumbled beside the door for the light switch.

When the light came on, I saw a familiar face pop up from beneath the sleeping bag. Darlene, Horace's girlfriend. Ex-girlfriend now, I supposed. Unfortunately, popping up brought her face-to-face with the owl, which had just landed on a nearby box. Darlene shrieked. Maybe the owl did, too, though if it did, Darlene drowned it out. At any rate, they both dived for cover.

"You can come out now," I said. "It went into the closet."

"It will get me!" came the voice from beneath the sleeping bag.

"No, it won't," I said. "Michael and I won't let it. Just crawl out and run for the door. We'll cover you."

Michael took up a karate stance and looked menacingly at the closet door.

The sleeping bag heaved itself up and scuttled out the door.

"So what do we do about him?" Michael asked, nodding at the closet.

"Is at least one of the windows open?"

"All of them wide open."

And without screens, of course—another item on our repairs and renovation list.

"Then we leave the lights on and let him find his own way back out into the darkness," I said. "Unless there's some compelling reason for him to stay—do you suppose we have mice?"

"I think if we had mice, we'd have found out by now," Michael said, "considering how many people have been sleeping on the floor."

"Good point," I said. "But let's not mention that, or we'll be up half the night chasing imaginary mice out of everyone's sleeping bags."

Outside, I found that a dozen of my relatives had surrounded Darlene and were trying to comfort her. My arrival sent her into a renewed frenzy.

"You knew!" she sobbed. "You knew that monster was out there all the time! How can you be so cruel?"

"I told you to keep your windows closed if you didn't want things flying in," I said.

"I thought you meant insects," she said. "Little insects. So I wore some mosquito repellant. I didn't expect to be attacked by a ravenous bird of prey! How can you—"

"Where are the scoundrels?"

We all started as Mrs. Fenniman emerged from her room, waving the antique cavalry saber she always kept under her bed for protection. Though considering how

soundly Mrs. Fenniman slept, I didn't think the local bur-
glars were in much danger. And come to think of it, tonight she was using a sleeping bag like the rest of
us—where had she put the sword?

"Gone," I said aloud.

"Dang," she said. "Never any fun around here."

With that, she jammed the point of the sword into one
of the floorboards and left it there, quivering, while she
stomped back into her room.

Mrs. Fenniman's arrival had startled Darlene into silence, but now she began to sniffle again.

"Now, now," Rose Noir said, putting her arm around
Darlene's shoulder. "I know it was a terrifying experience.
But consider what a wonderful omen you've received!"

"Omen?" Darlene said, with a sniffle. "That horrible
monster?"

"Many cultures consider the owl sacred," Rose Noir
said. "They were beloved by the goddess Athena, sym-
bolic of wisdom, and considered protectors of warriors."

She nattered on for a few minutes, relating bits of owl
lore from around the globe, in a strangely soothing voice.
Darlene began looking calmer, and one by one the rest of
the gathered relatives yawned, said good night, and returned to bed.

"Why don't you stay in my room for the rest of the
night," Rose Noir suggested eventually. "I'm sure Meg
will get the owl out of your room by morning."

Still sniffling Darlene made a visit to the bathroom—
though not until Michael had checked it and declared it
owl-free.

"I notice you didn't mention all the cultures that consider owls a bad omen," I said to Rose Noir once the bathroom door had closed behind Darlene. I knew a bit of owl
lore, too, thanks to Dad and SPOOR. "Like the ancient
Roman and early British belief that hearing an owl hoot

foretells death, or all the African countries that think the owl is too evil to name and just call it 'the bird that makes you afraid,' or—"

"I see no reason to dwell on the negative side of things," Rose Noir said, frowning at me.

Cousin Darlene emerged from the bathroom.

"I'll need my makeup kit in the morning," she said, and followed Rose Noir down the corridor, trailing her sleeping bag behind her.

"Yes," I murmured as the door closed behind her and Rose Noir. "And you might just get it back, if you tell me who you sold Horace's gorilla suit to."

"She didn't," Michael said. "How could she?"

"She did, and he dumped her because of it," I said.

"Good for Horace," Michael said.

Another item in the plus column. Michael not only tolerated my family, he actually liked them.

Some days, more than I liked them myself.

"Why not get Rose Noir to find out who got the suit?" Michael suggested. "Darlene will probably feel very grateful to her by tomorrow."

"Great idea," I said.

Just then Mrs. Fenniman's door flew open. She stomped out into the hall, wrenched the saber out of the floor, and disappeared into her room again. A few seconds later I heard a sharp thud. Michael and I both winced and glanced involuntarily at the gash in the hall floorboard.

"We need to refinish the floors anyway," Michael said, finally. "Let's turn in."

Chapter 24

Sunday morning dawned bright, clear, and unseasonably warm. I knew because I got to watch. I woke up just before dawn, started worrying about everything I had to do, and couldn't get back to sleep. I didn't hear any hooting owls or screaming cousins, but just listening for them kept me wakeful. And the eight-foot-tall windows that made the room so wonderfully light and airy faced east. Given our remote location, I hadn't made curtains a high priority. That would have to change.

Still, lovely weather. Perfect yard sale weather. Too bad that instead of a yard sale, we still had a crime scene in the backyard. I could hear voices—probably Cousin Horace and the local evidence technician showing the crime scene to the promised reinforcements from Richmond. A lot of reinforcements, from the sound of it. At least what I could hear over the renewed hammering from the roof.

I tried to focus on something positive. The bare wooden floors, for example. Beautiful hardwood floors;

at least they would be after someone (probably me) refinished them. One of the few things in the house that didn't need expensive major repairs. Just some elbow grease. Okay, a whole lot of elbow grease; probably more than I'd have to spare for months. But they were already beautiful in potential.

Or maybe I just liked them because they were bare. Only the sleeping bag, pillows, and an alarm clock to mar the beautiful emptiness; and I could roll up the sleeping bag neatly and put it and the pillows in the closet for the day.

Of course, I'd have to wait until Michael got up.

I talked myself out of going down to tidy the kitchen. The itch to tidy was only a symptom. Tidying the already tidy house wasn't what I really wanted.

I wanted to clear the two acres of junk out of our backyard, and I wanted to clear Giles of murder. The junk would have to wait until the police released the scene.

So what could I do about the murder?

I took out my notebook-that-tells-me-when-to-breathe. Which Michael sometimes calls my security blanket. He's not far wrong. It's certainly my way of imposing order on an unruly world. Whenever I feel overwhelmed, I take out the notebook and make sure I've written down everything I have to do or remember. No matter how dauntingly long the list is, I know I'll feel better once I have each task pinned down in ink and captured between the notebook's covers. In the last few months, especially when Michael was away on his acting trips, I sometimes felt the notebook was the only thing that kept me sane.

I'd been scribbling for a long time when Michael finally turned over and yawned.

"Morning," he said, with a sleepy smile.

In fact, a downright inviting smile, and I was tempted to rejoin him in the sleeping bag. Just then the boom lift platform appeared outside the window, carrying half a dozen of my uncles and cousins wearing plaid flannel shirts and toting saws. They waved cheerfully before settling down to the fascinating task of removing the dead oak branch.

Michael sighed and waved back.

"I've put curtains really high on my to-do list," I said. "And meanwhile, I need to ask you something."

"Ask away," he said.

"What do you know about Mrs. Pruitt?"

"Who?" he said, frowning and sitting up.

"Ginevra Brakenridge Pruitt," I said. Shouted, actually; the volunteer lumberjacks had started their chain saw.

"The Poet Laureate of Caerphilly?"

"Is she?"

"Well, not officially," he said. "And I suspect the administration would love to downplay her connection to the college, if it weren't for all that money she left them. The whole student demonstration thing was pretty embarrassing."

"Demonstration?" Caerphilly's students were notoriously apolitical. "When did the students demonstrate, and what did it have to do with Mrs. Pruitt?"

"Back in the late seventies," Michael said. "I wasn't here, but I've heard all about it. They protested against having to sing the school song at graduation."

"Let me guess: Mrs. Pruitt wrote it."

"All five interminable verses," Michael said. "The administration appointed a commission to study the suitability and political correctness of the lyrics, and declared a moratorium on singing it until the commission finished its work. And since the commission's last meeting was held in 1981 . . ."

"So that's why we all hum along instead of singing the

school song at college events," I said. "I've been meaning to ask."

"In my opinion, which counts for very little around the English department—"

"But a great deal here in the sane world."

"She's unreadable. Not that I've tried recently, but I did, back when I was new on campus, and hoping to make a good impression on people like Schmidt. I know that sounds pretty ridiculous," he said, frowning slightly when I began laughing.

"No," I said, wiping my eyes. "I'm laughing because I tried the same thing, before the first time you took me to a faculty bash. I looked up some of the people you told me were important and tried to bone up on their subjects. I should have remembered Schmidt from that. And you're right. She's completely unreadable."

"So under the circumstances," Michael said, smiling again, "I imagine the only person in Caerphilly who cares much about Mrs. Pruitt would be Arnold Schmidt."

"The world's leading scholar of her oeuvre," I said, nodding.

"Probably the world's only scholar of her oeuvre," Michael said. "He's built his career on analyzing her work."

Outside the window, the chainsaw sputtered into silence and was replaced by a lively quarrel between several of the amateur tree surgeons over where to make their next incision.

"Would he kill to protect his career?" I asked.

"I don't know," Michael said. "I suppose he might, but I can't imagine how Gordon McCoy could have anything to do with Mrs. Pruitt or Schmidt's career. Gordon doesn't—didn't do anything without a financial motive, remember, and how could you possibly make any money from a long-dead poetess nobody reads anymore?"

"Isn't the word 'poetess' rather antiquated?" I asked.

"And Mrs. Pruitt isn't?"

"True. Anyway, Schmidt said Gordon was rumored to have found a cache of Pruitt's papers," I said. "Which he wanted to buy, of course."

"Well, it's not as if he'd have any competition," Michael said. "The college certainly wouldn't care. But even at Gordon's prices, he could afford them. No need to kill for that. And I have a hard time imagining Schmidt doing anything violent. For that matter, I have a hard time imagining him doing anything even mildly energetic."

"Hmmm," I said. "Still, I have this feeling he's hiding something."

"Something reprehensible, I hope," Michael said, crawling out of the sleeping bag. "He's one of the department's worst snobs."

We heard a loud cracking noise outside.

"Timber!" several of the volunteer lumberjacks shouted.

I glanced up at the window, but couldn't see anything except several of my uncles flinching as something—presumably the dead branch—landed below, with a lot of crashing sounds. Also breaking glass sounds. Then the uncles glanced up at me with sheepish looks on their faces.

"How bad is it?" I asked, as Michael peered out of the window.

"We'd probably have had to replace that window anyway," Michael said. "Whoever owned the funnel cake truck will be upset, but it's not as if they had our permission to park it on our lawn, so we're probably fine."

"Damn," I muttered.

"I'll go down and deal with it," he said, reaching for his jeans. "So what are you planning to do today?"

"That depends on Chief Burke," I said. "If the crime scene people finish early enough, we might reopen the yard sale. But I'm not optimistic. At a minimum, it would be nice if they could finish processing all the boxes of stuff people collected, so we could get those off our hands."

"Seems reasonable." Michael said. "But not urgent."

"What if people change their minds?" I said. "What if they don't come back to pay for the stuff they've collected? What if they don't even come back to pick up what they've already bought, and we have to hunt them down to get them to haul it away?"

"Oh . . . I wouldn't worry too much about that," he said.

He was gazing out of the window. I walked over to take a look.

"Good grief," I exclaimed. We had at least as many people milling around in the front yard as we'd had inside the yard sale at its peak the day before. And they seemed to be spillover from the back and side yard. I strolled into the dressing room (and future master bathroom), whose window looked out over the side yard, including part of the yard sale area. Yes, wall-to-wall people.

Of course, they weren't all prospective customers. The trucks from the local affiliates of all three networks had returned, and with no one awake to fend them off they'd driven over the front lawn to get to the yard sale, leaving large ruts behind them. Good thing we hadn't done much landscaping yet.

Someone had put Spike out to resume his security duty, and half a dozen teenage boys had invented a new sport—climbing over the fence, running along as Spike literally nipped at their heels, and then leaping back to safety at the last minute. Caerphilly's answer to running with the bulls at Pamplona, and not a whole lot safer, if you asked me. Though the crowd enjoyed it, and for lack of anything interesting on the murder front, several of the news teams were busy filming it.

"Well, let's look on the bright side," I said. "I'm sure we can think of one."

"If the chief lets us reopen the yard sale today, we'll have an overflow crowd all ready to dash in and buy souvenirs," Michael suggested.

"And if he doesn't let us reopen for days?"

"The crowds will be even bigger when it hits the *National Enquirer*."

"Oh, and the college will love that," I said. "Professor Turned TV Star Hosts Murder."

He winced.

"Maybe I should stay out of sight until the reporters leave," he said.

"Good idea," I said. "Or wear your mask again, anyhow. But at least the circus out there has one bright side."

"And that is?"

"The only way I can think of to help Giles is to create reasonable doubt of his guilt," I said.

"Well, there's always fingering the real culprit."

"Yes, that would be nice, but creating reasonable doubt will be hard enough," I said. "So we need to poke a few holes in the stories of the other people who went into the barn. What Dad calls our skulk of suspects. And I've already spotted one of them in the crowd. Make that two. Chances are the whole skulk is here."

"And if some of them aren't?"

"I would find that highly suspicious and would try to find out why they are avoiding us, when I do catch up with them—which shouldn't be all that hard in a small town like Caerphilly."

"So who will you start with?" he asked.

"Depends on who is here," I said. "But I think I see the

person I'd like to start with. Over there by the Sno-Cone truck—the woman who was trying to buy the trunk. See you later."

I dashed downstairs and out into the yard.

Dad occupied our front porch-turned-stage, giving his spiel on the importance of owls in the ecosystem. Not that you could hear much of what he was saying over the boombox, which was playing The Fabulous Thunderbirds' version of "Who Do You Love?" while a chorus line of assorted owl-costumed SPOOR members performed a ragged but enthusiastic imitation of the Rockettes. Either Dad's fellow SPOOR members had shed their reticence overnight or Dad had recruited some more uninhibited owls, probably from the ranks of my family.

Nearby, having removed the offending branch, my lumberjack uncles had moved on to boarding up the broken window and shaking their heads over the remains of the funnel cake truck. The boom lift was once more swaying gently overhead, its four-person cargo equally divided between people busily snapping photos of the forensic crew at work and people staring greedily down at the piles of unbought stuff. Though apparently Chief Burke had forbidden Cousin Everett to take his customers directly over the crime scene today, because the platform was only wobbling along the edges of the fence. The ride would probably still offer some excitement, since Everett had delegated running the boom lift to Rob, whose ineptness with mechanical objects was legendary.

I saw Michael, on his way to join the crowd around the funnel cake truck, waylaid by Cousin Bernie, the most obsessive of the family's genealogists, who never really felt he knew someone until he had inspected at least half a dozen generations of his family tree. Cousin Bernie still regarded my father with profound suspicion because, through no apparent fault of his own, Dad had been orphaned as an infant. After a glass or two of wine at family gatherings, Bernie was often found staring balefully at Dad and muttering, "The man could be anyone."

I wondered how Bernie would react when he learned that Michael had spent nearly forty years on the planet without ever feeling the need to track down all sixteen of his great-great-grandparents.

I left them to it and looked around for the would-be owner of the trunk. As luck would have it, not only was she still loitering by the Sno-Cone truck, she came running over when she saw me.

"There you are!" she exclaimed. "There's no one else around here who can answer my question."

"I'd be happy to try," I said. "If you'd tell me what your question is?"

"Where can I pick up my trunk?" she said.

Chapter 25

"Your trunk," I repeated.

"The locked trunk I bought yesterday," she said.

Wasn't she getting ahead of herself? I didn't recall that we'd completed the sale yesterday. Not to mention the small detail that the trunk was evidence in the murder investigation. Was she serious?

"You mean the one the body was in?" I asked.

"That's the one," she said. "Where is it? My husband is waiting in the van."

"I'm afraid you can't pick it up yet," I said, frowning.

"How dare you—"

"No one can pick anything up until the police say so," I said.

"And when will that be?"

"I have no idea," I said. "When Chief Burke tells me, I'll spread the news."

"This is unacceptable," she said.

"Tell it to the chief," I said, through gritted teeth.

"I need the trunk now!" she said, stamping her foot.

"Sorry. Not much I can do."

"But what am I supposed to do when my auction ends?" she wailed.

"Your auction?"

"I've got it up for auction on eBay," she said. "I'll need to ship it to the buyer in eight days."

She must have deduced how I felt about the idea from my face—I certainly didn't say anything.

"It's my trunk!" she said. "I can do anything I want with it."

"It will be your trunk when and if you buy it," I said. "In the meantime—"

"How much was it?" she asked, pulling out her wallet.

"To tell you the truth, I don't remember," I said. "And right now figuring out who owns it is academic, don't you think?"

"Academic?" she echoed.

"After all, I doubt if the police will be finished with it for a long time," I said.

"How long?"

"Certainly not until after the trial," I said, with a shrug. "They'll want it as evidence."

"Oh, dear," the woman said.

"In fact, a lot of times they hang on to the evidence until after all the appeals are finished," I said. "It could be years."

She actually whimpered.

"But don't worry," I said. "As soon as the police give it back, I'll let you know. Tell me—did you see anyone else in the barn when you found the trunk? Leaving the barn, perhaps?"

"What does that have to do with anything?" she said. "I thought you said it's mine?"

"It's yours when the police let us sell it, yes—you were the first one to bring it to the cash register. But if we knew more about what happened in the barn, maybe that would speed up what the police are doing. So did you see any-one else in the barn?"

"Who should I have seen?" she asked.

I stared at her. Was she completely clueless, or shame-lessly eager to perjure herself in return for the trunk? Or possibly both?

I decided I was wasting my time. She probably wouldn't have noticed anything that didn't have a price tag on it, and even if she had, no sane person would be-lieve a word she said.

"Never mind," I said. "I'll let you know about the trunk when I hear from the police."

In the front yard, the SPOOR contingent had segued into a new number—The Four Tops doing "Reach Out," with the whole audience joining in to mangle the first words of the chorus into "Owl Be There."

On my way to check out their choreography, I passed Michael, still trying to escape from Cousin Bernie.

"But you can learn so much from knowing your ances-tors," Bernie was exclaiming.

"He's right," I said. "Like finding out that two of our Hollingworth ancestors had been hanged as horse thieves—so reassuring to know I could blame all my little peccadilloes on hereditary criminal tendencies. Which reminds me—Michael, Mother was looking for you."

"Right," Michael said, looking immensely grateful. "I'll go find her right away."

"The man doesn't even know his maternal grand-mother's maiden name," Bernie said, staring at Michael's departing back with horror.

"I'm sure he can look it up if he needs to," I said.

"He said perhaps he'd take an interest in ancestors when he had some prospect of becoming one himself," Bernie went on.

"Sounds sensible to me."

"For all you know, he could have hereditary lunacy in his family!" Bernie exclaimed.

"Probably does," I said. "He gets along so well with all of our clan."

"He could be anyone," I heard Bernie mutter, as I turned away.

By the time I reached the front yard, the SPOOR crew had wrapped up their final number and were receiving a well-deserved standing ovation. The mild-mannered barbershop quartet in pastel-striped jackets and jaunty straw hats waiting nearby for their turn on the stage looked quite morose. I understood how they felt. Dad and the Owlettes were a hard act to follow. In fact, most people were heading away from the stage and out into the shopping area.

The shopping area that wasn't even supposed to exist. Cousin Rosemary and the quilting aunt were back, along with most of the other volunteer vendors from yesterday afternoon, and a lot of new recruits. In fact, a secondary yard sale had grown up to take the place of the one the police hadn't finished with. It was still slightly smaller than the official yard sale, but that would probably change if the police didn't wrap up their forensics soon. The early birds had set up their tables along the front walk while the late arrivals had to content themselves with secondary aisles on either side.

About half of the vendors were people who already had tables inside the regular yard sale and most of the rest were people I'd turned down when it became obvious that our two-acre site was already overcrowded. Looking at the stuff people had brought out for the original yard sale, I'd have bet you couldn't possibly find a card table's worth of unwanted junk anywhere in Caerphilly, but obviously this crew was up to the challenge. As I stood and stared, openmouthed, three more cars drove up and disgorged people who promptly erected more card tables and covered them with clutter. Although, considering how brisk sales were at some of these tables, some people's notions of junk and clutter obviously differed greatly from mine.

Or perhaps the buyers were vehement environmentalists, determined to find some good use for everything their neighbors would otherwise throw away.

Along with the people cleaning out their attics, I noticed several women selling homemade jams, jellies, and assorted baked goods, and a man hawking miniature replicas of old-fashioned outhouses, complete with the traditional half moon cut in the door. If they were intended to serve some practical purpose, I couldn't figure it out, and they certainly weren't the kind of decorative knickknack I'd want to bring home, but people were buying them enthusiastically.

They were buying Cousin Ginnie's lingerie just as enthusiastically, from the number of those distinctive lavender and silver bags I kept spotting.

"This is better than the county fair!" I overheard one woman say to another.

"So does this go on every weekend?" the second woman asked.

I didn't stick around to hear the answer.

"Meg? Why so gloomy?" came Rob's voice from behind me.

"Oh, nothing much," I said, turning to find that, unlike most of the attendees, my brother had worn his costume again today. "Our yard's become a flea market, and the woman who fainted yesterday when we found Gordon's body in the trunk has recovered enough to badger me so she can auction it off on eBay, that's all."

"She'd make a bundle," Rob said. "You're not letting her have it, are you? You could sell it yourself."

"Rob!" I exclaimed. "Do you have any idea how tacky this is?" Perhaps being a successful entrepreneur was having a bad effect on Rob's character.

"Come to think of it, they probably wouldn't let you, anyway," Rob said. "They usually make you take down something if anyone gets offended by it."

"Bravo," I said.

"But I still don't see why you don't sell all this stuff on eBay," he said, waving his hand vaguely at the sale area. "Might be a lot less trouble."

"Not necessarily," I said.

"You wouldn't have to have this whole huge mob scene," he said.

I sighed, and tried to answer reasonably. And articulately. After all, perhaps there was some logical reason why he hadn't paid attention the first twenty times I'd explained this.

"No," I said. "I'd only have to photograph all the stuff, answer questions about it, pack it all up for shipment, and haul it down to the Post Office or UPS."

"Oh," Rob said. "Sounds like a lot of work."

"And, of course, some percentage of the packages would bounce back when people decided they didn't get what they thought they were buying. No thanks. At least here, everything is nonreturnable and people provide their own transportation."

"Okay, I suppose you're right," Rob said. "But you could make a lot more money."

"Money isn't everything," I said. "There's my sanity to think of."

"A bit late, if you ask me," Rob said, sniggering.

"Later," I said, with the dignity one develops after twenty-five years of ignoring a younger brother. Just then I saw a camera flash several times, and glanced up to see that one of the news photographers was taking pictures of

me and Rob against the background of Cousin Ginnie's
new booth. Rob sniggered and struck a more dramatic
pose. I winced. Did I really want the *Caerphilly Clarion*
to run a photo of me and Harpo Marx, apparently discussing the relative merits of a leopard-print nightie and a
red lace one?

And Cousin Ginnie's new booth—amazing. The police still had her original booth and its remaining contents
locked up with the rest of the yard sale and yet here she
was again, with a booth just as large and well-stocked as
the original. She was just handing over change to a customer, along with one of the lavender bags Michael had
mentioned, with little silver metallic hearts stamped all
over it. A rather large bag.

"Meg!" she called cheerfully. "Want to come and try a
few things on?"

"Um . . . maybe later," I said. "Nice bags."

"Aren't they? I did the hearts myself with a rubber
stamp. I think they add a nice touch."

"Very nice," I said. Also very distinctive. I had seen a
lot of them around the sale. Was it prudish or sensible of
me to think that if I bought something from her, the first
thing I'd do was hide the bag?

"You'd look great in this," Ginnie said, holding up a
piece of black lace that didn't look large enough to fit a Barbie doll. "It stretches," she added, seeing my expression.

"No thanks," I said.

"Don't wait until all the best stuff is gone!" she exclaimed, waving the wisp of lace at me. "Just the thing to
keep that young man of yours interested." I stifled the impulse to tell her we were doing just fine in that department.

"That reminds me," I said. "What's wrong with
Morris?"

"Morris? Nothing that I know of. Why?"

"He seems upset; that's all," I said.

"I admit, he hasn't been himself lately," she said, frowning slightly. "And I can't for the life of me figure out why."

"I think he's upset about your selling off your . . . clothes."

"You mean all these fripperies?" she said, waving at the rack to her right. "I told him I was going to."

"Yes, but I think he sees it as some kind of rejection."

"Rejection?"

"I was talking to him earlier," I said. "He was quite morose."

"Well, that explains a lot," she said. "I've been wondering what was eating him. A couple of months back I had to tell him to please slow down on the fripperies, just until I could clear out space for new stuff."

"You do have a lot of, um, fripperies," I said.

"Mercy! I've got at least this much more at home," she said, laughing. "After thirty years, I've got closets full of the stuff, and none of it something I can get a lot of day-to-day use out of."

"So you decided to get rid of some of it."

"I thought I'd start with the things I can't even get into anymore," she said. "After all, I'm not the woman I used to be. I'm more like two of her!"

She laughed again, and patted her rounded stomach in a matter-of-fact way I envied.

"I figure if I clear out the stuff I can't wear anymore, I can make room for the new stuff. After today, I should be set for another thirty years! Doesn't he see that?"

"Apparently not," I said. "He thinks it means that the passion has gone out of your marriage."

"Good heavens," she said, shaking her head. "What will I do with him? You can't imagine how hard it is to change his mind once he gets a notion about something."

"Actually, I bet I can," I said, glancing around her booth.

Luckily, a customer came up and gave me a chance to escape before I did something stupid, like offer to talk to Cousin Morris. After all, Michael had already offered to do that.

"Meg!"

I looked up to see Cousin Rosemary waving frantically at me. I had forgotten overnight what I was supposed to be calling her. I waved cheerfully, and pulled out my notebook-that-tells-me-when-to-breathe as I strolled over to her table.

"Meg!" she said. "I have some important information."

"What is it, Rose Noir?" I asked, after sneaking a peek at the notebook.

"It's about the murder!" she said.

Chapter 26

"About the murder," I repeated. "I see."

Since, as far as I remembered, Rose Noir hadn't been anywhere near the barn on Saturday, I had a hard time imagining that she could know anything useful. Had she overheard something? Perhaps two cops chatting about the case while waiting in line for Sno-Cones? Seemed unlikely. Still, you never knew.

"I should have warned everyone yesterday morning that something bad would happen," she said. "I heard an owl hoot Friday night."

"We have a whole nest of them in the barn," I said.

"An owl's hoot is always a dire omen."

"What happened to the sacred owl, beloved of Athena, protector of warriors?" I asked.

"And it all goes back to feng shui," she continued, ignoring what I thought was a very reasonable question. "I know in the long run your yard sale should have a very positive effect on the feng shui of your house. Though all those years of being packed with unwanted clutter probably left a lot of negative energy behind. I should probably do a house cleansing before you move in."

"Mmm," I said, noncommittally, while I tried to think of a tactful way of asking if a house cleansing merely involved waving around a lot of incense or if it included any actual scrubbing, and if the latter, whether she did windows.

"But, of course, in the short term having a yard sale, especially one so huge, means that you've gathered an immense amount of unwanted clutter here in one spot. Think of the incredible amount of negative energy that's created!"

"You think this had something to do with the murder?"

"Of course," she said. "You not only have acres of clutter, but you have all the greed and acquisitiveness that the yard sale has stirred up in the people who come here. It's absolutely toxic!"

"Sort of a psychic cesspool," I said, nodding. And rather like my notion of the evil Army of Clutter laying siege to the house. Of course, seeing eye to eye with Rose Noir on anything worried me. "I understand what you mean, but I'm not sure you could convince the police that it's a factor in the murder."

"Yes, but it is," she said. "I'm sure of it. I think you should think very seriously before agreeing to hold another yard sale."

"You know, you're right," I said. "I don't need to think about it at all. You've convinced me. No more yard sales for us!"

"Wonderful!" she exclaimed, clapping her hands.

"Now, if I could convince you to change your mind about selling me the lavender stuff."

Her face hardened, and I gave up. Probably not the time to approach her about interrogating Darlene, either.

Time to do something useful, anyway. Like finding some-one else to question.

The Hummel lady, for example. I was peering around, trying to spot her, when I ran into Dad.

"Looking for someone?" he asked. "An elusive sus-pect?"

"Just the Hummel lady," I said. "Have you seen her?

"Why?"

"I happened to overhear Chief Burke questioning her," I said. "She's the last person who admits to seeing Gor-don alive, and she claims that she saw Giles entering the barn as she left."

"Aha!" Dad said. "Then she's the prime suspect!"

"Not necessarily."

"The last person to see the deceased alive should always be the prime suspect!" Dad said. He read far too many mys-tery books, and was fond of making such pronouncements.

"I thought the prime suspect was always the person who found the body," I said.

"Well yes, them, too," Dad said. "Sometimes you have multiple prime suspects. And, of course, you can't over-look the deceased's spouse. You'd be amazed at how many people are killed by their spouses."

"I'm sure Mother appreciates your self-restraint," I said. "But for now, I just need the Hummel lady."

"Right," Dad said. "There she is."

He pointed, and I spotted the Hummel lady standing at one edge of the fenced-in area, studying the yard sale in-terior with a pair of opera glasses. She wore the same clothes she'd had on yesterday, including the strange hat with its bobbling flowers, so I deduced it was a costume of some sort.

Time to tackle the first prime suspect. I strolled over to the Hummel lady.

"Back again, I see," I said. "Looking for anything in particular?"

The Hummel lady fixed me with an evil look. Then her expression changed. I imagined that I could see the thoughts passing through her mind—the angry impulse to be rude to me replaced by the sudden, surprised realization that I might be useful, and a fleeting look of cunning before she arranged her face into a smile that I might have thought authentically sweet and friendly if I hadn't seen the whole sequence of expressions leading up to it.

"Oh, you know me," she said, as if we were old friends. "Just an old yard sale hound. I have to say, though, I do think it's much nicer when you don't have those nasty old professionals."

"Like Gordon, you mean?"

She blinked in surprise at the name, and then rearranged her expression into one of profound sadness.

"That poor man," she said, shaking her head. "Such a tragedy. But, yes, I do think that those antique dealers and pickers lower the whole tone of a yard sale, don't you think? Instead of a fun event it becomes something crass and commercial."

I stifled the smart aleck impulse to say that so far our yard sale hadn't proved nearly crass and commercial enough for me. For one thing, it wasn't true. I didn't care whether the sale was crass or classy; whether we made a huge profit or didn't even cover expenses, as long as we got rid of a few tons of stuff. And for another, I didn't think it would help me get her talking.

So I also refrained from saying that I thought the genuinely professional dealers and pickers improved the tone. With a few exceptions, like Gordon, they were a lot less trouble than the amateur bargain hunters. They showed up on time rather than early and went through the sale quickly and efficiently, gathering up large quantities of merchandise without trying to nickel-and-dime the sellers to death. I'd have been happy to have nothing but dealers and pickers if not for the large amount of junk we wanted to sell that no self-respecting picker would touch.

To her, of course, they were competitors who might snatch up some rare bit of Hummel before she could.

"Sorry you feel that way," I said. "Do you think that's why Gordon was killed—that someone resented him lowering the whole tone of the yard sale?"

"I'm sure I don't know," she said.

She paused, briefly, and then asked in an overly casual tone:

"What's going to happen to the stuff he was buying? Or had he already bought it when he was killed?"

"He collected a great heap of stuff, but he hadn't paid me a dime," I said. "So as far as I know, as soon as the police release it, we'll have to find someone else to buy it all."

"I see," she said. "If someone were interested in something that he might have gathered—"

"I'm afraid the trunk's already spoken for," I said. "A pity—the buyer will probably get a ton of money for it on eBay, but my conscience wouldn't let me keep it."

I deduced from her expression that she found the juxtaposition of "money" and "conscience" odd, if not downright unnatural.

"I see," she said. "If you happen to come across any little bits of china . . ."

"You can have any Hummel we have at a dollar the lot on one condition," I said.

"Yes?" she said, leaning forward eagerly.

"I want to know the truth about what went on when you were in the barn," I said. "Not the pack of lies you told Chief Burke."

"I beg your pardon," she said, drawing herself up with

apparent indignation. "Are you suggesting that I . . . would *lie*?"

"I happen to know more than Chief Burke about what went on in the barn yesterday," I said. Which wasn't exactly a lie. I was sure Chief Burke knew nothing about the fledgling owls, for example.

"Were you spying on me?" she asked.

"What makes you think that?" I asked, trying to strike the right note of nonchalance to convince her that the answer was yes. And then something struck me—she'd said "spying on me" not "spying on us." I decided to take a chance.

"Why did you make up a whole conversation with him when you never even saw Gordon?" I asked.

Her shoulders fell.

"If I'd known someone was watching, I'd have admitted that I never found him," she said. "I was afraid someone would think I'd killed him. I didn't know I had a witness who could clear me. You could have said something."

"I've told the chief everything I saw," I said. "Just what did you think you were going to accomplish, anyway?"

"I was searching. For any little bits of . . . Hummel," she said, forcing the last word out as if she were convinced that saying it aloud would jinx her quest.

"And you looked everywhere," I said.

"Except in the locked trunk, of course," she said. "I thought that must be where he'd put them. I even tried to force the lock open, but I couldn't. And then I heard someone coming in, and I thought I should leave."

I pondered. Okay, I wasn't surprised that she hadn't seen Gordon—I knew he had to be already dead and locked in the trunk when Giles entered the barn for the second time. But I was surprised that she'd admitted it so readily.

Unless she found admitting a lie easier than confessing

to murder. For all I knew, she'd killed Gordon before searching the barn, and was barely restraining her panic until she could find out exactly how much I'd seen.

She didn't look as if she was barely restraining panic. An urge to climb the deer-proof fence and scour the yard sale for Hummel, perhaps, but not panic.

"So if you didn't do him in and stuff him in the trunk, who did?" I asked.

"I have no idea!"

"Did you see anyone else in the barn?"

"Well—not *in* the barn."

"Then where?"

"I did see someone leaving just before I went in. But I have no idea who."

"Can you describe the person?" I asked, trying to keep my tone patient.

"No, not at all."

"Was it a man or a woman?"

"All I saw was this huge Mexican hat."

"Aha!" I said. "Professor Schmidt with the sombrero in the barn!"

"I beg your pardon?"

"Never mind," I said. "Thanks."

"So?" she said. "What about my reward?"

"Reward?"

"My Hummel!"

"The yard sale's still a crime scene," I said, slowly and carefully. "But as soon as they release it, you can have every bit of Hummel on the place."

"For a dollar?"

"For a dollar," I said. "In fact—what the hell—gratis. On me."

"Excellent," she said, positively beaming at me. I couldn't think of anything else to ask her, so I didn't object when she strolled off to study the stuff inside the fence from another angle.

I felt better already. As long as I could get her to repeat her story for the chief, it would create reasonable doubt of Giles's guilt. Gordon was already dead and locked in the trunk when Giles came in. Of course, finding the real murderer would be more satisfactory than creating reasonable doubt, but still, I'd already made progress.

Of course, now I had to scour the yard sale for Hummel. And it wouldn't be pretty if it turned out we had no Hummel at all. Perhaps I should scrounge up a Hummel or two to placate her, if it turned out no one at the yard sale was selling any. Make sure I had something to hold out as a reward for good behavior. Or would that look like a bribe?

I'd worry about it later.

I pulled out my cell phone and was about to dial Chief Burke when it occurred to me that so far I only had the Hummel lady's word. And she'd already lied once. Should I tell the chief now, or look for some corroboration first?

I shoved my cell phone back in my pocket.

First I had to find Professor Schmidt.

Chapter 27

I prowled through the crowd looking for Arnold Schmidt. It wasn't easy finding anyone, since both the crowd and the number and variety of vendors catering to them had grown exponentially. I saw people hawking vacuum cleaners, scarves, purses, home-grown vegetables, patented tear-free onion slicing machines, essential oils and incense, souvenir Caerphilly t-shirts and key chains, and bad imitation Rolexes. Someone was even trying to sell a litter of baby ferrets, which I hoped Dad, Michael, and Eric didn't see.

My relatives were still selling hot dogs, hamburgers, corn on the cob, and potato salad as fast as they could dish them out, but now the discriminating outdoor diner could also find homemade fried chicken, barbecued ribs, kebabs, tacos, gyros, sushi, crab cakes, and at least a dozen different varieties of sandwich, along with popcorn, ice cream, and Sno-Cones for dessert. No more funnel cake, alas, thanks to our volunteer tree surgeons.

I even spotted Cousin Sidney cruising up and down the road in his tow truck, dragging a float on which one of the dark horse candidates in the upcoming Caerphilly mayor's election was perched, wearing an Uncle Sam costume and haranguing the crowd through a megaphone. None of which exactly enhanced Sidney's effectiveness as a deterrent to the parking scofflaws, though it did add to the day's festiveness.

At one point, I heard several loud reports—they couldn't be gunshots, could they? Not loud enough, I thought, as I ran toward them. No, not gunshots. A cousin dressed as a bunch of grapes, with about a hundred purple balloons fastened to his clothes, had given too enthusiastic a hug to another cousin in a porcupine costume.

Sammy, the young police officer, who stood nearby guarding the gate to the original yard sale, hadn't been fooled. Or maybe, unlike me, Sammy had more sense than to run toward something that sounded like gunshots.

As I passed by his post, I saw Sammy sniffing the air and frowning.

"What's wrong?" I asked.

"Do you smell anything?" he asked.

I sniffed.

"Mainly charcoal-grilled hamburger," I said. "I could fetch you one if you're hungry."

"No, something . . . funny."

I sniffed again. This time, I caught a whiff of what I suspected was bothering Sammy.

"Oh, that," I said. "Nothing to worry about. Rose Noir is doing her household cleansing ceremony."

Sammy looked puzzled.

"Smudging the area to clear away the bad energy," I clarified, and looked around to see if I could spot the source of the odor. "Ah, there."

I pointed to the edge of the yard. Apparently Rose Noir had decided to make a wide circle, taking in the house, the yard sale, and all the assorted outbuildings. She was marching at a stately pace, waving her smudging stick to create elegant arcs and crescents of smoke. Her mouth was moving, so I gathered she was either singing or chanting, but I couldn't tell at this distance.

"What's that she's burning?" Sammy asked.

"Probably sage, cedar, sweetgrass—various herbs," I said. "Legal herbs," I added, remembering the time Mother had invited Rose Noir over to smudge the family house after the visit of a particularly unpleasant cousin. Rob had mistaken the odor of the smudging herbs for marijuana. I still wasn't quite sure if he'd been relieved or disappointed when he found out that his parents hadn't become potheads. I suspected Sammy had made the same mistake. He was still frowning suspiciously at Rose Noir.

Well, if he tried to report her, odds were the chief would set him straight, and if not, an unsuccessful drug raid probably wouldn't daunt this crowd. And maybe it was just my imagination, but the aroma of the smudging herbs seemed to lift my spirits. I strolled on, invigorated.

But I had no luck spotting Professor Schmidt. Apparently, apart from his lust for the phantom Pruitt papers, he was immune to the call of the yard sale. I revised my opinion of him sharply upward, even as I fretted over how much trouble I'd have finding him.

I did run into Dad, who gazed at me reproachfully.

"Your cousin Rosemary says she's disappointed in you, trying to sneak behind her back and use a scent that clashes with your personality," he said. His tone of voice made it sound as if he shared her disappointment.

"You didn't have to tell her it was for me," I said. "In fact, didn't I warn you not on any account to let her find out?"

"I didn't tell her, but she suspected you were trying to pull a fast one."

"Good grief, Dad," I said. "It's not as if I was disobeying doctor's orders, or faking a prescription. It's only her opinion."

"She feels very strongly about it, though," he said. "I don't think you can change her mind."

"Of course not," I said. "Sometimes I think this family has cornered the market on pigheadedness, and she certainly has her full share."

"Hmmm," Dad said. I suspected he was thinking that Rosemary wasn't the only one with a good share of the family pigheadedness.

"I'll just tell her that the cosmetic and soap shop in the mall carries plenty of lavender- and rose-scented stuff," I said. "And they don't have any qualms about selling it to me."

"But Rosemary is so proud of her bath oils, and she uses only the best-quality, all-natural materials!" he exclaimed. "Here. She gave me this. She says it's you."

He handed me a small brown bottle. I opened it and took a whiff. Mistake; the intense smell of eucalyptus and menthol made my eyes water so badly that I had to fumble blindly to replace the cap, but even so they couldn't disguise the strong undertone of heavy musk.

"Yuck," I said. "What does she think I am? A civet with a bad head cold?"

But Dad had disappeared. I made sure the bottle was screwed tightly shut and stuck it in my pocket. I'd deal with Rose Noir later.

Some of my younger cousins, while taking rides over the crowd in the boom lift, were amusing themselves by pouring their lemonades into their popcorn buckets, and then dumping the resulting soggy mess down on the crowd while making barfing noises. I told them to cut it out, and when they didn't listen to me, I had Rob deposit them at the feet of an irritated state police officer who still had patches of soggy popcorn clinging to his uniform and perched on the wide brim of his Smokey the Bear hat.

And I still hadn't found Schmidt.

"Bother," I said.

"What's wrong, dear?" Mother asked.

"As far as I can tell, everyone in Caerphilly is out here, except for the one person I need to talk to," I said. "I'll have to go into town to look for him."

"I don't suppose there's anything I could do to help, dear," Mother said.

"Actually, there is," I said. "Find me some Hummel."

"Hummel?"

"You know, those little china figurines? Little girls with rosy cheeks, little boys in lederhosen, puppies, lambs, kittens—"

"Yes, dear, I know what Hummel is," Mother said, with a touch of asperity. "I just didn't know you liked it. And it doesn't really go with that Shaker/Japanese décor your house has been requesting, does it, dear?"

"I don't like it," I said, hastily. "Loathe the stuff, and so does the house. Couldn't pay either of us to keep it around. But, at the moment, I need some. To bribe an informant."

"Ah," she said, nodding. "An informant with a certain amount of taste."

"Well, not my taste, but to each his own," I said. "So do you think you could get hold of some Hummel?"

"Ye-es," Mother said, nodding slowly. "I remember several shops in town that might have quite a lot of it."

"I don't need quite a lot of it," I said. "Just a couple of pieces. Maybe three, if you get a real bargain on them. Preferably not brand new. They don't have to be in perfect condition, either, as long as they're Hummel."

"Leave it to me, dear," Mother said, and turned to leave. Then she paused and remained staring thoughtfully at something.

At Rose Noir's booth. I winced. The booth décor suited Rosemary's business splendidly. Lots of ethereal flowers and little lace frou-frous, and great swaths of pink and lavender tulle hanging overhead. A nice environment for buying prettily scented cosmetics, but I couldn't see anyone living in it day in, day out, and I had the sinking feeling Mother could.

"Rosemary's new name," she said finally—and cryptically.

"What about it?"

"Shouldn't noir be noir?"

"Is that an existential question?" I said. "If so, ask me later. I'm in a very mundane, literal mode today."

"Sorry, what I meant was, shouldn't the word 'noir' have an 'e' on the end?" she said. " 'Noire,' with an 'e.' Because, grammatically speaking, 'rose' is feminine in French."

"You expect correct French grammar from someone who renames herself more often than she cuts her hair?" I asked.

"True," she said. "But someone should enlighten her."

"Don't look at me," I said. "I can't even get her to sell me the cosmetics I want. She doesn't think I'm a rose or lavender sort of person."

Mother studied me thoughtfully.

"No, dear," she said. "But you try."

I didn't even want to figure that one out.

"I'm going to town," she announced, as she strode away.

"So am I," I said. "Want a ride?"

"No, dear," she called back over her shoulder. "I think I'm better on my own. Or perhaps Michael can take me; he's not as busy as you are."

And also not as immune to your charm, I thought with a sigh, but I let her go. I strolled over to Rose Noir's booth to see if I could enlist her to help poor Horace.

"I have a favor to ask you," I said. "It's about Darlene."

"She went home," Rose Noir said, shaking her head. "She's still upset about the owl in her bedroom last night. I don't want to sound judgmental, but . . ."

Her voice trailed off as she shook her head, apparently despairing of saying anything non-judgmental about Darlene.

"But she's an idiot and Horace is better off without her," I said.

"Poor Horace," Rose Noir said, from which I deduced that she didn't exactly disagree.

"Poor Horace, indeed," I said. "A pity Darlene left. I was hoping you could ask her who she sold his gorilla suit to—after last night, I doubt if she'd tell me."

"Oh, I don't need to ask her," Rose Noir said, her face growing cheerful again. "I bought it."

"You? Why?"

"To give it back to Horace," she said. "I think it's terrible, trying to make someone give up a profound and meaningful part of his inner self."

I nodded. I wasn't sure how wearing a few yards of faded fake fur could be a profound and meaningful part of Horace's inner self, but I could remember when several of my prissier aunts had tried to convince me that the black-smithing I loved wasn't a respectable career for a woman.

"Do you want to give it back to him?" Rose Noir asked, reaching under her table and pulling out a large shopping bag.

"I wouldn't want to deprive you of the pleasure," I said.

I would defend Horace's right to his inner simian self to the death if need be, but I'd rather not have the aunts who sided with Darlene think I was the one responsible for returning his suit.

I went off to find my car and continue the search for Professor Schmidt.

Chapter 28

I had to wait while Cousin Sidney towed the three SUVs and one pickup truck that blocked the entrance to our driveway and put down some orange cones to save my space.

With any luck, Professor Schmidt would be in his office, and if he wasn't, I could cruise by Michael's office, borrow his copy of the departmental faculty directory, and get Schmidt's home address and phone number.

Caerphilly was quiet. Unusually quiet, even for a Sunday. Almost unnaturally quiet—probably because nearly everyone in town was out at our yard sale-turned-carnival. Normally I had to cruise for fifteen minutes to find a parking space within ten blocks of Dunsany Hall, where the English department had its offices, but today I had my choice of a dozen spaces by the front door.

I walked through the silent halls, sticking out my tongue and making faces at the closed doors of the Great Stone Faces, as Michael and I called the department chairman and all his stuffy cronies—all the diehards put-

ting such intense pressure on Michael's tenure committee
to turn him out in the cold.

Not a very mature thing to do, of course, but it helped
me stay polite when I had to encounter them in person.
And probably a lot safer to do today than during the
week. The assistant dean had once dashed into the hall
when I was sticking out my tongue at his door, and as part
of my effort to convince him that I was doing wrinkle-
preventing yoga facial exercises, I'd ended up standing on
my head in the faculty lounge for nearly half an hour. One
of those days when I went home wondering if perhaps the
best thing I could do for Michael's career was not to over-
come my commitment phobia and make an honest man
of him but to disappear completely from his life.

Though even my absence probably wouldn't help him
snag an office here in the oldest, most prestigious part of
the building. Professor Schmidt, of course, had a prime
space, only three doors down from the beastly department
chairman.

"Professor Schmidt!" I called, and knocked loudly before turning the knob. Which didn't budge. I frowned at
the door for a few seconds, and then, as I turned to leave,
my eye fell on a framed enlargement of a photo of Mrs.
Pruitt that hung beside his door, as if to remind passersby
of the importance of the poet on whom he was the
world's foremost expert.

Fashions in photography had certainly changed over
the years. The picture was a full-length portrait of Mrs.
Pruitt sitting in a chair, with an elaborately swagged drap-
ery and a potted palm behind her. Although sitting wasn't
quite the word—she was perched rather precariously, as
if she had only briefly alighted for the photographer's
benefit, and would be off on another flight of poetic fancy
in a few seconds. I kept expecting the chair to fall or
break. And she should have just looked at the camera,

smiled or frowned, and have done with it. Let the viewer see what she looked like without hamming it up. Instead, she was holding a slim book in one hand while she gazed soulfully at the ceiling, her other hand raised to place a single finger to her lips in a gesture clearly designed to suggest deep thought while slightly obscuring several of her chins.

Perhaps in its time it was considered a splendid likeness, and inspired droves of people to buy her books, but now it just looked silly. I could see why Professor Schmidt had to keep busy erasing the mustaches and sarcastic comments that each succeeding class of English students felt inspired to draw on the glass covering the photo. I hadn't bothered to study it before, and wouldn't today if not for the possibility that there might be some tenuous connection between Mrs. Pruitt and Gordon's murder.

But whatever the connection was, I wouldn't learn it from Ginevra's primly pursed lips, so I shrugged and moved on to the less exalted wing of the building where Michael had his office.

Also locked, though this was uncharacteristic. Of course, he'd probably started locking it since he'd begun keeping an ever-increasing amount of stuff in it, stuff that we'd moved out of our old basement apartment but couldn't yet take to the house.

Help was at hand, though. I glanced down the hall and saw that Giles's door was open. With any luck, he'd have a copy of the faculty directory.

When I reached his doorway, I saw Giles hard at work on a large stack of official Caerphilly College forms. I recognized the distinctive pale blue paper the administration liked to use—Michael swore it was so passing bureaucrats could tell at a glance if a faculty member was allowing the forms to pile up on his desk.

"Giles, Giles," I said. "You're hopeless."

He started at my voice, and then looked slightly relieved to see it was only me.

"Hopeless?" he repeated.

"Here we go to all the trouble of implicating you in the most shocking crime Caerphilly has seen in generations, all for the sake of enhancing your public image as an edgy, hip kind of guy," I said. "And you go and ruin it all by spending your Sunday chained to a desk doing paperwork?"

"Oh, is that what all this is in aid of?" Giles said, with an expression that I'm sure he intended as a smile, though it came off as more of a grimace. "If it's all the same, I'd just as soon return to my old image as a boring fuddy-duddy."

"I'll see what I can do," I said. "Speaking of which, may I borrow your faculty directory? I need to track down a suspect."

"By all means," Giles said, astonishing me by pulling the directory out of a pile of stuff without much hunting. "Looking for anyone in particular?"

I was opening my mouth to explain when the phone rang.

"Sorry," he said, gesturing to the phone. "It's the department chairman. I really ought to . . ."

"Want me to leave?" I asked, reaching for my purse.

"No, no," he said, with his hand over the mouthpiece. "Please don't; I want to ask you something, and he's probably just calling about tomorrow's faculty meeting. Dr. Snyder," he said, into the phone. "How are you?"

Unfortunately, Giles was wrong. For the next fifteen minutes, I heard his side of what was obviously a chewing-out by his department head. Not fair, really; it wasn't Giles's fault that the police unjustly suspected him of murder. Still, I felt bad, being present to witness his embarrassment. I made a motion to leave at first, but Giles waved me back into my seat. I pretended to be absorbed in the faculty directory for ten times as long as it took me to find and copy down Professor Schmidt's address, and when I grew tired of rereading the names of the stuffed shirts who had it in for Michael, I turned to the nearest bookshelf and feigned an intense interest in its contents.

Though once I made the effort to focus on the titles of the books, I found they were rather interesting. I deduced from the few authors' names I recognized—E.C. Bentley, Dashiell Hammett, Raymond Chandler, and S.S. Van Dyne—that I was seated next to Giles's collection of Golden Age mystery writers. I scanned the shelves for R. Austin Freeman and found him right at my elbow.

I'd seen these books before, of course, at least a dozen times when I'd visited Giles's office. But without the added interest of being associated with a murder, they hadn't particularly attracted my attention. Like most of the books in that section of the shelves, they were rather nondescript. So many faded linen bindings in muted shades of blue, brown, green, and red, with the occasional battered dust jacket, and now and then an empty space where a book was in use. The gentle patina of dust over everything further softened the colors. The whole effect was oddly soothing, rather like the bookshelves of some of my elderly relatives—except that many of Giles's books were neatly wrapped in plastic Brodart covers to protect them, while my relatives' vintage libraries were allowed to fade *au naturel*. I counted forty-eight volumes by Freeman, though some of them seemed to be different editions of the same title. The English and American editions, I suspected. I'd have opened a few to check, but I wasn't sure how Giles felt about people handling his treasures. Maybe I was overreacting to the protective plastic covers, but they did seem calculated to repel casual inspection.

I found myself wondering if he read them or just collected them, and also how much he treasured them for their own sake and how much for what he thought they said about him—that despite his rather mild and pedantic manner, he wasn't a stuffy old dinosaur like so many of the department's faculty. That he was, in fact, hip and cool, though in a low-key, bookish manner.

It worked for me. I liked Giles's office almost as much as his study. Apart from the familiar, comforting presence of the books, I liked the bits of academic clutter he had scattered about. Here a Civil War vintage sword—the English Civil War, of course—there a Tudor coin, or a battered piece of pottery that Julius Caesar might have held. Whenever I grew impatient with Giles, I reminded myself that underneath the slightly stiff exterior was the man with the wit and erudition to create this office.

Perhaps I appreciated his office all the more today because usually an even layer of dust covered everything, and today, the dust had clearly been heaved around by the police search. I saw clear spots and spots where the dust had been piled up like a snowdrift by moving objects around. Nearly every knickknack stood near but not precisely on the clear spot where it had been resting for months or years before the police arrived. Strangely enough, this added to the room's charm.

Okay, it was clutter, but there's clutter and clutter. Not all clutter was created equal. Even with the signs of the police search, I liked Giles's clutter. Classy, academic clutter. No more useful than any other clutter, perhaps, but I still had a hard time condemning it.

When I had the time—after the yard sale was over and Giles cleared of murder charges—I'd have to do some long hard thinking about my definition of clutter. And probably talk the subject over with Michael. I didn't want the house to be a place to keep our stuff while we went out to get more stuff, or however George Carlin had defined it. And I needed to make sure Michael felt the same way. If he didn't—

"Sorry about that," Giles said, when he was finally able to hang up. "Apparently I'm not Dean Snyder's favorite underling today."

"Here's hoping we can change that, and quickly," I said. "Have you seen Professor Schmidt today?"

"Arnold Schmidt? Not that I recall," Giles said. "Dare I hope that you're about to pin the guilt on him instead of me?"

"It's a possibility," I said. "Remember the woman in the flowered hat who identified you to Chief Burke as the person who was entering the barn as she left?"

"The dame who fingered me?" he said, in a bad imitation of an American gangster's accent. "You bet I remember her."

"She lied," I said. "Not about seeing you, but about talking to Gordon. I suspect he was already dead and locked in the trunk when she went into the barn."

"Good show!" Giles exclaimed. "If you can prove that, perhaps Chief Burke will start looking for the real killer!"

"I'll try," I said. "And since Arnold Schmidt was just leaving when she walked in—"

"Oh, please let it be him," Giles said. "He's the most insufferable snob in the department."

"I'll keep you posted," I said.

"Please do," Giles said. He returned to his paperwork, looking almost cheerful.

I felt a momentary twinge of irritation. Was Giles doing anything to help himself, or just sitting back and waiting for me to clear him? He could at least have offered to help me find Schmidt. The way Michael would, if he weren't back at the yard sale, trying to keep it under control while simultaneously humoring Mother.

Then I realized I was being too hard on Giles. Not fair to expect a mild-mannered, reclusive English professor to turn into Sam Spade in a pinch, even if he was a vintage mystery fan. And definitely not fair to compare him with Michael. Giles needed rescuing. And the next step was to tackle Schmidt.

Of course, first I had to find Schmidt.

Chapter 29

I headed toward Westlake, where Professor Schmidt lived. Like much of Caerphilly, it had been built in quaint, mock-Tudor style, but in Westlake the houses were closer to manors than cottages, and the lawns were so impeccable that I suspected the owners made their gardeners manicure the grass blades with nail scissors. A very posh neighborhood filled with astronomical mortgages and the department heads and professors emeriti who could afford them. Even full professors probably steered clear of Westlake unless they were independently wealthy or had a spouse with a well-paying job. Michael and I hadn't done much house hunting there, partly because we could never have afforded it, and partly because the houses there hardly ever went on the market anyway.

My route led through a part of Caerphilly I'd seen far too often since Mother's arrival a week ago, since it contained most of the town's antique stores. Including Gordon McCoy's Antique and Junque Emporium, though that was on the very fringes of the district, merging into a neighborhood of stores where normal people shopped

and restaurants that served iceberg lettuce instead of its
snooty Italian cousins. Out of curiosity, I took the street
that went past Gordon's shop.

How strange. Three of Caerphilly's small supply of
police vehicles were parked outside the Antique and
Junque Emporium, along with the chief's blue Chrysler.
Had the epicenter of the murder investigation moved
from our house to Caerphilly, unnoticed by the crowds
hovering around the yard sale? And for that matter, unnoticed by the various print and broadcast journalists?

I cruised past the shop at about ten miles per hour, but
I didn't see anyone, so I circled the block and came round
again. Still nothing to see, so this time, as soon as I
turned, I parked the car on the empty side street. If it
hadn't been for the police cars, I might have thought I was
in one of those science fiction flicks where the heroine
wakes up to find that everyone else has left the planet.

I strolled up to the front of the store, nonchalantly, and
peered in the open door.

Gordon's front room was just as I remembered it, a
cluttered warren without any apparent theme or organiza-
tion. Priceless antiques stood next to items I'd have assumed were tacky pieces of junk except that their
presence in Gordon's stock meant they were actually
valuable collectibles. Chinese brush paintings hung beside painted velvet renditions of bullfighters and paint-
by-number oils of puppies and kittens. Rare art pottery
and Ming vases shared shelf space with vintage Coke
bottles. Enameled samovars and hookahs shouldered a
humongous scale model of the Starship Enterprise, and
tiny bronze Degas ballet dancers loitered in corners with
the sort of elaborate, special edition Barbie dolls that
would probably run away screaming if a small child ever
tried to pick them up.

There were at least a dozen more rooms much like this one, though the most obscenely expensive stuff lived in the front room, where Gordon could show it off. And where it might catch the eye of a passing collector.

Come to think of it, that was the theme—stuff Gordon could sell for obscenely high prices.

Though one room always felt different—the one where Gordon kept the used and rare books. I remembered it as way in the back, so I had to go through five or six other rooms to reach it, but perhaps deep in the heart of the shop would be a more accurate description. Was it only my bias that made this room feel like a serene oasis in a chaotic jumble? Or did it reflect how Gordon felt about the books? Endicott, his former partner, did say books were Gordon's first love.

I could relate to that. I'd noticed in the last several weeks that books were among the few material objects I didn't feel ambivalent about. In fact—

Stop it, I told myself. I was on the verge of feeling sorry for Gordon, and apart from being a strange and disturbing feeling it wouldn't help me find his murderer. And I didn't have time to worry about it now. Chief Burke was standing inside the shop, and I'd lingered long enough at the door that he'd turned and spotted me. Too late to slip away quietly, so I waved and smiled at him.

"What's up?" I asked.

"Give me strength," Chief Burke said, rolling his eyes upward. Then he lowered them, fixed them on me, and frowned. "Just what are you doing here?"

"Rubbernecking," I said. "Morbid curiosity."

"Not trying to solve the murder case yourself?"

"I have every confidence that by the time you finish your investigation, you'll be convinced that Giles had nothing to do with Gordon's death," I said. "Of course, if

I come across any information that will help speed up the process . . ."

"You'll pass it along, instead of going off half-cocked and getting yourself in a world of trouble," Burke said. "Naturally."

He didn't sound as if he believed it.

"Naturally," I said. "So what's going on?"

"Someone broke into Mr. McCoy's antique store," Burke said. "I don't suppose you remember what you were doing last night around midnight?"

"Michael and I were over at Giles Rathbone's house, having sherry and discussing his case," I said.

"Having sherry with your boyfriend and my prime suspect," Burke said, nodding. "Figures."

"Why would you suspect me of breaking into Gordon's store?" I asked.

"Looks like your style," he said. "There wasn't anything missing or damaged, and he had plenty of things a real burglar would have taken—a fair amount of cash, not to mention some nice jewelry and silver. But whoever broke in last night just disarranged some of the papers in his office. I figure it was someone snooping around for information."

"And you assume that someone was me?"

"If you didn't do it, I apologize, and point out that it wouldn't exactly be out of character, and if you did, I do hope you were careful and wore gloves."

"I always do when I'm burgling," I said. "Incidentally, that was a joke."

"Hmmm," the chief said, studying me.

"What was the burglar looking for?" I asked.

"If I knew that, I'd know who did it, wouldn't I?" the chief said. "They were messing around in his business records."

"Maybe it was someone who felt cheated by Gordon,"

I suggested. "And wanted proof so they could file a claim against the estate."

"Like as not," the chief said, nodding. "Of course, that doesn't narrow down my field of suspects. I have yet to find anyone who didn't feel cheated by Gordon."

"Well, I didn't, but that's mostly because I never did any business with him," I said.

"Why not?" the chief asked. "Did you have something against him?"

"Not particularly," I said. "We had him in to look over Mrs. Sprocket's antiques before the yard sale, but since he'd usually offer about half of what the other dealers would pay, we never sold him anything. And you've seen the yard sale—you can imagine about how much we need to buy junk. Or antiques."

"So you'd have no reason to want him dead," the chief said.

"Apart from a few stray homicidal urges when he knocked on our door before dawn, no," I said. "Out of my life, yes; but I wouldn't have needed to kill him to achieve that, because I knew once we were through with the yard sale, he would be. Out of my life, that is."

"I see," the chief said.

"Does this mean that you're seriously considering the possibility that Giles didn't do it?"

"I'd be a fool not to look at a suspect who just waltzes right into my investigation," the chief said.

I decided to assume this was a subtle hint that I'd overstayed my welcome, so I wished him luck and left.

I glanced up and down the street when I stepped out of Gordon's shop, and could have sworn I spotted someone peering around the corner of the building at the end of the block and then ducking back when he saw me.

I sauntered to the other end of the block, turned the corner, and then ran as fast as I could. Luckily I didn't have to go all around the block. An alley halfway down the cross street ran through the block, giving access to the back doors of the shops on either side. I raced through the alley to the next cross street and then carefully stuck my head out.

The someone was peering around the corner again. He ducked back, and I recognized him.

Professor Schmidt.

Chapter 30

I waited until Schmidt peered around the corner again and was absorbed in whatever he saw. Then I crept up behind him.

"Looking for something?" I asked.

He jumped a foot in the air and uttered a rather undignified squeak. When he saw who it was, he tried to return to his usual pompous manner, but I decided I liked him better off balance.

"So, first you lie to Chief Burke, and now you're spying on him," I said. "Want to tell me why?"

"I beg your pardon," he said, but I could see he was nervous.

"Why don't you just tell Chief Burke what really happened in the barn?" I asked.

"What do you mean, what really happened?" he said. "I went there because Gordon offered to sell me some papers. He didn't have the papers with him, so I advised him to stop wasting my time and went away again. That's all that happened."

"Oh, sure," I said. And a sudden thought hit me—

Schmidt wasn't just eager to buy the papers from Gordon—he was nearly frantic. What kind of papers would make anyone that upset?

"And you didn't burgle Gordon's shop last night?" I asked. "I suppose that was one of his other blackmail victims."

It was a gamble, but it worked.

"Blackmail," he exclaimed. "What are you talking about?" But from the way he flinched and the fearful look on his face, I knew I'd guessed right.

"Oh, come on, professor," I said. "I know he was blackmailing you. I heard that much. But I don't understand what he had on you."

For that matter, I was having a hard time imagining Schmidt doing anything worth blackmailing about. Perhaps in his long-distant youth, before he'd become such a pompous jackass.

"Mrs. Pruitt," he said, finally.

I pondered that for a few moments. Were we talking about the same Mrs. Pruitt? The long-dead poetess? I'd seen the portrait, and all the photographer's art couldn't make her look like anything but what she was: a stout, hatchet-faced woman in her fifties. She'd been closer to ninety when she died, and that was still several decades before Professor Schmidt was born.

"Well, obviously it was about Mrs. Pruitt," I said. "But I'm not sure I understand the details."

He sighed, loudly, and stared at the ground for a while.

"And if I can't understand it," I went on. "Well, maybe the police won't, either, but I'll just have to take that chance, and tell them everything I do know."

That finally worked.

"As I'm sure you know," he said, "I've made Mrs. Pruitt my life's work."

I nodded encouragingly.

"Not just analyzing her work, but defending it."

"Defending it against whom?" I said.

"Her work has sadly fallen out of fashion," he said, indignantly. "It's become quite trendy to belittle her work. Not just its quality, but its originality."

"They find her work derivative?" I asked.

"Derivative would be a kinder way of putting it," he said. "There have been a number of articles written over the years that claim she was a plagiarist—that she took the works of more commercially successful poets and . . . well, changed enough of the words to make it look like a different poem, and passed it off for original work."

"And did she?"

"I've always contended that she was merely strongly influenced by her favorite poets," he said. "And that her profound reverence for them manifested itself in an unconscious imitation of their forms and meters."

I took that for a reluctant yes.

"But Gordon had something that proved otherwise, right?" I asked.

"He'd gotten hold of a box of books from her library," Schmidt said. "Books of poetry by Longfellow, Tennyson—people like that. A lot of the poems were all marked up in her handwriting, showing how she'd taken their poems and produced her versions. Changing a couple of words in each line, until it looked different enough to pass off as her own."

"Hard to defend that as unconscious imitation," I said.

He nodded slightly.

"Not exactly good for your career," I suggested.

He shook his head.

A wild suspicion hit me, and I decided to run with it.

"Especially if it came out where Gordon got them," I said. "However did you let them fall into his hands?"

He winced.

"It was my wife, and her damned decluttering," he said. "The damned box had been gathering dust in our attic for twenty years. And then, while I was off in England at a conference, she went to this damned class on getting rid of clutter."

"Really? Where?" I asked. Sounded useful, that class. Maybe I could go, and take my whole family.

"I don't know," Schmidt said, frowning. "One of those places that gives stupid classes for housewives with too much time on their hands."

"I see," I said, and hoped it didn't come out sounding too much like a snarl. I found myself hoping, for Mrs. Schmidt's sake, that he turned out to be the murderer and got a good, long prison sentence.

"Anyway, one of the stupid decluttering rules they gave her was if you hadn't opened a box for more than a year, you should get rid of it without opening it. The stupid cow called Gordon and had him clean out the whole attic."

"So Gordon not only had the goods on Mrs. Pruitt, he knew you'd found out about her plagiarism and covered it up," I said.

He nodded.

"Sounds like motive for murder to me," I said.

"Not really," he said. "I may have my shortcomings as a scholar, but I have a very well-honed sense of self-preservation. Why would I kill Gordon without getting back the evidence? Who knows who'll get hold of those books now that he's dead? But whoever it is, I very much doubt it will be anyone as greedy, grasping, and dishonest as Gordon."

"So I take it you don't have them?"

"Would I still be trying to find them if I did?"

Maybe, I thought, if you wanted to look less like a murder suspect.

"So someone else has them," I said aloud. "Or will get

them, whenever they turn up. And you're afraid that someone will make them public, and you're trying to get them first."

He nodded.

"So if you didn't kill him and you didn't get your books back, just what did happen between you and Gordon yesterday?" I asked.

"Nothing," he said.

"Try again."

He pursed his lips as if afraid something incriminating would slip out. I just waited.

"Nothing happened because he was already dead when I went into the barn."

Chapter 31

Yes! I thought. I hadn't entirely trusted the Hummel lady's story, that she'd never seen Gordon, but now I had independent confirmation that Gordon was already dead before Giles entered the barn. I wasn't sure whether to cheer, knowing that this was probably enough to clear Giles, or shake Schmidt for lying and helping to implicate Giles in the first place.

"He was already dead?" I repeated.

"Definitely dead," Schmidt said. "When I first walked in, I saw his stuff lying all around, and I figured he was there—maybe snooping in the hayloft, that was about his style. So I called out for him to come down, that we needed to talk about the books. And he didn't say anything. And I went over to the ladder to the hayloft and he was just lying there, dead, with this bloody bookend by his head."

"What did you do then?" I asked, though I was beginning to have a suspicion.

"I panicked. I was afraid someone would find him, and

know that I'd come into the barn to talk to him. I figured the longer it took them to find him, the less chance anyone would jump to the wrong conclusion and suspect me. So I thought maybe if they didn't find the body . . ."

"So you hid it."

"In the trunk," he said, nodding. "It was right there. And I put the bookend in, too."

"And you took the key with you and hid it in a bowl of old keys."

"Yes," he said. "I was just going to throw it away somewhere, but as I was leaving, I saw the bowl of keys on one of the tables, so I wiped the trunk key off and threw it in there."

"And you ran away without even looking for your books."

"I looked," he said. "They weren't there."

I studied his face. He looked embarrassed, depressed, defensive, hostile, and generally miserable. But I had no idea if he looked truthful. For all I knew, he could still be covering something up.

I wasn't convinced he didn't have motive for murder. But I also had a hard time imagining that he could bludgeon Gordon to death with the bookend. He looked like the sort of person whose idea of taking stern and decisive action was to write a querulous letter to the *Caerphilly Clarion,* and then whine for weeks if the editor pruned a single adverb. Perhaps I should let him fret for a while, and try to find either confirmation that Gordon had been dead already when Schmidt entered the barn or something to disprove it.

"So who do you think did it?" I asked.

He frowned.

"I don't want to cast undue suspicion on someone else," he said.

"Why not?" I said. "The more suspicion you cast on someone else, the less likely the police will focus on you."

"You're not telling the police!" he exclaimed.

"Give me a reason not to," I said. "Tell me who you think did it."

"Well, I don't know that he did it," Schmidt said. "But as I was coming in, I did see Ralph Endicott, leaving through the other door."

"Endicott—Gordon's old partner?"

"That's him. Seemed in a bit of a hurry, too," he added, warming to his subject. "And goodness knows, after everything Gordon did to him, he has no reason to like the man."

"Okay," I said. "If I can prove Endicott's the murderer, maybe the police won't have to find out what you did. At least not the part about Mrs. Pruitt's books."

"Thank you," Schmidt said. "You can't imagine how grateful I'd be."

I decided not to point out that my statement contained a very large "if" with a great big "maybe" attached. And it occurred to me that before I let Schmidt completely off the hook, it might be a good idea to find out if he had any influence with any of the Great Stone Faces. If so, maybe I could pressure him into using it to our benefit.

Did that thought make me as despicable a blackmailer as Gordon?

I'd think that through later.

"Stay away from Gordon's shop," I said. "If I hear anything more about a break-in, I'll tell the police everything."

"Of course," he said, hastily. "I was just about to go home. I realize what a mistake it was, thinking of breaking in."

"That's a load of owl pellets," I said, in lieu of a ruder word. He looked puzzled, and I decided to leave him that way. He walked off quickly, as if in a hurry to get away from me.

I was turning toward the alley when I suddenly decided that I was tired. Why go the long way round? Why not just march right past the front of Gordon's shop? If the chief saw me and wondered what I was up to, maybe it was time to tell him everything. I'd found proof that Gordon was already dead when Giles went into the barn. Let the police decide which of the other suspects was guilty.

I wouldn't even have to tell them about Schmidt. All I had to do was sic them on the Hummel lady, and they'd follow the same trail I did.

Of course, by the time I realized that, the police cruisers were gone and Gordon's shop locked up tight. So much for good resolutions.

Still, I could do something. I pulled out my cell phone and dialed the non-emergency number for the police station. The chief wasn't in, of course, but Debbie Anne, the dispatcher, apologized very nicely and said she'd give him a message if I liked.

"Tell him the Hummel lady lied," I said. "And he should talk to her again."

"The who?"

"Hummel lady," I said, and spelled it. "I don't know her name, but the chief will know who I mean. Or he can call me if he likes."

I felt much more cheerful. My conscience was clear. The chief couldn't accuse me of sneaking around behind his back—well, not as easily, anyway. And, meanwhile, maybe I could get even closer to the truth if I could find Ralph Endicott, the ex-partner. I had a feeling I knew where to look. The last time I'd seen him, he'd been lurking near the fence around the yard sale, scanning the merchandise with his binoculars and scribbling notes in a leather-bound notebook. I needed to get back to the yard sale.

Easier said than done, though. As I was making my way out of town, I thought I spotted Mother, disappearing into a shop. I circled the block again and cruised past the shop at five miles per hour, but I couldn't see anything, and I drove on, hoping I'd been seeing things. Even the thought of Mother entering that particular shop made me nervous. Not only was it a bastion of chintz and gilding, but there wasn't a single price tag in the shop, on the theory that if you cared about the price, you couldn't afford it and they couldn't be bothered with you.

And then I hit a giant traffic jam that blocked the road leading toward our house for most of the ten miles I had to travel. I thought I was home free when I finally inched past the spot where a replacement funnel cake truck had broken down on its way out to set up operations at our house, but, instead, the traffic got even worse. Not many people were leaving, but the few that did had to fight their way out. Enough cars had parked along the shoulders on either side that the already narrow road was down to a single lane for much of the last two miles, and the arriving cars gave no mercy. Here and there, arguments and even the occasional fistfight broke out. The fields on either side of the road were festooned with stranded SUVs and jeeps whose owners thought they could bypass the traffic by taking to the countryside, only to find they'd misjudged either their vehicles' ability to traverse deep mud or their own driving skills. Cousin Sidney and his tow truck would be tired but happy by the end of the day.

I finally made it in on the heels of an arriving state police cruiser and scared away a woman who tried to take my parking space when I removed the orange cones. Not bad considering that she was driving a Chevy TrailBlazer that could have eaten my little Toyota for breakfast. But she wasn't very good at what I called slow motion chicken. Her tank was new and spotless, and my heap showed definite signs of past close encounters with other vehicles, so when I kept moving forward into the space, slowly but inexorably, she eventually wimped out and backed away.

"I was here first!" she shrieked, as I was walking away from my car.

"I live here!" I shouted back.

"And that makes you special?" I heard her mutter.

The whole day was getting out of hand. Some of Michael's drama students had shown up and were presenting scenes from various plays by Shakespeare, using our front porch as a makeshift stage. The college chamber music ensemble was impatiently awaiting their turn, and from the noises emerging from the house, either someone had held a séance and offended the ghost of John Philip Sousa or the college marching band needed a lot more rehearsal before we let them onto the porch.

Apparently Rose Noir had finished smudging the circumference of the yard sale, and was now putting the finishing touches to her cleansing ceremony from on high, thanks to Everett's boom lift. I wasn't sure it was wise to supplement the herbal smoke with scattering dried herbs, but anyone who had stuck it out this long at the yard sale wasn't about to be put off by showers of potpourri. At most, a few people looked mildly annoyed as they brushed it off their shoulders like fragrant dandruff.

The volunteer vendors now completely filled the front yard and had begun to expand into the field across the road from us. Normally our front yard had a restful view of the field sloping at first gently, and then more and more steeply, up to a tree-crowned ridge. Now we had a ringside view of more ad hoc yard sale participants.

I found Michael observing this phenomenon with alarm.

"Mr. Early won't like this," he said. Mr. Early, the farmer who owned the field across the way, was a noted local curmudgeon.

"Maybe he's out of town," I said.

"Isn't October supposed to be a busy time for farmers?" Michael said. "Harvest time, and all that."

"I think it depends on what you're growing."

"What does Mr. Early grow?" Michael asked.

We both squinted at the field for a few moments.

"Beats me," he said. "Just looks like grass to me."

"Maybe it is just grass," I said. "I think I've seen sheep there."

"Are you sure?"

"Not really," I said. "I suppose that shows what complete city slickers we are. I'll ask Dad."

"You think he'll know?"

"Maybe, and if he doesn't, he'll have a great time finding out. Maybe he'll even befriend Mr. Early."

"That would be nice," Michael said. "Though from what I've seen of Mr. Early, it would probably be a first. Meanwhile, I think I'll go over and tell those people that they're trespassing on Mr. Early's land."

"You really think they'll listen?"

"No, but at least I can tell Mr. Early that we told them to leave," he said, as he strode off.

That might help. Though I thought managing not to be around when Mr. Early discovered the interlopers was an even better plan.

Chapter 32

The bad thing about the chaos currently infesting our yard, and now spilling over onto the neighbors' property, was that no one was in charge. Though there were still a few people around—mostly my relatives—who held on to the delusion that I was in charge, and could fix their problems and answer their questions.

The good thing was that these misguided souls were far outnumbered by people who didn't know me from Adam and didn't expect a damn thing of me. That was a comforting thought.

Probably a good idea to make myself scarce till things quieted down. And maybe when Chief Burke returned from his burglary investigation I could get him to clear out the squatters.

On the other hand, if we could just get him to open up the yard sale again, we'd have more customers than we'd ever dreamed of.

Michael reappeared, with Dad at his side.

"I ran into your Dad," he said. "You were right—sheep. Some special kind that grows expensive Yuppie wool."

"Isn't it wonderful?" Dad said, beaming.

"The sheep?" I asked. "What's so wonderful about them? I bet they're just as clueless as ordinary sheep."

"No, this!" Dad exclaimed, flinging his arms out with enthusiasm.

"Your dad is enjoying the yard sale," Michael explained.

"It's certainly surpassed my expectations," I said.

"Meg, do you suppose it would work if we have a modest admission fee next year?" Dad asked. "If we charge even as little as a dollar, we could probably fund our SPOOR operations for an entire year."

"You can charge as much as you like the next time we have a yard sale," I said.

"Excellent!" Dad said, and walked off beaming.

"We're having another yard sale next year?" Michael asked.

"I'd sooner reenact Lady Godiva's ride," I said. "Down fraternity row. You'll notice I said 'next time,' not 'next year.'"

"Ah," Michael said, nodding. "That sounds more like it. Though we may need to have another sale if we decide to use your mother's designs for the house."

"No," I said. "We are not selling off all our stuff to buy chintz or Louis Quatorze or whatever crazy stuff Mother's excited about this week."

"Well, wait till you see her drawings," Michael said. "I think she's finally trying to listen to what we want."

"Listening to what we want is nice, but designing something we can live with is quite another thing," I said. "Besides, what if what we want is to be left alone to muddle through decorating on our own?"

"Then we'll tell her thanks, but no thanks," he said, with a laugh. "After all, she can't bully us into redecorating. I'll go see what I can do about the trespassers."

With that, he headed off again in the direction of Mr.

Early's field. I shook my head. Obviously, he still didn't know Mother well enough.

I could worry about Mother later. Right now, I wanted to talk to Ralph Endicott. I even spotted him, standing across the yard. But as I was walking toward him, I saw Chief Burke coming toward me, a stern scowl on his face. I tried to look innocent, helpful, and glad to see him, while my brain raced to figure out what I could have done that would bring him all the way out here in such a bad mood. If he'd talked to the Hummel lady already, he should be pleased at what I'd found, not mad at me.

And why not simply tell him what I'd learned from Schmidt, sic him on Endicott, and be done with it?

I was opening my mouth to spill the beans but the chief spoke first.

"My people tell me they're finished in there," he said, nodding his head toward the fenced-in yard sale area. "So I thought I'd come out and tell you that if you want to re-open your yard sale, it's fine with us."

Before he even finished speaking a murmur went through the crowd. Half of the people stampeded toward the gate to the yard sale while the other half began shoving to get closer to where the chief and I were standing. And I suspected they didn't have too many questions to ask him.

"You didn't have to come all the way out here to tell us," I said. "You could have just called." I didn't add that it would have been a lot easier for me if he'd told me over the phone, where no one else could overhear him. Now we had to gather everyone and everything we needed to reopen with several hundred people underfoot asking why it was taking so long.

"Had to bring Minerva out, didn't I?" the chief said, glancing at the plump figure following him down the walk. "God forbid that the fool thing could open even five minutes before she got here," he added, raising his voice.

"Someone else might beat her to another confounded piece of Depression glass."

"You hush up and let the poor girl go take care of everything she has to do to open up again," Minerva Burke said. "And you might round up some of your men to help with crowd control, now that you've just blurted out your news in public and riled everyone up."

Chief Burke's frown deepened as he stomped off and issued orders to the various officers still on the scene.

"Men," Mrs. Burke said to me, shaking her head. "Makes you wonder where they all were the day the good Lord handed out common sense, doesn't it?"

I decided I liked Mrs. Burke.

"Of course, there's some of them better than others," she went on. "Don't you shilly-shally around too long over that young man of yours, now. He's a keeper, and if you don't do something about it, someone else will."

Of course, I might like Mrs. Burke better from a slight distance.

"Would you like to have some lemonade while you wait?" I asked, pointing to an area near the back door where Mother and several of her cronies had set up lawn chairs and folding umbrellas and were sipping lemonade and iced tea while observing the crowd's antics.

"Thank you, sugar," she said. "I believe I would."

It didn't occur to me until a few minutes too late that introducing the formidable Mrs. Burke to Mother might be a mistake. Not that they wouldn't hit it off. When I glanced over a few minutes later, I saw unmistakable signs that they were hitting it off far too well. And possibly plotting together. One of the things I liked most about Caerphilly was its location—close enough to Yorktown that I could see my parents as often as I liked, but far enough that they wouldn't be underfoot quite all the time. The last thing I wanted was Mother establishing a satellite office in my backyard, and I began to fear that she'd found just the ally to run it.

Not something I could worry about right now. It was eleven-forty. We needed to get this thing rolling.

I fled inside the fence to organize things, leaving Officer Sammy and Cousin Horace to guard the gate.

"Rob!" I called. "Get Sammy to give you the bullhorn and walk around announcing that we're opening at noon."

"Roger," he said, looking quite cheerful, as he usually did when he drew a job that required no strenuous exertion.

"And tell everyone who has a table to get in here ASAP, and everyone else to stay the hell away from the gate until noon," I added.

"Though not necessarily in those precise words," Michael suggested. "Any jobs for me?"

"Could you secure the barn?" I asked. "We don't want hundreds of people tramping through and trying to take pictures of the murder scene."

"Can do," he said.

With most of the friends and family on site helping and the rest quickly learning to make themselves scarce, we staffed the tables and set up the checkout by noon. I gave Sammy a nod and he and Cousin Horace opened the gates.

My last thought, as the shopping hordes descended, was that perhaps by the time I could think again, the chief would have solved the murder, and poor Giles would be free.

I thought, with a twinge of guilt, he might have an easier time of it if I'd had the chance to tell him about Schmidt and Endicott.

The next two hours lasted at least ten years. Each. But eventually Michael and Dad convinced everyone that nothing they could say or do would gain them admission to the barn. After that, the mere sightseers left in a huff; the media retreated to various corners of the yard, trying

to look inconspicuous, in the hope that we'd forget they
were there and leave the barn unguarded; and the rest of
the crowd settled in to do what they were there for: to
shop till they dropped. Only a few of them did it literally,
due to overexertion in the sun, and Dad was there to re-
vive them. But many more were staggering under the
sheer weight of their purchases, and my teenaged
nephews and their friends found a lucrative new business
opportunity: carrying boxes to people's cars and trucks.

I could see all sorts of small family dramas shaping
up. Did Aunt Cleo's sons know she was selling their
paintball guns? And did Mother know that Dad was buying them for Eric and his brothers?

Why was Aunt Verbena, who lived in a high-rise condo-
minium with her seven cats, buying several birdhouses and
bird feeders? Was this some scheme to cut her cat food bill
and, if so, should I report her to the Audubon Society?

And why was Michael spending so much time in
Cousin Ginnie's booth? I knew he'd volunteered to talk to
Morris, and I could see that he might need to talk to Ginnie as well in the process of patching things up between
them, but why would talking to Ginnie involve so much
inspection of her merchandise? That looked like shopping. Had I failed to make my feelings about secondhand
lingerie clear?

I tried to push these worries out of my mind and think
positive thoughts. Stuff was leaving. Someone actually
bought Edwina's entire wire coat hanger crop, the results
of nearly a century of uncontrolled breeding. And the
same person walked off with the wallpaper collection—
full and partial rolls of every wallpaper ever used in the
house, any one of which would be a strong contender in a
"world's ugliest wallpaper" contest. If only unloading the
unused wallpaper would be my last sight of them—I had a
feeling some of those ghastly patterns would haunt my

dreams for weeks once we began stripping down the walls. But—positive thoughts. The rolls were leaving.

And the clock hands were moving, however slowly. Though the end of the yard sale didn't mean I could rest. There was still the murder. I heard people talking about it, but none of them mentioned any exciting new information on the case. So, since Chief Burke wasn't using the information I'd given him, I was impatient to use it myself.

"You should take a break," Michael said to me, not for the first time.

"I will in a few minutes," I said.

"I'm serious," he said. "You look beat."

"I am, and I'm going to rest. Just not yet. Not until I check three more people out."

Michael glanced down the line.

"Is the third guy someone particular?" he asked, in an undertone.

"Gordon-you-thief's ex-partner," I murmured back. "I want to talk to him."

"Gotcha," he said. "I'll shuffle about getting ready to take your place until you're finished with him."

The next two people took forever, but then Ralph Endicott stepped in front of me.

Checking him out took quite some time, too. Which surprised me. I didn't remember that he'd been carrying around all that much stuff before the murder, but now he had two full boxes.

Had Gordon's death freed him from the worries and problems that had kept him from opening his new shop? And if so, was that a sufficient motive for murder?

Still, checking him out gave me time to study him before I tried to talk to him.

"Let me help you carry that to your car," I said, when he'd paid for his purchases and Michael had taken my seat.

"Oh," he said, surprised. "If you're leaving anyway."

"Taking a much-needed break," I said.

We walked along for a few minutes without speaking, though not exactly in silence, since the entire choir of the New Life Baptist Church, more than a hundred voices strong, was belting out "There Is a Balm in Gilead" from on and around the front porch stage.

We passed my cousins Basil and Cyril, who were blocking one lane of the road as they tried to load a small truck's worth of stuff into the trunk and nearly nonexistent back seat of a Miata. At least one twin was loading stuff, while the other tried to prevent Cousin Deirdre from splashing their twin moose heads with paint.

We walked nearly a quarter of a mile toward Endicott's car before I felt our surroundings were quiet enough for him to hear me and private enough for me to say what I wanted to say.

Of course, there was still plenty of time. No wonder he'd accepted my offer of help—he'd parked more than half a mile from our house. I spent a few moments trying to devise a subtle, diplomatic way to open up the subject, but I finally decided that I was too tired and hungry to be subtle, not to mention cranky because he had stuck me with the heavier of the two boxes, so I just dived right in.

"Look," I said. "I know what you did in the barn."

His head whipped around to look at me, and he dropped the box he was carrying. It landed with a rich and varied medley of crashing and tinkling noises that went on for several seconds after impact.

Endicott didn't even notice.

Chapter 33

"I beg your pardon," Endicott said, in a shaky voice.

"I said I know what you did in the barn. Not everything, of course," I added. "But enough to know that you lied to the cops."

I felt a twinge of guilt as I said this, since my conscience reminded me that I hadn't exactly told the cops everything either. But, at least, I was only committing sins of omission. Not even omission, really—delay. I hadn't told the chief any bald-faced whoppers under direct questioning.

Endicott finally appeared to notice the fallen box, and squatted down beside it.

"I don't know what you're talking about," he said, his eyes fixed on the box flaps and his hands poised over them, as if he were trying to get up enough nerve to open the box and view the damage within.

"Come on," I said. "I know what you told the chief—you were snooping in the stuff Gordon had dragged into the barn—his stash, I think you called it. And he caught you, and had a good laugh at your expense, and you left. Only we both know that's not exactly how it went."

"I didn't kill him," he said. "If you saw what I did, you'd know that."

"Then what the hell were you doing?"

"I was just hiding the body," he said. He abandoned the idea of examining the breakage, picked up the box, and began walking, briskly. But not so briskly that I couldn't keep up, despite the weight of my box.

"Hiding the body?" I repeated.

"He was already dead when I found him," he said, over his shoulder. "I walked in and found him lying there, dead, in the middle of the barn floor, and I knew if anyone else walked in and saw us there, they'd think I killed him. Everyone knew how much I hated him. So I thought if I could only hide the body—to make sure it wasn't found right after I left the barn . . ."

"So you hid it," I said. "Where?"

"Farther back in the barn," he said. "Right beside the ladder to the loft."

I nodded. That tallied with what Professor Schmidt had said.

"And then you just strolled out and pretended nothing had happened. And lied to the police."

"I was in shock!" he said, with a shudder. "I get queasy at estate sales, just thinking about the possibility that someone might have died in the house—I'd never even seen a dead body before, much less touched one."

"And why should I believe you?" I said. "You lied about talking to him, and let an innocent man get arrested."

"Well, I'm innocent, too, and if I told the truth, I'd have been arrested," he said. "I figured with all those forensic things they can do nowadays, they'd find the real killer soon enough."

"Oh, and a town like Caerphilly has a big budget for forensics, right?" I said. "And with all the murders they have here, they probably have some really experienced, top-notch evidence technicians, too."

As I said it, I apologized mentally to Cousin Horace, who was a pretty decent evidence technician. But Endicott didn't know that. And it was true about the budget. I'd been to Caerphilly County Board meetings, so I knew how miniscule the chief's budget was, and thanks to Dad's passion for anything connected with crime, I had a fair idea how far into the hole the forensic part of the weekend's investigation had probably put the county, to say nothing of the overtime costs. Maybe that was why the chief was so eager to arrest Giles.

Just as Endicott was visibly eager to get away from me. He kept walking faster, no doubt hoping to lose me, and by now we were traveling at a brisk jog, our boxes clinking rhythmically as we ran.

"I'm sorry," Endicott gasped out, finally. "It's not as if I had a lot of time to think it through."

"And you had a good reason to want him dead," I said. "He was costing you money—and threatening to cost you more, wasn't he?"

"Not enough to kill him," Endicott said, in a shocked tone. "Only a few thousand dollars. I could well afford that. How do you think I've managed without a shop for nearly two years? I deal in antiques—well, not as a hobby; I try to keep things very businesslike. But I don't need to make a living at it. I don't need the money; I inherited enough money to live quite comfortably."

"And enough money to hire a top-notch defense attorney if you need one," I said. I was starting to worry about all the running we were doing. I was getting seriously winded, and I had about twenty years' advantage on Endicott.

"If it comes to hiring a lawyer, yes," he said. "Though I hope it doesn't. Think of the scandal."

"What about his keys?" I asked. "And his wallet?"

"I beg your pardon?" he said, glancing back.

"His keys and wallet were missing," I said. "Did you take them?"

"Good heavens, no," he said. "What do you take me for, a petty thief?"

He sounded more offended than when he thought I was accusing him of murder.

"Besides, only an idiot would steal Gordon's wallet," he said. " 'Who steals my purse steals trash,' and all that."

"He didn't carry a lot of money?"

"If they outlawed plastic Gordon would starve," Endicott said.

"The keys are a different matter," I said. "He had some valuable stuff in the shop. I know; I've been there."

"Well, yes," Endicott said. "I suppose if you're after the stuff in the shop, his keys would be worth stealing. But not to me. I still had my own key to the shop, though I doubt if Gordon remembered that."

"Wouldn't he have changed the locks when you sold him your part of the shop?" I said.

"Any normal person would have. Not Gordon," Endicott said. His words were starting to come out in short, staccato bursts. "Too cheap and too lazy. I hung onto the key just after the sale. In case he ever tried anything really devious. Like trying to fake my signature on something. And I never got rid of it—the key."

We were both slowing down now. Endicott stopped suddenly, put the box down, and squatted by it, panting. I dumped my box on the ground beside his. What had he bought, anyway? I didn't recall selling him anything this heavy. Had he shoplifted Rob's discarded barbell set while I wasn't looking?

He was still avoiding my eyes. I studied his face, what I could see of it, and tried to decide if he was telling the truth. I had thought he was only resting, but after panting for a few minutes, he reached into his pocket, pulled out a set of keys, and stood up, bracing himself against the side of a parked SUV.

"Lend it to me," I said, holding out my hand.

He glanced up, startled, and clutched his key ring to his stomach.

"Just the shop key," I said. "I'll bring it back in a few days."

"But—I haven't got it right now," he said.

Light dawned.

"No, you gave it to Arnold Schmidt, didn't you. To keep him from telling Chief Burke that he saw you coming out of the barn just before he found Gordon dead," I said.

"How did you know that?" Endicott asked, looking genuinely puzzled, and perhaps slightly fearful.

"So if you didn't kill Gordon and take his keys and wallet, who did? If you can tell me something useful, maybe I won't have to tell Chief Burke all about this."

He looked as if he was thinking, hard. But his face didn't have the look of someone desperately trying to invent something that would save him. More the look of someone who was trying to convince himself he had to do something he didn't really want to do.

"I don't want to get anyone in trouble," he began.

"You already have," I said. "Tell me what you know."

"I don't know anything for sure," he said. "It's only a vague suspicion."

"I'll take a vague suspicion if that's all you've got," I said.

"Well . . . when I came in, I saw Carol leaving."

"Gordon's wife?"

"They were separated," Endicott said. "And if Carol had had her way, they'd have been divorced a year or two ago."

Which meant they'd split up about the same time Endicott and Gordon had stopped being partners. Was that only a coincidence?"

"Was it an amicable separation?" I asked, even though I thought I knew the answer.

"Amicable," Endicott snapped. "Hell, no. You've never seen anything so vicious. He fought her over everything—the house, the shop, the bank accounts. And she kept trying to convince the judge that he was hiding assets from her."

Now that he'd made up his mind to talk, I wasn't sure I could stop him if I wanted to. Not that I did, of course.

"And was he?" I said. "Hiding assets?"

"I wouldn't put it past him," Endicott said. "He tried to pull a few stunts like that when we broke up the partnership. And I wasn't going after every penny I could get, the way Carol was. I just wanted to get clear of him as fast as possible. She was really holding his feet to the fire. Not that I blame her. The things that woman put up with! He started fooling around on her before the honeymoon was over—can you believe that?"

"Only with difficulty," I said. "Most women would have better taste than to fool around with Gordon. And most men, too."

"But you see why she'd want the keys," Endicott said, eagerly. "She'd been trying everything to find out what he'd hidden, and where, and with the keys, she could go into the divorce court fully armed, so to speak."

"Though she'll be going into probate court, not divorce," I said.

"True," Endicott said, as if this were a new idea.

"Wait a minute," I said. "Wouldn't he have changed

the keys when Carol filed for divorce? How can you be so sure your key still fits?"

"We changed them the first time she filed for divorce, five years ago," Endicott said. "I was the one who arranged it. As far as I know, he never gave her a copy of the new one. The reconciliation never went that well."

Which could mean that Gordon had been working on hiding his assets from Carol for five years. No wonder Carol was so upset.

"Could she have killed him?" I asked.

He fell silent. I suspected that he wasn't agonizing over how to answer my question, only how he could avoid answering it. For whatever reason—friendship, shared suffering, perhaps a hint of romantic attraction—Endicott didn't want to point the finger at Carol. But the longer he paused, the more loudly I could hear the answer he wasn't giving. Yes, she could have killed Gordon.

"I'll talk to her," I said. "See what she says."

"Don't—" he began.

"Mention that you ratted on her," I said. "I won't. As it happens, I was already planning to talk to her. It wasn't exactly a surprise when you mentioned her name. I saw her going in and out of the barn, too, you know."

Though until I'd talked to Endicott, I had no idea when she'd gone into the barn and thus no idea if she was a valid suspect.

We put the boxes in the back of the SUV and Endicott drove off, a little too fast, as if he was glad to get away from me. I thought for a while, and then pulled out my cell phone to call Chief Burke.

"I'm busy," he said, when I got him on the phone. "This had better be important."

"Did you get—"

"I got your message, yes. Was there anything else?"

Got it, and from the stubborn sound of his voice, wasn't doing a thing about it. I'd been waffling about whether to tell him about Schmidt and Endicott, but if he was going to be mulish . . .

"I was just wondering if it had occurred to you that whoever has Gordon's keys might try to use them again," I said.

"Come again?"

"How do you know that whoever burgled the shop last night wasn't interrupted before they found what they were looking for or did what they were trying to do?" I said. "And whoever did it still has his other keys—house, car, who knows what."

"If you're worried that someone will break in somewhere and steal evidence, you can stop worrying," the chief said. "We've taken measures to secure the premises he owned or rented, and I don't just mean stringing up a lot of pretty yellow crime scene tape. And if you're the one who has the keys and you're angling to find out if it's safe to use them, it's not, so do me a favor and snoop someplace else. I hate arresting well-meaning amateurs for interfering in my investigations."

"Don't worry," I said. "I don't have Gordon's keys, and I have no intention of breaking in anywhere. Scout's honor."

"Were you ever actually a Girl Scout?" he asked.

"Briefly," I said. "And it was Dad's fault I got kicked out."

"That I can believe," he said. "Behave yourself."

With that he hung up.

I felt better. I wasn't sure whether the chief was telling me the truth, or just what he thought would scare me off, but if Professor Schmidt really was running around with a working key to Gordon's shop, my conscience was clean. I'd warned the chief. If Endicott was telling the truth, it was probably Carol who'd tried to burgle the shop last night.

I got Carol's number from directory assistance and tried to call it. No answer. She might be back at the yard sale. And even if she wasn't, I had a feeling I knew where she'd strike next. And when. Odds were she wouldn't strike until after dark. And right now, dark felt a long way off. I could hear several voices calling my name, back at the yard sale.

In fact, long before I got back to the yard sale, I heard gunfire from the direction of the house. Cursing Endicott for making me use up so much energy already, I started running back.

Chapter 34

I made it back a lot faster than I'd come, but even so, I heard several more gunshots before I reached the house and could see what was happening.

I was reasonably sure they were gunshots rather than, say, car backfires or more bursting balloons, because each sharp sound was followed by a short burst of hysterical screams. At least I hoped they were only hysterical. Surely people would be screaming longer and louder if anyone had been injured, wouldn't they? And fleeing in far larger numbers.

So far, traffic heading away from the house was light—I'd only had to dodge two cars, twelve pedestrians, and a sheep. Though the sheep did puzzle me, until I remembered the trespassers in Mr. Early's field. I sped up a little. I'd have sped up a lot, but running with Endicott's heavy box earlier had taken a lot out of me.

I arrived to find that the crowd had completely blocked the road for several hundred yards, and the police were trying to clear a path for the patrol car that was inching its way through. I spotted someone in the back of the car—

our neighbor, Mr. Early. He was shaking his fist at the crowd and shouting. The closed car window and the clamor from the crowd drowned out what he was saying, but I could guess what he was unhappy about.

The crowd milling about in front of our house contained a rather large number of sheep. Dad would probably insist on calling them a flock of sheep, but I would argue that they needed to be a lot more cohesive to qualify as a flock. Not to mention better behaved—could these really be the same sedate sheep I remembered dotting the pasture across the road and waddling slowly up and down the hillside? These sheep appeared enraged, or perhaps possessed. Okay, perhaps they were merely spooked at finding themselves in the midst of a large, noisy, unruly crowd of humans. But I had never imagined sheep capable of charging into people and knocking them down. And they were larger than I thought sheep were supposed to be. Giant economy-sized sheep. Did I have the wrong idea about sheep, or was Farmer Early breeding some kind of mutant fighting sheep?

The New Life Baptist choir was belting out an enthusiastic version of "Rise Up, Shepherd, and Follow." Easy for them to take this philosophically; they were up on the porch, where only the most demented of sheep was apt to venture.

I panicked briefly when I saw red splotches on several of the sheep, but I quickly realized that it wasn't blood. Apparently Cousin Deirdre had found a new supply of paint and was running about happily spattering the fleeing sheep.

I spotted Michael at the edge of the chaos, looking tired, and possibly in need of rescue, since he was talking to one of my uncles.

"No," I heard him say as I drew near. "I don't think I've ever lived anywhere that had a 4H Club I could have joined."

"No experience with sheep, then?" the uncle said.

"I've eaten quite a few," Michael said. His tiredness probably made his voice sound a bit more savage than he intended.

"I don't really think that's going to be helpful here," the uncle said, sidling away.

Michael nodded to me and stood staring at the passing sheep.

"What happened?" I asked.

"I warned them that they were trespassing," Michael said. He was panting slightly, as if he'd been running around after the sheep. "Did they listen?"

"Of course not," I said. "They're idiots."

"Some of them started taking down the fence, to make it easier to get to their booths and tables," he said. "You should have seen how surprised they were when the first few sheep came trotting down the hill. And then when Early showed up with his shotgun and started firing over their heads and yelling about trespassing . . ."

He fell silent and rubbed his face with his hand, as if exhausted. I put an arm around his waist and we stood together for a few moments watching the crowd.

Both sheep and humans were dispersing. The music dissolved into shrieks when a particularly bold sheep trotted up onto the porch, sending the choir members fleeing in all directions.

On the plus side, by evicting the unauthorized bazaar from his field, Mr. Early had convinced many people that the fun was over for the day. Except for the customers lined up at the yard sale checkout, people were mostly heading for their cars.

On the minus side, once they got to their cars, they weren't having much luck departing. Every few yards, you could see a sheep standing on the road, gazing thoughtfully into the distance, seemingly unaware that half-a-dozen cars were lined up behind it, honking their horns and shouting at it. No sooner would one sheep amble off the road than another would saunter out.

But there were really only a small number of sheep playing in traffic. Where had the rest of them gone?

"What are we supposed to do about all this?" Michael said. He wasn't puffing anymore, but he still sounded tired. "They're incredibly stupid, and trying to get them all to go where you want them to go is nearly impossible, but the minute one of them does something destructive, dangerous, or just annoying, every single one of them goes and does the same damned thing."

"All true," I said. "But we can't do anything about the people, so let's talk about the sheep."

"I was talking about the sheep," he said, with a faint ghost of a smile.

"They're a problem, too," I agreed.

I spotted several of my relatives in the crowd. And, unfortunately, they had spotted me. They were pointing at me and waving, and heading this way. Probably to ask me what I planned to do about the sheep.

"Come on," I said to Michael. "I have an idea."

I strolled over to where Officer Sammy was standing, with Michael in my wake.

"Hey, Sammy," I said. "Could you help me with something."

"I'll sure try," he said, with his eager, 250-watt smile.

"I figure by now they have Mr. Early down at the station, being arrested or arraigned or whatever."

"And we need to get our sheep together," Michael put in.

I winced. Sammy frowned.

"Your sheep?" he said.

"Mr. Early's sheep," I said, pointing to one of the woolly fugitives that happened to be passing by. "His sheep have escaped their pasture, and we're trying to round them up and put them back."

"That's good," Sammy said, nodding.

"Only we have no idea how many of them he has," I said. "We can't very well know when we've found them all if we have no idea how many we're looking for."

"No problem," Sammy said. "I'll call down to the station and get a count."

While Sammy made his way through the throng to his patrol car, I greeted any relatives who came looking for me with orders that they each go and catch a sheep. Preferably several sheep. As I expected, most of them hurried to comply, and the rest, when they realized that I was asking them to work, made themselves scarce.

Fifteen minutes later, Sammy showed up leading a sheep and bearing the news that Mr. Early had two hundred and twenty-one head of sheep.

"And I suppose each of those heads is attached to a separate sheep body," I said, letting myself slouch against the fence. "And every blessed one of them is rapidly trotting away in a completely different direction from every other sheep in the flock."

"On their eight hundred and eighty-four beastly sharp little hooves," Michael said, rubbing the shin one of the sheep had kicked.

"Only eight hundred and twenty-eight beastly sharp little hooves," I corrected.

"Did I multiply that wrong?" Michael said, frowning. "It's been a long day."

"Your multiplication's fine, but you forgot to subtract the ones we've already caught."

"That's right," he said. We both turned to look behind us at the pasture. So far, the combined efforts of our amateur shepherds had only corralled thirteen sheep. Fourteen, with Sammy's contribution. And from what I could see, those fourteen were the fattest, slowest, most sedentary of the flock. Most of their more nimble comrades had already disappeared over various horizons, with or without panting humans in hot pursuit. All except for a small cadre of guerilla sheep who remained lurking near the road, ready to take their turns blocking traffic.

"Fifteen," Michael said, as Dad and Rob arrived with another sheep to add to the collection.

"Dad," Rob said, when they'd shoved their catch through the gate. "My arms itch."

I glanced over and saw that not only was Rob scratching his arms rather obsessively, but his face had begun to swell.

"Oh, damn," I said.

"Do you suppose Farmer Early sprays some kind of dangerous chemical on his sheep?" Rob asked.

"No," I said. "He didn't have to; nature already did."

"What do you mean?" Dad asked.

"Lanolin," I said. "The wool is full of lanolin. Remember how careful Mother had to be when he was a kid? He got hives from even a trace of lanolin."

Perhaps the wrong thing to say in front of a hypochondriac.

"I can feel my throat closing up," Rob said, clutching his Adam's apple with one hand while still scratching with the other. "I'm going to die, aren't I? Killed by a sheep overdose."

"You've probably outgrown some of your sensitivity," I said.

"I've got my bag up at the house," Dad said. "Come on; I'll give you a shot of antihistamine."

"Should we call an ambulance?" Michael asked. I noticed that he was scratching his arms, too. And for that matter, so was I. They were starting to itch rather fiercely.

Power of suggestion, or was prolonged contact with live lanolin factories bringing out an allergic reaction in those of us who'd never had a problem before?

Dad and Rob had begun trotting toward the house, and most of our volunteer helpers trailed after them. I hoped Dad wouldn't run out of antihistamine, given how many hypochondriacs we had in the family.

Chapter 35

"Should I go find some more sheep?" Sammy asked.

"Not just yet," I said. "Can I borrow your bullhorn?"

"Sure," Sammy said. "It's in my car."

"I'm sure you know what you're doing," Michael said, as we followed Sammy to the police cruiser. "You always do. But just how is a bullhorn going to retrieve any sheep?"

"It won't," I said. "But they will."

I pointed at the people still milling about the premises. Fewer than before, of course, but still far too many of them.

"We're offering a bounty of twenty dollars per sheep," I added.

"But that would cost—"

"In the form of a gift certificate redeemable at next weekend's continuation of the yard sale."

"I bow to your ingenuity," he said.

Ten minutes later, the yard was empty of all but the customers checking out. And many of them were jostling with impatience to get out and join the sheep hunt.

"I certainly hope you're not counting this sheep bounty as a yard sale expense," Barrymore Sprocket said.

"We'll talk about it later," I said.

"Because I certainly can't authorize—"

"Later!" I snapped.

Barrymore retreated, still grumbling.

"Meg," Michael said, sounding worried. "What if someone tries to bring in ringers to claim the bounty?"

"What, you mean like goats or cows?" I said. "I think we'd notice."

"No, like someone else's sheep."

"Are there many other sheep around?"

"Oh, yes," Sammy said. "I can think of at least a dozen other farmers in the county who have sheep. Not as many as Early, of course."

"Then how are we supposed to tell them apart?"

"Well, most of the farmers don't have Lincolns."

Since the only vehicle I'd ever seen Mr. Early driving was an enormous battered pickup truck, I assumed this was a brand of sheep.

"Okay, how can we tell Lincolns from other sheep?" I asked.

"They're bigger than most sheep," he said. "And they have longer wool. And they're kind of square."

"You can't blame them," Michael said. "It's hard to stay up with all the trends, stuck out here in the country they way they are."

Sammy blinked once and then focused on me.

"Square-shaped," he said, carefully. "You know, blocky and rectangular, rather than round and—"

"Right," I said. "Fleece-covered tanks. I'm sure this all makes sense to a farmer, and maybe it would to us if we had a couple of non-Lincoln sheep around for comparison, but we don't, so how can we tell if our bounty hunters are bringing us Mr. Early's sheep or rustling someone else's sheep?"

Sammy blinked.

"You could always look at the ear tags," he suggested, as if talking to a small child.

Sure enough, all the sheep were sporting bright yellow plastic ear tags. I winced when I saw that they'd been permanently attached to their ears with a sort of plastic grommet, but then reminded myself that it was probably no worse than having one's ears pierced.

And each tag had a unique number, along with Mr. Early's name.

"So all we have to do is write down each tag number, and we'll know which sheep we have," I said. "And if anyone found a sheep with any other ear tag, they'd know it wasn't Mr. Early's and they wouldn't bring it here."

"Unless they were city slickers who didn't know any better like—like a lot of these tourists," Sammy said, looking at Michael and me as he spoke. "Of course, you could get locals cutting off the tags and trying to pretend the animals had lost them. Which happens, but not too often because there are pretty stiff penalties for stealing livestock, so—"

"Sammy," I said. "I have a great idea! Why don't you stay here and check in the sheep as people return them. I doubt if any sinister sheep rustlers would try to fence hot sheep with you in charge, and if they did, you could arrest them!"

"Okay," Sammy said. "But I think it would be a good idea to give them each a receipt, with the ID numbers of the sheep they turn in marked on it. Down at the station, we always like to give people a receipt when they turn in lost or stolen property."

"Excellent idea," I said. "And we'll keep a carbon, so

we can make sure no one tries to sneak any sheep out one end of the pasture and then bring them in the other to earn more than one bounty for them, which is what I bet a few people would try if we didn't keep track."

"I would never have thought of that," Michael murmured.

"No wonder you hate faculty politics so much," I said. "You have no sense of deviousness. Come on—let's do a census of the sheep we already have."

Easier said than done. While the ear tags were a vivid yellow that was hard to miss, reading the numbers on them required us to get closer than the sheep liked—close enough to get kicked or butted, especially since by the time we finally caught up with our quarry, we were usually too tired to take evasive action. The captive sheep, which I had previously dismissed as the most dim-witted and sedentary members of the flock, proved remarkably deft at eluding us on their home ground.

From the amount of sheep dung waiting to surprise the unwary passerby in the flat part of the pasture, I deduced that the sheep must spend a lot of time hanging out there, which probably accounted for my remembering that I'd seen them. Once they escaped from the flatlands to the slope beyond, as half of them did before we could get their numbers, the dung gave way to sneaky hidden rocks, all accompanied by patches of thorns and brambles, conveniently placed so you could hardly help landing in them when you tripped over the rocks.

We never would have gotten the last two sheep identified if Dad hadn't returned from tending Rob and used his powerful birding binoculars to read the tags from afar. He offered to search the rest of the pasture for any sheep that might be still lurking out of sight, and we gratefully took him up on it.

"What's Eric doing?" Michael said, pointing. I broke

into a run, with Michael and the lanky Sammy behind me. One of the sheep appeared to be dragging my nephew behind him. At least it was moving too slowly to be dangerous. Though why Eric didn't simply let go of the sheep's tail I couldn't imagine.

Until I got closer and realized that Eric was trying to rescue Spike, who had chomped onto the sheep's left hind leg and refused to let go. Or perhaps Eric thought he was rescuing the sheep from Spike. Since the sheep appeared calmly oblivious to her two hitchhikers, I suspected Spike had nothing but a mouthful of wool. His readiness to let go when Michael grabbed him confirmed my suspicion.

"You're letting my sheep go!" Eric wailed, as I picked him up and tried to dust him off.

"Don't give up the sheep," Michael said, nodding.

"I'll take it back to the pasture," Sammy said. He captured the sheep and strolled off leading it with an ease that astonished me. How long did you have to live in the country before you learned how to do things like that?

"What on earth were you doing?" I asked Eric.

"Spike was helping me catch the sheep," Eric said. "Good dog."

Since Spike's only previous encounter with sheep had been in a culinary context, I didn't approve of casting him in a real-life remake of Lassie.

"That's nice," I said aloud. "But Spike's pretty fierce. Maybe we should keep him away from the poor sheep."

Just then, Spike proved my point by biting Michael.

"Okay," Eric said. "I'll take him back to his pen."

Before I could stop him, he reached out and picked up Spike. Spike not only refrained from biting, he curled up in Eric's arms and behaved angelically all the way back to his pen. Though I did suspect he was smirking at me and Michael.

Michael went off to solve the traffic jam by removing as many sheep as possible from the road, while I returned to the checkout table.

An hour went by. Maybe two. Or maybe it was only ten minutes. All my running around after sheep and suspects had worn me out, and I was starting to make embarrassing mistakes in simple arithmetic.

"I think a dollar is too much for this," a woman announced, thumping a large, ungainly ceramic object on the table in front of me.

I studied the object. It appeared to be a cross between a candelabrum and one of those strawberry pots with ten or fifteen different holes for the plants to stick out. Perhaps it was intended to be a vase in the shape of a stylized octopus. Whatever it was, someone had painted it in color combinations even a kindergartener would find gaudy.

"I agree," I said. "But that's the price."

"Can't you reduce it to fifty cents?" she said. "Since it's the end of the day and all?"

I thought of explaining that it might be the end of the day, but the yard sale would probably be continuing next weekend. But that would probably start a long discussion.

"Okay, on one condition," I said.

She snapped to attention.

"You can have it for fifty cents if you go out and find something else on sale for a dollar that's just as large and hideous," I said. "If you can do that, I'll give you both things, two for fifty cents. Otherwise it stays a dollar."

She frowned for a second. Then she picked up the vase or statue or whatever it was and raced back out into the yard sale.

"But it has to be something really hideous, remember," I called after her. "And I get to decide if it's hideous enough!"

The next customer stepped up and plunked two large cardboard boxes on the table. But instead of efficiently emptying her boxes so I could add things up, she handed me a plate. A rather ordinary china plate.

"How much for this?" she asked.

I turned the plate over. Yes, it had a price tag.

"Fifty cents," I said.

"Can you do twenty-five for it?"

I looked at her two large boxes. And then at the long line of people waiting to check out. Waiting and watching.

"No," I said, shaking my head. "But I tell you what—"

I broke the plate over my knee and handed her the larger half.

"I can do twenty-five for this," I said.

Apparently she wasn't in the mood for bargaining. She ignored the proffered plate, unloaded her two boxes without attempting to dicker, and paid the total in silence.

I left the two halves of the plate at my elbow, just to keep people motivated.

A long afternoon.

"Hello, dear."

I glanced up to see that my next customer was Mother, carrying the hideous lamp shade, its garish colors glowing in the afternoon sunlight like some strange tropical fungus.

"Where were you planning to use that?" I asked, pointing to the lamp. And then I braced myself, hoping that the answer wouldn't be "In your living room, dear."

"Good heavens," Mother exclaimed. "You really didn't think I'd use that on a lamp!"

"Isn't that usually what one does with lamp shades?"

"But not one this vile," Mother said, recoiling from the lamp shade, as if the possibility of using it for interior decoration was a new and profoundly disturbing notion.

"Then why are you buying it?"

"For my costume, dear," she said. She placed the lamp shade on her head and struck a pose. The lamp shade was so huge that it dwarfed her slender figure. She really did look like a tall floor lamp afflicted with the ugliest of all possible shades.

"Oh, I see," I said, trying to sound merely enthusiastic rather than profoundly relieved. "Is Dad going as a lamp, too?"

"We didn't think it quite suited," she said. "He's wearing Eric's old warped skis and going as a rocking chair."

"Wonderful," I said. "You always think of the most unusual costumes."

Mother beamed at that. And it wasn't a lie, either. How nice to have reached the age where I found my parents' enthusiasm for wearing outlandish costumes endearing; as a child, of course, it had been only one of many reasons I'd found them mortally embarrassing.

"How's it going?" Michael asked, appearing in front of me instead of a customer. I glanced over and saw that Mrs. Fenniman and Rob were helping the next customer drag a small mountain of boxes over to my table. I took a deep breath.

"We're getting there," I said, nodding at the large pile of sales receipt carbons on the table.

"How about the sleuthing?" he asked, in an undertone.

"Well, it obviously hasn't been going anywhere for the last several hours."

"If you needed to get away from the sale, you should have told me," he exclaimed.

"There's nothing more I can do before sundown anyway," I said. "But if you'd care to help me with a surveillance this evening."

"I would be delighted," he said, with a bow. "Who are we tailing?"

"Carol McCoy," I said.

"The grieving widow?"

"She's not grieving," I said. "She's probably celebrating Gordon's demise, and she may have caused it."

"Then I dislike her on principle."

"Because she might be a murderer?"

"Because she's contributing to your unreasonably negative view of matrimony, which is an honorable estate, and so forth. You look beat. Why don't you knock off now? I can finish up, and you can take a hot bath, and maybe even a nap."

"You're just trying to get on my good side," I said.

"Always," he said, with a smile.

I glanced at the woman with the mountain of boxes, and the umpteen other customers behind her. I was about to pull my usual stiff upper lip routine, deny being tired, and insist on staying to the bitter end. But, dammit, he was right. I was beat.

"You're an angel," I said. "Just give a yell if anyone needs me for anything."

"On the contrary, I will kill anyone who tries to bother you," he said. "See you at sundown."

Chapter 36

Things really were winding down. I was only stopped half a dozen times on my way to the house.

And a large amount of stuff had left the yard. I tried to focus on that, and not on the fact that we hadn't gotten rid of nearly as much stuff as we would have if the yard sale had been open all weekend. Think positively. We'd probably unloaded several tons of stuff.

I also tried to shake off the thought that we'd released several tons of noxious clutter into other people's lives. Should I feel guilty, I wondered, remembering Rose Noir's feng shui advice. Only if it really was clutter, I decided.

Now that I had time to breathe, I remembered a few customers who made me feel good about the yard sale. The woman in neat, though slightly worn, clothes who'd looked so pleased at her box full of children's toys and books. The elderly woman clutching a vase exactly like one she remembered from childhood visits to her grandmother. The two college students who'd been so happy with their armloads of vintage clothes. Not to mention all the cheerful people carrying around Cousin Ginnie's telltale lavender and silver bags.

And Cousin Ginnie herself. I'd have to ask Michael later what he'd said to Morris. Evidently it worked. For the last several hours, he and Ginnie had been minding the booth as a team, beaming merrily every time they rang up a sale and giggling together in between times. Planning new feats of lingerie shopping with the proceeds, perhaps. At least they were happy.

So what if some of our customers took their purchases back to languish unused in houses already filled with clutter? Not my fault. If they hadn't come to our yard sale, they'd have found another. I resolved to work on being grateful for the gift of empty space we were getting from the sale, and not condemning people with different attitudes toward stuff.

Maybe that was a decorating theme I could give Mother. Stencil William Morris's motto in the front hall: "Have nothing in your houses that you do not know to be useful or believe to be beautiful." And then work on matching the rest of the décor to that philosophy.

When I reached the back door, I turned to survey the crowd and realized that one of the few people I hadn't spotted was Carol McCoy. I pulled out the cell phone and tried her number again. No answer. Not a problem. We'd tackle her tonight.

I cringed when I glanced at our makeshift kitchen table and saw a large shopping bag sporting a tag with my name written on it in large, loopy letters. An elegant lavender bag decorated with silver hearts. I considered ignoring it—I wasn't sure I wanted to know which of Cousin Ginnie's fripperies someone thought I would like. Then again, better to get it over with while Cousin Ginnie was still here and could take returns.

I peered in and breathed a sign of relief when I found it wasn't lingerie, but cosmetics. A small ocean of Rose Noir's handmade cosmetics, all scented with lavender, rose, or lavender and rose. Bath salts, bath oils, powder, body lotion, shampoo, room spray—the works.

I picked up the business card tucked under one corner of the bag. A note on the back read, "Thanks for letting me participate in the yard sale—RN." And the card now read Rose Noire. I had to look close to see that the final "e" was inked in, so carefully had it been done.

"Good grief," I said. "I hope Mother didn't traumatize her too badly."

Okay, Rose Noire didn't surrender unconditionally. Nestled at the very bottom was a small brown bottle marked: "Eau de Meg. Ingredients: cinnamon, cloves, and just a hint of very, very light musk."

I wondered briefly if Rose Noire had been shopping at Ginnie's booth, or just borrowed a bag. Not something I needed to know. I grabbed the bag—I needed both hands to lift it—and took it with me to the second floor, where for the next hour I proceeded to set a terrible example as a hostess by hogging the bathroom and using up a good portion of the available hot water.

I then retired into the master bedroom. I didn't expect to nap, but I rested, soothed by the welcome sounds of car doors slamming out in the yard, and car engines disappearing in the distance. The occasional baaing of sheep made me tense up at first. But once I decided that each baa meant another of Farmer Early's sheep returning to the fold, I found them soothing—all the benefits of counting sheep, without the bother of arithmetic. I relaxed again. Inside the house, my relatives scuttled up and down the halls, obviously planning some sort of outing. When they knocked on the bedroom door, I played possum.

I tried to forget all about everything outside. About

Mother and her determination to decorate the house. Though I realized, with the clarity that sometimes comes on the verge of sleep, that perhaps I was being so stubborn because it felt as if she wanted to design not just our house but our entire lives. I'd try to explain that to Michael later, I thought, shoving the subject aside.

I also tried to push the murder out of mind, because I started getting angry if I thought about Endicott and Professor Schmidt and the Hummel lady all messing with the crime scene, lying to the police, and digging a deeper and deeper hole under poor Giles's feet. And, of course, I tried to forget about the yard sale.

For some reason, I found myself thinking about Sophie, the barn owl, and her mate, whom Dad had probably also named, though I didn't know what. At nightfall, the barn owls would swoop silently out into the darkness and begin their night's hunting, ridding the nearby farms of any number of rodents. Just as Michael and I would steal out after sunset to rid Caerphilly of another kind of vermin.

Of course, all Sophie had to do was swoop down and pounce on the rodents. Michael and I would be trying to track down Carol and wring the truth out of her. Probably a confession of murder, unless she pointed the finger at still another lurker in the barn. And even if she did, I wasn't sure I'd believe her. I should have seen it all along. And Chief Burke definitely should have seen it—she was always the most logical suspect.

Interrogating Carol was difficult, but she had confessed to the murder and was apologizing nicely for ruining the yard sale when someone began shouting my name and interrupting us.

"Meg?"

Okay, I'd dropped off to sleep after all, and dreamed I was interrogating Carol. Apparently counting sheep by proxy really worked. It was dusk, and Michael was shaking me awake.

"I wasn't sure I should wake you—"

"Except that you knew I'd be furious if you didn't," I said. "Come on. The game's afoot, as Sherlock Holmes and Dad would say."

Just for the heck of it, I tried calling Carol's number as we went downstairs. No answer. I didn't really expect one. I reminded myself that she wasn't deliberately trying to dodge me. Though she might be trying to dodge the police.

The house was strangely empty. Not that I was complaining. It just seemed too good to be true. Downstairs, we found Dad and Rob in the kitchen. Dad was sitting on the floor in the center of the room, doing something with aluminum foil. Rob was examining the ceiling lamp with great concentration.

"No thanks," Rob was saying. "It was a lot of fun when I was a kid, but I think you should save your pellets for Eric."

"Well, if you're sure," Dad said.

Now that I was closer, I could see that Dad was wrapping owl pellets in aluminum foil. I decided Rob had the right idea. The ceiling lamp was fascinating.

"Do you remember dissecting owl pellets when we were kids?" I asked Rob, in an undertone. "Because I don't."

"No," he said. "Unless it was so traumatic that I've blotted it out of my memory. I've never been all that keen on animal droppings."

"Owls are birds, not animals," I said. "And owl pellets aren't droppings, they're—"

"Yeah, I know," Rob said. "They barf them up. Doesn't make it a whole lot better, knowing they're owl spit instead of owl—"

"Never mind," I said. "I might want to eat again one of these days."

"Oh, that reminds me," Rob said, in a more normal voice. "Are you up for pizza at Luigi's?"

"Maybe later," I said.

"You would have to mention pizza," Michael said. "I'm trying to remember when I ate last."

"The whole family's going," Rob said. "In fact, most of them are already there. I'm just waiting for Dad to get ready."

"Later," I repeated.

"Aw, come on," Rob said. "Pizza. Celebration. What's the problem?"

"Michael and I have to be . . . elsewhere," I said.

"Right," Michael said. "Maybe we'll join you when we're back from . . . elsewhere. I'll grab something we can eat on the way."

He opened the refrigerator door and began rummaging.

"Just ignore these," Dad said, waving a foil-wrapped object. "I'll move them later."

Rob shuddered.

"You're not just leaving the cashbox lying around," Barrymore Sprocket said. I glanced over to find him standing in the doorway behind us, looking shocked and indignant.

"I thought we'd lock it up," I said. "And do the accounting in the morning."

"I was hoping to report to the family," he said, "on the results of the sale so far."

"He's got a point, Meg," Dad said. "We really ought to take care of that before we start celebrating. If you have something else to do, I'll stay behind and count it."

"And I'll help him," Barrymore said.

"But Dad—" Rob said.

"Have them put the tab on our Visa," Dad said, thereby showing that he knew the way to Rob's heart: free food. "Your mother will be there to sign. And have them deliver a pizza for us. How about a sausage and mushroom—will that work for you, Barrymore?"

I didn't stay to the end of Barrymore's explanation of what sausage would do to his stomach.

"We'll be back later," I said, and headed for the driveway.

On the way, we passed Rose Noire loading her leftover merchandise into her car. Actually, she was sitting cross-legged on a large box supervising while Officer Sammy and a gorilla-suited Horace loaded the car.

"And it's important not to let ridicule and social pressure prevent you from expressing your true nature," Rose Noire was saying. "I expect some people to laugh when I explain that in a previous life I was one of the sacred cats in the temple of Bastet."

"Narrow-minded people," Horace said. "The Egyptians considered the ape sacred to Thoth, the lord of books."

"I like cats," Sammy put in, hastily.

Michael and I waved and continued on to the car. Michael's car, which wasn't as blocked-in as mine, though we did have to drive across part of what had once been a flower bed to get out.

"That flower bed was in the wrong place anyway," I said.

"That's the spirit," Michael said. "So we're off to Carol's house," he added as he maneuvered his car off the grass and onto the driveway. "I trust you know where it is?"

"I have no idea," I said. "That's not where we're going. Head for the Spare Attic."

"It'll be closed by now," Michael said, but he didn't argue with me, and at the end of our driveway he turned right, not left. A left turn on our small rural road took us to civilization, or at least to the town of Caerphilly, and from there we could pick up the main roads that led west to Richmond, south to Yorktown, or north to D.C. A right turn led us even farther out into the countryside until the road finally dead-ended five miles away at Caerphilly Creek. Apart from the nearby farmers and anyone unfortunate enough to be living in converted 1920s motel rooms at the ramshackle Whispering Pines Cabins, the only reason anyone ever had for going past our house was to visit the Spare Attic.

Chapter 37

The Spare Attic was a clever name for a fairly utilitarian place. The same local businessman who'd turned the Whispering Pines Cabins from a hot sheets motel into a residential hotel soon realized that many of his unfortunate clients had more stuff than they could possibly fit into their dinky cabins. So he'd bought the old abandoned Brakenridge textile mill, dirt cheap; thrown up inexpensive chain-link partitions in the central factory floor; and rented out the resulting storage units at exorbitant prices.

At least he'd tried to charge exorbitant prices until a lack of renters forced him to realize that apart from the tenants at the cabins, not many people wanted to rent his bins.

When old Ezekiel Brakenridge, Ginevra's father, had built the factory in the nineteenth century, he'd doubtless put it on the banks of Caerphilly Creek for a good reason, though I didn't know whether he needed the creek for power or just liked to have a convenient source of running water to pollute. But the mill was even farther from town than we were—probably about fifteen miles. However much people in town needed storage space, most of them balked at driving that far for a bin. And the people nearby were mostly farmers who had plenty of barns and outbuildings for storage—as we would, once the Sprockets were out of our lives and we could bring our possessions onto the property without the risk that Barrymore and his kin would redefine them as Sprocket family heirlooms. So for now we'd rented a bin for our overflow stuff. At least the stuff that wouldn't suffer from the Spare Attic's lack of sophisticated climate controls—in fact, its almost complete lack of any heat or air conditioning whatsoever.

I considered it a benefit that only about half the units were rented. The slow pace of business had forced the landlord to postpone his plans to erect a second, third, and fourth tier of bins atop the original tier. Given his reputation for shoddy construction, I hoped we wouldn't need a bin by the time the upper tiers rose and then inevitably collapsed.

Or by the time the owner realized that a few well-placed sparks could turn his sagging business into a lucrative insurance claim.

But in the meantime, it was just what we needed for our temporary overflow.

And probably just what Gordon needed to hide any number of valuable assets from the covetous Carol.

"No one here," Michael said, as we pulled up.

"That's good," I said. "Let's find someplace to hide the car."

"There's an old dirt road that goes down by the river," Michael said, "popular with the more wayward students as a lover's lane."

"That should work as a hiding place," I said. "And you know about this lover's lane because . . . ?"

"Prudish members of the administration periodically try to make being caught there punishable by expulsion," he said, with a grin. "Forcing wild-eyed radicals like me to battle these encroaching forces of repression."

"Now I know why you're so popular with the students," I said. "And if we run into any of your wayward students?"

"On Sunday night?" he said. "They'll all be home trying to do their Monday class assignments at the last minute."

"It's been a few years since you were student, hasn't it?" I said, with a laugh.

"Not that long," he said. "So if we run into anyone, just do your best to look furtive and disheveled. In fact, now that they've cleaned it up, I heard Caerphilly Creek is quite lovely by moonlight. If we have time before Carol arrives . . ."

"Perhaps after we deal with Carol," I said.

He pulled the car off the lane at a picturesque spot where the creek widened and deepened into a tree-shaded pool that made me wish momentarily that it was still summer and warm enough for skinny-dipping. Then I focused back on the task at hand.

I grabbed my key ring, in case the key to our bin proved useful, and a flashlight, since the sky was not only moonless but rapidly clouding over. We both had our cell phones, of course, in case we wanted to report Carol, though I hoped we could pick her brain first. We crept back up the lane to the Spare Attic and found a place to hide behind an abandoned Dumpster.

"So why are we after Carol," Michael asked, in a whisper, once we were settled. "And why do we expect her to show up here?"

I brought him up to date on my day's snooping, as he called it.

"Incredible," he said. "Three people wander into a crime scene and can think of nothing better to do than mess it up. No wonder the chief's having a hard time getting to the truth."

"Well, I don't think the Hummel lady realized it was a crime scene," I said.

"No, but Ralph Endicott and Arnold Schmidt did," he said. "And how do we know any of them are telling the truth?"

"We know the Hummel lady is telling the truth because of Schmidt," I said. "And what Endicott said validates Schmidt's story."

"And makes Carol look like a murderer," he said.

"Unless Endicott's lying."

"True," he said. "And if you ask me, we should keep looking at Endicott. His story's rather suspicious, isn't it? Being harassed by Gordon's creditors doesn't sound like much of a motive for murder, does it?"

"You suspect him because he doesn't have much of a motive?"

"I suspect him because even though he doesn't have much of a motive, he still hid the body. I think there's more going on that we don't know about."

"Sorry," I said. "That's all I could find out."

"Hey, you did better then Chief Burke."

"Still, we remain suspicious of Endicott until we find out whether Carol's story validates or contradicts his."

"And if her story contradicts his, how do we decide who to believe?"

"I'll worry about that when we get there," I said. "First we have to find Carol."

"And what if Carol points the finger at yet another of our yard sale customers?"

"Then we'll hunt them down next," I said. "And badger them until we have the truth."

Just then we heard a car approaching. We drew back behind the Dumpster and watched as a battered Toyota Corolla crawled slowly across the parking lot and disappeared down the dirt lane.

"Preparing their Monday class assignments," I said, nodding.

"I hope they don't grab the swimming hole," Michael grumbled.

"I just hope they don't recognize your car."

We both burst out laughing at that, and were still suppressing the occasional giggle when we heard another engine.

The hulking shape of a large SUV turned into the parking lot and pulled up in front of the old factory's front entrance. I couldn't tell the make or color in the dark, but when its door opened, the dome light let me recognize the person inside.

"Carol," I whispered.

We watched as she got out of the car, wearing a black-and-white warm-up suit and pink-and-white running shoes so clean they practically glowed, even in the near darkness. What the well-dressed amateur burglar will wear. She looked all around to see if she was being watched—a fairly useless maneuver when you're the one holding a flashlight in the middle of an unlighted parking lot. Then she tiptoed over to one of the tall, multipaned windows that filled most of the front of the building. She glanced around again, and then pulled out the crowbar that she'd been unsuccessfully trying to conceal beneath the warm-up jacket.

"I've always wondered if this place had a security alarm," Michael murmured.

"I haven't," I said. "I just figure we're lucky it has four walls and a roof that doesn't leak all that much."

Carol looked up at the window. She could probably reach the glass with the crowbar, but climbing in would be a challenge.

Evidently Carol had done her homework. She returned to her SUV and hauled out a small stepladder. She set it up beneath the window and climbed up, so she had a much more comfortable angle for wielding the crowbar, and then she bashed in enough of the panes and surrounding window frame to create a hole large enough to let her enter.

"Okay, so either it's a silent alarm or there's no security," I said.

"Let's go," Michael said.

"Hang on a second," I said, tugging at his sleeve.

A few seconds later, the front door opened. Carol stuck her head out, looked around, and vanished inside.

"Now let's go," I said.

"Why would she do that?" Michael asked.

"Maybe she's not just planning to inventory Gordon's stuff," I said. "Maybe she's planning to haul stuff away, now that she's found it. Why carry things down the ladder if you can just march right out the front door?"

We darted across the open space between the Dumpster and the front door and crept inside.

There was a small vestibule inside the door, and beyond it, an archway led to the cavernous three-story main body of the former factory. A light came on in the open area. Not a lot of light, but enough that Carol could spot us if we weren't careful. Michael and I stayed in the vestibule and peeked out to see what Carol would do.

Chapter 38

The old factory building looked a lot different by night.

By day, and as long as the temperature wasn't extreme, it wasn't all that unpleasant. It had been built with great banks of windows, to save on lighting costs, which meant that during the day, natural light filled the huge central area. But now, with only a few widely spaced 25-watt bulbs providing light, it was uninviting. In fact, downright spooky.

I'd have turned on my flashlight if I wasn't afraid of Carol spotting us. We waited to see what she would do.

Ahead of us, Carol turned on her own flashlight and started down the first aisle, waving the flashlight from side to side in what appeared to be a pointless fashion, until I realized that she was checking the bin numbers on either side as she went. As she swung the flashlight back and forth, huge chain-link shadows loomed up and subsided around us, along with a variety of other odd shadows, harder to identify and thus infinitely more sinister. Although they'd probably turn out to be odd bits of furniture and little-used skis and exercycles. I wondered, briefly, how much of the stuff at our yard sale had come from these bins or others like them; and how much would end up here after a year or so. Ah, well. Not my problem.

Following Carol would be tricky. The chain-link dividers provided security, but not a lot of cover. Here and there, a bin tenant with a more highly developed sense of privacy—or possibly something definite to hide—had hung curtains of some kind inside their bin, so you couldn't readily see the contents. The curtained-off bins would provide a little cover, but not necessarily enough.

"Let's go," Michael whispered, as the light moved away from us.

"Not yet," I whispered back. "She's on the wrong aisle. She'll figure that out any second now and turn around."

"What if we lose her?" He was visibly twitching to follow.

"We won't lose her," I said. "I know where she's going, and no matter whether she's taking stuff or just doing an inventory, it'll take time. Besides, this is the only exit, unless she wants to smash a few more window panes."

Sure enough, a few seconds later, the swaying light steadied and headed back our way. We pulled back into the shadows of the vestibule and watched as Carol emerged from the first aisle. She checked the numbers at the head of the second and third aisles, and then disappeared, correctly, down the fourth.

"Come on," I whispered, as I slipped out into the open area.

We crept along the aisle, keeping a safe distance behind Carol. Her flashlight beam continued to swing back and forth until she was about two-thirds of the way down the aisle. Then it steadied, and I heard keys rattling. Michael and I stopped and crouched in the shadows about twenty feet away.

"Now?" Michael whispered.

"Not quite," I said.

I waited until I heard the hinges creak as the chain-link door opened. Then I stood up and turned on my own flashlight. Carol froze when the beam hit her. She was holding a key ring in her hands, and had just hooked the open padlock on the chain link of the door.

"Carol, Carol," I said. "Closing time was hours ago."

She shaded her eyes with her hands, trying to see us.

"Chief Burke won't like this," Michael said.

"I bet he will," I said. "He's been looking for the keys that were taken from Gordon's body."

It was only a guess, but I saw from the way she winced that I was right.

"Let's just give him a call," I said.

"Roger," Michael said, taking out his cell phone.

"No, please," Carol said. "Let me explain."

"Okay," I said. "Start explaining."

"Just an idea," Michael said. "But why don't we take the explaining outside? Just in case anyone has already called the cops about Carol's unauthorized entry."

"Good idea," I said. "First, give me Gordon's keys."

I stepped closer to Carol and held out my hand. She balked, but finally surrendered them. I took them from her, using the hem of my shirt, to avoid messing up any fingerprints or leaving any, and got Michael to give me his handkerchief to wrap them in.

Gordon was one of the sneaky few who'd curtained his bin. Not surprising. He had one of the largest-size bins, and while most of the stuff in it was packed in boxes or shrouded under tarps, the few things I could see didn't look like cheap junk. Carol would probably be much wealthier as a widow than she would have been as a divorcee. Assuming she wasn't also a murderer. The jury was still out on that.

I closed the door to Gordon's bin and clicked the padlock shut.

"Lead the way," I said to Michael.

We set off, with him preceding Carol and me following. Halfway down the aisle, a sudden thought hit me.

"Stop for a second," I said. "Did I lock up?"

"Yes, of course," Michael said.

"Are you sure?" I said, raising my eyebrows and hoping Michael got the message. "I'm not sure the padlock clicked."

"Well, not absolutely sure," Michael said, looking puzzled, but deciding to agree with me.

"I'm not either," I said. "I'll check; you and Carol wait outside."

I ran back to Gordon's bin, unlocked it, and rummaged around for a few minutes. It didn't take me long to find a box, near the front, with GBP lettered on it with a thick, black Magic Marker. Sure enough, it contained a stack of old, musty poetry books. I opened one at random and saw FROM THE LIBRARY OF MRS. GINEVRA BRAKENRIDGE PRUITT, printed in old English lettering on an ornate Victorian bookplate.

Although I knew I shouldn't take the time, I couldn't resist flipping through a few pages of the book—a fairly conventional poetry anthology from the turn of the century, featuring all the usual names. Suddenly I noticed that someone had been scribbling, in ink, on one of James Russell Lowell's poems. I had to choke back laughter when I realized that the unknown book defacer had been hard at work changing nouns, adjectives, and verbs, transforming Lowell's "What Is So Rare as a Day in June" into the far more pedestrian "What Is So Fine as a Morn in May."

I flipped through a few more pages, spellbound by Mrs. Pruitt's temerity. Surely eminent poets throughout the English-speaking world must have rolled over in their graves when she published these travesties. In fact, so many of them must have been spinning so rapidly that I was surprised no scientist had yet spotted a correlation between Mrs. Pruitt's publication dates and periods of unusual seismic activity.

"Hail to you! Proud student!" (presumably written on the occasion of someone's graduation) would have made the normally blithe spirit of Percy Bysshe Shelley wince. Lord Byron would probably have consulted his solicitor upon reading what she did to "She Walks in Beauty," but I suspect Edgar Allan Poe would only roll his eyes upon reading "Once upon a midnight bleak, while I studied, tired and weak." Then again, maybe he'd have hit her up for beer money. And probably have gone thirsty, judging from her revision of Tennyson's "The Lotus-Eaters" into a tract in favor of Prohibition. (" 'Temperance!' he cried, and pointed at the bar, 'My trusty axe will bring that downward soon.' ")

I snapped the book shut, realizing I'd already spent too much time on it. At least now I had that much more confirmation of Professor Schmidt's story. And since the bin where Michael and I were storing our stuff was only one aisle over and a few bins down, I decided to make sure the box didn't disappear, just in case we didn't have the only set of keys.

After locking Mrs. Pruitt's books in our bin, I hurried out to the parking lot. It suddenly occurred to me that if Carol tried to escape, Michael wasn't the best person to have guarding her. I'd have no qualms about knocking her down and sitting on her if necessary, but Michael might have a sudden attack of chivalry.

Chapter 39

"All secure," I reported, when I emerged into the parking lot.

Carol and Michael stood face to face, beaming their flashlights at each other. Carol's feet were planted firmly and she frowned at Michael. His back was to me, and he appeared to be pointing something at her, in addition to the flashlight. Okay, I knew he hadn't brought a weapon, but I didn't know about Carol. What if after I'd left them alone, she'd pulled a gun and he'd had to disarm her? Then I relaxed. He wasn't holding her at gunpoint. More like cell-phone-point.

"Carol was thinking of leaving," he said, as I came closer. "But I convinced her to stay and talk to you first."

"If you call the cops, I'll tell them you were trespassing, too," she said.

"But we were following you, Carol," I said, aiming my flashlight at her face. "And we are bona fide customers. You, on the other hand, appear to have broken into the building and used a stolen key to access someone else's bin."

"It's all mine now," she said.

"Only if you didn't kill Gordon," I said.

"How could I possibly kill him?" she hissed.

"You were in the barn with him," I said.

"I was not!"

"Then why did Ralph Endicott say he saw you leaving?"

"He didn't!"

"He did, and he's not the only one who saw you there," I said. "I saw you there myself. So give me one reason to believe you didn't kill him."

"I couldn't have!" she wailed.

"Why not? He cheated on you, and now he was trying to cheat you out of your fair share of the property by hiding half his assets in there," I said, jerking my head at the building. "Why couldn't you have killed him?"

"Because he was already dead when I got there!"

"Not another one," Michael muttered.

"But you told Chief Burke you talked to him," I said. "You were fairly specific about your conversation. I heard you. Are you saying you lied to the cops?"

She sighed and slumped as if suddenly exhausted.

"I figured if I claimed to have found him dead, they'd think I did it," she said. "Don't they always suspect the person who finds the body?"

"It's not as if you were the only one to find the body," I said. "People spent the entire morning finding it and hiding it again."

"They did? Well, how was I to know that?" she said. "I was standing there, looking at his dead body, and all I could think of was that everyone in town knew how much I hated him. Half of them had heard me threaten him, when I'd lost my temper. I figured if they found me with the body, they wouldn't bother looking for the real killer. I was terrified. Hysterical. So I ran out."

"Without even thinking about what you should do."

"Exactly!" she exclaimed.

"But not before taking his keys."

"Out of his pocket, no doubt," Michael added. "Must have been pretty tough, hysterical as you were. Reaching down, touching the body of a dead man—a murdered man—and hunting around until you found his keys."

"I didn't have to hunt," she said. "I knew he kept them in his right back pocket. He was lying on his face; I didn't even have to move his body."

Despite the dim light, she must have read the look on my face.

"Not much, anyway. Okay, it was pretty awful, having to roll him over like that, but I figured it was my one chance to find out what the bastard was hiding from me, and where he was keeping it. I'd been trying for over a year, and that damned lawyer of his kept blocking everything I did."

"But why were you still so worried about finding his hidden assets?" I asked. "You didn't have to worry about losing out on the property settlement. All you had to do was inherit."

Unless he'd made a will that disinherited her, of course. But I had a hard time imagining Gordon being that organized, and I suspected, from the look on her face, that she felt the same way.

"Yeah, whoever killed him did you a big favor," I went on. "Unless you did yourself a big favor."

"I say she looks good for it," Michael snarled, in his best imitation of a hard-bitten PI from a noir flick. I had to pretend to cough to cover my grin, but Carol took him quite literally.

"I didn't do it, I tell you!" she wailed.

"Give us a reason to believe you," I said.

"You won't believe me," she said, shaking her head. "No one will."

"We might if you told the truth about what you did and saw in the barn," Michael said.

"Especially if you saw anything that would help identify the real culprit," I said.

She looked back and forth between the two of us, the flashlight beam moving with her head.

"I saw someone taking something from Gordon's body," she said. "His wallet. And then he slipped out the other door, just as I came in."

"Who was it?" I asked.

"You see!" she exclaimed. "I knew you wouldn't believe me."

"I didn't say I didn't believe you," I said. "I just asked who you saw."

"It was your tone of voice," she said, pouting. "You're using a very hostile, accusing tone of voice."

"That's probably because I feel slightly hostile," I said. "After all, you just admitted that you saw someone leaving the murder scene with Gordon's wallet in his hands and you didn't do a thing about it."

"Why should I?" she said. "It's not as if Gordon ever had much in his wallet worth stealing. Probably a few dollars and his famous rubber checkbook."

"It never occurred to you that the person you saw might have done more than steal the wallet—that he might have been Gordon's killer?"

"Of course," she said. "But what if the chief didn't believe me? And what if the killer did? Do you think I want a cold-blooded killer knowing I'm the only witness who can put him away?"

"So you say nothing, and let a cold-blooded killer roam the streets while an innocent man rots in jail," I said.

"He's not in jail," Carol said. "He's out on bail."

"No thanks to you," I said. "I know why you didn't tell anyone—you just wanted to get a chance to snoop in Gordon's stuff, and you didn't care what happened to anyone else. So who was it?"

"Who was who?"

"Who took Gordon's wallet?" I snapped.

"I don't know!" she said.

She took a step back. Probably because she'd seen my free hand clutch involuntarily into a fist.

"Try again," I suggested.

"I don't know his name."

"Describe him, then."

"It was that creepy little man who was helping you run the yard sale," she said.

Creepy little man? The only men who'd been helping me, apart from Michael, were Dad and Rob, and while they both had their detractors, I couldn't imagine anyone calling either of them a creepy little man.

"What creepy little man?" Michael asked.

"That Lionel Barrymore person," she said.

"Barrymore Sprocket?" I asked.

"That's the one," she said.

"And you didn't even bother mentioning this!" I exclaimed. "If you had, they would never have arrested Giles! Tell me exactly what you saw."

"Meg," Michael began. I gestured for him to be quiet. We had Carol talking; why interrupt her?

"I didn't really see anything else," she said.

"Meg—we really need to go back to the house," Michael said.

"But—"

"Meg," Michael said. "Barrymore Sprocket was helping your father count the yard sale proceeds, remember?"

Chapter 40

"Oh, great," I said. "We've probably left Dad alone with the murderer."

"I'll go get the car," Michael said, running toward where we'd hidden it.

"Give me your car keys," I said to Carol. I shoved my flashlight into my pocket and held out my right hand while pulling out my cell phone with the left.

"Use your own car," she said, hugging her purse to her body.

"We're using our own car," I said, as I dialed 911. "You're waiting here for the police, and I'm taking your car keys with me to make sure you do it."

Carol picked that moment, when I was distracted and the light from Michael's flashlight was disappearing into the distance, to turn off her own flashlight and make a run for it.

"Oh, no you don't!" I yelled, launching myself at her.

Apparently the 911 operator answered the call while I was airborne.

"A-a-i-i-e-e!!"

Carol screamed when I knocked her down, and kept screaming at intervals while I relieved her of her keys and hunted through the leaves and gravel of the parking lot for her flashlight and my cell phone. As a screamer, she was right up there with Fay Wray for volume and drama but, luckily for me, she tended to go all out on each scream and then have to rest and catch her breath for long seconds. In between her screams, I convinced Debbie Anne down at the police station that Carol was merely hysterical, and that the real danger was at the old Sprocket farm, which was what most locals still called our house.

"I'll send someone over as soon as possible," she said.

"Can't you get word to any of the officers who are still at the crime scene?" I asked.

"Oh, Meg, I'm sorry," Debbie Anne said. "When the chief gave the go-ahead for y'all to resume your yard sale, he took away some of the officers, and the rest all came back with Mr. Early when they arrested him. I think he sent everyone home for a good long rest. Even Sammy called in to say he was going home, now that all the sheep were back. But don't you worry; I've sent pages out to every single one."

Wonderful.

"Just tell them to hurry," I said. "Before there's another murder."

Carol was still screaming, though with increasingly longer rest periods, when Michael pulled up, spraying gravel all the way to the front door of the building. He didn't stop—just slowed down and threw the door open, and he hit the accelerator about a second after I landed in the passenger's seat, with my cell phone and both sets of confiscated keys still in hand.

"Are those Carol's keys?" he asked.

"And Gordon's, too," I said. "Damn! Dad's cell phone isn't answering. We really need a phone at the house. Damn the Sprockets, anyway."

"What about Rob? Or your mother?"

"Trying them," I said. In fact I was cycling through the entire family phone list, with no luck.

Just by way of a change, I dialed a few Sprockets whose numbers I had in my cell phone, and on the third try I reached a Sprocket instead of an answering machine.

"Do you know where Barrymore is?" I said, cutting off his complaints about being awakened.

"Barrymore?" the sleepy Sprocket said. "Still locked up in Deep Meadow where he belongs, I hope. Why?"

I hung up.

"Barrymore's a jailbird," I said. I recognized Deep Meadow as one of the Virginia State prisons.

I tried Chief Burke's direct line, only to find myself forwarded to the dispatch office. Debbie Anne gave me another perky reassurance that she was sure one of the officers on patrol would be there any minute.

"Any minute," Michael repeated, when I relayed this to him. "We'll be there any minute ourselves."

"Damn," I said. "I should have talked to Sprocket. I'd almost forgotten that he'd even been in the barn."

"Don't blame yourself," Michael said, as he rounded a corner on two wheels.

"But I should have remembered it," I said. "And I know why I forgot. He came over and told me that he couldn't make Gordon leave the barn, so I should go and do it. And I had no reason to suspect him, because when he did it, I didn't even know Gordon was dead."

"And he probably did."

"He definitely knew, the bastard, because he probably did it. And what's more, I bet he was trying to set me up to be the one who found the body."

"Didn't succeed, though," Michael said.

"He did succeed in making me think he was harmless."

The house was in sight now. And completely dark, except for a single light in the kitchen. Apart from my car, there were only two vehicles in the driveway. Both apparently belonged to some relative or other; I'd seen them around for the past several days. Under other circumstances, I'd have been thrilled to find the road outside our house empty except for the deep, muddy ruts along both sides, and the yard littered only with debris, and not with hundreds of people. But now, I swore as I wondered what had happened to the several dozen relatives who'd been underfoot every minute of the last week. Had they all gone out to eat pizza on Dad's tab? I hoped he was with them.

The only unusual note was the sheep lying in the middle of our driveway, placidly chewing its cud.

"Damn!" Michael said, as he braked and swerved onto the grass to avoid it. "I thought Sammy said he'd gotten them all back."

"Maybe he miscounted, or maybe Farmer Early did," I said. "We'll worry about her later."

"Just what we need," Michael muttered. "More sheep thrills."

I ignored him. I was racing up the steps to the front door by this time, with Michael on my heels. I pulled out my keys to get in, but Michael reached past me and shoved the door open.

The front door unlocked and hanging open—I didn't like the looks of this.

"Hello?" I called. "Anyone home?"

I heard only echoes. I ran back to the kitchen. Empty.

"Shall I call Luigi's?" Michael asked.

I shook my head and pointed to the half-eaten sausage and mushroom pizza on the table. Evidently Dad had gotten his favorite pizza after all.

I walked back into the central hallway and listened. Apart from Michael's footsteps as he moved from the kitchen to the dining room and then the living room, I could hear nothing but the muted sounds of insects outdoors. Quiet. Too quiet; why weren't we hearing police sirens by now?

"Dad?" I called up the stairs.

I raced through the upstairs floors while Michael checked the basement. We met again in the kitchen.

"Do you suppose he finished counting the money and went to Luigi's?" Michael suggested. "Maybe that's why the carryout pizza's not finished. I'll call and check."

"Maybe I should check the yard sale area," I said, peering out, though the entire yard was dark and still.

"Hello, Mrs. Langslow!" Michael said. "No, not now—something's come up. Look, is Dr. Langslow there? Damn. Sorry. What about Barrymore Sprocket?"

Or was something moving in the yard, I wondered. I pulled the curtain aside to get a better look. I realized I'd left my flashlight in the car, and turned to get it. I'd need it for searching the yard.

"Your mother says your dad and Barrymore still haven't gotten there, and they assumed they were still here counting the money," Michael said, with his hand over the mouthpiece. "Shall I call the police and tell them—"

"Eeeeeeeeeeeeeeee!"

Chapter 41

Michael almost dropped his phone when a bloodcurdling shriek pierced the night. I bolted for the back door.

"That came from the barn!" I said.

"We should wait for the cops," Michael said, though I noticed that he was sprinting after me rather than following his own advice.

"Eeeeeeeeeeeeeee!"

"I'm not standing around waiting for the cops while Barrymore Sprocket commits another murder!" I said, just as I slammed into another sheep.

"Careful!" Michael said, a little late.

I planned to have a word with Sammy about his sheep counting abilities, next time I saw him. The sheep baaed reproachfully, scrambled back to its feet, and sauntered off. I had to catch my breath again before I could get up, and Michael beat me to the gate.

As we stumbled through the yard sale area toward the barn door, I berated myself for leaving the flashlight behind. There was still plenty of junk to stumble over. We plowed through the junk by brute force, and I was sure both my shins were bleeding by the time we made it to the barn.

We burst inside and by the faint light of a fallen flashlight on the ground we saw Dad, bound with clothesline and gagged with packing tape, lying in the middle of the open center area.

"Dr. Langslow," Michael said, dropping down beside him. "Are you okay?"

"Take his pulse," I said. "Better yet, keep your eyes peeled for Barrymore Sprocket, and I'll take his pulse."

"Right," Michael said. He stood up, and I could see him looking around for a weapon.

Dad's pulse was steady, and after a few moments, his eyelids fluttered.

"Dad," I said. "What happened?"

"Growf!"

We all jumped—well, Michael and I, at least—and turned to see Spike, stumbling clumsily out of his bed and stalking toward us, growling. Which wasn't unusual—Spike tended to be even grouchier when he woke up than the rest of the time. Not the first time I'd been glad to have a fence between us.

Dad made noises.

"Hang on a minute, Dad, I'll rip the gag off."

"Ow!" he exclaimed. And then his face grew serious. "No! Look out!" he pointed with his chin.

Michael and I whirled, and Michael raised the weapon he'd found—a broken bicycle tire pump. But Dad appeared to be pointing at Spike.

"Eeeeeee!"

The shriek again, but not as loud now. And coming from someplace outside the barn.

"It's only an owl," Michael said, lowering the bicycle pump slightly. "I think."

"A great horned owl," Dad said.

"Dad, what happened?" I asked, as I worked at the knot in the rope on his wrists. "Who tied you up?"

Though I suspected I already knew the answer. Glancing around, I saw three plastic milk crates placed upside down, as if someone had been using them for tables or stools. Our cash box lay on the middle one, its lid open and all its compartments bare.

"Sshh!" Dad said, putting his finger to his lips. "Barrymore. Went thataway!"

He pointed to the barn door—the back door, not the one we'd come in.

We heard a clank outside, as if someone had tripped over a saucepan.

Michael and I looked at each other.

"Can you untie your ankles, Dad?" I said. "While Michael and I see if we can catch him."

Dad nodded cheerfully, though he didn't lean down to begin working on his feet. Instead, he lay back and stared solemnly up at the rafters, as if looking for something important. I grabbed Dad's flashlight, but turned it off. No sense letting Barrymore know precisely where we were.

Well, help should be on the way—should damn well be here already, for that matter—and the most important thing was to keep Barrymore Sprocket from doing any more damage, I thought, as Michael and I crept out of the barn.

I heard another faint clang from the far side of the yard sale enclosure. I smiled to myself. Barrymore appeared to be stumbling away from the gate, rather than toward it. Perhaps he'd taken a wrong turn on his way out of the barn.

He'd need to get back to the gate to leave. So maybe we should just make our way to the gate and wait for him to stumble into our hands.

Unless he planned to pull up a couple of the stakes

holding the fence to the ground. If he tried enough of them, he might find a couple that were loose enough to give way. Or he could cut a hole in the fence. Maybe that was the noise we were hearing—Barrymore making himself a new gate.

I moved forward, and I could hear Michael, a few feet to my right, following suit.

We had the advantage of numbers. But Barrymore had the advantage of the terrain, I realized, as I knocked over something that sounded like a stack of aluminum pie pans. He was the proverbial needle in the haystack. We probably couldn't see him unless we got right next to him, and he could easily slip by us while we stumbled in the dark.

Then again, Barrymore couldn't see any better than we could. Which meant there was always the possibility that we'd all three stumble around the fenced-in area till dawn, like inept players in a giant game of blindman's bluff.

One of us should watch the gate.

I turned around and headed back, but I must have gotten off course, because after about three feet, I ran into the deer fence.

Over to my left, I could hear Michael getting tangled in a nest of coat hangers dangling from something overhead.

Or was that Michael, knocking over the stack of glass objects to my right?

Long moments of silence followed as we all stood still and tried not to breathe too loudly.

Chapter 42

My eyes had adjusted to the dark. If I got close enough, I could see objects silhouetted against the sky. Not clearly—the sky was only a shade lighter than the objects. But I could see vague shapes looming up ahead of me as I moved around.

Unfortunately, this didn't help me navigate safely through the clutter, since most of the things lying in wait to trip me crouched close to the ground, where I couldn't see their silhouettes. It wasn't even reassuring, since to my overactive imagination most of the looming shapes looked remarkably like thugs wielding cudgels.

I steered by sound, aiming for a point midway between the coat hanger sound and the breaking glass sound.

The figure to my left knocked over a lamp—I heard the light bulb explode on impact with something hard.

The figure to my left tripped over something, fell, and muttered, "Damn!"

I couldn't tell if it was Michael or Barrymore. And apparently we'd all three stopped to listen.

All I heard was a sheep baaing, as if startled. Closer

than I expected. Had the sheep gotten inside the yard sale fence? If they did, they could do a terrific amount of damage. We'd probably have to throw a ton of stuff away.

Yay, sheep.

Just then, I heard someone stumble a few feet ahead and to my left.

"Michael?" I called.

"Over here," came his voice, from somewhere behind me.

Something slammed into me, hard, and knocked me into a pile of stuff.

"Get him," I shouted.

I heard clanking and scrambling behind me as Michael gave chase. From my new position, flat on my back, I realized that I'd been felled by the portable toilet door, which someone hiding inside had suddenly slammed open to make a run for it. And when I fell, I'd knocked over a large plastic bin. I was lying in a heap of spilled toys. Every time I tried to get up, I'd slip on some of the marbles, and every time I fell again, another half dozen toy soldiers would bayonet me with their tiny sharp weapons.

And then, when I paused to catch my breath, I realized that I could still hear the clacking of marbles and the faint grunts that suggested the miniature soldiers might also be attacking someone else, perhaps six feet away.

Barrymore.

I waited a few seconds until I was sure I had a fix on his position, and then launched myself toward him. I wasn't trying to stand up, just land on top of him, so this time the marbles helped.

"Oof!" he exclaimed, as I knocked the breath out of him.

"Got him!" I shouted, as I pulled his arm behind him and sat down on his back.

"Hang on!" Michael shouted.

"Meg!" my captive gasped. "It's me! Rob!"

I switched on the flashlight to reveal the swollen face of my brother. I hoped the swelling was only left over from his allergy attack, and not something I'd done.

"What happened to you?" I asked, standing up.

"I've been stumbling around trying to find whoever tied up Dad," Rob said. "I keep falling over stuff."

"Barrymore Sprocket," Michael said.

"Is that who it is?" Rob said.

"If we've been chasing Rob, then where's Sprocket?" Michael said.

I played the flashlight beam over the junk around us. Michael and Rob held their breath.

"Not out here," I said.

"Then where—"

Just then, we heard a yelp of pain from the barn, followed by frantic barking.

"Spike?" Michael muttered, turning his head toward the sounds.

"Dad?" Rob said, sitting up.

"Barrymore!" I exclaimed, and sprinted for the barn, closely followed by Michael. Rob, apparently, had injured his foot in falling, and followed more slowly.

Inside we found Dad, still lying peacefully on his back, looking at Spike's pen, where Barrymore Sprocket was backed up against the barn wall, ducking left and right in a vain attempt to dodge Spike so he could reach the fence and make a break for freedom.

"Stop where you are and I'll call him off," I said.

"The police are on their way!" Michael added.

Barrymore hesitated, and perhaps he might have surrendered, but just then we heard another ghastly shriek, and a feathered missile plummeted from somewhere high up in the barn, heading for Spike.

"Look out!" I said, throwing the flashlight at the owl. Spike yelped and dived for cover, while Barrymore Sprocket seized his chance to leap over the fence.

"Leave him alone, Sophie!" Michael shouted. The owl swooped back up again, and Michael ran after her, waving the bicycle pump. I vaulted the fence and scooped up Spike.

"I've got Spike," I called. "Don't worry about Sophie—stop Barrymore."

Michael ran after Barrymore, and I ducked as another shriek announced that Sophie hadn't given up.

Only it wasn't Sophie. Instead of a small barn owl, with its winsome, heart-shaped face, a much larger owl was staring down at us from the rafters. Its beak looked sharper as well as larger, and the feathers around its face were arranged in a pattern that resembled a perpetual frown. It looked slightly cross-eyed and more than slightly annoyed, and I deduced from the large tufts of feathers sticking up on either side of its face that I was looking at a great horned owl.

"Look out!" Dad shouted. The owl moved. For some reason, I was expecting it to plummet, beak first, like a hawk. Instead, it launched itself, feet first, for all the world like a kid jumping into a pool and hoping to splash as many bystanders as possible. All that was missing was the cry of "Banzai!" Of course, it made sense. The talons were its weapons. I'd probably have stood transfixed as it flew into my face, but just then Spike bit me and made a run for it, and I tripped and fell out of the owl's path while trying to catch him. Even so, I felt the owl swoop by me; and something sharp raked my cheek. I hoped it missed my eyes. The owl swooped past, and I scrambled into the corner where Spike had retreated, putting myself between him and the owl, and grabbing his water bowl to serve as a shield. The feathered fury swooped past again, and then disappeared.

"Meg!" Michael called. "Are you all right?"

"It flew out the door," Dad said. "Magnificent!"

"I'm fine," I said. "What happened to Barrymore Sprocket?"

"I've got him," Michael said. "Where's Rob?"

"Limping around outside," I said.

I made sure both eyes were working properly, and fingered the owl gash in my cheek and the Spike bite on my arm, both of which were bleeding, though neither badly enough to kill me. I vaulted back out of the pen, grabbed one of the milk crates, and threw it down over Spike, to keep him from becoming an owl hors d'oeuvre. Then I walked over to where Michael was.

"I thought you said you had him," I said. He wasn't holding Barrymore down. He was standing at the foot of the ladder leading to the loft, staring up.

"I've got him cornered," he said. "He scurried up the ladder."

"Barrymore!" I called. "Come on down."

We stood with ears cocked toward the loft, but heard no sound from Barrymore."

"Come on," Michael called out. "You have to come down sooner or later. There's no other way out."

I heard a rattling noise from above.

"Unless he uses the rope and pulley in the hayloft door and rappels down," I said. "Which, unless I'm mistaken, is what he's doing."

"Damn," Michael said. "I'll run outside and catch him. You guard the ladder."

I took his place at the foot of the ladder, and decided that instead of just waiting, I might as well climb up. Not that I thought we had much of a chance to catch Barry-

more. It was a long way around to the hayloft door.
Maybe if it took Barrymore several minutes to get up his
nerve—

Too late. I heard a motor start up outside.

Then again, that couldn't possibly be Barrymore's car,
unless his car needed the mother of all tune-ups. It
sounded more like a small generator. I jumped off the ladder and ran to the back door, where the noise came from.

"Don't worry!" Rob called. "I've got him!"

He had climbed into the cab of the boom lift, started
its motor, and was slowly swinging the arm and extending
it, aiming the raised platform at the hay loft door. Was he
planning to catch Barrymore, crush him against the side
of the barn, or just scare him silly? Whatever he planned,
the sight of the boom lift platform creaking and lurching
toward the barn was pretty terrifying. Barrymore, who
had climbed halfway down the rope, began climbing up
again, a lot faster. He looked scared and he didn't even
know, as I did, how singularly inept my brother was with
mechanical objects. How well could Rob possibly have
learned how to operate the boom lift?

The platform hit the side of the barn a few feet below
Barrymore. The barn stayed in place, though I could hear
bits of rubble falling inside, and the impact threw Barrymore off balance. He fell six feet onto the platform, and
Rob immediately raised the arm, taking the platform
higher and higher until it was perched forty feet above the
ground at the end of the fully extended arm.

"Good job," I said, and ran back inside to make sure
Spike and Dad had survived the falling rubble.

Dad was lying peacefully, legs still bound, and I deduced from how loudly Spike was barking that he was
still safe under the plastic milk crate.

"Are you okay?" I asked Dad, as I started to untie his
legs.

"It was amazing," Dad said. "I've never seen a great horned owl that close."

"I've never wanted to," I said. "After I untie you, can you patch my cheek?"

"Are you okay?" Michael asked, running back in. "You're bleeding."

"She'll be fine," Dad said, peering at my face. "It's only a superficial laceration. Though we should clean that wound as soon as possible. Owls eat a lot of carrion, you know."

"Thanks for sharing that," I said, as I finished untying Dad's feet. "There; you're free again. Let's fix my wound."

"Should I call 911 and tell them to send an ambulance?" Michael asked.

"No, but call and ask Debbie Anne why the heck none of the police have arrived yet," I suggested.

"Wasn't that cool?" Rob asked, strolling into the barn.

"Very cool," I said. "Why aren't you keeping your eye on Barrymore?"

"Relax," Rob said. "He's forty feet in the air in the boom lift. He's not going anywhere."

As if on cue, we heard the boom lift's engine start again.

"I turned that off," Rob said, in a puzzled voice.

"And Barrymore's probably turned it back on," I said, heading for the door.

"How could he?" Rob protested. "He's up on the platform."

"There's another set of controls up on the platform," I heard Dad saying as I ran out. "So you can maneuver it from up there."

"There is?" Rob said.

Michael and I sprinted for the gate, but Barrymore had already swung the platform away from the barn and toward the driveway, lowering the boom arm as he went. By the time we cleared the gate, he was already climbing off the platform, and by the time we reached Michael's car, Barrymore's car had disappeared over the crest of the hill. At least I hoped he'd taken his own car. Odds were any car he stole would belong to one of my more easily annoyed relatives.

"We could go after him," Michael said, running around to the driver's side and trying, in vain, to shoo away the sheep that had curled up next to his door.

"We could let Chief Burke and his men go after him," I said. "Where is Chief Burke, anyway?"

"Not answering his phone, last time I tried," Michael said.

"Sorry about that," Rob said, strolling up. "I didn't know about the controls on the platform."

"What are you doing here anyway," I asked. "I thought you were in town, having pizza."

"I brought Dad his pizza," Rob said. "Did you know that Luigi's doesn't deliver this far out of town? You may want to rethink this living out in the wilderness thing."

"At last!" I exclaimed, seeing a caravan of three police cars speeding toward us.

"What in tarnation is going on out here?" Chief Burke exclaimed, leaping out of his car.

"Barrymore Sprocket attacked Dad, stole the yard sale proceeds, and went thataway," I said. "Incidentally, he's probably also Gordon McCoy's killer."

"Went thataway?" the chief repeated. "Blue Honda Accord? We'll cite him for reckless driving when one of my officers catches him. He must have been going over a hundred when he passed us. Pity we didn't know what he was up to."

"If you'd gotten here sooner . . ." I began.

"We'd have been here fifteen minutes ago if some

blasted farmer hadn't let his silly sheep get out and wander all over the road again," Chief Burke said. "If I find out who's responsible, I'll throw the book at the lazy rascal."

"We tried to call your cell phone," Michael put in. "But we didn't get an answer."

"Stupid sheep," the chief said. "Where's Dr. Langslow?"

"In the barn," I said.

The chief stormed off toward the barn.

"What's with him?" I asked Sammy. "He doesn't usually lose his cool like that."

"He dropped his cell phone while we were chasing the sheep off the road," Sammy explained, "and one of the sheep stepped on it. He's that provoked."

"So what's with the sheep, then?" I asked. "I thought people had brought them all back. Were these someone else's sheep?"

"No, they were Mr. Early's sheep," Sammy said, with a frown. "Are you sure the gate was closed?"

"Who knows?" Michael said. "And even if it was, I wonder if maybe our volunteer fence menders didn't fix it as well as they thought they did."

"A sheep fix?" I suggested. They ignored me.

"Well, maybe it will cheer up the chief if the sheep slow Barrymore Sprocket down," Michael suggested.

From the direction of the barn, we heard a crashing noise, followed by a reproachful baa.

"Blast that sheep!" the chief exclaimed.

Chapter 43

Things were quieting down again. The police were mostly gone, and a couple of neighboring farmers rounded up by Sammy fixed the break in a fence and put the sheep back in their pasture again.

The yard sale was battened down for the night—in fact, for the five days it would have to wait until its continuation next weekend. When my relatives began arriving back from Luigi's, quivering with excitement and curiosity about the night's events, I channeled their energy into rigging up some floodlights, hauling as much of the yard sale stuff as possible into the barn, and covering the rest with tarps.

When we finally finished that, everyone else drifted off to bed, but I was still too wound up to sleep.

"What's wrong?" Michael asked, when he came down to the kitchen to see why I was still up, sitting at my laptop.

"I just remembered that the truck from Goodwill was supposed to get here at eight A.M. tomorrow," I said. "To take all the unsold yard sale stuff. I just called and left a voice message apologizing for the short notice, and asking to reschedule for next Monday. I should have called sooner; they may still show up."

"Then we'll tell them to come back next week," he said. "Don't worry; they probably heard the news. They'll figure it out."

"And I e-mailed an updated version of the ad to the *Caerphilly Clarion*, asking them to run it again this Friday," I said, drawing a line through the item in my notebook. "And also an updated announcement to the college radio station. Can you think of anything else we need to do?"

"Nothing we need to do tonight," he said. "Let's worry about it tomorrow."

"I don't want to worry abut anything tomorrow," I said. "I just want to sleep late tomorrow. In fact, never mind late. I just want to sleep."

"Sounds fine."

"And then do nothing for the rest of the week."

"Also fine," he said. "Or maybe we could do something fun."

I nodded. I was shutting down the laptop. I hadn't thought of anything urgent that needed doing, and sleep was becoming really appealing.

"Maybe before your parents leave town we could go out to that antique mall with your mother and—"

"Do we have to do that this week?" I asked. "Shopping isn't usually something I do for fun, especially shopping with Mother, and right now the idea sounds only slightly less horrible than taking a bus tour of the lower three circles of hell."

"But your mother—"

"Will live if she has to go antiquing by herself."

"Fine," he said. He sounded irritated. "Just blow her off."

"Michael—"

"Couldn't you at least take an hour or two to look at what she's found?" he asked. "I only spent the whole past week hauling her around town, and listening patiently to every crazy idea she came up with and then trying to talk her out of them all without hurting her feelings. And trying to explain what we wanted instead."

"It never occurred to you just to tell her that what we want is to be left alone to do things ourselves?"

"She's your mother, dammit," he said. "I was trying to be nice to her."

"Can't we be nice to her, and also tell her nicely that we don't need a decorator right now?"

"Have you even looked at her drawings? The latest ones—the ones she's done this week, based on what I've been telling her?"

"No; she hasn't mentioned any drawings."

"She probably figures you'll reject them without even looking at them. Why do you have to be so negative? She's only trying to help."

"Oh, and that's supposed to make me feel better? That she's only trying to help; she doesn't actually set out to drive me crazy?"

"Forget it," he said, turning and striding out of the room. Something about his tone scared me.

"All right," I called after him. "If it's so damned important, I'll look at them!"

"Don't put yourself out on my account," Michael snapped back. His steps clattered down the stairway, and then I heard the front door slam.

I walked out into the hall, and then noticed that several of the visiting relatives were peering out of the doors of their rooms, and Mrs. Fenniman had crept halfway down the staircase from the third floor.

I ducked back into the room and closed the door before

any of them could ask what was wrong, where was Michael going, and had we had a fight. I hoped my relatives wouldn't come knocking on my door, trying to cheer me up by sympathizing with me and reviling Michael. Or telling me Michael was right and I was a fool for arguing with him. Worst of all, some might take Michael's side and some mine, and we could end up with an all-night debate up and down the hallway. Which, knowing my family, is probably what would have happened if it hadn't been past two A.M. already.

Should I go after Michael? Not until I was sure I had my own temper firmly under control, or I'd only make it worse. Luckily, I hadn't heard his car start. I went over to the window. He wasn't in the driveway. Maybe he'd just gone out to the barn to cool off.

I took a deep breath and decided I was calm enough to cope, so I opened my door and peered out. The lurking relatives had vanished. I emerged and went downstairs to the kitchen. I peered out the kitchen window, but I couldn't see anyone out back. More to the point, I didn't hear the inevitable noise Michael would have made, trying to find his way through the remaining clutter to the barn.

Then I spotted something on the door-turned-table, near the leftover pizza and the now-empty cash box. One of Mother's design notebooks.

I could feel my temper heating up again. But my curiosity kicked in, too. I walked over and opened it.

On the first page, in Mother's neat printing, were the words, "Preliminary designs. For discussion only. Subject to client review. No work to begin until client signoff obtained."

Okay, maybe Mother had gotten the message after all. I stifled a small inclination to feel guilty and flipped the page.

The first sketch was obviously a design for the master bedroom. I stared at it, transfixed.

Not because it was horrible. It wasn't. It wasn't bad at all. In fact, I rather liked it. It didn't really look like one of Mother's designs. It was way too simple, and there wasn't a square inch of chintz in sight. I could see elements of Japanese, Mission, and Arts and Crafts styles in it, but it wasn't completely any of those things. It was simple, serene, uncluttered, and beautiful. And at the same time, I could tell there was a lot of storage space hidden away under the serene surface, which was a really smart idea. Michael and I still had plenty of stuff, and I didn't see us getting rid of it all, no matter how much of a convert I'd become to simple living and spare, minimalist décor.

I had to hand it to Mother. She'd come up with exactly the kind of design we'd have done ourselves, if either of us had had the time to work on it. Or the talent.

Of course, if we told her to go ahead with her design, there was always the issue of whether it would look like this when she finished adding all those little touches that occurred to her along the way. And whether we could talk her into something equally to our liking for the several dozen other rooms in the house. And whether we could afford even this room. And how long we'd have her underfoot, and whether any of us would survive with our sanity intact.

Not to mention my belief that, given a chance, Michael and I could do something with the place that suited both of us just fine. It might take longer and it might not be as breathtakingly beautiful as Mother's design, but it would be our home, done by us, not merely a beautiful house that someone had decorated for us. Assuming we survived as an us. And then—

But why let quibbling spoil a beautiful moment of guilt? I owed Mother an apology. But first, and more important, I owed Michael one.

I'd been so focused on one urgent cause after another—emptying the house, organizing the yard sale, rescuing Giles—that I'd been losing sight of the real reason I was doing all this. That it was all supposed to be for us.

It would serve me right if Michael decided he'd had enough of the grouchy, hyperactive Meg he'd seen in the last few months, the commitment-phobic Meg who changed the subject every time he tried to talk seriously about our future together, the—

Of course, that was the moment when I heard a car door slam, followed by his engine starting and the screech of tires as he roared out of the driveway and down the road.

I raced back up to our room, found my purse, and ran down to my car. And then lost valuable time when I had to run back in to ransack the house for ten minutes, till I found where I'd dropped my keys instead of putting them in my purse where they belonged.

I headed for town. I didn't need to rush—I had no chance of overtaking him now. Even in his usual good temper, he'd race along the long, empty road to town. And catching up with him while he was still angry wouldn't be productive anyway. And it wasn't as if I'd have to wander around looking for him. If it were day, he could have gone to the gym, or the faculty lounge, or even Luigi's for a beer. But this time of night about the only place he could go was his office. If he drove around for a while to cool off, he'd eventually end up there.

Caerphilly didn't exactly roll up the sidewalks at dusk, but at two-thirty on a Sunday night (or Monday morning), it was almost eerily deserted. I didn't see another car the whole way into town. I heard one, several streets off, when I was nearing the campus, but since it was too noisy for Michael's well-tuned car, I found myself relieved when it faded in the distance. After all, Barrymore Sprocket, who had seemed so harmless and turned out to be a cold-blooded murderer, was still at large somewhere. Though surely somewhere far from Caerphilly, if he had any sense.

Not a single car parked in front of Dunsany Hall, but then Michael could have parked in the adjacent faculty garage. I didn't have a card for that, but I did have the key code to get into the building. I took the front steps two at a time, punched in the code, and slipped inside. I walked softly and didn't turn on the lights. I didn't want Michael to hear me coming and storm off again.

And maybe with a fugitive at large it was better not to advertise my presence in a deserted building.

For that matter, maybe I should have a weapon ready, in case I ran into Barrymore Sprocket. A quick search through my purse and pockets produced nothing particularly useful. For want of something else, I fished out Rose Noire's bottle of "Eau de Meg" scent. It was small enough to throw but hard enough to hurt if it hit, and I didn't much care if I broke it. Perhaps, if I held it menacingly, I could convince someone that it was mace. And I loosened the top, so I could throw the contents more easily. Self-defense through aromatherapy—it might not stop an attacker but at least the menthol and eucalyptus might slow him down for a few useful seconds.

Clutching the small bottle and looking over my shoulder every few seconds, I tiptoed down the hall.

Chapter 44

But Michael wasn't in his office. The door was unlocked, which was odd, but the lights were off and he wasn't there.

Should I check the men's room? The soda machines in the basement?

I didn't really want to. Michael's office was familiar, and gave the illusion of safety.

I peered out into the corridor. Farther down, I noticed light spilling out of an office door that was slightly ajar. Giles's office. I relaxed slightly. Michael had probably come to his office to stew until his anger passed, seen the light in Giles's office, and gone down there. Maybe he was venting to Giles. No, that wasn't really much like Michael, and it would certainly be out of character for Giles. They were probably just talking. Not a bad thing. Talking with Giles always put Michael in a good mood.

I found myself smiling as I walked down the corridor. Maybe they were even celebrating. We hadn't seen Giles since we'd unmasked Barrymore Sprocket as the killer.

So Michael probably got to tell him the good news. I'd join them, and bask in my share of the credit. He would probably be incredibly grateful and thus glad to see me as well.

And catching up with Michael while he was with Giles wasn't a bad idea. We couldn't make up very satisfactorily with a third party around, but then we weren't likely to continue the quarrel, if he hadn't cooled down. I could probably find a way to run up a truce flag without Giles even realizing what was happening.

But when I reached Giles's office, it was empty, too. No, empty was the wrong word for anything so full of books and other objects. Temporarily unoccupied, I thought, with a smile. And even in my current anti-materialistic mood, I didn't lump in books with mere clutter. Right now, a room this filled with anything else would repel me, but Giles's office was still inviting. I sneezed a few times—the book dust again.

The harsh fluorescent overhead light was off, so the light came from a single old-fashioned lamp on the paper-strewn desk. His chair was pushed back, as if he'd just stood up. An ancient radio, nearly hidden among stacks of books and papers on the credenza behind the desk, played something I vaguely recognized as Mozart, though I couldn't have named the piece. Probably the college station's regular Sunday night classical program.

But where was Giles? And was Michael with him? Surely Giles wouldn't have gone far leaving his door unlocked and his light and radio on. He had far too many valuable books on the shelves, not to mention all the assorted antique objects littered among the books—the familiar academic clutter, all the coins, potsherds, and ancient weapons Giles collected, but in an off-hand, casual manner, quite unlike the fervor with which he accumulated books.

I sneezed again. More dust in the air than usual, apparently.

Odd. Most of the shelves looked the same as they had this morning, but one entire bookcase had been recently dusted. The one containing his golden age mystery collection—including the R. Austin Freeman books.

And for some reason, that shelf looked different than it had the last time I'd looked at it—was it only earlier today? I closed my eyes and tried to visualize what the shelf had looked like—the muted colors of the cloth bindings and the slightly frayed and faded dust jackets.

When I opened my eyes again, I realized what was different. Right in the middle of one shelf, among all the muted and faded colors, was a vivid red dust jacket I didn't remember seeing this morning.

I bent to look at it.

The Uttermost Farthing, by R. Austin Freeman.

Closer up, I could see that it wasn't brand new, but it was in much better condition than the other Freeman dust jackets. Its color, behind the plastic cover, was intense and unfaded, its edges crisp and sharp. Was it a much later book, or perhaps a reproduction?

In either case, it hadn't been there before. I'd have noticed that intense red. Especially since it would have been at my elbow this morning, when I was contemplating Giles's collection of Freeman books. I remembered that there had been at least one gap in that shelf, and now it was completely filled. I'd certainly have noticed the title, thanks to its association with the murder, and I think, despite my wariness of the protective plastic cover, I'd have pulled it out and examined it.

As I did now.

Copyright 1914, so it wasn't a newer book. And close up, I could see the minute signs that it wasn't brand new. Not a reproduction. Definitely a much healthier twin to the half-burned book Horace had found in his grill. In fact, a near-mint-condition copy of the book's first edition. I felt a brief pang of sympathy for the book, which showed all the signs of having survived more than ninety years on this planet unread, and for that matter, rarely opened. I thought briefly of my own less rarified library. I tried to take reasonable care of books, but still, some of my books showed signs that I hadn't always given them kid glove treatment. My complete Sherlock Holmes bore light flecks of the spaghetti sauce that had been a staple of my diet during the lean years right after college. My collection of paperback mysteries included more than one that had accompanied me, literally, into the bathtub. Occasionally, when I reread *The Lord of the Rings,* I would turn a page and dislodge a few glittering flakes of the rock candy I'd been eating obsessively during that long ago Christmas week when I'd first read them. They were probably less valuable, those books, but I had the irrational notion that they were happier.

If only books could talk, I could ask them. And I could ask this book what it had seen. I had the sinking feeling it would tell me it had witnessed a murder.

"He pulled a switch," I said aloud. Giles had been telling the truth for the most part. He'd only lied about one thing—the worn, inferior copy was the one he already owned, and it was Gordon who'd found the infinitely more desirable mint copy I now held in my hands.

Well, lied about two things, I realized. He'd also killed Gordon. After all the trouble I'd taken to prove he hadn't.

I walked over to the desk, still holding the Freeman book, and reached for the phone to dial 911.

"I'm, sorry, Meg, but I can't let you do that."

I turned to find Giles standing in the doorway, holding a gun. One of his elegant little antique dueling pistols.

Chapter 45

I wondered, briefly, if I should grapple with Giles. Try to
take the pistol away from him. Or maybe just run away.
After all, the gun was over a century old; what were the
odds it still worked, or that Giles was a good shot, or even
that he had enough nerve to shoot me?

Not good enough. Something about the look in his eye
stopped me. He looked more capable than the usual Giles.
And a lot less sane. Or perhaps I was seeing Giles clearly
for the first time. He stepped into the office and inched
along the side, keeping his back to the wall and his eyes
fixed on me.

The Mozart piece ended just then, and the announcer
told us what it was and who played it, in the molasses-
smooth tones classical radio announcers cultivate, especially the late night ones.

That's the ticket. Calm, soothing, rational.

"Giles," I said. "Be reasonable. Let's talk."

He shook his head.

The announcer's voice changed and cracked slightly,

revealing his youth. Of course, now he was talking about something a lot more newsworthy than Mozart.

"A spokesperson for the Caerphilly Police Department reported that state and national authorities have been called in to assist with the search for a fugitive suspected in the murder of local antique and book dealer Gordon McCoy," he said.

Giles chuckled.

"Chief Burke stated that the fugitive was to be considered armed and dangerous," the announcer said.

"Barrymore Sprocket," I said, nodding. "He stole the yard sale proceeds, and everyone thinks he's the killer. Let's just leave it that way."

He shook his head.

"You'd never do that," he said. "I know you better. You couldn't live with yourself until you told the truth, even though it would make you look foolish, after all the time you spent trying to prove I didn't do it."

"And succeeding," I said.

"Don't think I'm not grateful," he said. "But I just can't let you undo all that effort."

"Giles, you're not a cold-blooded killer!"

"No, I'm not," he said. "I didn't mean to kill Gordon. I struck him in a moment of anger, that's all. And ran away."

"Accidentally carrying the mint condition copy of *The Uttermost Farthing*."

He nodded.

"And then you came here, switched the books, and returned to our yard sale with your battered copy. Why? You'd gotten clean away—why not stay away?"

"I had to put a copy of the book back," he said. "After all, you knew he had it. Other people might have overheard."

"I knew he had a book he thought you wanted," I said. "I didn't know it was *The Uttermost Farthing*. I don't recall him ever mentioning the name. I might not even have remembered R. Austin Freeman if the burned book hadn't reminded me. If the subject ever came up, you could have picked any book at the yard sale and claimed it was the book he wanted to sell you; I'd never have known the difference."

"Damn," he said, his face falling slightly. "If I'd known you were that clueless—damn."

Dad, who read far too many mysteries for his own good, was fond of saying that murderers frequently gave themselves away by their efforts to cover up their crimes, but I decided Giles might not appreciate the observation, so I held my tongue. The radio had gone back to its classical program, and more calming Mozart filled the silence.

"At least I knew precisely how to get myself cleared," he said, after a few moments. "I knew if I just made sure all the incriminating evidence came out right at the start, so you could hear it, you couldn't resist trying to prove me innocent."

"My well-known weakness for rescuing strays of all kind," I said, with a sigh.

"Well, yes, along with your tendency to think you know best and the rest of us just have to come around to your opinion."

I winced. Yes, Giles knew me too well—a lot better than I knew him. He'd played me perfectly.

"Annoying traits," Giles said. "I always found Michael remarkably cultured for an American, but I never could fathom what he saw in you." And what I heard in his tone made it all the more insulting—not hate, or anger, but puzzlement and vague distaste.

Not to mention the ominous past tense. I suddenly remembered the open door of Michael's empty office. Why was the door unlocked if Michael hadn't been here? Was Giles up to something in Michael's office?

Or had Michael already been here and run into Giles

and his lethal little antiques. Surely if he'd done something to Michael, I'd have found—

I shoved the thought away.

"Not to change the subject," I said. "But just how do
you think you can get away with killing me?"

"There's still a dangerous fugitive at large," he said,
nodding toward the radio. "The police will find me, dazed
and half conscious on the floor of my office, and learn
that their fugitive wrested the gun away from me, shot
you with it, and then coshed me over the head before fleeing with whatever cash and small valuables we had. Now
put the book down."

I glanced down, and realized that I was unconsciously
holding *The Uttermost Farthing* in front of my heart.

"It won't work," I said.

"Why not?" he asked.

"Because I won't let you get away with it," Michael
said, from the doorway.

Giles and I both started. I felt a flood of relief at seeing
Michael alive and well. And then almost immediately
wanted to kick myself for the missed opportunity. By the
time it occurred to me to jump Giles while he was still off
balance, he wasn't.

"Michael," Giles said, shaking his head. "I'm sorry,
but you can't talk me out of this. Step over beside her."

"So you can shoot us both?" Michael said, without
moving. "Is that what you want? Our blood on your
hands?"

"Not to mention all over your books," I added.

"The police are on their way," Michael said. "I called
them just now. Even if you shoot us both, they'll catch you."

Giles was glancing back and forth between the two of
us. He narrowed his eyes and focused on Michael for several beats. Then he shook his head.

"No," he said. "You wouldn't stop to call the cops when you saw she was in danger. You'd just dash in and try to bluff me into giving up."

I resented his underestimating Michael's intelligence. At least I hoped he was underestimating it. Michael looked calm and confident, but then, he was an actor. He got paid to look calm and confident.

"Do you realize what you're doing?" Michael began. "Gordon was an accident. But if you shot us, there would be no way you could pretend it was an accident. Not to the police and not to yourself."

He was talking in a calm, soothing voice and, I hoped, distracting Giles. Good. Because while I hoped Giles was wrong, and Michael had sensibly called the police before barging in to rescue me, I wasn't counting on it. I waited till Giles was completely focused on Michael, and then I made my move. Unfortunately, Giles wasn't as distracted as I thought.

"Oh, no you don't," he exclaimed, grabbing the antique sword with his left hand, before I could get more than one step closer to it.

And then he focused back on Michael. He didn't exactly turn his back on me, but he clearly wasn't watching me closely.

Bad decision. Just because I didn't have a weapon didn't mean I wasn't dangerous.

When Michael, who was a far more astute judge of my character than Giles, made a sudden feint to distract him, I tried again. I flung the contents of Rose Noire's little perfume vial at Giles's face. As I hoped, he flinched when the liquid hit him, and then the eucalyptus and menthol made his eyes water. He didn't drop the sword or the gun, but he didn't react quickly enough when I scrabbled at the book stand behind me.

You'd think an English professor would remember the old adage about the pen being mightier than the sword. The twenty-pound abridged edition of the Oxford English Dictionary made just as good a weapon as a saber. And a lot tidier; no messy blood to deal with.

Giles dropped both sword and gun and keeled over when the dictionary hit his head. A stack of books cushioned his fall—not that I particularly cared at the moment—and Michael tied him up with a long telephone cord while I called 911 with my cell phone.

"I did already call," Michael said. "I'm a lot more practical than Giles thinks, you know."

"Yes, I know he already called, Debbie Anne," I said into the phone. "But tell the chief to hurry. We have the real murderer this time."

"You see?" Michael said.

"I never doubted you," I said. "But I couldn't pass up the chance to let the chief know that we caught his murderer."

"We did, didn't we?" Michael said, with a smile. "As a team, we're not half bad."

And then, since Giles was not only tied up but still unconscious and the police wouldn't show up for at least a few minutes, we seized the chance to end our quarrel in a much more satisfactory fashion.

Chapter 46

Chief Burke must have been in the next county. Most of the Caerphilly police force, two state troopers, and several dozen rubberneckers had arrived before he did. The tiny, book-filled office started to give me the creeps—or maybe it was the presence of the man I'd considered our friend before he almost became our murderer—so I convinced the cops who had arrived to let Michael and me wait for the chief on the building's front veranda. We were standing arm in arm behind a huge white marble pillar, peeking down at the growing crowd, when the chief finally pulled up and began climbing the long front stairway.

"Did you catch Barrymore Sprocket?" I asked when he arrived at the top.

"Yes," the chief said, sounding rather grumpy as well as out of breath. "Spotsylvania County picked him up half an hour ago. We'll look pretty silly when we have to tell them he's the wrong man."

"He's not the wrong man," I said.

"He didn't kill Gordon McCoy," the chief said.

"He did take Gordon's wallet, not to mention our cash box, and he knocked Dad out and tied him up," I pointed out. "Which means he's wanted for grand theft, assault and battery, and interfering with the scene of a crime, right? Just because he's not the killer doesn't mean he isn't a criminal."

"I suppose," the chief said. "Thank goodness those bulletins always say alleged anyway."

"And when you put the bulletin out, I was alleging like mad that Barrymore was the killer," I said. "Not your fault."

"Hmph," the chief said, and turned to go inside.

"You forgot to ask him about the money Sprocket stole," Michael said.

"We can worry about that later," I said. "The money's not that important. And if we don't get it back from Barrymore, there are plenty of other Sprockets."

He nodded.

"I should have known he couldn't be trusted, the minute he walked in," I said.

"I recall that you didn't trust him," Michael said. "You saw through Sprocket almost as soon as you met him. Not like me. I've known Giles for seven or eight years, and I never suspected he'd do something like this."

"Not your fault," I said.

"No, it is," he said. "I should have realized something was wrong when he didn't immediately warm to you."

"Not his fault," I said.

"Yes, it is," Michael said. "If he wasn't smart enough to like you for your own sake, he should at least have tried harder for my sake. I'm better off without a friend like that."

He sounded tired and depressed. And to cap it all off,

we saw the department chair and vice chair whispering over at one end of the veranda, and occasionally glancing our way.

"Already planning which of my detractors to appoint to my tenure committee," Michael said. "Well, the hell with them. If they kick me out, it's their loss."

"The hell they will," I said. "Wait here."

Ironically, when Giles was about to kill me, the campus had been completely deserted, but now the crowd, drawn by the police sirens, was increasing by the minute. The police were keeping most of them, including the reporters, down in the street, but a growing number of faculty members had shown up and were milling about the veranda, exchanging misinformation. Including, oddly enough, Professor Schmidt. I walked over and pulled him aside.

"Can we talk for a minute," I said.

"What about?" he said. But he must have guessed. He followed me, glancing over his shoulder, until we were out of the crowd's earshot.

"Mrs. Pruitt," I said. "The cover-up has to stop."

He closed his eyes, as if I'd just announced my intention of executing him.

"Of course, I understand what happened. In your youthful enthusiasm for your subject, you succumbed to the temptation to hide the books. And, no doubt, you've regretted it ever since, but have been unable to find a way out of the trap you devised for yourself."

He eyed me warily, as if not sure where I was going.

"But now, you have a chance to make a fresh start!" I exclaimed. "You can disarm suspicion by being the one to reveal to the world the discovery of these new primary sources."

"Of course before I can do that I need to find these exciting new primary sources," he said.

"Don't worry," I said. "I'll give them to you."

"And just where am I officially supposed to have gotten the damned things?" he asked.

"From me," I said. "I found them in Mrs. Sprocket's attic. Or possibly her barn."

"Where did she get them?"

"I have no idea," I said. "You'd be amazed what I found in her clutter collection, and I have no idea where she got any of it. Who cares? I found this box of books, and when I saw Mrs. Pruitt's bookplates in them, I contacted you immediately, because I knew you were the world's leading authority on her work, and I thought you would like to have them. Little did I know that these books would revolutionize Pruitt scholarship. You will analyze them, in a series of articles in all the usual scholarly journals, and show the world that you're humble and honest enough to reverse your opinion when new facts come to light. It'll probably breathe new life into your career."

I could see a glimmer of hope in his eyes. And also a lot of suspicion.

"What possible reason could you have for helping me?" he asked.

"No reason whatsoever," I admitted. "But I'm very keen on helping Michael."

He frowned, puzzled.

"I'm sure if he knew, Michael would share my belief that you deserve a chance to make this right," I said. "Just as I'm sure if you think about it, you'll come to share my belief that Michael deserves tenure."

"Ah," he said.

"So provided you snag the soon-to-be-vacant slot on Michael's tenure committee, I see no reason to bore the public with any other version of events."

He studied me through narrowed eyes.

"Done," he said.

He strolled away, looking happier than I could ever remember seeing him. I returned to where Michael was standing and put my arm around his waist.

"Professor Schmidt looks disgustingly cheerful," he said, leaning his head on mine. "Is he already gloating over Giles's downfall and my future departure?"

"No," I said. "I think we'll find that his close brush with murder and the possible notoriety of being a suspect has given Professor Schmidt a change of heart."

"He has a heart?" Michael said. "Who knew?"

"So if you hear that he's lobbying to replace Giles on your tenure committee, don't worry," I said.

He blinked. Then he smiled.

"You're up to something," he said.

"Always," I said.

"You want to share?"

"You're better off not knowing," I said.

"You know," he said. "I think you're much better at faculty politics than I am. If you won't misconstrue this as a sexist remark, or an attempt at pressuring you into something you're not ready to consider, or anything unfortunate like that, may I say that you have all the makings of an excellent faculty spouse? Assuming that's a role you might possibly consider performing at some future point."

I took a deep breath.

"I think it's a role I might be very interested in performing, on one condition."

"Name it," he said, suddenly sounding much more serious.

"Neither of our mothers gets to plan the wedding."

"Done," he said.

He leaned over, pulled me behind a pillar, and kissed me. But a couple of titters from the knot of faculty members nearby broke his concentration and he frowned, at them and at the crowd milling about in the street. Including the reporters.

"My car's down there," he said, gesturing toward the street. "Why don't we leave Chief Burke to wrap up his loose ends, and go home to discuss this more privately?"

"Home's a bad idea," I said. "By now, we'll probably have at least fifty friends and relatives there, waiting to hear all about what happened."

"Oh," he said, his face falling. "I hadn't thought of that."

"On the other hand," I said, starting down the steps. "I have it on good authority that Caerphilly Creek is lovely by starlight."

Keep reading for an excerpt from
Donna Andrews's latest
Meg Langslow mystery

No Nest for the Wicket

COMING SOON IN HARDCOVER
FROM ST. MARTIN'S MINOTAUR

"Move," I said. "You're blocking my shot."

The cow chewed her cud and gazed at me with placid bovine calm.

"Go away!" I ran toward her, waving my arms wildly, only to pull up short before I ran into her. She was bigger than me. Half a ton at least. Maybe three quarters.

I turned my croquet mallet around and prodded her black-and-white flank with the handle. Not hard—I didn't want to hurt her. I just wanted her to move.

She turned her head slightly to see what I was doing.

I prodded harder. She watched with mild interest.

"Hamburger!" I shouted. "Flank steak! Filet mignon!" She ignored me.

Of course, those words held no menace for her. Mr. Shiffley, her owner, was a dairy farmer.

I walked a few yards away, feet squelching in the mud. I could see why the cow insisted on lounging where she was. The evergreen tree overhead protected her from the March drizzle, and she'd claimed the only high ground in sight.

I glanced down. My croquet ball was sinking into the

mud. Did Extreme Croquet rules allow me to pull it out? Probably not.

The little two-way radio in my pocket crackled.

"Meg—turn?" my brother Rob said.

"Roger," I said. The cow still lay in front of—or possibly on—the wicket, but I had to move before the mud ate my ball. Didn't mud that ate things count as quicksand? I set down the radio and whacked my ball. It bounced off the cow's flank. She didn't seem to mind. She had closed her eyes and was chewing more slowly, with an expression of vacuous ecstasy.

"Done," I said, grabbing the radio before it sank. "I need a cow removal here at wicket nine."

"Which one is that?" Rob asked.

"The one by the bog."

"Which bog?"

"The one just beside the briar patch. Near the steep hill with the icy stream at the bottom."

"Oh, that bog," Rob said. "Be right over."

I pocketed the radio and smiled menacingly at the cow.

"Be afraid," I said. "Be very afraid."

She ignored me.

I leaned against a tree and waited. The radio crackled occasionally as Rob notified the scattered players of their turns and they reported when they'd finished.

In the distance, I heard a high-pitched cackle of laughter that meant my team captain, Mrs. Fenniman, had made a difficult shot. Or, more likely, had just roqueted some unlucky opponent, which she told me was the technical term for whacking someone's ball into the next county. Annoying in any croquet game, but downright maddening in Extreme Croquet, where the whole point was to make the playing field as rugged as possible. On this field, being roqueted could mean half an hour's detour through even boggier portions of the cow pasture.

I pulled the cell phone out of my other pocket. Time to see what was happening back at the house. The construction site that would eventually be a house again, if all went well. Today we'd begun demolition of the unrepairable parts, and it was driving me crazy, not being there. I'd left detailed instructions with the workmen, but I didn't have much confidence that they'd follow them. They were all Shiffleys, nephews of Mr. Shiffley the dairy farmer. Everyone in Caerphilly knew that if you wanted some manual labor done you hired a Shiffley or two—or a dozen, if you liked; there was never a shortage. They were cheerful, honest, hardworking, and reliable, as long as you didn't need anything done during hunting season.

Everyone in Caerphilly also knew that when you had Shiffleys on the job you needed someone else in charge. Not that they were stupid—some were and some weren't, same as any other family—but they were stubborn and opinionated, every one of them, and you needed someone equally stubborn and opinionated telling them what to do. Me, for instance. I was not only stubborn enough, but thanks to my work as a blacksmith, they halfway respected my opinions about related crafts like carpentry and plumbing. Michael, my fiancé, would do in a pinch, as long as he remembered to suppress his innate niceness. Unfortunately, Michael was in town, attending the dreaded all-day Caerphilly College faculty meeting. We had Dad in charge. I was worried.

"Come on, Dad, pick up," I muttered as his phone rang on unanswered. I heard rustling in the shrubbery—either another competitor approaching or Rob arriving for cow removal. Either would cut short my time for talking.

"Meg! How's the game?" Dad exclaimed, when he finally answered.

"I'm stuck in a bog with a cow sitting on my wicket," I said. "How's the demolition going?"

"Fine the last time I looked."

"The last time you—Dad, aren't you at the house?"

"I'm up at the duck pond."

I closed my eyes and sighed. Two weeks ago, when I'd left Dad in charge of another crew of Shiffleys to install the new septic field, he'd talked them into excavating a duck pond. Apparently Duck, my nephew's pet duck, needed a place to paddle while visiting us. Or perhaps Dad thought Michael and I would soon acquire ducks of our own. Anyway, he'd sited the pond uphill from the septic field, but in a spot with exceptionally good drainage— so good that the pond didn't hold water. Which hadn't stopped Dad from trying to keep it full.

"Let's talk about the pond later," I said. "I need you to keep an eye on the demolition crew. See that they don't get carried away with the sledgehammers."

"Roger," he said. "I'll run right down. Oh, about those boxes in the front hall—the Shiffleys can work around them today, but next week—"

"The boxes will be long gone by next week," I said. "The professor from UVa should come by before five to haul them off; keep an eye out for her, will you?"

"Roger. By the way, speaking of the duck pond—"

"Gotta go," I said. "Rob's here for the cow."

I had spotted Rob peering through some shrubbery.

"Man, I thought last month's course was tough," Rob said. "Who set this one up?"

"Mrs. Fenniman," I said. "Possibly with diabolical assistance. Did you bring Spike?"

"Right here," Rob said. He pushed through the thicket and set down a plastic dog carrier. He'd gouged a small notch in its door opening so he could put Spike inside without detaching the leash. Smart.

I peered in through the mesh.

"Cow, Spike," I said. He growled in anticipation. I

could see he'd already done cow duty elsewhere—his fluffy white coat had disappeared under a thick layer of mud.

"Here we go," Rob said, grabbing the leash. "Go get her, Spike!"

A small brown blur shot toward the cow, barking and snarling. The cow must have met Spike before. She lurched to her feet with surprising agility and trotted off.

Annoying that an eight-and-a-half-pound fur ball could strike fear in the heart of a cow when I couldn't even keep her awake.

"I'll just move her a little farther while we're at it," Rob said. He grabbed the dog carrier and ambled off.

"Not too far," I said. "And remember, you're supposed to get the milk out of the cow before churning it."

"Don't worry," Rob called over his shoulder.

I hadn't been worrying, only hoping Spike wouldn't chase the cow quite so far off. Cows were welcome as long as they refrained from lying on the stakes and wickets—Extreme Croquet rules defined any livestock on the course as walking wickets. Hitting the ball between the legs of a standing cow would give me a much-needed extra shot. I didn't want Spike chasing her toward a rival player.

Yes, the cow had been lying on the wicket. I bent the battered wire into an approximation of its original shape, pounded it into the ground, and leaned against a tree to await my turn.

But before it came, another player arrived. Henrietta Pruitt. I smiled and hoped it looked sincere. Mrs. Pruitt was captain of the Dames of Caerphilly, a team whose members were all big wheels in local society. I had no idea why they were here. When the *Caerphilly Clarion* ran the article announcing that Mrs. Fenniman had planned an Extreme Croquet tournament, I thought the townspeople would either laugh themselves silly or ignore the whole thing. Instead, we'd had to make room for two local teams.

Either they were too embarrassed to withdraw when they learned this wasn't a normal croquet tournament or they really wanted to play Extreme Croquet. All day they'd slogged through the mud as if born to it. Maybe I'd misjudged them.

"Well, fancy meeting you here," Mrs. Pruitt said. "After you passed me a few wickets ago, I thought you'd be at the finishing stake by now."

Damn. Apparently I'd had the lead for several wickets and never noticed. Of course, someone else could have passed both of us while we were stuck in various bogs.

"This wicket's tough," I said.

Not for her. Her ball sailed through on the first try, avoided the roots, and rolled down to tap my ball with a firm but gentle click.

"Good shot," I said. "All that golf and tennis pays off." Maybe if I flattered her she wouldn't roquet me.

"Yes," she said. She looked left, down the hill toward the icy stream, then right, toward the briar patch. "It's important to keep in shape, isn't it?"

She raised her mallet. I closed my eyes and tried not to wince at the sharp crack that sent my ball flying.

I plunged into the thorn bushes to find it while Mrs. Pruitt played on. I dodged poison ivy, cow pies, protruding roots, and the bleached and scattered bones of a sheep.

Suddenly I found myself perched on the edge of a steep bank, looking down at a gulley filled with more thorn bushes and, by way of a change, lots of sharp pointy rocks.

"I think I'll take a detour," I muttered. But before I could retreat, the bank crumbled, and I found myself sliding down toward the thorns and pointy rocks.

My mallet hit me in the stomach when I landed. For long seconds I lay with my eyes closed, fighting to breathe.

"Meg! Turn!" my radio said.

I opened my eyes to answer and found myself staring into a pair of blue eyes. Strands of long blonde hair fell around them, partly obscuring the woman's face but not the eyes, which stared at me with unnerving intensity.

"Are you all right?" I wheezed, shoving myself upright.

No, she wasn't.

Someone had bashed in the back of her head.

I started when the radio crackled again.

"Meg? Your turn," Rob said.

"Not now," I muttered, although not into the radio.

I squirmed farther from the corpse while fumbling in my pocket for the cell phone, and whacked myself in the stomach again with my own mallet.

My mallet. I glanced at it, and then at the dead woman's head. Maybe I was jumping to conclusions. Maybe she'd just fallen, as I had, and been less lucky. Hit her head on one of the rocks.

I inched over so I could see her head wound. Then I held my own croquet mallet as close to it as I could.

Looked like a match to me.

For a horrible moment I wondered if I'd done this accidentally when I fell. No, my mallet showed traces of mud and leaves—more than traces—but no blood. I took a deep breath and checked the woman's wrist. No pulse, and while she was still warm, she definitely wasn't body temperature. She'd been dead before I fell.

But not long before. Which meant the killer might still be nearby. I dropped her wrist, scooted away until I had my back against the bank of the gulley, and flipped open the cell phone to call the police.

Debbie Anne, the dispatcher, shrieked and dropped the phone when I told her why I was calling. In a few seconds, Chief Burke was on the line.

"You're reporting what?"

"A murder," I said. "Female, blonde hair, blue eyes, late thirties. Tall, I think, though that's hard to tell—she's lying down. Not someone I know."

"You're sure she's dead?"

I glanced up and met the blank blue eyes.

"Yeah, someone bashed her head in," I said. "But send an ambulance if you don't believe me."

"And you have no idea who she is?"

"I don't know her, and I haven't searched her for an ID."

"Keep it that way," he said. I nodded. Though now my curiosity was aroused—most women carried a purse, but when I stood up and scanned the area, I didn't see one.

"The ambulance is on the way," the chief said. "And I'm sending a couple of deputies to secure the scene— just where is the scene, anyway?"

"Somewhere in Mr. Shiffley's cow pasture," I said. "The boggy part, near the stream. Have the deputies stop at the house and someone can probably lead them up here. Dad, or maybe one of the other players."

"Other players?" the chief said. "Good Lord, please tell me you're not out there playing paintball again."

"Not paintball," I said. "Croquet."

"In Fred Shiffley's pasture? What's wrong with your back yard?"

"Too tame," I said. "This isn't normal croquet. It's Extreme Croquet. You have to play it in extreme conditions. Mr. Shiffley's pasture's perfect—plenty of hills, trees, rocks, quicksand, thorn bushes, poison ivy—"

"Something your family invented?" the chief growled.

"Actually, something Mrs. Fenniman read about in

Smithsonian magazine," I said. "Extreme sports are very big these days, you know."

"Sounds damned strange to me," he muttered.

I agreed, but family loyalty kept me from saying so.

"Fred Shiffley know you're doing this?" he asked.

"We have his permission," I said. "In writing."

Which was true. Dad got along beautifully with the neighboring farmers. I wasn't sure whether his endless curiosity about every detail of farm life had won them over or his free medical advice, but he'd charmed them into letting us play—not just Mr. Shiffley but also an OK from Mr. Early, who owned the nearby sheep pasture where another croquet game was currently going on.

Unless the other game had ended earlier than ours. What if it had, and the other players wandered over to watch our game? I needed to call Dad and—

"Minerva's here," the chief said, interrupting my worrying. "We'll be out as soon as we can."

Minerva? Much as I liked Mrs. Burke, I wondered why he'd bring her to a crime scene. Not my business to pry.

"Fine," I said aloud. "What do you want me to do until the officers arrive?" I was hoping he'd order me to come back to the house. Away from the body.

"How much of a crowd do you have gawking at the body?"

"No crowd at all," I said. "This isn't exactly a spectator sport."

"The other players aren't standing around gawking?"

"The field's at least two acres," I said. "I can't even see the other players at the moment."

A short silence.

"I'm sure it will all make sense when I see it," he said, finally. "Don't touch anything till I get there."

With that he hung up.

"Meg!" my radio squawked. "Your turn."

I realized Rob had probably been calling me all during my conversation with Chief Burke. I grabbed the radio.

"I'm still looking for my ball," I said.

I heard tittering. Probably from Mrs. Pruitt and the other dames.

"Try closing your eyes and letting the ball call to you," said another voice. My cousin Rose Noire—Rosemary Keenan to the IRS and our mothers. "Imagine the ball emitting a guiding beacon of white light."

"Can we get on with it?" Mrs. Pruitt snapped.

"Not until I find my ball," I said. "And no sneaking extra shots while I'm looking—everyone stays right where they are—understood?"

"Roger—everyone, report your whereabouts!" Mrs. Fenniman said, in her best field marshal voice. "Claire and I will stay here by the turning post."

Claire, presumably, was the woman I still couldn't bring myself to call anything but Mrs. Wentworth—wife of the history department chairman.

"We'll concentrate on beaming positive energy for your search," Rose Noire said. "Won't we?"

"Or if you want some real help, give us a call," Mrs. Pruitt said. I heard her in the background, rather than directly, so evidently she was with Rose Noire.

"Could someone please come and chase this cow away?" Lacie Butler whined. "I think it's planning to attack me."

"Good grief; it'll be killer rabbits next," I muttered—though not into the radio. I'd never met anyone as timid and anxious as Lacie. I hadn't quite decided whether I felt sorry for her or just found her terminally annoying. Maybe if I ever ran into her when she wasn't gophering for Mrs. Pruitt and Mrs. Wentworth, I'd find out.

"I'll bring Spike," Rob said.

"Oh, would you?" Lacie exclaimed. Lucky for us

Lacie was a good fifteen years older than Rob, and married to boot. That breathless, damsel in distress routine was exactly what my overly susceptible brother fell for—if the damsel was beautiful and on the fair side of thirty.

"I'll be right over as soon as I chase Duck away from wicket three," Rob said.

"Oh, did she lay another egg?" Rose Noire asked.

"Just sitting on some smooth rocks," Rob said. "But we don't want her getting used to nesting on the field."

No, especially now that the field had become a crime scene. I put the radio down and tuned out the continuing chitchat from the other players. I opened my cell phone again and called Dad.

"I'm up at the house," he said, before I could speak. "I'm keeping a close eye on them—you don't have to worry about a thing."

Except perhaps Dad looking too closely over someone's shoulder and getting accidentally whacked by a sledgehammer. Or the very real possibility that the Shiffleys would mutiny against their unwanted overseer and go home to sulk. That was the downside of working with the Shiffleys—they were quite clannish. Offend one and you offended them all, and fat chance getting anyone to do your carpentry, plumbing, wiring, treecutting . . .

"That's nice," I said. "We have another problem."

"What?"

I took a deep breath. Dad, an avid mystery buff, wouldn't see a problem but a golden opportunity to kibbitz on Chief Burke's investigation.

"We have a suspicious death," I said. "Chief Burke is on the way, and he needs our help."

"He needs me to examine the body," Dad said, jumping to a predictable conclusion. "My medical bag's in the car—"

"Examining the body comes later," I said. "First we secure the crime scene and prevent suspects from leaving."

"Okay," he said. "What suspects?"

"The croquet players in the other field, for starters," I said. "And anyone else who looks suspicious."

I remembered the half-dozen Shiffleys swarming over the house, each armed with a sledgehammer that looked remarkably like a croquet mallet.

"Including the Shiffleys," I said with a sigh. "And anyone else who's been hanging around today."

"Will do," Dad said. "Cousin Horace just drove up— I'll get him to help me."

"Good idea," I said. Cousin Horace was a crime scene technician with the sheriff's department in my hometown of Yorktown. Like many of my relatives, he'd been spending more and more time here in Caerphilly lately— though in Horace's case, I suspect the attraction wasn't me but Rose Noire, with whom he was smitten.

"If you get a chance, could you call the teams who are supposed to show up tonight and head them off?" I added. "Odds are we won't be playing tomorrow, with one field being a crime scene and all. But don't tell them why we're rescheduling. In fact, don't tell anyone."

"Of course not," Dad said. "So where is the body?"

"On the croquet field," I said, which was sufficiently vague to keep him from trotting up here to inspect it. "Oops! Gotta go; talk to you later."

As soon as I hung up, I wished I hadn't. What an hour ago I would have called peace and quiet settled over the gulley, only now it felt like oppressive silence.

I glanced over at the dead woman and realized that I resented her for getting murdered practically in my backyard. Illogical, and I didn't like myself for feeling that way. After all, she didn't ask to be murdered here. Mrs. Fenniman was a much more logical target for resentment, wasn't she? It was her fault I was out here playing Extreme Croquet instead of back at the house minding my own business. She'd organized the tournament and browbeat me into playing hostess.

Of course, I didn't have to go along with her plans. I'd gotten better at saying no to my relatives' crazier projects, but I still wasn't very good at continuing to say no until they heard it.

How long did it take to get here from town, anyway? And was it early enough to head off the other teams or were they already en route—perhaps already here to complicate things even more? I glanced at my watch. Almost three.

"We keeping you from something?"